Charlie Owen enjoyed a thirty-year career in the police service, serving with two forces in the Home Counties and London, reaching the rank of inspector. His previous novels are *Horse's Arse*, *Foxtrot Oscar* and *Bravo Jubilee*, all of which have been highly acclaimed and are available from Headline.

Praise for Charlie Owen:

'Charlie Owen is a talent. This is the first book since *Layer Cake* to have an authentic voice that exposes the dark and eccentric world of English street crime' Guy Ritchie

'It's like *Life on Mars* without the time travelling' *Zoo* magazine

'Will have you gripped from page one. The characters, the plotlines and the dialogue are so vivid' *Daily Record*

'Charlie Owen has a talent for humorously exposing the dark world of British street crime' *Leicester Mercury*

'If you love dinosaur DCI Gene Hunt in TV hit *Life on Mars*, you'll find this violent, yet hilarious thriller a delight' *Peterborough Evening Telegraph*

By Charlie Owen and available from Headline

Horse's Arse
Foxtrot Oscar
Bravo Jubilee
Two Tribes

TWO TRIBES

CHARLIE OWEN

headline

First published in 2009 by
HEADLINE PUBLISHING GROUP

First published in paperback in 2010 by
HEADLINE PUBLISHING GROUP

3

Cataloguing in Publication Data is available from the British Library

ISBN 978 0 7553 4571 7

Typeset in AGaramond by Avon DataSet Ltd,
Bidford on Avon, Warwickshire

Printed in the UK by CPI Mackays, Chatham, ME5 8TD

Headline's policy is to use papers that are natural, renewable and recyclable products and made from wood grown in sustainable forests. The logging and manufacturing processes are expected to conform to the environmental regulations of the country of origin.

HEADLINE PUBLISHING GROUP
An Hachette UK Company
338 Euston Road
London NW1 3BH

www.headline.co.uk
www.hachette.co.uk

To Carol and Richard – with love.

Author's Note and Acknowledgements

This will be the final novel in the saga of life at Horse's Arse. I have made this decision for a number of reasons. Firstly, the idea was only ever for the series to be a trilogy, but then I decided that it was appropriate to finish the story towards the end of what I have always considered to be the last decade of true vocational coppering – the 1970s.

I had thought of going on to write about the 1980s, but the sequel to the best ever TV series about policing, *Life on Mars*, confirmed what I have long suspected – that the 1980s just aren't sexy! Not yet anyway. If that changes, then I'll rethink my plans, but the fact remains that young men and women joined the police in the 1970s, before Lord Edmund-Davies's pay review in 1978–9, to be coppers. The pay and conditions prior to that review were poor – so it had to be a vocation. And we certainly didn't join up to become Human Resource Managers, or Policy Implementation Managers, or any of the myriad non-operational posts that now infect the modern police service. We joined to police the streets, which appears to be something that fewer and fewer cops do today.

Hats off to the men and women at the sharp end today who can be sure of only one thing. That behind them, safely cocooned in their offices, are battalions of pencil-pushers busily micro-managing them (9–5 Monday to Friday) and analysing the ins and outs of a cat's arse to assist their own climb up the greasy promotion pole. The policing pyramid is upside down.

However, it is too easy to blame the police service for all the ills that currently affect them and for their alienation from the public they serve. Successive governments of both political persuasions must take the lion's share. In my view, the Labour governments of Tony Blair and now Gordon Brown, introduced more meaningless legislation, targets and bureaucracy than any of their predecessors. The slavish way in which many Chief Officers embraced New Labour also contributed to the malaise. There were few, if any, dissenting voices as politically astute Chief Officers around the country dropped to their knees in the name of Human Rights and Home Office audits.

Whilst I have dedicated this book to my brother and sister, I owe huge thanks to the usual suspects who reminded me of past events and procedures. To Paul Dockley for his invaluable insights into the role of a

Senior Investigating Officer in the 1970s, and to Teresa Richardson, Neil Wallis, John Bateman, Matt Holt, Mick Duggan, Andy Williams, Stuart Gibson and Paul Chinnery, who all fall into that category. My eldest daughter, Lucy, transferred my written manuscript into a Word document and saved me hours of work; thanks, darling, the cheque's in the post! I also owe a great debt to Martin and Tracy Kosmalski and their daughters Jo and Gemma, and to Tony and Val Jourdan and their sons Richard, Charlie, Ben, Toby and Alfie.

Finally, I must again thank my editor Martin Fletcher for his patience and understanding whilst he waited for me to deliver this last book, and Ross Hulbert, the Headline Publicity Manager. Martin, it's been an amazing journey and I've had a blast. Thanks for everything.

This novel is from start to finish entirely a work of my imagination and the characters, companies and their actions in the story are fictional.

Chapter One

The bloody woman was driving him mad. It was a muggy, early-June evening in Handstead New Town, and in common with most of the residents, the Haywards had all the windows in their nicotine-stained terraced house wide open to catch what little breeze there was. But it wasn't the sound of passing vehicles or kids playing outside that kept distracting sixty-three-year-old George Hayward from the television news. It was her fucking shoes.

As he strained forward in his battered armchair to try and catch what the newsreader was saying, he shot a venomous look at his one-armed wife sitting in a similarly decrepit chair on the other side of the room. Fucking great – he'd missed it now. On the main BBC evening news as well, not the poxy local news on *Look North*, read by that old poof in the cheap wig. The story had reached the main national news channel, and right after an interview with Prime Minister James Callaghan they were showing footage of the trouble at the engineering works in

Handstead. Crowds of shaven-headed yobs were pushing and shoving with lines of coppers – and he'd missed every word the reporter had said. All because of her fucking shoes. She'd lit up another fag and was blowing a cloud of smoke up to the naked bulb hanging from the toffee-coloured ceiling when he banged the arm of his chair, violently upending the overflowing ashtray attached to a leather strap draped over the arm.

'Brenda!' he bellowed, leaning towards her, his leathery face puce with anger.

She barely acknowledged him, concentrating as she was on picking at the livid red scabs on the stump of her left arm, her cigarette clamped between her lips and her eyes screwed up against the thin plume of smoke drifting lazily upwards.

'What now?' she said without looking at him, before peering closely at the sores on the stump.

'Your fucking shoes, woman – stop rubbing them together, will you?'

'What you on about?' she replied, looking up quizzically at him.

'You're rubbing your fucking shoes together and I can't hear the telly,' he shouted back. 'I've missed the whole report on that picket line, couldn't hear a bloody thing because of the racket you're making.'

'My shoes?' she asked, laughing as she spoke. 'How can they be upsetting you? Get a grip, you silly old bugger.'

'It's nothing to laugh about, you scabby old cow,'

bawled a now irate George Hayward. 'We're on the national news and you're rubbing your bastard new shoes together like some fucking moneylender and I can't hear a thing. Shut the fuck up, will you?'

'Oh piss off, and don't call me scabby, you pissy old twat.'

'Pissy? Who're you calling pissy, you sour-faced, one-armed old bitch?'

'I might only have one arm now, but at least I can control my bladder. Jesus, you smell like a tom cat.'

Soon the insults and threats were being screamed at full volume across the room, and as happened fairly regularly, the Haywards' neighbours eventually tired of the noise and called the police. The Late Turn Yankee One took the call, and twenty minutes later the hugely unimpressed crew were refereeing the couple's heated verbal bout. The smell in the Haywards' house made breathing difficult. It was a combination of their long-term support of the tobacco industry eighty times a day, and their recently deceased dog, but mostly it was the ammoniac fumes, coming from George. It was an appalling combination.

'Jesus Christ,' gagged the older of the two coppers, his eyes watering as he stood between the two rancid protagonists.

'Now listen, you two old buggers,' he went on, 'this has got to stop or you're both going to get locked up. This is the second visit we've had to make this week. What's going on?' He immediately regretted asking the question.

In fact, any question was a mistake. It invited an answer, when all he and his mate wanted to do was to get out into the fresh air.

The Haywards both took this as their cue to start again at full volume, causing him to step in once more.

'OK, OK, that'll do. Billy, take Mrs Hayward into the kitchen. George, you stay here with me. I want a serious chat with you.'

Reluctantly, the younger cop followed Brenda out into her greasy kitchen, desperately trying to avoid looking at her stump. But that was an impossibility, and she caught him gazing in appalled fascination. It was akin to watching a public execution – you knew it wasn't the right thing to do, but there it was and you hadn't seen one before, and well, you know . . .

'Lost it a few years ago now,' she said proudly, picking at the remains of an elderly plaster. 'Got it stuck in a paper baler.'

'Jesus, I'm s-sorry,' stammered the young cop, ashamed that he'd been caught staring. 'Anyway, what's up with you and your old man? I thought at your age you'd be past all that scrapping.'

The youngster was acutely aware of the ludicrous nature of their conversation. He was nineteen years old, just out of Training School and living in the police station section house, and here he was about to pry into the lives of a couple who'd probably been together since the Black Plague last swept across Europe, and trying to give them some marriage guidance tips. At Training School, all the role-playing exercises for domestic disputes had ended with the 'married couple' politely thanking the cops for their advice in getting their marriage back on track and with peace restored, but in reality back at Handstead, officers almost always ended up having to lock someone up or risk getting a slap themselves from the warring parties, who always sided against the cops. Cops hated domestic disputes for precisely that reason – they were on a hiding to nothing.

'Oh it's him, Officer,' began Brenda Hayward. 'He's such a miserable old git. Moan, moan, moan, always belly-aching about something I've done, or not done.'

'What was it tonight?'

'My fucking shoes, can you believe it? My shoes were squeaking and he said he couldn't hear the news on the telly. And he called me a scabby old cow. Pissy old bastard keeps wetting himself, you know, Officer. Fancy a cuppa?'

The young cop had clocked the grimy sink overflowing with encrusted cups and crockery as they entered the kitchen and had quickly worked out that he ran enough of a serious risk to his health merely by being in the house. Having a cuppa with the Haywards was as advisable as a black-cab ride in Belfast.

'You know what, if it's all the same to you, darling, I'll give it a miss this time,' he said hurriedly, glancing up as his colleague and smelly old George appeared at the door.

The Haywards were well known to the local cops,

usually as the recipients of the almost endless harassment meted out to them by the neighbourhood yobs. Their ancient Reliant Robin three-wheeler car was regularly rolled on to its roof at night, they lived in dread of Bonfire Night week, and they had both fallen foul of the fearsome burning bag of dog-shit trick. It was only in recent months that their loud arguing and bickering had necessitated other visits from the police.

'You two need to sort yourselves out,' said the older cop benevolently. 'You ought to be sticking together rather than fighting.'

'It's him, Officer,' protested Brenda. 'He's got absolutely no consideration for me at all. I might as well not be here.'

'You won't be much longer, you keep carrying on,' retorted her husband.

'You know we've been married over forty years and the dirty old bastard still uses my toothbrush without asking, even though he knows it pisses me off,' she continued.

'You know a better way to get dog-shit out of a pair of trainers, I'm all ears,' replied George, arms outstretched imploringly.

'See what I mean?' she shrieked.

'Jesus Christ, will you two pack it in?' moaned the older cop, motioning to his aghast colleague that it was time to get out of the festering hovel. 'If we have to come back, you're both going to get locked up for the night, OK?'

The Haywards sullenly acknowledged the warning but said nothing, preferring to look daggers at each other as the cops left.

'Be nice to each other,' reiterated the older cop as they reached the welcome fresh air. 'I'm not joking – any more from you two and it's the cuffs for both of you.'

As the door closed behind them and they breathed deeply what passed for fresh air in Handstead, the sound of the Haywards bickering again could be clearly heard.

'Do a GOB entry when we get in, Billy,' instructed the older cop as he unlocked the area car. 'If we're not back this shift, someone else will be. Silly old buggers.'

Whilst the United Kingdom as a whole was being throttled by industrial disputes as rebellious unions flexed their considerable muscle, the dispute that had caught the BBC's attention and which had been missed by George Hayward, was a very local affair. In truth, it had nothing to do with union activity – indeed, the Electricity Workers Union had distanced themselves from it once they had learned the true facts – but everything to do with naked racism.

Red Star Electrics on the Ridgemount Industrial Estate was a family-owned business that had first set up in Handstead twenty years earlier. Then, two Sikh brothers had run it and they had, not unnaturally, employed a largely Asian workforce. However, the securing of a massively lucrative contract with the

National Health Service manufacturing wall sockets and ceiling extractors, coupled with the demise of the petro-chemical industry in the town, meant they had taken on many of Handstead's homegrown workers. The very same homegrown workers whose militancy and work-shyness had contributed significantly to the petro boys pulling down the shutters and crossing the North Sea.

Amongst those fortunate enough to secure jobs with the Sikh family business was Wallace Moffatt. He was an obese forty year old who used his considerable bulk to threaten and intimidate in his role as the local EWU shop steward. What he lacked in intelligence he made up for in brute ignorance and animal cunning, and with his shaved head that resembled a pink cannon ball and malicious little piggy eyes, he was a formidable opponent.

Moffatt's role as the unopposed shop steward seemed to be mainly to antagonise the longsuffering owners of the business and to do as little real work as possible. Despite his name, he was clearly not local, with a rough Welsh accent that got thicker as he got angrier and louder. And getting angry was what he did best, with his jowly face getting redder and redder, beads of perspiration forming in his thin eyebrows and on his upper lip, and the veins in his temples standing out like blue snakes.

Very little was known about Wallace Moffatt. He was married with a couple of daughters, lived on the infamous Park Royal Estate, and had previously worked for the petro-chemical company – but other than that, his background was as sketchy as a book on the Swiss Navy. What was not in doubt though was his rabid racism and hatred of anyone unfortunate enough not to be white. Not for him mere hostile looks and mumbled insults. He spent his waking hours venting his considerable spleen at the Asians and Africans he worked with and for, and always at the top of his voice. His membership of the still fledgling racist group the Albion Army was also well known and proudly claimed by him, and it was his blatant racism that had led to the dispute at Red Star Electrics. The dispute had run for over a year now, with little prospect of a resolution. Moffatt's early involvement in the lengthy picketing had, needless to say, attracted the attention of the local police and Special Branch – but the man was apparently squeaky clean, with not even an unpaid parking ticket to his name.

Things had come to a head in April the previous year when Moffatt had reduced a young, female Asian worker to tears with a prolonged racist outburst on the shop floor. Confronted by one of the owners, he continued in the same vein and had been summarily dismissed. Moffatt had then led a walkout from the factory of most of the white workers; the majority of whom returned within a few days when the background to his sacking became common knowledge.

Most of his white co-workers knew which side their bread was buttered, and the Sikhs were fair employers. Few workers were prepared to risk their own livelihoods to support an obnoxious bully like Moffatt. So the stalemate and stand-off ensued, with the fat shop steward and his few supporters pledging to picket the factory until he was reinstated. As the EWU distanced themselves from him, he turned to his real alma mater, the Albion Army.

Formed in 1970, the Albion Army was still looking to make a name for itself. Believing the National Front to be too left wing, it had picked up some decent publicity the previous year in London, when a march had deteriorated into a riot, but what the leadership needed was a *cause célèbre* – and that was when Wallace Moffatt nailed himself to the cross and martyred himself in the name of white supremacy.

Every day since he had been dismissed, the Albion Army had maintained a vocal picket in the cul-de-sac leading to the main gates of Red Star Electrics. Sometimes there were as few as five shaven-headed cretins shouting abuse at the employees as they arrived for work or left to go home. Other days, they would turn out several hundred strong, and on a number of such days they had physically prevented staff from passing through the gates.

The intimidation of workers – be they black, Asian or white – was intense, and sickness levels amongst staff began to rise as they chose not to endure the journey through the baying mob. The business was suffering and the Sikh owners turned to the police for help as workers reported that they were being followed home and their cars and houses vandalised. It was an impossible task using just local resources, and as the BBC News had quite clearly shown, the few cops deployed to deal with the pickets were being quickly overwhelmed most days, and occasionally getting a good kicking into the bargain.

Radical changes were needed – and they were on their way.

Chapter Two

Two hours after the Late Turn area car crew had left the warring Haywards to get on with it, D Group mustered for their night duty. The evening had remained sticky and muggy, and all the windows in the muster room were wide open to let in some air. The threadbare curtains hung limply and the information bulletins and Police Mutual Assurance Society posters remained unread and motionless on the noticeboards as the room resolutely refused to cool down. Several dozen battered blue plastic chairs were scattered haphazardly around the room in front of an ancient wooden lectern, behind which the huge, grey-haired Sergeant Andy Collins was leafing through a pile of paperwork before he addressed his troops, who had entered the room in ones and twos.

They were an extraordinary bunch but perfectly suited to the town they policed. Handstead New Town had sprung up like a bad dream around the historic Old Town, and had all but consumed it. It was a classic example of urban planning undertaken by thirty-somethings wearing red-rimmed spectacles who'd never have to live there. The idea behind the New Town was sound and philanthropic – get the impoverished masses out of their squalid tenements and into proper homes with indoor toilets and glass in the windows. But the idea soured when Manchester City Council, in what the Greater Manchester Police saw as an enlightened moment, decided it was just too good a chance to miss and deported vast numbers of their most troublesome tenants out to this brave new world in the sticks.

Soon the looming tower blocks of Handstead, with their endless echoing corridors, blind corners and dark recesses that could only have been designed with the intention of increasing robberies, became no-go areas to all but the unemployable feral youths who plagued the town. Their reputations as violent criminals spread beyond the locality, and by the late 1970s, Handstead New Town had acquired the reputation of being the biggest shithole in the county.

Its phonetic code, Hotel Alpha, had been bastardised by the local cops to 'Horse's Arse'. Over time, every cop in the county came to know it by that name. Handstead New Town was the filthy tissue that the old whore Manchester had wiped herself on and chucked over her shoulder. It was a town crying out for some firm, innovative policing, but as was the norm, the police answer had been to use it as a dumping ground for their own malcontents. It became a punishment posting, a Devil's Island – and so the two sides that faced each other on a daily basis had very similar attitudes and outlooks. The local population was policed with extreme prejudice and the majority of the residents regarded the cops with identical disdain.

That said, once the cops had adjusted to the fact that they were doomed to spend the rest of their careers in the arsehole of the world, a kind of Canute-like pride enveloped them. They began to take a perverse pride in where they worked, revelling in the comments of colleagues around the county who'd rather eat their own feet than work in Horse's Arse.

The lifespan of a uniform police group at any station was cyclical. Groups would spend time gelling and refining themselves until they each had a unique identity – some had reputations as thief-takers, others as good fighters, a few as being brutal and corrupt – and then they would begin to fracture and disperse as cops got promoted or posted to specialist units, and the evolutionary process would begin again. Except at Horse's Arse, where the only way out came via a sacking, prison sentence or a medical discharge. Even promotion for a Horse's Arse officer was unlikely to lead to escape. Of the five Inspectors and twelve Sergeants at the station, 90 per cent had served there as PCs.

D Group was a perfect example of a group at its absolute peak of destructive power. Its members were, to put it mildly, an eclectic bunch of malcontents and reprobates, some of whom stayed only just on the right side of right and wrong. But not one of them was corrupt. The thought of taking a backhander to let a bad guy walk away was a complete anathema to them all. The bad guys of Handstead, and there were plenty to go round, were there to be locked up as regularly as possible – given a good hiding too, when appropriate – and the cops were prepared to bend the law until it nearly snapped to get them locked up.

It was not unusual for the local yobs to find themselves listening to colourful and largely fabricated accounts of their drunken misdemeanours at court, but they generally shrugged their shoulders and accepted it as part and parcel of the unique way of policing that existed at Handstead. Both they and the cops knew that whilst the offence they were now appearing at court for was significantly a work of fiction, there were a good half-dozen other crimes for which they had never been held to account. PC Sean 'Psycho' Pearce, one of D Group's most infamous members, summarised the arrangement very nicely: 'I've never fitted up anyone who didn't deserve it.'

Andy Collins looked up from his paperwork at his group sitting opposite him and was about to make a start on his muster when the door opened and Inspector Hilary Bott, the station's Deputy Commander, walked in. Collins could barely contain his surprise at seeing the desk warrior at such an hour, nor his contempt for her. He rolled his eyes to the ceiling as the visibly nervous Bott strode towards him with a steely glint in her eyes.

'Fuck me, ma'am – you shit the bed or something?' shouted a voice from the back of the room, which Collins recognised immediately as Psycho's. This had disaster written all over it, worried Collins. Jesus, Bott still had a dreadful stammer, courtesy of an outrageous stunt pulled by Psycho last year, which had led to the old witch being sedated in her toilet and taken to hospital.

'Evening, ma'am,' he eventually offered. 'Why are you here?'

'I'm g-g-going to take the night duty muster,' she stammered, ignoring Psycho's earlier question. 'Mr Stevenson decided it would be a good idea if I got to know all the uniform groups here in my capacity as his D-Deputy, so I thought I'd do a night shift with you. Now, where's the G-GOB and collators' bulletin?'

Clever man, that Chief Inspector Stevenson, mused Collins as he moved to one side to allow Bott behind the lectern. He knew Stevenson found the woman to be an insufferable pain in the arse and took every opportunity to send her off on improbable errands and assignments. Getting her to work a night shift with D Group was inspired; there was a good chance she wouldn't survive it.

Collins looked again at the group, all of whom were glaring at Bott with the notable exception of Psycho, who was beaming merrily, apparently delighted to see her. 'Oh fuck,' said Collins quietly to himself.

'Evening, ma-ma-ma'am!' shouted Psycho, aping her stutter, which brought shrieks of laughter from some of the others. Bott looked up nervously at Collins for some moral support. He sighed deeply, and took the cigarette out of his mouth.

'Shut the fuck up, Pearce,' he said, before turning back to Bott and hissing at her, 'On you go, boss, but make it quick, please.' He now stood slightly in front of the lectern, daring the group to try it on again, but confident none of them would. However, Psycho was still smiling and that worried the shit out of him.

'Thank you, S-S-S-Sergeant Collins. Now listen up please, l-l-l-l-ladies and gentlemen,' she said, 'these are your beats for the n-night.' And then she proceeded to run through the sheet that Collins had just prepared.

There were no surprises. Yankee One was to be crewed as usual by the Brothers, PCs Henry Walsh – known as H – and Jim Docherty; the original Odd Couple. H, a public schoolboy, and Jim, an ex-Para, were as close as shit to a blanket and no one could work out why. They were, on the surface, the unlikeliest of friends but the pair were inseparable and probably the most belligerent of all the cops at Horse's Arse. They had one simple approach to all policing problems – violence. No preamble or questions, just wading in, fists flying. This was all well and good when the wheels had already come off, but very inconvenient when things were nicely under control. The others on the group regarded them warily, such was their penchant for fighting at every opportunity, always welcoming them at full-on Wild West-style pub fights, but dreading the approaching two-tone sirens of Yankee One at a peaceful situation.

The Unit beat vehicles, Two One and Two Two, were to be crewed by PCs Alan 'Pizza Face' Petty and John Jackson (JJ), and PCs Andy 'the Mong Fucker' Malcolm and Ally Stewart. WPC Amanda 'the Blood Blister' Wheeler was given the front office for the night, PC Ray 'Piggy' Malone got the dirty van, Andy Collins was the street supervisor, Sergeant Mick Jones was the night duty Custody Sergeant and PC Dave 'Trog' Hooper his gaoler. And Inspector Jeff Greaves would be the night duty Inspector but no one, not even his guardian angel, Andy Collins, had a clue where the mad bastard was.

Greaves was a career detective who'd been busted back to uniform and sent to the penal colony, and he was now two-thirds of the way into his master-plan to get a medical discharge from the Job. His plan was known to very few, certainly not to Andy Collins, and Greaves now played the role of a broken window-licker as he progressed towards the final act in the play – wetting himself publicly as he received his Long Service and Good Conduct medal.

It was virtually unheard of, not to get a Long Service and Good Conduct medal if you reached twenty-two years of service. Coppers with the most appalling discipline records to their names would shamelessly present themselves at elaborate ceremonies at Headquarters and listen politely as a senior officer they barely knew waxed lyrical about the exemplary service the be-medalled hooligan had completed. It was a ludicrous charade, but one that Greaves intended to exploit to the full. His decline into mental breakdown at Horse's Arse had been carefully planned and choreographed. He had walked to work in the pouring rain wearing slippers, turned up dressed to play tennis or wearing a pilot's leather flying helmet, and spent hours talking to noticeboards.

It was well known to all that Greaves was as mad as a fish and a complete liability, but Andy Collins was very old school when it came to his Inspector. He would not hear a word said against him and protected him from senior officers like a mother hen. He would hide him away in the senior officers' dining room if the bosses were about, or put him in his car in the garages to avoid questions being asked if he was having a particularly mad day.

Whilst Greaves was the figurehead leader of D Group, Andy Collins was the true power – but Collins would never claim that accolade. Greaves was well aware of what Collins was doing for him and had resolved that once he had pocketed his index-linked medical pension, he'd tell him everything and thank him properly.

'OK,' continued Bott, as she briefly looked up at the simmering mob in front of her. 'Got a few m-memos from Division that you need to be aware of. First one's from M-M-M-Mr Findlay.'

There was an audible groan as the name of Chief

Superintendent Phillip 'The Fist' Findlay was mentioned. Collins was even more perturbed to notice that Psycho was the only one not to join in the groaning, but continued to grin manically.

'He's got wind of the fact that officers are using inappropriate ph-phraseology on the main set channel which has got to stop. Apparently officers are routinely referring to g-g-g-gypsies as "pikeys" . . .'

At this there was a loud chorus of other choice phrases, upon which Collins stepped forward and raised a threatening finger at the group. Reluctant silence ensued and Bott continued.

'As I was saying, g-g-g-gypsies are being referred to as "pikeys" – and worse. Mr Findlay has instructed that in f-f-f-future they're to be known as Caravan Utilising Nomadic Travellers.'

The group exploded in raucous laughter and Bott again looked up at Collins who was glaring at Psycho. The latter was laughing louder than any of the others and it was obvious who was behind the memo.

'Now what?' asked the bewildered Bott.

'The memo's a fake, ma'am,' sighed Collins wearily.

'A fake? W-What do you mean?'

'Have a look at it, for God's sake. Caravan Utilising Nomadic Travellers? It's a mnemonic.'

'Mnemonic?'

'Cunt, for Christ's sake,' yelled Collins. And, 'Shut the fuck up, you lot,' he continued at the group.

Bloody Psycho. The man had previous for bogus memos, usually purporting to be from Bott herself. His last one 'from her' instructed that officers were to expose their genitals to her rather than salute if they met her out on the ground. He was a bloody menace.

'How d-d-dare you sp-sp-sp-speak to me like that!' complained Bott loudly above the din. Her stammer was getting worse as she got stressed, and the complaint took a lot longer than it should.

'I'm not swearing at you, boss,' explained the exasperated Collins. 'Someone's slipped in a bogus memo for you to read. The mnemonic you've just read out spells *cunt* – sorry, ma'am.'

'Oh,' replied the crestfallen Bott, peering closely at the false memo. 'It looks real enough. That's definitely Mr Findlay's sig-sig-signature.'

Collins looked daggers at the celebrating Psycho at the back of the room. The maniac had a job lot of signed blank memos ready for all occasions, and once he'd spotted Bott wandering about the nick so late at night, he'd rightly assumed that she would put in an appearance at the night-duty muster. It was a real bonus that she'd decided to take the muster herself.

The unfortunate Hilary Bott was unaware that she too was now one of the doomed, living dead of Horse's Arse. She had been sent there by the recently retired Chief Constable Daniels with a brief to bring about some changes in the zoo. Under his care and patronage, she had enjoyed some protection, but now he had gone she was lost. Even under his wing, she had suffered badly at the hands of the uniforms at Horse's Arse. Psycho loathed her, seeing her as the living embodiment of everything that was wrong with the Job – female *and* an Inspector. And she had to be a rug-muncher, he reckoned, since even he, with the morals of a tom cat, was unsure whether he could shag her.

Bott was a very unattractive woman in her late forties who cut her own mousy blond hair, making her look uncannily like Colonel Rosa Klebb of *From Russia With Love* fame. She was chubbily overweight but her real problem was that she had no idea how to deal with individuals like Psycho. She had arrived at the nick with great plans to bring about change and reform, and immediately fallen foul of the Subdivision Commander of the time, who viewed any change as akin to the end of the world. He had undermined her at every opportunity and even tried to fit her up over a problem in the cell block where prisoners had been gassed by a vehicle in the rear yard.

Her real Nemesis, however, had always been Psycho, who had waged a psychological war against her from day one. That had culminated in Bott knocking herself out in her private toilet in her office, being sedated and taken to hospital. The strain of it all had left her with a terrible stutter, but she was back and determined to get on with the job Daniels had given her. Unfortunately, the new

Subdivisional Commander viewed her with as much disdain as his predecessor, and her life at Horse's Arse continued to be a misery.

'I'll deal with this from here if you like, ma'am,' said Collins gently, taking the memo from her and guiding her towards the muster-room door with a spade-like hand on her back. 'Why don't you go up to your office and I'll pop in after I've finished to let you know how things are going.'

'Very well, Sergeant Collins,' replied Bott imperiously as she tried to recover some face. 'I think I'll g-g-go back to my office and g-g-get on with some paperwork. I'd like to see you after m-muster to discuss some operational plans I've g-g-got.'

'Of course, ma'am, an excellent idea,' murmured Collins as he ushered her out, holding the door open for her. And once she had gone, he wheeled round and shouted. 'Pearce, you fucker!', pointing viciously at the beaming Psycho. 'You do that again, I'll snap your fucking back.'

'Hey, Sarge, if I knew what you were on about . . .'

'Fuck off – we both know it was you. What really pisses me off is you thought you could turn me over with your stupid memo. You mind your step, Pearce, I'm watching you.'

Psycho didn't respond – there was little point. He had never intended to upset Collins; he held the man in enormous respect, and had only ever wanted to humiliate

Bott again. But sometimes there was some collateral damage; there was always that risk, but he vowed to be more careful in future. Andy Collins was not a man to fall foul of. Not for nothing had the power of his punching earned him the nickname of 'the Anaesthetist'.

As Andy Collins finished off the muster, Hilary Bott hurried back to her office on the first floor, where she intended to lock herself in for the night. As she pushed through the double doors into the corridor she was surprised to see a light shining under the closed door to Chief Inspector Stevenson's office. She hadn't noticed it earlier. She was in two minds whether to knock or not, so wary was she of Stevenson, who had joined in the ongoing persecution of her by convincing her that he needed to masturbate regularly during the day as part of a medical condition.

Finally, she plucked up the courage and knocked timidly on the door. There was movement inside, and then after a long pause she heard Stevenson shout, 'Who is it?'

'Only me, sir,' she replied, with her ear pressed to the door. 'May I come in?' She never bowled in without waiting to be summoned in case she blundered in on Stevenson, mid-wank.

After another long pause, he called out, 'Come in, Hilary.'

She opened the door and peered cautiously in, relieved to note that Stevenson appeared to be fully dressed as he rummaged through his desk drawers. She sniffed at the telltale smell of whisky and cigarettes in his tatty office.

'You're here late, sir,' she said, as she took a step inside but not venturing any further in case he suddenly dropped his trousers and pulled the top off one.

'Had some paperwork to sort out and a meeting with the DCI. What do you want, Hilary?' Stevenson asked dismissively, without looking up from what he was doing.

'Nothing in particular, I just saw your light on. Thought you'd like to know I was doing a night shift.'

'A night shift? Who with?' he said urgently, looking at her for the first time.

'D Group, why?'

'Are you fucking mad?' snapped Stevenson. 'Five groups to choose from and you went for that lot? Jesus Christ, Hilary, most of them should be in prison. What's the matter with you – got some sort of death wish?'

Before she could reply, the man exclaimed in triumph and dropped what he had been looking for on his desk. Bott looked in horror at the tube of lubricating gel and a pair of latex surgical gloves. He then cracked his walnut-sized knuckles and began to loosen his belt buckle.

'Oh my God,' gasped Bott, backing away towards the still-open door.

Stevenson glanced up at her. 'Sorry, love, I'm due one on the hurry-up,' he said. 'You can stay if you want.'

'Oh my God,' she repeated, before stepping out into the corridor and shutting the door firmly.

Replacing his props, Stevenson smiled to himself as he heard her running into her own office, the door slamming and locks being fastened before a chair was scraped across the floor and obviously jammed under the door handle.

Retrieving his glass of Scotch from his top drawer, he slumped back in his chair and grinned broadly as DCI Dan Harrison strolled out of the toilet on the far side of the office. He too held a glass of Scotch.

'You better be careful, Pete,' he laughed, as he retook his seat in the armchair opposite the desk. 'One day she's going to complain about you.'

'Her word against mine, Dan,' replied Stevenson casually. 'Besides, everyone knows she's a nutter. Never going to go anywhere, is it?'

'You're probably right, mate,' Harrison agreed, getting wearily to his feet and draining his glass. 'I best be off – got an early start tomorrow.'

'You want one for the road?' asked Stevenson, opening his bottom drawer and bringing out his bottle of Laphroaig.

Harrison held up his hand. 'Not for me, mate, we had plenty upstairs earlier. That'll do me.'

Placing his glass on Stevenson's desk, he walked to the coat-hooks on the back of the door where his suit jacket hung.

'Much going on with the uniforms lately?' he asked.

'Pretty quiet on the grand scale of things. Usual pub fights but nothing special. Had another flashing this lunchtime.'

'Same guy?'

'No question, wearing the Zorro mask again,' Stevenson grinned.

'Hmm, he's good for far too many for comfort. What's that so far – a dozen?'

'Got to be – maybe more.'

'What do your guys call him – Pork Sword Man?'

Stevenson laughed. 'That's him, always got a boner on. Got to give him that.'

Harrison grimaced. 'I'm worried we're going to get some pressure soon to take him out. Reckon it's time to put something together to deal with him. We can have a chat about it tomorrow – we'll get a CID-uniform operation on the go, OK?'

'Yeah, sounds fine,' yawned Stevenson. 'I'm about all day, so pop in when you're ready.'

'Night, Pete,' said Harrison, opening the door. 'Keep it in your trousers.'

Dan Harrison and Peter Stevenson were the senior officers that Horse's Arse needed, and in their year together in charge of the CID and uniforms respectively, they had made a huge difference. Harrison was a portly forty-five-year-old career detective who had sacrificed his marriage and family on the altar of his career. He had little to interest him now outside of the Job, preferring to spend as much of his time as he could working. Which was why he was still at the nick so late. Admittedly, he and Stevenson had been in the station bar on the top floor from about 6 p.m., but they had been talking Job, not socialising, before they'd adjourned to Stevenson's office for a nightcap.

Harrison lived alone in a studio flat on the edge of town, had few friends outside his circle of work colleagues, and hadn't seen his two daughters for nearly three years. The old school photograph of his girls in a frame in his office was the only indication anyone had that there had been anything in Harrison's life other than being a detective. He seemed to be ever-present at the nick, appearing as if by magic at any situation that was of interest, always looking to put one over on the bad guys.

He wasn't afraid to bend the rules to achieve that either. Faced with the potential of a Turkish crime family member getting a grip on the drugs trade in Handstead, Harrison had had no qualms in using the senior members of that family to remove the troublesome and ambitious local Turk from the scene – permanently. He ran a network of unregistered and unscrupulous informants with a combination of inducements and threats of exposure to their community – and got impressive results. Harrison appeared to vindicate the ethos that the ends justified the means.

Peter Stevenson had only been at Handstead a little over a year, also as one of Chief Daniels's men but with a brief to sort out the local hooligans – those who lived on the estates rather than the hooligans in the uniform! He too had been an unqualified success, leading as he did by example and from the front. So much so, that within his first month in the post, he had led the firearms team in a shoot-out with members of the notorious Park Royal Mafia, who had attempted to rob a gunsmiths in the nearby village of Tamworth. Stevenson and his team had blown three of the Mafia to pieces, sending out a clear, unequivocal message to the criminals of Handstead: the town was under new management, who were prepared to fight fire with fire.

A big, red-faced Scot who liked a drink, Stevenson inspired fear and respect in equal measure in the civilian and uniform staff who worked for him. He could fairly claim that he never asked his staff to do anything he hadn't done or couldn't do himself. Domestically, he was happily married with a young son, but he too put in the hours. Like so many of the cops at Horse's Arse, initially he'd been in despair at his move there, but as he adapted to the way things were done, he had come to realise there was nowhere else he'd rather be.

Five minutes after Harrison had left, Stevenson slipped a coat on over his uniform, turned out the lights in his office and headed home. For the next eight hours, Horse's Arse was to be placed in the not so tender care of D Group.

Chapter Three

The girl was drunk. Not off her face, falling down drunk, but probably well over the drink-drive limit. Certainly drunk enough to do things she wouldn't normally do, like starting to walk home from the party as she did now. She had phoned for a taxi from her friend's house, but the prospect of a forty-minute wait made up her mind. It was a warm night and nice and dry – the walk would only take her half an hour and do her the world of good.

Saying her goodbyes around half-past midnight, she set off towards the town centre where there was a better chance of grabbing a cab, kicking her shoes off fairly quickly and continuing barefoot along the cool pavements. She passed no one nor saw any vehicles between leaving the house and arriving at the edge of Stream Woods, which lay between her and the town centre. Sober, she would never have done it but with a drink inside her and keen to get home, she decided to take the path through the woods.

Stream Woods was only about a quarter of a mile deep, and the path had been tarmacked. It was well lit along its entire length until it opened out in Bishops Rise, but the huge rhododendron bushes and trees growing at the edges of the path made it feel claustrophobic even on the brightest of days. However, she could take fifteen minutes off her barefoot journey by going that way; there was no one about and it was a beautiful evening. A crescent moon hung in a velvet black, star-studded sky, and the only activity as she turned on to the path were bats flitting around the buzzing halogen streetlamps.

She was about 200 yards along the path when she stopped and took a cigarette from her bag. As she clicked the flame of her lighter and leaned forward to inhale, she heard the bushes behind her suddenly explode as something came crashing out of them. She then felt a huge blow to the back of her head. She was vaguely aware of pitching forward on to the path, smashing face-first into it, crushing her still unlit cigarette into her forehead. Not quite unconscious, she sensed a figure standing alongside her – she could see men's black lace-up shoes – and then strong hands grabbed her by her long hair and dragged her quickly off the path and into the bushes. She couldn't move, felt no pain either from the blow or being dragged along by her hair, and then realised she was lying face-down in the undergrowth. She could smell the pine needles on the ground.

Her eyes were still open, though fixed on the middle

distance, and she could hear footsteps crunching in the undergrowth nearby; then came another vicious blow to her left temple. She was still not completely unconscious and able to comprehend that her skirt and knickers were being ripped off, as though by some wild beast. Then she felt a huge weight on her back and hands on her buttocks, and then a searing pain as she was penetrated. He went at her like a madman and she felt the blows to the back of her head as he battered her during the rape. Eventually, she felt him ejaculate – but not directly into her; he must be wearing a condom.

There was a part of her brain that refused to submit to the beating she was getting, and small details were still registering with her. She felt him pull roughly out of her and then he was saying something and the footsteps began crunching around near her. It could have been hours later, but was probably only seconds before she felt another, worse, pain as the hands grabbed her buttocks again and something hard and cold was rammed into her anus.

And then that one stubborn part of her brain surrendered and she slipped into welcome unconsciousness.

Whilst the girl was being brutalised, the Brothers killed a man. Shortly after 1 a.m., Pizza and JJ were cruising the Park Royal Estate when they responded to a rendezvous request from Yankee One to the Tamworth Road crossroads. It was unusual for them to ask for a meet, and intrigued, Pizza had made his way there quickly. The radio was relatively quiet and he and JJ chatted amiably until they rounded a corner and the headlights of Two One lit up a scene of carnage.

'Oh fuck,' said Pizza quietly, as he and JJ gazed at the catastrophe. JJ stared open-mouthed.

In front of them were Yankee One and Bravo Two Two, and off to the side, the Brothers, along with Psycho and Malcy, crouched next to a body lying on the verge. Clearly visible nearby was a mangled bicycle.

'Oh fuck,' repeated Pizza. 'Stay here, JJ. Keep an ear on the radio,' he said, getting out of Two One. He trotted over to the others and JJ wound down his window to try and hear what they were saying. He was too far away, but from the body language of the group he could tell they were desperately worried. He was about to disobey his instructions when Pizza jogged back and got into the car. His face was grim.

'What happened?' JJ asked.

'The Brothers were racing Two Two. Came round the corner and took out that cyclist,' Pizza said tersely.

'Oh no! How is he – have they called an ambulance?'

'No point. Dead as a fucking doornail.'

'Fucking hell, have they called anyone?'

'You're joking, aren't you? They call anyone, the Brothers are going to prison.'

'What? What the fuck are they going to do then?'

'Clear it up,' replied Pizza simply.

'Clear it up?'

'Yeah, clear it up. You keep your mouth shut, JJ, you understand? We weren't here – we know fuck all about this. It didn't happen.'

'What?' shouted JJ, unable to believe his ears and terrified he was now being railroaded into a conspiracy of grotesque proportions.

'I said, you keep quiet, JJ,' hissed Pizza in a menacing tone JJ had never heard from him before. 'You saw fuck all, and you say fuck all. You never *ever* talk about this to anyone, understood?'

'Oh God,' JJ said desperately, slumping back in his seat.

'Not a word, OK?' reiterated Pizza.

'OK, OK,' replied the devastated JJ, his stomach feeling leaden. 'But this is all wrong.'

'We've got to stick together,' said Pizza, as he watched what was happening ahead of them. 'We don't, we're all fucked.'

As the pair looked on, the Brothers, Psycho and Malcy bent down to the lifeless corpse in the grass and took hold of an arm and leg each. Then, swinging in time and one of them counting, 'One, two, three!' they swung the body high over the hawthorn hedge and into the adjacent field. In the headlights, JJ could see it appeared to be the body of a young male wearing a combat jacket.

'They can't be serious,' he said, looking imploringly at Pizza. 'They can't just chuck him in a field.'

'Got no choice, JJ,' replied Pizza, looking at him. 'Got to get rid of him.'

As he spoke, they saw Psycho put on his uniform black leather gloves and then dispatch the mangled bike over the hedge after its owner.

'Holy shit,' breathed the appalled JJ as Pizza started up Two One and began to reverse into a field entrance to do a three-point turn.

'We were never here, JJ, we know fuck all about anything and no one can prove otherwise,' said Pizza, as they headed back towards the glittering lights of the town.

They drove in silence with not even radio traffic to puncture the atmosphere. Pizza only had two and a half years' service under his belt, but in that short period so much had happened to him he felt he'd lived a lifetime. It was not unusual for cops at Horse's Arse to see and do so much more than their colleagues elsewhere in the county, but Pizza had been to hell and back – which made him exceptional.

Two years earlier, whilst still an unloved and derided probationer, he had watched as his partner that day, Dave 'Boyril' Baines, had been shot alongside him in a flat in the Grant Flowers tower block. And then the shooter had blown her own brains out all over the wall.

Baines had died in Pizza's arms desperately trying to tell him something, and since his death, Pizza had been plagued by a dream. He would be in a crowded room and spot Bovril on the far side, again trying to say something to him, and as Pizza barged his way through the mêlée to get to him, he would wake up bathed in sweat, grinding his teeth in frustration. He kept getting closer, but after two years he still wasn't there.

It wasn't all gloom and doom though. Some good had come out of Baines's death. At his funeral, Pizza had met a friend of his, with whom he now lived. She had been pregnant at the time they met, but Pizza had fallen in love with her the moment he laid eyes on her, and now doted on her little son, whom he regarded as his own. He had insisted that the boy be christened David in honour of his murdered friend. It was all very cosy and convenient, but Pizza lacked one piece of the jigsaw, and it was something that the lovely Lisa Jones was dreading him finding out.

Dave Baines and Lisa had been much more than just friends – he was the father of little David, but had died unaware of the fact. There was no chance Pizza would ever find out unless she told him, and Lisa saw no point in rocking the boat now. They were so happy together – but she knew Pizza was having the dream regularly, and that worried her enormously. Many a night Pizza had woken with a shout and dripping with sweat, and she had stroked him back to sleep as he murmured, 'He's trying to tell me something, he's trying to tell me something.'

Whilst Pizza appeared blissfully happy with their domestic arrangements, for Lisa, the dream was a ticking time bomb. Professionally, Pizza was a made man. Prior to the murder of Baines he had been a non-person, as all probationers were, undergoing an unofficial rite of passage. But his exposure that day to the murder, the fact that he survived alongside Baines, and his subsequent eloquent and determined appearance at Manchester Crown Court during the trial of many of the senior members of the Park Royal Mafia, had cemented his place on the group. The others knew he was sound and could be trusted to do the right thing, whatever that might be. It was the way things were done on police groups, both uniforms and CID. You had to prove yourself first, and once you had, you were a fully paid up and respected member for life.

Pizza was also developing into a decent street cop with an innate sixth sense for sniffing out when something was wrong. Keen to learn from the others, he was a tireless worker and had eagerly seized on the ethos by which the Brothers swore – the harder you work, the luckier you get.

Young JJ was virtually a mirror image of Pizza as he had been at the same stage of service. Now twenty years old and with a year's service under his belt, he was still undergoing his rite of passage but was a long way towards achieving his goal of acceptance. He was fortunate to have a tutor such as Pizza who'd been there, done it and got the T-shirt. He'd made huge progress in his first year, particularly after he'd proved himself to be a phenomenal streetfighter during an enormous punch-up with a crowd of football hooligans. He was born to it, with extraordinary fist speed and spatial awareness – both crucial factors in a street brawl. Psycho had given him the nickname JJ after that blow out, the first step on the rocky road to full membership of any group. But he still had a way to go, though the omens were good.

JJ was also a great storyteller and regularly had the group in stitches as he recounted some of the goings-on in the section house at the nick where he had recently moved. He'd particularly impressed Psycho with an account of how he'd spiked a greedy colleague's food – something the infamous poisoner Psycho had taken a note of, for future reference. Living in the section house was a notoriously mean PC from A Group, Chris Wade, who made it a point of honour to pay as little for his food as possible, or preferably not at all. He had cultivated a relationship with a curry house in the town centre where he now ate for free, and it was not unknown for him to be having cold onion bhajis for breakfast.

One evening, as some of the residents had been watching TV, Wade had asked whether they fancied a curry, which he could get cheap. He'd taken £5 off each of those present and duly returned with a huge box of assorted curries and side dishes, which appeared to be a good deal for all concerned, but which of course had cost Wade fuck all. At the end of their feast, Wade had asked everyone if he could keep the leftovers as he was Late Turn for the rest of the week, and no one had objected – after all, he'd got them this great deal. Wade had then packed what remained of his ill-gotten gains into the communal fridge.

The following day, when JJ had popped into the curry house to get a menu for his own future use, the staff had innocently revealed Wade's crime. JJ didn't mention it to anyone else, but determined that Wade would pay. On returning to the section house, he'd nipped over to the girls' corridor where he knew one of the WPCs kept a large, shit machine of a hamster. He had quickly upended the cage with the rodent squeaking in protest against the bars, and emptied the contents of the bottom of the cage into a plastic shopping bag. Returning to his room, he had carefully extracted several dozen huge hamster droppings, which he then stirred into the aluminium curry boxes, marked up *Chris Wade's – do not touch* in the fridge.

JJ made a point of trying to be present in the following days as Wade ploughed through his hamster biryani and turd tikka masala before he told everyone, including Wade, what had happened.

'Fucking genius!' Psycho had exclaimed. 'Like your style, boy.'

Once JJ had revealed his story, another of the section house PCs had also put his hands up to a spot of poisoning. He had discovered that Wade's girlfriend, who stayed over from time to time, had decided it was OK to use what she liked from the fridge without asking, and was regularly slurping from bottles of lemonade kept there. She had become ill soon after, much to everyone's huge amusement. You played by the rules in the section house or suffered the unpleasant consequences.

Now though, JJ was under huge pressure. They'd opened the door to their exclusive club just a crack; given him a nickname after he'd proved himself as a fighter. But now they were asking him two, far more testing questions. Could they really trust him? And how far would he go to earn that trust?

Chapter Four

'Late Turn brought one in for burglary who's fucking us about,' said Sergeant Mick Jones to the two detectives who were leafing through the custody records of the clips over the chalk detention board.

DCs Bob Clarke and John Benson, the night duty CID team, turned to look at him.

'Fucking you about, how?' asked Benson, his eyes sparking in malicious anticipation. He was a big man with a full Frank Zappa-style moustache and dressed down for night duty in just a pair of jeans and a buttoned-up dark Ben Sherman T-shirt. His huge arms bulged in the short sleeves.

'Can't or won't talk English,' replied Jones. 'We've tried all sorts but he just keeps on with "No understand English". Don't recognise the accent either.'

'White or black?' asked Clarke, who was smaller than his colleague, with collar-length hair parted to one side and similarly dressed down in jeans but wearing a more formal pink shirt with double cuffs and cufflinks. Once a detective, always a detective.

'White,' continued Jones. 'Eastern European maybe?'

'What do you think, John?' asked Clarke, turning back to the custody sheets and looking for the papers relating to their next victim. 'One for Doctor Saint Moritz or your schlong?'

'Definitely Captain Schlong,' replied Benson, glancing up at him with a wide smile. 'Give us the cell keys, Sarge. We'll just pop down and sort this out,' he called over his shoulder.

The cells were pretty full with the usual assortment of drunks and fighters, and the noise from the cell passage was clearly audible from where they were standing. The detectives stood looking at the chalkboard with the names of the prisoners scratched on with their alleged offences and arresting officer's collar number alongside until the gaoler, Trog Hooper, strutted over and handed them the bunch of large keys.

'Be gentle with him, boys,' he muttered, before disappearing into his side room to put the kettle on.

The two detectives walked down into the gloomy bowels of the cell block, lit with dull yellow ceiling bulkhead lights. The walls were painted with a shiny cream paint; shiny to aid with hosing off the blood and shit that invariably covered them. As they approached the main cell gate, the smell of sickly sweet industrial-strength disinfectant became stronger, but still failed to completely mask the smell of vomit and human excrement. It was a smell that the gaolers like Trog who worked permanently in such an environment, could never really get out of their noses. It seemed to seep into the pores of the skin and stay there.

'Cell four,' advised Clarke as they locked the gate behind them and moved into the cell passage. The long corridor had ten cell doors, each with a small chalkboard outside for the name of its current occupant. It was lit now by the sinister red glow of the night lights, which threw a positively demonic hue on it. The occupants of the cells had heard the visitors approaching and the banging and shouting had intensified.

Ignoring the bedlam, Benson peered through the inspection hatch to cell four before unlocking it and stepping inside, followed closely by Clarke, who pulled the door almost shut behind them. The detectives looked down at a middle-aged white male wearing black trousers and a dirty white long-sleeved shirt, lying on the high bench bed on a blue plastic mattress with his hands behind his head. Making no motion to move, he smiled up smugly at them. Swarthy and unshaven, with heavy sideburns, his face just screamed dishonesty and could only have been loved by his mother.

'Looks like a fucking pikey to me, Bob,' remarked Benson casually.

The man rolled into a sitting position. 'No speak English, no understand,' he said mockingly.

'Hmm, is that right?' said Clarke, flicking through the arrest sheets he'd brought down with him. 'Let's see, shall we? Nicked at half-past nine coming out of the back of a house in Abbots Grove with a couple of chequebooks and a bit of cash. White male, name, address and date and place of birth unknown. Not much to go on, is it?'

'No speak English, no understand,' repeated the man, looking at the floor but grinning broadly.

'What's the plan here, pal?' asked Benson, sitting on the bench alongside him and leaning back against the wall. His immense bulk so close had made the prisoner feel immediately uncomfortable and he shuffled himself away before replying.

'No speak English, no understand,' he said, but he'd stopped smiling. Something about these two visitors told him he had trouble on his hands.

'You know what, John?' said Clarke from the door. 'I reckon he thinks that if we can't find out who he is or interview him, he'll walk away from this. We'll just get bored and give up; too much like hard work for a silly little job like this.'

'Think you might be right, Bob,' said Benson, leaning away from the wall and going close to the man's face. 'I reckon I'm going to have to fuck some sense into him.'

'No speak English, no underst-stand,' stammered the man, wide-eyed as Benson got to his feet and stood in front of him.

'Oh, you speak English well enough, my old son, and

you definitely understand it well enough to comprehend that I'm now going to fuck you up the arse until I'm a hundred per cent sure you do.'

Benson began to unbuckle his jeans and then dropped them around his ankles before he pulled his boxers down to his knees – causing the man on the bench to gasp out loud. Benson had a cock like a baby's arm holding an orange, which explained his nickname of 'Donkey'. It wasn't the first time he and Clarke had employed the Captain Schlong routine to deal with a difficult prisoner, and it appeared to be working again. The terrified man had jumped on to the bench seat and had backed away against the wall, unable to take his eyes off the fearsome beast being massaged into life in front of him. Fully awake, it could probably consume a piglet.

'I'm going to be leaving you with an arsehole like a blood orange if you don't suddenly remember how to speak English,' continued Benson, eyes fixed on the trembling man.

'No, no, I speak English very good,' he blurted out. 'What you want? I give you everything, plenty information. What you want?'

'Good lad,' laughed Benson, putting the monster away and pulling his jeans up. 'We'll be back soon to take a full and frank confession from you – and I mean the fucking lot, understood?' He fastened his belt buckle with a flourish and stared at the man.

'Understood?' he said, louder.

'I give you everything, you keep trousers on, OK?' the man replied, all the colour drained from his face.

As the two detectives slammed his cell door shut behind them, he slumped back on to his mattress and wondered to himself whether remaining in Romania would have been the more sensible option.

Benson and Clarke returned to the booking-in area and dropped the keys on to Jones's desk. He was on the phone so they waited for him to finish.

'Forget the prisoners, boys,' he said as he hung up. 'You're wanted down at Bishops Rise. Two One's got what sounds like a nasty rape job.'

A little after 3 a.m. DCI Dan Harrison walked into the CID main office where Clarke and Benson were at their adjacent desks.

'What we got?' he asked, hanging his suit jacket over the back of a chair. His face was crumpled and drawn from lack of sleep and he'd clearly not had time to shave before he left the flat. His hair was sticking up and needed a wash, but his eyes were bright and alert – this was what he lived for. He had been dressed and out of the door within five minutes of the phone by his bed ringing. He could wash and shave later. The first few hours of any enquiry were crucial and he wasn't going to waste time on his ablutions.

'Nasty one, boss. Sorry to drag you out of bed, but we thought you'd want an early heads up,' replied Clarke. 'Don't know anything about her yet. Uniforms found her in Bishops Rise at one-forty a.m., naked from the waist down and been given a right horrible beating.'

'Definitely raped?'

'Put money on it. Bleeding badly front and back doors. Nose and a cheekbone probably broken, both eyes closed, cuts and bruises all over her face. She's had a terrible time.'

'She telling us anything? Where it happened?'

'Not a thing. She's in shock but she'd probably not be able to say much anyway; both lips are smashed up. She's a real mess.'

'Shit, we need a scene quickly,' sighed Harrison. 'Where is she now?'

'Downstairs in the doctor's room. Surgeon's on the way.'

'Who's with her?'

'One of the night shift WPCs – she's been told to try and get her talking.'

'Not been to hospital?'

'No, not yet. We wanted to get her seen here by the surgeon. We can take her there later.'

'OK, when's the surgeon due here?'

'About now; it's Doc Dougan.'

'Thank fuck for that. Listen, we've got to get a scene from here. Where was she found?'

'Bishops Rise, top of the path out of Stream Woods.'

'Let's start there. Get the uniforms working away from where they found her back into the woods. She missing any property?'

'Don't know yet. Obviously minus her bottom half, trousers or skirt and knickers.'

'She have a handbag with her?'

'Not that we've seen.'

'OK, tell them they're looking for a skirt or trousers and knickers and a handbag, but could be anything else. They find anything, give us a shout. Bob, give Control a ring. I want a unit of the Patrol Group available to me from first light. We got a SOCO here yet?'

'Yeah, Graham Lightfoot is downstairs waiting for the Doc.'

'Great. I want statements tonight from the uniforms who found her and I want a fucking scene quickly. Let's go and see her.'

Harrison and Benson hurried downstairs to the cell area where they found the SOCO having a smoke with Trog Hooper.

'Graham, I want some early photos of her,' said Harrison.

'Already done, boss,' replied Lightfoot, grinding his cigarette out under his shoe. 'She's a fucking mess. Done twenty shots already,' he said, checking the counter on his Celica camera.

'Excellent. Doc Dougan should be here any moment. Stay close to him, he knows what we need. John, let's go and see her.'

As they entered the doctor's room, a small office just off the cell corridor which smelled cleaner than the rest of the cell block, it was difficult not to gasp or pass comment on the girl's appearance. She sat trembling on a chair at the far end of the office, hunched forward and head down, a rough grey blanket wrapped around her shaking shoulders. Her hair was matted with dried blood, and large clumps appeared to have been torn out. Even with her head bowed they could see her face was one huge bruise, covered in drying cuts, both eyes completely closed, her mouth a bloody, puffy lump. Her bare legs and feet were covered in dirt and scratched, and a small pool of blood was forming on the floor at her feet from the steady trickle that ran down the inside of her left calf and off her ankle.

Both men were genuinely shocked. They'd seen plenty of victims of brutal sex attacks in the past, but this poor girl was, by a distance, the worst. She'd been beaten to within an inch of her life. The only small consolation was that she was still alive and could perhaps tell them what had happened, but Harrison wasn't holding his breath. The attack had taken place in the open air, he still didn't know where, and what little forensic evidence that may have been available to him was now at the mercy of the elements, nature, wildlife and of course the wildlife of Handstead that walked on its hind legs.

'Tell the uniforms to look for clumps of hair as well,' he whispered into Benson's ear.

'She been able to tell us anything yet?' he asked the Blister, who was standing with her back against the wall. She shook her head sadly.

Harrison crouched down alongside the girl and looked compassionately at her before he spoke.

'Darling, I'm so sorry for what's happened to you. My name's Dan Harrison, I'm the Detective Chief Inspector here, and I give you my word I shall do everything I can to catch the creature who did this to you,' he said softly. 'I know that right now, the last thing you want to do is talk to anyone, but I'm going to need some details about you and where you've been tonight. But you take your time; you talk to my officer here when you're ready. I've got a police doctor coming to see you – he's a good man, trust me – and he will examine you and get me some evidence of what's happened to you.'

He saw the girl shudder as he talked to her and knew that what he was saying was registering. On top of the brutal attack, an intimate examination by a male doctor often proved too much. Harrison gently touched the shaking girl's shoulder.

'Listen, sweetheart,' he whispered, 'I'm going to get him, I promise you. Be strong – help me.'

The girl stopped shaking and slowly turned her swollen face towards the soft voice in her ear.

'Mandy Blackstock,' she mumbled painfully through swollen and cut lips and broken teeth. 'I'm Mandy Blackstock.'

'Take it easy, Mandy, take it easy. You're safe now and we're on your side from here on,' Harrison told her. 'I'm going to get on with what I've got to do to lay hands on this bastard, but my officer's going to be staying with you, so you give whatever you can to her, OK?'

The girl nodded tearfully.

'I'll be back to see you a little later. Be strong for me, Mandy.' Then Harrison got awkwardly to his feet, his knees popping and cracking, and walked over to the Blister. 'Stay with her, talk to her and write it all down, OK?'

WPC Amanda Wheeler nodded and held up her notebook and pen to confirm she was ready to go. Having sat in with dozens of rape victims over the years, she was very aware of the importance of an early account from the girl. She had put her time in with the recently disbanded Women's Police Department, which dealt with the victims of sex crimes and children and very little else; it was an area of police work at which she could rightly claim to be an expert. It was also an aspect of the Job from which most male officers would run a mile.

'Soon as I get any more I'll let you know, boss,' she said to his back as he hurried out of the door to supervise activities out on the ground.

Both uniform Inspectors currently on duty at the nick were blissfully unaware of the events unfolding around them. Hilary Bott was barricaded in her office where she intended to stay until it got light and the beasts and ghoulies had gone away, and Jeff Greaves was getting himself comfortable for a kip in the Inspector's office where Andy Collins had guided him just after 10 p.m. He was stretched out in his chair with his feet up on the desk, shoes off and his hands behind his head, quietly running over his future plans to get out of this fucking place and get a real job, when there was a knock on the door. He quickly got into character.

'All the rabbits have been fed, don't be cross with me!' he called weakly, quickly getting his feet off the desk.

The door opened and Andy Collins peered into the office. He smiled warmly at his lunatic Inspector.

'Sorry to bother you, boss. Need to bring you up to speed on what's going on, if that's OK?'

Greaves smiled back and nodded. It killed him to keep pulling the wool over Collins's eyes, but needs must.

'Nasty rape came in from Bishops Rise. We've got the girl downstairs and Mr Harrison is in and coordinating everything.'

'Good, good,' murmured Greaves, relieved to hear that the DCI had everything under control.

'The surgeon's been called, but there's a bit of a problem,' said Collins slowly.

'How?'

'He's been nicked by Traffic.'

'Nicked?'

'Yeah, a pair of right pricks bagged him in the rear yard.'

'For fuck's sake!' exploded Greaves in a rare display of lucidity. 'Who's the surgeon?'

'Doc Dougan.'

'You are fucking joking,' said Greaves, getting to his feet. 'Doc Dougan?'

'Afraid so, boss,' replied Collins.

'Right, where is he?'

'We've put him in the detention room with the door open. Couldn't use the doctor's room, the rape victim's in there.'

'Fucking hell, Andy, we can't put him in there – he's one of the good guys. Stick him in an interview room or somewhere and start getting some water down him.' Greaves began to lace up his shoes which he'd pulled out of his bottom drawer.

'How pissed is he?' he asked.

'Jesus, boss, you know the Doc. He's had a drink and he's probably over the limit, but he's got a hobnailed liver. We phoned him and got him out of bed to come and help; apparently he'd been at a dinner with surgeons from around the county so he'd had a few. You know the Doc.'

Greaves certainly did know Doc Dougan – very well indeed. They went back years – initially on a professional basis, latterly as close personal friends who drank together regularly and played golf. Such good friends were they that Doc Dougan, in his capacity as a Force Surgeon, was lined up to give evidence on Greaves's behalf to prove his suitability for a discharge from the Job on medical grounds.

'Do you know the arseholes who nicked him?' asked

Greaves firmly as he followed the loyal Collins out of the office.

'Not their names, boss, but I recognise their faces. They're part of the crew that plot up around the town trying to bag pissed coppers – a pair of real cocks.'

Collins was referring to the very real threat to the careers and livelihoods of the cops at Handstead who stayed late to have a drink and then drive home. The heavy drinking culture there was well known, and officers at the northern Traffic base had set out to nick as many of their own as they could. So far, they'd laid hands on two PCs who had been fortunate to keep their jobs, but it was a gauntlet that the cops at Handstead seemed prepared to run after every Late Turn shift.

The hatred felt towards the Traffic cops who rarely brought real prisoners in was intense and on a par with the sheer loathing held for the rubber-soled Complaints and Discipline Department. Most divisional street cops could barely bring themselves to speak to a Traffic officer who did a job that seemed totally alien to them. How the fuck could anyone get excited about reading a tachograph and then shafting a hardworking lorry driver who'd exceeded his permitted hours of work? Where was the buzz in knowing the required depth of tread on a car tyre and costing an otherwise law-abiding motorist a fortune in fines? What was wrong with someone who reported a driver for exceeding a 50 m.p.h. speed limit by 20 m.p.h. at 4 a.m. on a deserted road? What value did any of them bring to the party? When did they last look in the boot of the car with the dodgy brake-light and find all that nicked gear? It didn't happen because being a real cop wasn't something that appealed to most Traffic officers. Drive nice fast shiny cars and fuck off the motorists was about the sum of it, and it was a work ethic that the cops at Horse's Arse simply couldn't get their heads round. Not that the feeling was dissimilar elsewhere, but the enmity between the cops at Handstead and the humpty-backed child molesters from the Northern Traffic base was intense.

As Greaves and Collins entered the booking-in area they could immediately see Doc Dougan sitting forlornly in the adjacent detention room. He looked up as he heard the movement outside but made no sign that he had recognised his old drinking partner.

'Give me the arrest sheet for Doctor Dougan, please,' Greaves asked Sergeant Jones. 'Where's the arresting officer?'

'Just popped out to give Jesus a tug for carrying an overweight load probably,' said Jones, handing over the sheets as asked. 'What a pair of twats . . . talk of the devil,' he finished as he noticed the two social lepers walk back into the room. Greaves spun on his heel and fixed the two Traffic cops with a glass-eyed smile.

'Evening, gents. You the two who nicked the police surgeon?'

'That's right, sir, positive test following a moving traffic offence,' replied one of the Traffic cops. He had a heavily pockmarked face, legacy of a well-deserved bout of childhood chickenpox, and blackheads the size of saucers along his bulbous red nose. It was a face that Greaves felt he could punch all day.

'Moving traffic offence?'

'Yeah, excess speed along Bolton Road East.'

'What speed?'

'Forty miles an hour, wasn't it?' the nun-raper asked his companion as the continuing questions started to concern him.

'Yeah, forty.'

'Forty miles an hour, in a thirty limit at three forty-five in the morning, after we'd called him out of his bed? You do know who he is, don't you?' said Greaves, glancing at his watch.

'It's thirty miles an hour, twenty-four hours a day, sir. That's the law, we just enforce it.'

'Of course you do, of course you do. Without fear or favour, I'm sure. Were you interfered with as a boy?' he said quietly.

'What was that?' asked the pockmarked Traffic cop.

'I said, can I see the roadside test? We'll need to deal with this by the book, as I'm sure you'll appreciate. Where was the test administered?'

The Traffic cops were expecting the question and smiled knowingly.

'In the rear yard, boss, but we're within our rights to administer the test as the original offence was committed on a public road.'

'Of course, I wasn't questioning your professionalism. Just your parentage,' he finished quietly again.

'Sorry, what did you say?' said Scarface's fat colleague, who looked like a five-pound bag of shit in a three-pound bag.

'I said, can I see the tube?'

Suspiciously, the Traffic cop held the incriminating glass phial out for Greaves to look at, but significantly did not hand it over. Greaves made no attempt to reach out for it, although he peered closely at it. The crystals along its entire length were bright green – evidence of a very positive test for alcohol in the breath.

'OK, thanks. Let's get on with this, shall we? Sergeant, have we got another police surgeon on the way?'

'Doctor Payne should be here in a couple of minutes,' replied Jones.

'Excellent. Come on, gentlemen,' Greaves said, walking dramatically into the detention room. Doc Dougan got to his feet and said nothing.

'Good morning, Doctor Dougan, I'm Inspector Greaves, the night duty Inspector here at Handstead.'

'Good morning,' said Dougan politely, keeping his eyes on Greaves, and studiously ignoring the Traffic cops who stood close behind him.

'Doctor Dougan, you've been arrested on suspicion of driving whilst over the alcohol limit, having provided a positive specimen of breath. Is that correct?'

'Quite right, I'm afraid, Inspector.'

'OK, I need to administer another test here at the station just to confirm the first test. Will you provide another specimen of breath?'

'Of course.'

'You got a kit?' asked Greaves, turning to the Traffic cops.

Needless to say they had, the pockmarked one pulling the small green plastic box from a pocket in his high visibility yellow jacket. Greaves took it from him and sat alongside Doc Dougan. Opening the box, he took one of the clear glass phials from its plastic lugs and began to carefully saw it along the small serrated piece of metal in the side of the box. He cut into both ends before he inserted one into a small slot and gently snapped the end off. He then pushed the other end into the slot and smiled as the fat Traffic cop leaned right in to make sure he wasn't trying to put in a previously used negative test, or do something else untoward.

The Traffic cop then suffered what numerous motorists had endured at the hands of cack-handed cops. With a vigorous arm movement, Greaves snapped off the small glass top, which shot up out of the box and into the right eye of the cop. He jumped back squealing, clutching at his eye as his mate moved towards him.

'Fuck, sorry about that. You OK?' asked Greaves.

'It's in my fucking eye,' he yelled. 'Fuck me, you've blinded me.'

Greaves and Dougan got to their feet and joined the

other Traffic cop fussing around him. Another figure appeared in the doorway of the detention room and the three with 20/20 vision turned to see who it was.

'Trouble?' asked a smiling Dr James Payne.

'Poor chap's got glass in his eye,' said Dougan sympathetically to his young colleague.

'Better have a look at that first,' said Payne, putting his briefcase on the raised bench and walking over to the injured Traffic cop, who was making whimpering noises, his hand clamped over his eye. After much moaning and persuasion, Payne got to have a look.

'Hmm, nasty one,' he eventually declared. 'You'd better get him down to A and E now. That'll need to be flushed out properly,' he said to the other Traffic cop.

'Can't you do it here?' he replied suspiciously.

'It's got to be done properly, under the right conditions. This is the last place you want to be poking around in someone's eye.'

'Just get me down to the fucking hospital, will you?' groaned the injured officer to his mate. 'This is caning me.'

'You can leave the rest of the procedure to us,' said Greaves brightly as the two cops hurried out of the detention room. 'Pick up the paperwork from me later.'

The pockmarked cop glanced back at him with a look that spoke volumes, but wisely he kept quiet. As they left, Greaves was sure he could see the slime trail on the floor behind them.

'See you later,' he called, as the door out to the rear yard slammed shut behind them. He waited until there was little chance of them returning unexpectedly before he went back to the detention room where Dougan and Payne were sitting on the bench chatting quietly. They smiled as Greaves walked in and stood in front of them.

'Nice shot, Jeff,' laughed Dougan softly.

'I knew he couldn't resist coming close to make sure I wasn't trying anything on, but getting him in the eye was a real bonus. What the hell happened, Doc?'

'This is all about you, I'm afraid, Jeff.'

'Me? What you on about?'

'I was over at Tubbenden Road police station a couple of nights ago and had a chat with the gaoler there. He gave me a heads-up about a bounty the Traffic division have put on me.'

'A bounty?'

'Apparently, one of the hierarchy at Headquarters has got the raving hump about me lining up to give evidence on your behalf when you go for your medical discharge hearing. I'm told they've put a hundred quid up to the Traffic officer that gets me for drink driving. It's no secret I have the odd tipple. That pair were parked up at the bottom of my road waiting for me – followed me all the way here.'

'Were you speeding?'

'What do you think, Jeff? With the information I'd been given and aware of them within minutes of leaving home? I was bang on thirty all the way, but I guess they need that hundred more than we know.'

'What a pair of arseholes,' scoffed Greaves. 'Listen, Docs, we need to find a way out of this. Got a problem with that?'

Dougan said nothing, but Payne smiled broadly and patted his partner and professional mentor on the shoulder.

'Doc Dougan said you'd have a solution, Inspector. What's the plan?'

'We need to be a bit swift, gents, so let's get on. Doctor Dougan, you have the option of providing me with a specimen of urine or blood. Did I hear you say you'd go for the blood option?' he said formally.

'You certainly did, Inspector.'

'Doctor Payne, Doctor Dougan has opted to provide a specimen of blood for analysis. Would you do the honours, please?'

'Of course, Inspector,' said Payne with a broad grin, opening his briefcase as Greaves pushed the detention-room door closed with his foot. From his desk, Sergeant Jones saw the door shut, smiled knowingly and got on with writing up his arrest sheets.

'This is going to hurt me a lot more than you, Doc,' said Greaves, unbuttoning his shirt cuff and rolling up the sleeve before offering his arm to Dr Payne.

There was silence as Payne inserted a needle into a big vein in the crook of Greaves's arm before he carefully filled two small clear glass phials. He shook them vigorously before placing them on the lid of his closed briefcase. As he wrote quickly on some adhesive labels, Greaves applied the round plaster he had been given over the small puncture wound and rolled his sleeve back down.

'You know the routine, Doc; which one do you want?' he asked.

Dougan picked up one of the phials and slipped it into his trouser pocket. 'Just a thought, Jeff,' he said. 'You haven't been taking any of that shit I've been prescribing for your madness, have you? If you have, it'll probably come back over the limit for drugs.'

Greaves laughed. 'No worries there, Doc, clean as a whistle – not even an aspirin. Let's get you bailed out before Cyclops and Blubber Man get back.'

'Are you about tomorrow morning Doc?' asked Payne.

'I can be, why?' replied Dougan.

'I've got a couple of cremation certificates that need countersigning.'

'I never turn my nose up at some ash cash, James, you know that,' laughed Dougan.

'I can meet you at the morgue about ten if that's OK?'

As the two police surgeons discussed the financial benefits of unexpected death, Jeff Greaves finished off the paperwork for the blood procedure. Twenty minutes later, Doc Dougan was safely tucked up at home in bed, whilst Dr James Payne started his examination of the unfortunate Mandy Blackstock in the doctor's room.

Once he'd finished his statement for the blood option procedure, Greaves tucked the submission form in with the other bogus sample in its grey cardboard box, signed and sealed it, and eventually deposited it in the fridge in the cell block for transportation to the lab later that day. Notwithstanding the fact that Doc Dougan was a mate, what Greaves had done for him, he would have done for any of the police surgeons who attended Horse's Arse on a regular basis. They were the good guys who needed to be looked after, but he counselled himself to watch his step.

Any more good deeds like this and people might begin to suspect there was fuck all wrong with him.

Chapter Five

Shortly after 5 a.m., Dan Harrison was in his office drawing up a list of actions for the forthcoming investigation when his desk phone rang. It was Andy Collins in a phone box in Bishops Rise.

'What you got, Andy? Got a scene for me?'

'Reckon so, boss, about two-thirds of the way along the path into Stream Woods. We've got her handbag on the grass verge and an area of smashed-down undergrowth. Looks like some clothing in the bushes but we've not been in there.'

'Well done, mate, I'll get a SOCO down to you. I can't send Graham Lightfoot, he's with the victim, but I've got another on standby at Headquarters. You got it taped off?'

'All done, boss, both ends and further back into the woods on both sides. Tell the SOCO to meet me at Bishops Rise – I'll walk him down.'

'Thanks, Andy. Speak to you later.'

Harrison put the phone down and then dialled the cell

block, drumming his fingers impatiently before Sergeant Mick Jones picked up.

'Jonesy, it's Dan Harrison. How's Doc Payne getting on?'

Jeff Greaves had telephoned him earlier to let him know of the enforced change of police surgeon, but Harrison wasn't overly concerned. He'd worked with Payne before and trusted him.

'He's just finished – washing up, I think. Graham Lightfoot's just completing the exhibit bags.'

'I need to speak to one of them quickly.'

'Graham's here, hold on.'

A couple of seconds later, Graham Lightfoot came on the line.

'Hey, boss, all done.'

'What's the score, Graham?'

'It's a nasty one. Raped her and shoved something up her backside for good measure – fucking animal.'

'Any idea what?'

'The Doc's money's on something like a bottle. She's going to need stitches.'

'We got any forensics?'

'Fuck all. Looks like he used a condom.'

'Bollocks. Any blood that's not hers?'

'Hard to say. You saw her, she's covered in blood but I reckon it's all hers.'

'Any good news for me?'

'Sorry. She's a terrible mess. Doc reckons her nose is

broken, possibly both cheekbones. Both eyes closed, maybe one of the eye-sockets fractured, both lips smashed up and most of her front teeth knocked out. And that's before you start to write up her injuries downstairs. She's covered in cuts and bruises.'

'Jesus. Any teethmarks – did he bite her?'

'Not that we've found.'

'Is she able to tell us anything yet?'

'We've got her name and address. She left a party in Windmill Gardens some time after midnight, was taking a short-cut through the woods and remembers getting walloped from behind by someone who came out of the bushes. She was conscious for most of the attack but didn't get even a glimpse of him.'

'Fucking hell,' sighed Harrison, who desperately needed a break, even a little one, to start a meaningful investigation. At least he now had a potential scene to get into, and maybe some witnesses from the party she'd left. Maybe, with a bit of luck, he mused, the rapist had been at the party and had followed her to the woods. It was a start, if nothing else.

'OK. Thanks, Graham. What's the plan for Mandy?'

'Doc wants her in hospital as soon as possible. He's called an ambulance.'

'Make sure the WPC goes with her, will you? Keep her talking, get whatever she can give us. Give me her address. I'll go and let the family know what's happened a bit later.'

He took down the details and after hanging up, rang

the Control Room at Headquarters where a SOCO was waiting to be deployed.

'There's a Sergeant Andy Collins waiting for you in Bishops Rise. He'll take you down to what I hope is the scene,' Harrison told him. 'It looks like he raped her wearing a condom and used something like a bottle in her backside. We're also looking for her lower-half clothing and clumps of hair. Keep in touch, OK?'

'I will, boss. I'll get back to you soon as I've got anything,' replied the SOCO.

'Good lad. Put the Control Inspector on, will you?'

After a brief wait, Harrison spoke again.

'DCI Dan Harrison, I'm the SIO for this rape at Handstead. Have you got me a unit of the Patrol Group lined up for later yet?'

'Yeah, you've got the local mob, Unit Three, all called out for a seven a.m. briefing at your place. Anything else you need?'

'No, that's all for now. Appreciate your help.'

He hung up and glanced at his wristwatch. Five-fifteen. It was almost completely light now and he could hear the early-morning traffic, outside on Bolton Road East, already beginning to rumble. He slumped back in his chair, closed his eyes and let out a long, loud sigh. His head was clear now; he'd got his investigation on track very quickly. He had hopefully got his scene under control and he had some enquiries to get going which might throw up a suspect. But he wasn't holding his breath. He had seen too many rape enquiries where the offence took place in the open air and the offender was a stranger, disappear into oblivion as lead after lead petered out after hours of frustrating work.

Christ, he needed a break. Actually what he really needed was a drink. Opening his bottom drawer, Harrison pulled out his ever-present bottle of Bushmills and a cut-glass crystal tumbler. He poured himself a large one and held the glass under his nose, inhaling the smoky aroma deep into his nostrils, feeling it creep across his sinuses and behind his eyeballs. He took a long sip and sat back in his chair as he enjoyed a few moments' peace and quiet before what promised to be a very long day.

He had dozed off and was dreaming about his lost daughters when the phone rang, making him jerk upright like a man getting his first shock in the electric chair. Heart thumping, he picked it up and croaked his name. The brief snooze had made him feel even more tired, and the Bushmills lingered in his stale mouth. As he answered he glanced at his watch. Six-fifty.

'Morning, boss, it's Phil Gilbert from the Patrol Group.'

'Nice and early, Phil – I like that,' laughed Harrison. 'Got a shedload for your boys this morning. See you in the muster room in ten minutes, OK? Congratulations on your promotion, by the way. Didn't you fancy a move away from the group?'

'No, I was happy to stay, sir. It's what I know,' replied Gilbert. 'Great opportunity to do things my way.'

'Good for you. See you in a bit,' said Harrison. He put down his phone and began to rummage through the desk drawers until he found the elderly toothbrush and tube of Euthymol toothpaste. Rolling his shoulders to get the tiredness out of his body, Harrison strolled into his toilet to complete his rudimentary ablutions.

Shortly after Harrison began briefing the Patrol Group, D Group started to return to the nick as they were relieved by Early Turn officers out on the cordons around the rape scene in Stream Woods. It had been a long, boring night and the lack of activity had left them all tired and dispirited. Still, it had stayed warm.

After dropping their kit into their lockers, they bade each other farewell, returned to their own cars and headed home. JJ was particularly quiet, still stunned by what he had seen and become an unwilling party to, out on Tamworth Road. Returning to his room in the section house, he lay fully clothed on the bed, his head spinning. Sleep for him would be an impossibility.

Psycho was also very subdued, but it had nothing to do with the shift they had just completed. He was in love, but all his efforts to win the heart of his intended had so far met with abject failure. He was absolutely smitten with WPC Anne Butler, who worked with C Group at Handstead. His religious mania over the last year had all been part of his master-plan to get into her knickers, once he had discovered she was a member of the Christian Police Association, but as her resistance continued, Psycho had begun to drop the act and revert to what passed for normality for him.

Anne had long been the object of his purely physical intentions, until she had attended a Dwarf Throwing drink with D Group and revealed another side of herself to Psycho that had bowled him over. Not only was she beautiful to look at, she also told some of the dirtiest jokes he'd ever heard. And even better, she now lived alone, since her jealous boyfriend had walked out on her after that drink, when he'd found the remainder of the group's whip-round safely concealed in her bra cups. But despite her availability, she had so far resolutely kept the pining Psycho at a good arm's length. His morose behaviour had been noticed by the group, but only Malcy knew the reason behind it.

'Come on, Psycho, get a fucking grip,' he cautioned his friend as they walked out to the garages to their cars. 'Plenty more fish in the sea.'

'I know, Malcy,' replied Psycho mournfully, 'but she's got right under my skin. She's pulling my fucking chain.'

'Have you been out with her lately?'

'Yeah, took her for a drink last week before we started nights.'

'Well, there you are then. She's not blanking you, is she? She's just taking things slowly, one step at a time.

Let's face it, she's hardly likely to jump straight into another relationship after that arsehole she's just got rid of.'

'I know, you're probably right. I wish she'd give me a clue, one way or the other.'

'Have you told her how you feel about her?'

'Jesus, no, of course not!' exclaimed Psycho.

Malcy stopped walking and faced his mate, hands on hips. 'Fucking hell, Psycho, don't you think she might actually feel the same way about you, but needs you to break the ice, make the first move?'

'You reckon?'

'I don't know, but why don't you give it a go?'

'What, tell her I really like her?'

'It's a start.'

'I couldn't,' said Psycho quietly as they resumed walking. 'What if she doesn't feel that way?'

'Then you're no worse off, are you, but at least you'll know where you stand.'

'I couldn't.'

'I worry about you sometimes, Psycho. Is it just a shag you're after?'

'God, no,' protested Psycho. 'I mean, that would be nice – the old pods need emptying and no mistake – but no, she's really special.'

'Well, why don't you get rid of your dirty water with the Blister. I'm sure she'd oblige – she usually does.'

'Oh no,' grimaced Psycho, genuinely appalled. 'I

couldn't go near *that* again. Those days are behind me, Malcy.'

'Yeah, right,' scoffed his mate. 'She gets her bearded clam out to you and you'd turn it down?'

Psycho shuddered at the memory. 'Damn right,' he said firmly. 'She's got piss flaps like a gutted trout.' He then smiled dreamily before continuing, 'You just know that Anne's going to be like a mouse's ear down there.'

Malcy shook his head as he opened his Mini. 'See you tonight, mate,' he said as Psycho reached his nearby, dilapidated Mark Two Ford Cortina that bore the scars of his numerous escapades whilst pissed.

'You reckon I should do something about my appearance?' Psycho called out.

'Like what?'

'Well, you know. This fucking birthmark,' he replied, putting his hand over the large port wine stain on his face.

'Never noticed it,' said Malcy. 'You could get your fucking hair cut and have a shave – that should do it.'

Psycho got into his car and watched as Malcy drove out of the garage and up to the high, razor-wire-topped gates, which eventually opened slowly, allowing him to race away up the slip road towards Bolton Road East. Malcy would catch a few hours' sleep before his daily pilgrimage to the Falconer Hospital fifteen miles away at Kray Hill to sit with his crippled wife. Psycho was the only member of the group to know the truth behind Andy Malcolm's appalling nickname 'the Mong Fucker' which had followed him on an enforced transfer to Horse's Arse, but at Malcy's request he'd kept it to himself. Malcy was a classic example of rumour and innuendo becoming accepted truth, and it was a nickname he was saddled with for the rest of his career. It was cruel and undeserved, but that was how it was in the Job, and there was absolutely no point in trying to explain it away. That's what guilty people did.

Psycho got into his Cortina and fired up the knackered engine. It finally burst into life, sounding like an old tractor, belching out clouds of acrid black smoke. Keeping the revs high, Psycho followed Malcy's route out of the nick and eventually joined the heavy rush-hour traffic crawling along the main road.

He had a slow journey, not getting back to his flat until just before 8 a.m., parking up on the ruined grass verge outside. Ten minutes later he was sipping at a mug of tea before he went to bed when he looked out of his sitting-room window and finally saw what he'd been looking for, for a very long time. Not Anne Butler with her mouse's ear, but the owner of the dog that kept shitting on the grass outside his bedroom window. Psycho had been clearing up piles of the stuff for weeks. Some warm nights, the smell from outside his window was so overpowering he'd cleared the mess up in his pants and slippers. And now, there was the fucking little shit machine curling another one off right under his window again, and joy of joys, there was its owner standing on the path, looking furtively round to make sure no one was watching. Psycho ducked out of sight – he had a plan.

Once he saw the longhaired, dishevelled owner saunter off, Psycho dashed out of his flat and through the front doors of the block into the garden. There it was, a pair of curled, sausage-sized turds right under his bedroom window. Quickly he scooped them up in the blue plastic garden trowel he had bought specifically for this job, and then strolled nonchalantly down the path out on to the pavement and after the dog and its scrote of an owner. Keeping well back, Psycho followed the pair for a couple of hundred yards up to the council estate at Rushland Avenue, attracting questioning looks from passers-by at the extraordinary sight of an obviously off-duty copper in half-blues, wandering along the pavement in his slippers carrying a trowel full of dog-shit. Nothing was said; this was Horse's Arse, after all, where the unusual was always expected.

Psycho stopped as he saw the dog and its owner enter a peeling red door. The house was typical of the others in the street. The garden was rubbish-strewn and overgrown, the metal window frames rotting away and the window in the front door replaced with a sheet of plywood following a drunken dispute inside. Large lumps of the grey pebbledash had fallen away from the front of the house, giving it the appearance of a face with a skin disease.

'Scumbag,' muttered Psycho, as he marched up the path to the house, kicking a used nappy into the long grass before hammering loudly on the door. After ten seconds' loud banging, a very angry-looking man flung the door open. It was the same man Psycho had seen with the dog. In his late twenties, his long dirty hair hung to his shoulders either side of his pale, drawn face that bore all the signs of the habitual glue sniffer. His pale, watery eyes glared at Psycho and he looked ready to go for him, but Psycho's huge frame and aggressive stance made him step back. The man was one of Handstead's vast lost legions of the unemployable, and Psycho knew exactly how to deal with him.

'What the fuck are you knocking on my door for?' shouted the waster. 'Fuck off!'

'You let your horrible little turdmaker shit on my garden again, you greasy little cunt, and I'm going to feed it to you,' snarled Psycho, before he raised his right arm and flicked the blue garden trowel at the man. The latter raised his arms in automatic self-defence, but the two turds were already airborne and splattered into his face and chest with a satisfying slap. Horrified, he stared down at the mess on his grubby green T-shirt.

'No one's going to notice if it had a shit in this dump, so you keep it away from my place,' continued Psycho, before he took a step forward and, carefully avoiding the shit on the man's face, planted a huge right-hander between his eyes. The man flew backwards and landed in the shabby hallway. The commotion had alerted the shit machine itself, which came scuffling in from the kitchen at the back of the house and froze when it saw Psycho standing menacingly in the doorway. The small dog emitted a weak bark of defiance before Psycho growled, and it clammed up before very obligingly cocking its leg and pissing into the hair of its prostrate owner.

'Good lad,' observed Psycho cheerfully, before he tossed the garden trowel into the hallway, stepped outside and slammed the door shut behind him. As he walked briskly away down the path he could hear the dog owner screaming in rage at his incontinent hound but significantly, he didn't come after Psycho. He had recognised him as an off-duty cop and was well aware, as were most of Handstead's criminal, wastrel underclass, that the cops here played by a different set of rules that were made up as they went along.

If Psycho had hoped that his bit of sport with the dog owner would help him sleep, he was sadly mistaken. As usual he was wide awake by midday and sitting morosely in his sitting room listening to Mel Carter crooning 'Hold Me, Thrill Me, Kiss Me'. His neighbours were heartily sick of hearing it at all hours of the day, but none had yet seen fit to confront the lovesick beast.

Chapter Six

Psycho was wandering restlessly around his flat and the rest of D Group were all tucked up in bed when the Pork Sword Man struck again that lunchtime. It was a beautiful warm afternoon with a light breeze, and office workers had baled out of their stuffy offices in the town centre to sit on the grass banks and lawns around the church. Soon the grass was full of chattering, laughing groups enjoying an hour's break from the daily grind. The three girls from the local branch of North Manchester Mutual Assurance Society were no exception. They'd bought some filled rolls in the baker's in the pedestrianised precinct, and some crisps and cans of Panda pop in the newsagent's. They were now spread out on the cool grass in the shade of a large yew tree enjoying their picnic when they heard the call from behind them.

'Hey, bitches, get some of this,' shouted the coarse voice.

As one, they turned in the direction of the voice and

there he was – Pork Sword Man in all his magnificence. Such was his appearance that the descriptions they subsequently gave at the enquiry office at the nick were sketchy at best. All they could agree on was that he had a huge erection and a Zorro mask over his face. They hadn't noticed what else he was wearing and couldn't even be sure of his skin colour until they remembered his cock. He was definitely white, but man, he was a big boy. They hadn't even noticed where he'd gone after he'd flashed them, such was their shock. Once they'd recovered, one of the girls had phoned 999 from the phone box outside the nearby Post Office, but with all the Early Turn cops still tied up at Stream Woods on the cordons and other enquiries, the three girls had reluctantly agreed to attend Handstead nick in person to report another appearance by Pork Sword Man.

The enquiry office was busy as it usually was at lunchtime, and the girls stood impatiently in the sweaty airless room as the harassed front office PC dealt with the daily detritus of life in Handstead. Ten minutes later, they were next up and listened enthralled as the red-faced man at the counter had his turn. He was apparently the recent victim of a burglary, as he explained to the uninterested and unhelpful PC.

'So if you've already reported it to us, why are you back?' the PC asked laconically.

'Because I've got another offence to report,' the man hissed.

'Which is what?'

'The fucking pictures and the attempt on the lives of my family. Dirty fucking bastards,' he fumed.

'What are you on about? What pictures, what attempt?'

'The bastards nicked everything of value except our camera, which was under the bed. Thank fuck, it had all our pictures in it of our holiday to Spain last year – hadn't got them developed yet.'

'Yeah, and?' asked the exasperated PC.

'Well, we got them developed yesterday,' shouted the man, pushing a wallet of photos under the counter. 'Go on, look at them.'

The three victims of Pork Sword Man casually took up position along the counter to get a better look at the photos the bored PC was leafing through and which had so enraged the burglary victim. As he had feared, the majority of the photos were mind-numbingly boring. Pictures of Dad pouring jugs of Sangria down his neck, all the kids scorched pink by the pool, Mum in a sombrero playing the maracas, Mum with her hooters out.

'This one?' asked the PC, showing some interest for the first time and holding it up for the packed enquiry office to see.

'Oh fuck, forgot about that one. No, not that one, keep going, keep going,' the man said angrily. Then he shouted, 'There you go – that one!' and motioned urgently from behind the armoured glass.

'Interesting,' said the PC, holding it up closer and peering at the glossy picture.

'Interesting be fucked,' bellowed the red-faced man, on the verge of wigging out completely. 'That's the fucking burglars.'

'On your camera?'

'Yes, on my camera,' he replied testily. 'And look what the bastards are doing.'

'I *am* looking. What are they doing?'

The man mumbled a reply, but neither the PC nor the engrossed audience on the other side of the glass could hear it.

'Doing what?' repeated the PC, holding the picture aloft and turning it to view it from different angles. A sea of heads in the enquiry office moved with him. The man again mumbled a reply.

'You'll have to speak up,' said the PC.

'Yeah, fucking speak up, we can't hear at the back,' shouted a voice from the front doors of the nick.

The man went into meltdown. 'Are you fucking blind?' he raved. 'The bastards have taken pictures of themselves with our toothbrushes jammed up their arseholes. We've been using the fucking things for the last two weeks.'

'Oh, got you now,' said the PC, as his light-bulb brain engaged, leafing through the photos in front of him. 'I thought they looked like arses but couldn't work out what the blue and red things were.'

'And yellow and green,' said the man wearily as the enquiry office erupted in raucous laughter. 'Bristle end in as well, the dirty bastards.'

'Hmm, not nice,' agreed the PC, bundling the photographs together, replacing them in the wallet and pushing it back under the glass.

'What are you going to do about it?' asked the incredulous man, glancing irately at the still laughing crowd behind him.

'Sorry, but I'm pretty sure it's not an offence in itself to stick a toothbrush up your arse. They haven't actually stolen the toothbrushes, have they?'

'What about the pictures themselves – don't you want them?'

'Well, if we ever start taking arse-prints or photos, I suppose they could be helpful, but right now they're of no use to us. Listen, I've got your details and I'll pass this information on to the investigating officer, but I doubt it'll help much. My advice to you, sir, is to buy some new toothbrushes, get yourself home and get gargling with some strong antiseptic mouthwash. Sorry. Now – who's next?'

Half an hour later, the three girls had given their report, arrangements were made to take statements from them later, and another crime had been marked up to the Pork Sword Man's account. As they made their way slowly back to work in the sunshine, the girls were still shrieking with laughter at the assault on the oral hygiene of the burglary victim and his family. What had happened to him was not, in fact, uncommon. Something about the very act of burglary seemed to generate a desire in many of the perpetrators to leave an unpleasant, lasting reminder of their visit. It was not unknown for burglars to shit in beds that they carefully re-made, or piss in a pair of shoes, or to leave booby traps for later such as stuffing a plimsoll into the U-bend of a toilet where it would unfurl and block the entire system.

Burglars were regarded by the police as the most loathed of criminals, after any that involved children in their crimes, and the guilty parties could generally expect pretty harsh treatment from the police, on the rare occasions they got locked up. The Romanian burglar still waiting in the cells for the CID to interview him was not expecting any favours from the police, simply praying that whoever interviewed him kept his trousers on. That would have been taking things too far, even for a burglar.

Shortly after 2 p.m., Dan Harrison was back in his office, writing up his log on the progress to date with the rape investigation. Under the circumstances, it could have been worse. The night duty uniforms had indeed found the scene and the SOCO had recovered some clumps of hair and the remains of a blood-stained bottle which Harrison was praying would give him some forensic evidence. He was expecting a call from the lab any time now. Women's clothing and a handbag – all its contents apparently intact – had also been found, bagged up and rushed to the lab for immediate examination.

Mandy Blackstock was safely in hospital and sedated, with her distraught family, whom Harrison had visited personally just after 8 a.m., by her bedside. The Patrol Group and DCs Clarke and Benson were busy tracking down and interviewing everyone present at the party, but so far no one had seen Blackstock after she had left the house. It was looking more and more likely that they had a stranger rape on their hands, and they were notoriously difficult to detect – especially without any forensics, and everything so far was pointing to a big fat zero on that score.

He was scribbling away furiously, glancing occasionally at his phone, willing it to ring, when DCs John Benson and Bob Clarke appeared at the open door. They didn't knock and Harrison motioned for them to come in.

The two detectives, who had now been on duty since 10 p.m. the previous evening, slumped into the chairs in front of the low coffee-table and closed their eyes. They looked shattered, with dark bags under their eyes, faces drawn from a lack of sleep. Getting up, Harrison shut his office door and then returned to his desk, producing his bottle of Bushmills and three glasses. Clarke and Benson heard the clinking of glasses and opened their eyes.

'Just a nightcap, boys,' grinned Harrison. 'Give me a quick update on your enquiries and then get yourselves home for a kip. You back on at ten?'

'Afraid so,' groaned Clarke, taking a glass from his boss and sipping appreciatively at the whiskey.

'How'd you get on?' asked Harrison, returning to his desk and perching on the front of it.

'Pretty good. The party was held by a friend of Blackstock's called Rita Corrigan,' said Benson, leafing through a small black notebook he'd taken from his jacket pocket. 'She was able to give us the names and addresses of everyone there, all thirty-eight of them. The patrol have already visited twenty-six of that lot and taken statements from them, but there's nothing of any use to us yet. Some of them were aware that Mandy had left the party, and Rita said goodbye to her, but no one saw her after she walked down the path.'

'Have any of the friends got any form?' asked Harrison hopefully.

'Yeah, a couple, but nothing significant to this enquiry,' replied Benson. 'One got a conditional discharge for drunk and disorderly last year, one has previous for criminal damage to a road sign, and a couple have juvenile cautions for shoplifting.' He saw the disappointment in Harrison's face and said, 'There's still another twelve to get hold of, boss. You never know, we might strike gold yet.'

'Be nice, wouldn't it?' said Harrison grimly. 'Come on, you two, you've done your bit for today and kicked the arse out of my overtime budget at the same time. Get yourselves away – I'll probably see you back here later.'

'You not going to have a kip, boss?' asked Clarke,

getting stiffly to his feet and handing his empty glass back to Harrison.

'Maybe later. I'm on a roll now and I want this job tidy before I do anything else. I'm hoping to get a result from that bottle we got back, otherwise we've got fuck all. I promised that poor kid I'd lock this bastard up and I fucking will,' said Harrison firmly.

Clarke and Benson didn't respond to his boast. They were experienced detectives who knew that rapes like this were either cleared up very quickly or not at all. The absence of any forensics generally meant the latter – all three of them knew that, but Harrison was determined not to leave any stone unturned before he admitted defeat.

The first twelve hours of any enquiry were crucial to the outcome and Harrison had not wasted a minute of his time. He'd already pulled in all the G87s (intelligence reports) for every night-time stop of people on foot in Handstead over the last week and every HO/RT1 (driving documents producer) given to drivers after midnight over the same period. They would all get a visit from his officers to account for their movements, and as his enquiry foundered, the driver of every vehicle stopped anywhere in the county after midnight could expect a knock on the door.

The Force Intelligence Bureau had also been tasked to come up with the details of every convicted sex offender living in Handstead, who would all be brought in for questioning simply on the grounds of modus operandi – once a pervert, always a pervert. It was a last resort in many police investigations where they had no immediate leads. Round up the usual suspects and sometimes you got lucky.

Chapter Seven

Temporary Chief Constable Paul Chislehurst stared grimly at the colour television playing in the corner of the meeting room on the seventh floor at Headquarters. He was a worried man on a number of counts. He and his two Assistant Chief Constables and the Detective Chief Superintendent (Crime) were watching a recording of the earlier BBC lunchtime news and yet another scathing account of the inability of the local police to deal effectively with the Albion Army picket at the Red Star Electrics factory.

Around the country, industrial disputes were on the verge of bringing down the government, the dead remained unburied and the rubbish lay in uncollected mountains in every town – yet the BBC had led their bulletin with the report on the dispute at Handstead, which was all about racism. The smug reporter had even quoted 'well-placed sources at the Home Office' who were apparently suggesting that the local Force might soon have to seek the assistance of their big neighbours in the Greater Manchester Police.

What really bothered Chislehurst was that he was starting to look ineffectual and out of his depth – which he patently was. The Chairman of the Police Authority had not been slow to phone him and remind him that his appointment to Chief was only temporary; the Police Committee were looking to him for some clear leadership and direction, and above all an end to the outrageous picketing and intimidation taking place at the factory.

Chislehurst had inherited the post as Chief purely on the grounds that he had been the Deputy to Chief Constable Daniels when the old boy had suffered his stroke at the Golf Society dinner and subsequently retired on medical grounds. Daniels's retirement had left a huge vacuum at the top of the Force. He had served at every rank, being one of the few Chief Officers ever to have reached the top rank in the same Force that he had originally joined. Chislehurst, however, was a 'butterfly' who flitted from Force to Force in search of promotion with no real allegiances to anyone other than himself. He had actually started as a PC with the local Force, but was now on his third stint, having wandered around Forces in the North of England like a gypsy looking for drives to tarmac.

Daniels had been a good detective; Chislehurst had made his name in Personnel and the Traffic Divisions, which told you everything you needed to know. Now he was required to deal with a situation on his ground that was simply beyond him. He had a game plan and it was a simple one – to shift as much of the blame as he could, and make his appointment to Chief Constable a permanent one. Which was where his Assistant Chief Constables would come in useful, and they knew it, along with Detective Chief Superintendent John Mills (Crime). Chislehurst was ready, willing and able to shaft all three of them, if it helped him get where he wanted to be.

Chislehurst was so out of his league it was painful. He wasn't a decisions man as Daniels had been, preferring to seize on the innovation of the senior officers he had inherited and take for himself any credit that accrued. He had at least recognised that he needed to create some sort of identity for himself, but his efforts on that score had proved disastrous leading to the nickname his senior command team now knew him by.

On his first morning in post he had breezed into Headquarters, graciously accepting the congratulations and plaudits being showered on him with an imperious wave of his hand, and made his way in the lift to his suite of offices on the seventh floor. He was desperate to make an impression, albeit a totally false one, on his troops as a man of the people, one of them, not afraid to get his hands dirty. As he entered the outer office where his personal assistants and staff officer sat, the solution came to him in a moment of blinding inspiration. When his staff officer, Inspector Mick Hetherington, got to his feet to welcome him, Chislehurst spotted the huge pile of post on Hetherington's desk. After limply shaking his hand, Chislehurst indicated the pile of unopened mail.

'What on earth is that lot?'

'The daily post, I'm afraid, sir.'

'Well, I can see that,' blustered Chislehurst, immediately taking umbrage at the unintended sarcasm. 'Post for whom?'

Hetherington was taken aback at the Temporary Chief's reaction to his perfectly polite answer. Clearly he was going to have trouble with this twat who had been totally anonymous during Daniels's reign.

'It's all for you, sir,' he replied.

'My post? Why the hell are you opening it?' asked Chislehurst, the solution to his problem becoming clear.

'Why? Well, because that's my job, sir. Mr Daniels used . . .'

Chislehurst held up his white, manicured hand to stop him.

'I'm not interested in what Mr Daniels did, Inspector. You're under new management now and I intend to deal with my post myself. Understood? From now on, *I* deal with my post.'

Hetherington frowned at him. 'Are you sure, sir? It's going to mean an awful lot of work for you and I'm sure you've got better things to do with your time.'

'Nonsense,' snapped Chislehurst, striding purposefully towards the open door of his office, smiling at his middle-aged secretary who was also standing to greet him. That look on her face, he told himself, was the expression of someone who had recognised a man with his finger on the pulse.

'What a cunt,' murmured Janet Braithwaite as Chislehurst back-heeled his door shut behind him.

Inspector Hetherington chuckled as he began to scoop the pile of mail up in his arms and returned it to the sack by his desk.

'Hasn't got a clue, has he?'

The following morning, Chislehurst had again bowled into the office freshly coiffured and fragrant, full of the joys of spring.

'Post's in your office, boss,' called Hetherington as the man passed him in a waft of expensive cologne.

Janet Braithwaite and Hetherington smiled at each other from their desks and waited for the explosion once the door had shut.

'What the . . . ?' they heard, and then Chislehurst threw open his office door. 'Inspector Hetherington, what the hell are all these post bags doing in my office?'

'It's your post, sir.'

'My post? There must be a dozen bags. What do you mean, my post?'

'Fifteen bags actually, sir, and it's all for you, I'm afraid. I've weeded out anything not addressed to you.'

'Fifteen bags?' shouted Chislehurst. 'I haven't got time to open fifteen fucking sacks of mail. What's going on?'

Hetherington then patiently explained to him that 99 per cent of all mail received at Headquarters was not unnaturally addressed directly to the Chief Constable. The Force received hundreds and hundreds of letters every day for every department in the Force, from catering to uniform supplies, radio workshops to fleet maintenance – and all were addressed to the Chief Constable. His staff officer would spend a couple of hours a day weeding the wheat from the chaff to ensure he only saw what was directly relevant to him, but Chislehurst in his complete ignorance had been unaware of that role.

'Get it out of my office and sort it out,' he eventually grumbled, not looking his staff officer in the eye. 'I'm far too busy to be buggering about with this.'

Janet Braithwaite and Mick Hetherington slowly hauled the bulging post sacks back out to their office annexe and winked at each other.

'What a cunt,' Janet reiterated quietly, and so Postman Pat was born.

'So, Chief Superintendent Mills,' said Chislehurst, switching the TV off with a remote and turning to look at his silent, anxious management team. 'This Red Star Electrics is getting seriously out of hand, by the looks of it. What are you doing about it?'

Mills's position couldn't be clearer, as he was well aware from looking at the expressions on the faces of the Chief and his two Assistants.

'This lot is down to you, old son.' He also knew why he'd been called to this meeting, and it wasn't to have tea and biscuits with the Chief, so he'd done some preparation.

'Got a meeting with Chief Superintendent Findlay and his team planned for later today, Chief,' lied Mills. 'I hope to have a draft solution for you by end of play today or first thing tomorrow.' There was no meeting planned yet but there certainly would be, once he got out of the conference room. Although he was the same rank as Findlay on paper, Mills's role as Detective Chief Superintendent (Crime) put him above Findlay in the pecking order and the shit line when it began to roll downhill.

'I see,' said Chislehurst, unconvinced. 'What options will you be looking at?'

Bastard, thought Mills. Time to bullshit.

'We're going to explore the viability of continuing as we are . . .'

'But that's not working, is it?' interrupted one of the ACCs.

'No, but we need to understand why,' Mills went on defiantly, 'as well as exploring other options.'

'Such as?'

'An increase in the resources we deploy there, some kind of intelligence-gathering exercise, maybe bringing in some sort of mutual aid for the long haul.'

'Mutual aid?' stormed Chislehurst. 'You can forget that straight away. No way we're calling in another Force to help out. It'll look like we don't know what we're doing. Not a chance.'

The audience sat quietly as they digested the truth that Chislehurst had expressed. There was no doubt in anyone's mind that Chief Daniels would have had a robust solution to the problem, but the tiller now lay in Chislehurst's dead hand and their boat was heading for the rocks.

After a pause, Chislehurst got to his feet.

'Thank you, gentlemen,' he said awkwardly. 'I'd like your ideas as soon as possible, Mr Mills. Today ideally, but certainly by nine a.m. tomorrow. We'll meet back here then to discuss your plans.'

With a heavy heart, Mills hurried back to his office on the fifth floor and slammed his door. Slumping in his chair he quickly ran over his options, which were few and not great. Eventually he picked up his desk phone and phoned Chief Superintendent Phillip Findlay, Divisional Commander for B Division. Needless to say, 'the Fist' was not in his office and it was ten minutes before he called him back.

'You wanted me, John?' he asked.

Ignoring the temptation to say something sarcastic, Mills gave him chapter and verse on the meeting he'd had with Chislehurst.

'We've got to come up with a solution or our arses are in a sling,' he said, emphasising the words 'we've' and 'our' so Findlay was left in no doubt that any failure would be shared or more likely heaped on his shoulders.

'Shit,' replied Findlay, who'd been expecting and dreading a call about events in Handstead. The subdivision was something he tried not to think about, preferring to leave it to Pete Stevenson and Dan Harrison. His abdication of responsibility was a well-known disgrace, but the time for accounting was fast approaching. Such was his detachment from events at Handstead generally that he harboured a massive misunderstanding about his nickname 'the Fist'. He had got it into his head that it had something to do with his firm approach to dealing with crime. In fact, it was a nickname that had followed him into the Job from his time in the Navy – namely, the Electric Throbbing Sailor's Fist. Every reference to him was usually prefaced with the phrase, 'that wanker'.

'What are you doing there?' asked Mills.

The true answer would have been, 'Fuck all,' but Findlay was a skilled survivor. Whilst he owed most of his promotions to his position within the Freemasons, he was also a canny operator who could see when he was on offer.

'We've upped the number of officers on duty during working hours and we are monitoring the situation.'

'Monitoring the situation – what the fuck does that mean? Jesus Christ, Phillip, the fucking wheels have come off. I want you, Dan Harrison, your uniform Chief Inspector and the Patrol Group Inspector in my office at four p.m. We're not leaving until we've got something drafted for me to give the Chief tomorrow morning, OK?'

'I've got appointments from half-three onwards,' whined Findlay.

'Fucking cancel them,' said Mills firmly, before he slammed the phone down.

Chapter Eight

'There ain't no black in the Union Jack,' chanted the crowd of approximately forty skinheads clustered around the main gates of Red Star Electrics as the dozen or so cops present tried to push them back to allow the main gates to open. The level of abuse began to rise sharply as the gates opened fully to allow the battered forty-seater bus to swing out of the factory compound and into the cul-de-sac.

'You fucking Paki bastards,' screamed the largest of the thugs, none other than the obnoxious Wallace Moffatt who'd been drinking all day in the Park Royal pub with a few hardcore lieutenants and had only just returned to the picket line for the 5 p.m. home run.

The owners had recently begun laying on transport for their workers to try and protect them from the intimidation they were experiencing, collecting them in the morning and dropping them off at locations that changed every day, but inevitably the bus was being followed and the workers too, when they got off. The thirty-five staff on board the bus looked straight ahead, trying to ignore the hatred and vitriol being hurled at them, many of them wondering how much longer they could endure this gauntlet every day.

Working at Red Star Electrics was becoming extremely unpleasant, and some workers had voted with their feet, preferring to claim unemployment benefit to risking their health. Which was precisely what Wallace Moffatt and the Albion Army were seeking to achieve. Their original intention to see Moffatt reinstated had long since been usurped by the desire to put the company out of business and bankrupt its Asian owners. The latter could no longer even be sure that the bus owners would continue to make themselves available, as the intimidation and threats had spread to their own staff, with their premises and two buses vandalised.

As the ancient, dark green Mark Two Dennis bus moved slowly through the boiling mob and away up the road, several of the skinheads raced off to get their own vehicles to follow.

The police had tried to stop this by shutting all roads behind the bus as it left, but it was slow and the Albion Army members had simply parked up outside the industrial estate with plenty of time to catch the bus up once it had left. Not much was going right for the police, but now that the Fist was taking a personal interest in policing tactics, a brave new dawn beckoned. Or didn't.

'Same time again tomorrow morning then, Wallace?' asked a tall skinhead in a long-sleeved Union Jack T-shirt and mirrored aviator sunglasses. He and Moffatt were standing hands on hips watching the bus as it turned left and disappeared from sight.

'Reckon so, Andy, reckon so. We've nearly cracked it here, you know.'

'You think so?'

'Fucking right. I've heard the bus company are on the verge of pulling the plug here. Apparently their drivers and staff are being terrorised and they've had enough,' replied Moffatt with a chuckle and knowing grin. 'Terrible, isn't it?'

His companion laughed. 'Nothing the rag-headed bastards don't deserve. Still, you going to keep the pressure on down here?'

'Bloody right I am. You heard from your mate at the nick? Any developments there lately we need to know about?'

'Fuck all – haven't heard from him for weeks. Got to keep his head down and his nose clean, I guess. Want me to try and have a word?'

'Yeah, be useful. They don't seem too interested right now and it might be that could change. Be a good thing to know if that was going to happen any day soon.'

'I'll try and get hold of him, but it's pot luck though. If he's not on duty I can't reach him.'

'What's he do, anyway?'

'Not sure. He's in an office somewhere. He's not really a mate, I just bumped into him at the snooker club and got chatting. He's on side with us though; given us some useful stuff, hasn't he?'

'Yeah, yeah. Keep him sweet, OK?'

The two men began to mingle with the other dispersing pickets, making arrangements for the following day's picket and a big drink tonight. They'd had a good day in the warm sunshine, spent a lot of it drinking, hurled some good verbal abuse at the Paki bastards and their white scum accomplices, and felt they were only a few weeks or months away from breaking the company. And the Albion Army hierarchy were delighted with the television coverage of their ongoing picket which was now getting mentioned on every news bulletin, local and more importantly, national.

An hour earlier, Chief Superintendent John Mills had pulled his chair up to the desk in his office and faced the hastily summoned B Division management team. He was pleased to notice that Findlay looked very worried, as he had every reason to be. Dan Harrison just looked exhausted.

'You OK, Dan?' he asked.

'Long couple of days, boss,' answered Harrison. 'We've got a nasty rape on the go.'

'Yeah, saw that on the bulletin this morning. How's it going? You need anything from us?'

'It's still early days – got an external scene so we're scratching about a bit. Absolutely no forensics on what we've found so far.'

'Hmm, not good,' agreed Mills. 'Nothing from the victim, I assume?'

'Not a thing. Attacked from behind and hammered black and blue. It's a vicious one.'

'Is she in hospital?'

'Yeah, Handstead General.'

'Keep me in the loop, Dan; let me know if there's anything we can do from here. I don't think we've met,' Mills said to Pete Stevenson.

The big red-faced Scotsman got to his feet and took the proffered handshake. 'Chief Inspector Pete Stevenson. I transferred in from Tubbenden Road last year.'

'Oh yes, I remember you now. You were on the team that took out the Park Royal boys who went after the gun shop at Tamworth, weren't you?'

'That's it. Quite an introduction to life at Handstead,' laughed Stevenson, retaking his seat.

'Inspector Phil Gilbert,' said Gilbert, getting to his feet. 'Patrol Group.'

'Thanks for coming, everyone,' continued Mills, not that he'd given any of them a choice. 'We've got a problem and we need a solution today.'

No one said anything, so he continued.

'Events at the Red Star Electrics factory are out of control. The TV and press people are all over it and the

Chief's worried we're starting to look silly. No one's talking about what the dispute's all about, just that the police can't control the violence down there. How do we deal with it? And you can forget about bringing in more cops from outside the county on mutual aid.'

'It would be very useful if we had an idea of what their objective was,' offered Findlay.

'I think it's pretty obvious what they're after,' snapped Mills impatiently. 'Close the factory down and get lots of publicity for themselves at the same time. "White jobs for white people" or something, isn't it? What do we know about this Wallace Moffatt creature, Dan?'

'There's very little on file about him. No previous, but he's an obnoxious fat twat who's a fully paid up member of the Albion Army. He lives on the Park Royal Estate, married with a couple of kids but fuck all else.'

'Do we know how he's communicating with his masters, getting his instructions?'

'No, but I doubt he's getting much direction from them. He's very much his own man. What's happening at Red Star is pretty much all his own work. The Albion Army are happy to send down some hired help occasionally and claim all the publicity they can, but he's running the show.'

'How can you know that?' asked Mills quietly, sensing that Harrison had more to give up. There was a long pause as Harrison flicked through the contents of the manila-coloured file on the desk in front of him.

'I've got someone inside and close to him,' he finally said, looking Mills straight in the eye.

'Go on,' prompted Mills, quickly weighing up the implications of what Harrison had just told him. As usual, Harrison was clearly doing his own thing at Handstead. Infiltrating an undercover officer anywhere required sanctions at a very senior level, and he as the DCS (Ops) would certainly have been aware if Harrison had gone through the proper channels. He hadn't and he didn't, but if it gave him a Get Out of Jail card there were ways of covering it up.

'I could see this getting messy about five months ago, so I put one of my guys in there. He's living on the Park Royal and hanging around daily with Moffatt. Moffatt's convinced he's got someone at the nick who holds the same views as them, gives them some low-level information from time to time. Of course he has – it's me.'

'Fucking hell, Dan, you can't just run operations like this without telling someone!' exploded Mills. 'How long has he been there?'

Harrison examined his file closely. 'He moved into a flat on the Park Royal Estate on the sixth of January, started appearing on the picket lines soon after that.'

'Five months?'

'Yeah. His cover story is that he was dismissed from the factory a few years ago, before Moffatt got there, and as virtually none of the pickets are employees, no one's spotted him as a wrong 'un. Now he wants to get his revenge on the Sikhs who binned him. Moffatt's welcomed him with open arms.'

'Who's financing this enterprise – paying for the rental on the flat and his expenses?'

'I'm covering his expenses out of my overtime budget at Handstead. The flat's not costing us anything; all done through a mate in the Council Housing Department.'

'Jesus Christ. Did you know about this, Phillip?'

Findlay had no choice but to hold his hands up to knowing the square root of fuck all. 'No,' he admitted weakly.

'Fucking hell, Dan, you're well out of order on this one,' fumed Mills, 'but we might be able to make something out of it.'

'That's the way I saw it as well, boss,' replied Harrison, who appeared unconcerned by the furore his revelation had generated.

'Why the fuck didn't you tell someone subsequently, get it sanctioned?'

Harrison's reply was unspoken but eloquent. He merely looked over at Findlay and then back to Mills. It was enough, and not the first time he'd deliberately kept Findlay and Headquarters in the dark on an operation he was running. He'd done it last year when he'd taken out a large LSD factory on the edge of town because he knew Findlay couldn't hold his own water, let alone keep a secret.

'Right,' said Mills, nodding and understanding. 'How do we use this to our advantage now?'

'I had a chat with Pete earlier,' said Harrison. 'Our plan is to engineer a show-down with the Albion Army, a bit of a set-piece battle with all the planning done beforehand so we come out on top.'

'Engineered through your man?'

'Yeah, and then that's where Phil and his boys come in.'

'The Patrol Group? They're only thirty-odd strong.'

'At the moment, boss, that's right. But I've got an idea to dovetail in with Mr Harrison's plan,' piped up Inspector Phil Gilbert. 'Ever seen the film *Zulu*?'

Mills was speechless. Stevenson and Harrison seemed unmoved by the question; clearly it had been discussed prior to the meeting, but Findlay obviously had not been privy to the scheming. He was doing what he did best – gaping like a goldfish and hoping no one asked him a question.

'*Zulu*? What in the name of God are you talking about?' Mills asked irritably.

'One of the finest films ever made in which the tactics of the Zulu warriors are shown in excellent detail. I saw these tactics used to very good effect in Handstead last year, which is where I got the idea. A Zulu fighting buffalo formation was used to take out a numerically superior group of football hooligans. You may remember it?'

'Fighting buffalo formation?' queried Mills desperately. 'What football hooligans?'

'The Leeds Service Crew, sir,' prompted Stevenson with a broad smile. 'They were taken out at the

Stonehouse pub by D Group and the Patrol Group using those tactics. They locked up thirty plus – a magnificent performance.'

'That's where I got the idea from, for these Albion Army pickets,' Phil Gilbert said enthusiastically. 'I've brought a copy of the video for you to watch, sir, so you can get an idea of what I propose. The scene I need you to concentrate on is just before all the soldiers start singing "Men of Harlech" – really stirring stuff.'

Mills stared at them all as though they'd gone mad.

'What you're suggesting then,' he said, 'and stop me if I've misunderstood, is that on the basis of a scene in a war film, we take on the Albion Army in a prearranged battle that we set up through an unauthorised under-cover officer who's now a drinking buddy of the main protagonist. Have I got it right? Is this what I tell the Chief?'

'Probably not in those terms, boss,' laughed Harrison. 'How about this? We're in a position to infiltrate the pickets and we can do it quickly. Get it sanctioned and everything. Then we increase the size of the Patrol Group and arrange for them to receive some unspecified specialist training with the aim of bringing the dispute to a close on one day.'

'How big does the Patrol Group need to be?'

'I would suggest at least four hundred, but it's only going to be a temporary thing,' said Gilbert. 'Once the problem's solved, we revert to three units of ten and a

Sergeant, and the others return to their divisions. It'd be a one-off.'

'Over what period?'

'Once we've got the bodies, two weeks' training maximum and we're ready to go.'

'What sort of training?' queried Mills.

'Watch the film, boss, it'll all become clear,' Gilbert told him, pushing a videotape across the desk.

Mills picked it up and looked sceptically at the case. 'This is utter madness,' he said.

'This is Handstead, boss,' Harrison reminded him. 'This could work. We get our reputation back, the dispute's done and dusted, and God forbid, the Chief gets his job permanently. I'll give you a hand to write up the briefing paper, if you like. I just happen to have a draft with me here, actually,' he finished with a broad smile, opening his manila file again.

Chapter Nine

'Who's the undercover officer then, Dan?' asked Findlay as they travelled down in the lift to the main Headquarters reception.

'It's a secret,' said Harrison simply, as the doors opened and they made their way out across the crowded foyer and past the large display cabinets filled with trophies for long-forgotten competitions.

'What do you mean, it's a secret?' protested Findlay. 'I'm your Divisional Commander and I expect to be fully briefed on what you're doing.'

Harrison stopped and faced Findlay with a look of utter contempt on his face.

'Listen, sir,' he sneered, 'I wouldn't give you the steam off my shit.'

As he spoke, Stevenson put a hand in Phil Gilbert's back and guided him onwards. He knew what was coming and the fewer people who heard it the better.

'You're a complete cock and I'm tired of you fucking up

my operations whilst you boast to your trouser-rolling mates about jobs going off on your ground. Jobs you know fuck all about or understand because you've never done a day's coppering in your life. You want to know who the undercover officer is, you ask Mr Mills. Now fuck off.' And with that, Harrison turned and strode away, leaving Findlay standing forlornly in the car park like a jilted bride.

Harrison then joined Stevenson and Gilbert in the unmarked Cortina they had travelled over in together. He settled himself in the back, the other two looking at him from the front.

'Everything OK?' asked Stevenson with a grin.

'Yes. Now let's get back to the nick, we've got a lot to get done.'

Harrison strode back into his office in a buoyant mood, his tiredness forgotten as he got his teeth into something. His good humour didn't last long, for Bob Clarke appeared at his open door with a pile of folders in his arms and a bothered look on his face.

'Don't spoil my day, Bob,' said Harrison. 'Tell me you've got someone locked up for the rape. You get any sleep today?'

'Yeah, got a few hours, boss, but nobody's locked up yet. We're working on it.'

'Good lad. What's up? You look worried.'

'Been up in the FIB (Force Intelligence Bureau) doing

some background on the rape,' replied Clarke, coming into the office and sitting in one of the armchairs at the front of Harrison's desk.

'Ready for a quick one?' asked Harrison, producing his bottle of Bushmills from his desk. Without waiting for an answer, he poured two large glasses and pushed one across the desk to Clarke. Once he'd settled again and taken a sip, Harrison continued.

'So, tell me about your trip to the FIB. What's that all about?'

'Just a gut feeling, that's all, boss. I've pulled all our undetected rapes going back to 1970.'

'How many is that?'

'Fourteen.'

'Christ, fourteen undetected in eight years. Not great, is it?'

'No, not great – but that's not what's bothering me.'

Harrison raised his eyebrows. He trusted Clarke's instincts and was beginning to feel distinctly uncomfortable.

'Go on,' he said.

'Of the fourteen, I've discounted six for various reasons, but there are eight with a distinct pattern.'

'Pattern? What are you saying here, Bob?'

'I think we've got a serial rapist and Mandy Blackstock is his latest victim.'

'Oh fuck,' sighed Harrison, topping his glass up with a generous measure. 'What's the pattern? How have you linked these eight?'

'OK, all eight took place outdoors, in or near woods.'

'Right.'

'All eight took place within a four-hour window of ten at night and two in the morning.'

'OK.'

'All eight girls were attacked from behind.'

'Yes.'

'All eight were badly beaten up, before, during and after the rape.'

'Go on.'

'In all eight there was zero forensics. Five of the SIOs on the files comment that the suspect probably wore a condom.'

'Any more?'

'Afraid so. Incidentally, Mandy Blackstock is the second to be raped in Stream Woods. Vanessa Baker was attacked there on the eighth of June 1971.'

'What about the bottle he stuck up Mandy Blackstock? Any of the others suffer anything like that?'

'No, but I believe we're talking about a gradual escalation of the violence as the crimes continue. I think our guy has taken it up a level with Mandy.'

'Go on – why do you think that?'

'Before I go on, boss, I don't know if I ever told you about the FBI guy who did a lecture on my CID refresher last year? He was the dog's bollocks, doing some sort of work on serial killers and rapists. "Profiling" or something, he called it. Anyway, he'd looked at dozens of serial offenders, all devious cunning bastards who understood about leaving nothing behind. You know – always gloved up, always use a condom, which they take along already opened so they don't have to worry about the wrapper. They try and commit their offences outdoors where any scene can be destroyed quickly, deliberately or inadvertently. That sort of detail. But even these creatures fuck up sometimes, and often it's because they like to keep a memento.'

'A memento?'

'Yeah, they're trophy hunters. They leave absolutely nothing of themselves at the scene or on the victim. The crime is meticulously planned and committed to the smallest detail – they don't want to get caught, they're having too much fun – but they sometimes take something with them as a keepsake. Something to remind themselves of the good times they've had.'

'Where does our man fit in with that theory? Mandy Blackstock hasn't lost anything, has she?'

'I've been through the SOCO inventory and spoken to the SOCO who did the scene, in person this afternoon. There's nothing gone from her handbag, but she is missing something.'

Harrison's heart was thumping as he asked, 'What?'

'Her knickers. We've not found them. The SOCO didn't find them and just made an assumption that she hadn't been wearing any, but I've spoken to Mandy. She was. She can remember them being literally torn off her.'

'They could be anywhere in the woods.'

'Unlikely. We found and secured the scene within a couple of hours of the attack and we've had the Patrol Group doing a fingertip search in a hundred-yard radius of the scene. I'm convinced her knickers have been kept by our man. They're his trophy.'

'What about the other eight girls?'

'I've pulled the SOCO inventories on all of them. Without exception, every girl lost an item the night they were attacked. Items of clothing, or small bits of jewellery, but all lost at least one thing. Cilla Cooper in 1976? They never found her bra but I read her statement and she describes the guy tearing it off with his teeth. He kept it, boss – he keeps something from all of them.'

'Oh God, Bob,' said Harrison in a tired voice. 'Listen, we need to go through those previous rapes with a fine-tooth comb. I've got a horrible feeling you're absolutely right, but I want to be a hundred per cent sure before we up the ante, all right?'

'I've made a start already. I'm reading statements and cross-referencing with the inventories. All the girls were local so hopefully if we need to clarify anything they'll still be around.'

'Get John to give you a hand, Bob, but I need full focus on this job first, OK? Did you get anything from the FIB method index?'

'We've got a couple of blokes living locally. They're lined up for visits on the hurry-up but these are old convictions for rape – fifteen and twenty-two years old.'

'Anything interesting out of the G87s or HO/RT1s?'

'Nothing, but we'll follow them up. If I'm right, boss, there's no way our man would have taken the slightest risk and got a pull from a copper before or after the attack. He understands how an investigation like this works, he knows what we'll be looking for. He got there on foot and he'll live within a couple of miles' radius. I'd stake my house and pension on it.'

'Fuck me, Bob, I'll look at you in a different light from now on. All I ever did on my CID courses was get pissed and go shagging. You've actually listened to something you were being taught. Trouble is, I'm not sure I'm very happy you did. Ten minutes ago I had one difficult rape on my hands – now I might have eight . . . Cheers, mate,' said Harrison with a wry smile.

Clarke got up to leave, but paused.

'I don't understand why the connection hadn't been made before, boss,' he said quietly. 'We had one in July 1976 in Garston Woods. Never found her tights.'

Harrison gave him a sideways glance that spoke volumes.

'Easiest not to sometimes, Bob, isn't it? Let's face it, if you're right and we've got a serial rapist on our hands, you're not going to be very popular if we don't lay hands on him. There's going to be a few SIOs and senior officers looking very stupid and they won't thank you for it. Who was the SIO on the Garston Woods job?'

Clarke flicked through his papers. 'DI Steve Sumner,' he said.

'I rest my case,' said Harrison. 'Sumner was a useless, lazy bastard who probably did the bare minimum on it. And now he's a DCI on the Regional. He won't thank you for raking over old coals, so let's get it right, OK?'

'Will do, boss. Catch you later.'

After Clarke had left, Harrison closed his office door, took his tie and shoes off and stretched out in the armchair Clarke had vacated. He had poured himself another large drink and pondered on the day he'd had so far. Clarke's news had really thrown the cat amongst the pigeons, but it needed to be looked at thoroughly. Last thing he needed was a serial rapist on the loose with nothing to go on. At least his plans for Red Star Electrics looked healthier. Detective Chief Superintendent Mills would be presenting the plan to the Chief the following morning and he was confident they'd get the green light to run with it. He was due to meet with his undercover officer at ten o'clock that evening; plenty of time to get home, change his clothes, have something to eat and take a shower. Oh bollocks – and then of course there was Zorro, he couldn't just ignore him. He resolved to speak to Pete Stevenson first thing the following day to set up an operation using the uniforms. His own guys were going to be fully committed for the foreseeable future with their rapist.

*

PC Phil Eldrett stared glumly at the flickering screen of his television but saw nothing. He was miles away, lost in the misery of his failed marriage and missing his two young sons. The Job had destroyed his relationship with his wife in a way that the Army had never been able to. As a member of 14 Intelligence Company, his two tours of Ulster had involved unbelievably dangerous work, often on his own, deep in South Armagh's bandit country. He had been away from home for weeks at a time, never talking about where he'd been or what he'd done when he got home and prone to some dark periods of depression. But his wife had always consoled herself that one day he'd leave the Army and get himself a normal job, and then they could start to live as a proper family.

Sarah Eldrett had been overjoyed when Phil had bought himself out and joined the local police force. Sure, he'd been working shifts but she and the boys saw him every day and they planned their lives around his shifts. They'd never been happier. But then the Job picked up on his surveillance background and began utilising his skills on operations here and there. Such was his expertise, he was known as 'the Shadow', and he began to spend more and more time away from home again. His silences and depression returned to haunt him and the spark went out for his wife as her dreams died.

What had started as a friendship with a male colleague at the supermarket where she worked part-time soon developed into a full-blown affair. Eldrett had long suspected it was going on but had never confronted her as he was desperate to make their marriage work, but the wounds had been too deep on both sides and Eldrett had eventually moved back to live with his mother.

His first Christmas apart from his sons had traumatised him, and in the early hours of New Year's Day 1978 he had found himself in his car in the deserted car park of a supermarket seriously considering the idea of swallowing a bottle of painkillers he had with him. His personal life was in tatters but at least he had his job, which he'd thrown himself into, working all the hours he could so that all he had to worry about doing was working and sleeping. He could eat at work if he chose, and the last thing he wanted was time on his hands to dwell on what he had lost.

His mother had quickly tired of having him under her feet and encouraged him to find somewhere of his own. Initially he'd welcomed his solitude, but now he craved someone to just say hello to, or goodnight, or even just to nod at, to acknowledge that he was still alive. Now, stuck in this ropy flat that stank of the cooking from the Chinese restaurant two floors below, glancing at the remains of his disgusting meal from the same venue, congealing in its aluminium trays on the table in front of him and sipping from a can of beer in front of a flickering TV with dodgy vertical control, he was close to tears. How the fuck had it come to this? he fumed to himself. He had had it all, a wife and sons he adored, a career he loved, a nice tidy house that was their home. And then the Job had pissed all over their happiness by offering him something to do again, something at which he excelled. He could always have said no, but for reasons he didn't fully understand, he had said yes instead. It was all his fault, and he began to well up.

Suddenly, a soft knock at his front door slapped him out of his self-pity. Turning off the TV and quickly gathering up the remains of his Chinese to drop in the overflowing bin in his small kitchen, he hurried to the door and peered through the small spy-hole. Smiling, he unfastened the security chain, shot the bolts at the top and bottom of the door and then stood back to allow his visitor to enter. The tall, bulky man pushed past him with the collar of his jacket turned up and a New York Yankees baseball cap pushed low over his eyes. Tufts of grey hair were visible at the man's neck.

'You're early, boss,' said Eldrett. 'Fancy a brew or a beer?'

'I'll have a beer thanks, Phil,' said Dan Harrison, pulling the baseball cap off his head and running his fingers through his hair. 'We've got to have a chat, young man. Things are going to change down at Red Star Electrics, and very soon.'

Chapter Ten

D Group mustered again at 10 p.m. None of them appeared to have slept well during the warm day, but JJ in particular looked like shit. He'd clearly been awake all day worrying himself sick about what he was now party to. As he'd got more tired and irrational he'd convinced himself it was only a matter of time before he got nicked and his fledgling career ended before it had had a chance to get going. Psycho also looked tired and subdued, having spent most of the day humming along with Mel Carter and pouring bottles of Heineken down his neck. The Brothers looked pale and sinister as usual, which had absolutely nothing to do with lack of sleep, and PC Ray Malone – Piggy – was covered in the remnants of the meal he'd eaten before leaving for work. He had clearly gorged himself again. He'd belched loudly a couple of times, which had cleared an exclusion zone around him, and now the concern was that his rear end would soon come into play. Should that happen, the effect on people's health wouldn't be confined to his colleagues, as a testy PC Ally Stewart had been quick to remind him.

'You keep a lid on your fat arse, Piggy. You drop just one and I swear I'll kill you,' he hissed from behind a hand as a Spaghetti Bolognese-flavoured belch attacked his senses. 'Just one and you're dead.'

Ally had sat down next to his fellow Scot Andy Malcolm and continued to mutter murderous threats. He was worried he'd be paired up with the flatulent porker for the night, despite previous pleas to Andy Collins to keep him and Malcy together. Generally, Collins had kept him away from Piggy, but nothing could be guaranteed. Ally had classic Small Man syndrome – plenty of aggression with very little to back it up. He seemed to be in a permanent state of simmering anger, which made him hard to warm to, and he subsequently existed on the margins of the group. He'd teamed up with Malcy when he'd transferred on to the group simply on the grounds that he too was Scottish, but Malcy felt no real allegiance with him. If there was anyone Malcy would rather spend time with, it was Psycho. Still, Ally was a decent grafter and there was less chance of getting into deep shit with him alongside: into trouble, definitely, as his syndrome reared its ugly head, but nothing like the shit that Psycho regularly found himself in.

Malcy had spent most of the afternoon at the hospital with his wife Karen, which had left him tired and despondent. The scale of her disability had destroyed her mentally, and she had spent their time together crying and talking of killing herself. It had almost been a relief to leave her, to go home and get ready for work, and he hated himself for harbouring such disloyal feelings – but her despair was starting to destroy him as well.

When Ally got up and announced he was going for a piss, this gave Malcy the chance to shift and sit alongside his silent, brooding mate.

'You OK, Psycho? You're very quiet,' he said.

'Couldn't sleep, Malcy. You see Karen today?'

'Yeah,' he replied flatly.

'Not good?'

'Getting worse. She was talking about topping herself, asking me to help her do it.'

'Jesus. How?'

'Pills. Said I'd been to enough suicides to know what it would take. She asked me to get her a load of Paracetamol.' He hung his head in abject misery.

'I'm sorry, Malcy,' said Psycho sincerely. 'What are you going to do?'

'Well, I'm not going to help her, that's for sure, but I'm worried she'll do it on her own. She's gone to fucking pieces, Psycho, she's all over the place. And there's fuck all I can do or say to her to help.'

Psycho didn't respond. There was no magic way to alleviate his friend's anguish. Either Karen adjusted to her new paralysed life or she'd go mad and die. As Psycho pondered that awful predicament, Malcy spoke.

'How's things going with you and the lovely Anne?'

'They're not,' replied Psycho bluntly.

'You phoned her?'

'Not recently.'

'Well, maybe you should, mate. For all you know, she's waiting for you to do just that. You've got to give her a bit of a break, Psycho. You're asking her to take a big step into the unknown with you.'

'What the fuck is that supposed to mean?' snapped Psycho, turning to face Malcy, his face colouring up in anger.

'Whoa, whoa,' replied Malcy, raising his hands in a gesture of surrender. 'All I'm saying is that you and I know you've turned over a new leaf and that you're serious about her. But all she knows about you is what everyone else knows about you i.e. you're a beast that'd shag a hole in the wall if you had to. Mate, you're a bit of a legend, but that reputation may not be doing you any favours with her. What if she's heard about you using the whores down at the railway sidings? Not going to look good, is it, and I'll bet there'll be plenty of people queuing up to tell her if she didn't know.'

'I haven't shagged a tom in months,' said Psycho more calmly, as he acknowledged the commonsense that Malcy was talking.

'You and I know that, but chances are, all she's going to hear about is what you used to be like. There's only one way you're ever going to be able to win her over, if that's the issue.'

'Go on, what?'

'Tell her everything.'

'You've got to be fucking joking. *Everything?* She wouldn't have anything to do with me ever again.'

'Maybe not the gory details, but you're going to have to put your hands up to a mucky past and tell her you've changed because of how you feel about her. She'll certainly respect you for acknowledging it happened, because trying to lie about it or deny it will fuck you.'

'Jesus, how do I start to tell her that? I can't just turn up at her house and tell her I used to get my tanks emptied by the hookers, can I?'

'We need a plan,' said Malcy, feeling happier in himself now that he was taking part in something positive, albeit on someone else's behalf. 'We definitely need a plan. Leave it with me.'

'Yeah, right,' mumbled Psycho, entirely unconvinced but devoid of any positive ideas himself. 'A plan.'

Ally returned to the muster room and sat back in his chair, casting dark looks at the whispering Malcy and Psycho like a jealous girlfriend. Wisely, however, he said nothing, as he was well aware that Psycho wasn't that keen on him and he had no desire to encourage the monster to carry out a previous threat – namely to snap his spine and pull his ears off if he didn't stop moaning.

'OK, you lot, listen up,' called Andy Collins as he glanced at his wristwatch. 'Time we got going. Well done all of you, with the rape we picked up this morning. Mr

Harrison's left a note for me, passing on his thanks. That was the scene we located in Stream Woods. The girl's in Handstead General in a bad way – no suspects or descriptions as yet, but Mr Harrison's asked that we put in plenty of stops on pedestrians and vehicles overnight. You never know, we might get lucky. There's not much in the GOB for today, but Pork Sword Man put in an appearance again at lunchtime down by the church in the town centre. Mr Harrison will be getting an operation together so anyone interested in some overtime on your days off, let me know.'

'What sort of operation?' asked Pizza, who looked relaxed and refreshed in contrast to most of his colleagues.

'His memo talks about a honey-trap job.'

'Honey trap?' queried JJ.

'Yeah, they'll put some WPCs out as bait with the boys plotted up in the vicinity, and hope he picks on our girls. Had a few results in the past, but it's a long shot,' said Collins.

'Which WPCs?' continued JJ.

'I'll have some of that,' interrupted the Blister from the back of the room as she stubbed her cigarette out on the floor. The others turned to gaze at her in astonishment. She glared back at them defiantly, her squat, sixteen-stone body crammed into a tight shirt and tunic that appeared ready to burst open at any moment. Her pumpkin-shaped, puce red face that had given her the nickname of 'the Blister', glowed brighter than usual under her untidy mop of tightly permed black hair, as she stood her ground against the others.

'And why not?' she answered loudly to the question that their incredulous faces asked.

'Fuck me,' bellowed Psycho, their self-appointed mouthpiece, 'I didn't know Pork Sword Man was blind as well.'

'What the fuck's *that* supposed to mean?' stormed the Blister, getting to her feet.

'The whole idea of a honey trap is to attract the guy, not scare him off. He catches sight of your wound on display, he's going to be off with his dog like a shot.'

'Shut the fuck up, Psycho!' yelled Collins from behind his lectern as the group dissolved into a raucous mob, the Blister shrieking madly as she swore vengeance on Psycho.

'You fucking bastard,' she screamed, as JJ and Pizza held her back.

'You've got some nerve, Psycho,' said Malcy as Collins desperately tried to restore order. 'You never seemed too fussy when you were pumping her up.'

'That was before, that was before,' insisted Psycho. 'Before I fell in love. I wouldn't touch her with a barge-pole now, for Christ's sake.'

'I suppose you were talking from a position of authority when you mentioned the sight of her fanny frightening off Pork Sword Man.'

'God's pyjamas!' exclaimed Psycho, leaning back in his chair and closing his eyes at the horror of the memory.

'She's got a fanny like a hippo's yawn – a real three-bagger.'

'Three-bagger?' wondered Malcy.

'Yeah. One over my head, one over hers – and a spare in case either of us lost one.'

'What a gent,' sighed Malcy. 'I thought you and the Blister had a decent arrangement going there.'

'Thing of the past, Malcy – I've moved on,' said Psycho, brightening up. 'First thing tomorrow, I'm going to give Anne a ring.'

Andy Collins eventually restored some order and glared at Psycho.

'Anyone,' and he emphasised the word, '*anyone* who wants some overtime to help take out the Pork Sword Man, let me have your names at the end of the muster. I've got your name, Amanda, thank you.'

The Blister steamed quietly at the back of the room as Collins endeavoured to get the muster finished as quickly as possible and get his officers out on the ground before it kicked off again. The Blister was used to being the butt of a lot of abuse over the years she had been in the Job, but Psycho's two bobs-worth had really got to her. She and Psycho went back years and had a loose arrangement that as and when either of them felt the need, they'd end up in bed for a quick shag. And that was it. They'd never been out for a drink together as a couple, and barely spoke to one another other than to arrange a shag. But it worked for both of them, and certainly from her point of view, provided welcome relief from the tedium of living with her elderly mother who moaned endlessly about everything. It wasn't the first time she'd been publicly insulted by him. She had endured months of ridicule when he'd shown around a series of embarrassing Polaroid photos he'd taken when she was pissed, and once he'd found out about her similar ongoing arrangement with Sergeant Mick Jones, endured a grilling from an irate Jones who'd overheard Psycho telling the group about a dry-arse fuck he'd given her.

The Blister knew she was no oil painting and was well and truly on the shelf now, but she always felt that Psycho owed her some respect. Which he always failed to recognise. She was aware of his infatuation with Anne Butler, and whilst she regretted the fact that he was unlikely to be knocking on her door again, she wished him well. She knew how lonely he was – as lonely as she – and didn't begrudge him his potential happiness. But some respect for her wouldn't go amiss. She resolved to face him up soon.

Collins assigned the group to their vehicles and beats, and to Ally's undisguised joy, paired him up with Malcy for the night. Piggy got the dirty van on his own which was entirely appropriate. The only recipients of his flatulence that evening would be the prisoners and drunks slung in the back. There were two Late Turn officers present, due to work through until 2 a.m. to support the night duty officers on what promised to be a busy shift on a warm, late June evening.

PCs Dave Carter and Roy Bentham often worked overtime with D Group. They had a similar work ethic and policing style, and enjoyed the inevitable mayhem that ensued when D Group had charge of the sub-division. They had been assigned foot patrol in the town centre to keep an eye on the two pubs that occasionally kicked off, and to supervise the drunken hordes that would shortly descend on the hamburger van parked up in the lay-by opposite the cemetery. It was an appropriate location, considering the hygiene standards maintained in the van.

D Group wandered up to the front office to collect their vehicles' keys and exchange their laminated pink and blue cards for their two-piece, light blue plastic Pye radios. The receiving unit had a heavy duty clip to attach it to the inside of the lapel of a tunic, whilst the transmitting unit went into a trouser pocket, or in the case of the WPCs, into a handbag with the ridiculous dildo-sized truncheons they were issued with. Not only did the Pye sets not work very well, but they were lost regularly in their dozens every time their owners did anything remotely energetic. Personal radios were still very much in their infancy and only marginally better than two tin cans attached to a piece of string.

The Blister had, as usual, been assigned to the front office, from where she stared daggers at Psycho as he collected the keys for Bravo Three Four, the rural beat vehicle. Collins had assigned him to this beat with a clear warning.

'I'll be checking the pubs out there, Psycho, and if I find you serving behind a bar, I'm going to knock you out. Understood?'

He understood very well. Collins was probably the only man in the station he wouldn't cheerfully fight. He'd seen the power of his punching on many an occasion.

Shortly after 10.30 p.m., Carter and Bentham were strolling through the pedestrianised town centre shopping precinct remarking on what a soulless, depressing place it was. Those shops that hadn't long ago gone out of business and been boarded up, the hoardings fluttering with faded and torn fly posters, had as neighbours nothing but estate agents, building societies, charity shops and discount stores. Until three years ago, a market had been run in the town square every Wednesday, but that had given up and sought a more profitable location. The presence of so many estate agents and building societies defied all logic, so depressed and rundown was the town, with the town centre perfectly epitomising all its ills.

Once these few businesses closed at the end of the working day, the precinct became deserted, save for the regular drunks and the hardened drinkers who used the two pubs that somehow defied the odds and had stayed in business. The two PCs had visited both pubs and found them half-empty with little sign of any potential trouble. It promised to be a very dull and uneventful four hours' overtime, but at least it was warm.

The pair were genuinely relieved to walk round a corner to see the plate-glass window of a discount chemist's shop shattered. Glancing through the gaping hole into the darkened shop they could see obvious signs of looting behind the prescription counter, but no sign of any intruders. Despite that, they put in a call for a dog van to check it out.

'Wait one, please. Any dog unit take a possible intruders on premises, Handstead town centre?' broadcast the main Force Control Room operator.

Heading south on the motorway, PC Bob Young and Alfie in Delta One jumped at the chance of a bit of action.

'Delta Hotel, show Delta One en route, ETA five minutes,' shouted Young, before he hit the twos and blues. 'Hold tight, Shithead, we've got a job.'

Sitting in the front passenger seat, police dog Alfie went potty as the two-tone siren went on and he began to try and leap out of the half-open window to get after someone. Young landed a couple of punches into the huge animal's ribcage as he powered the van towards the Handstead exit slip road.

'Sit down, you daft bastard, we're not there yet,' he yelled.

If the Brothers were the odd couple on the block, Young and Alfie ran them a very close second. Like the

Brothers, these two were isolated from their colleagues because of their reputation for violence – particularly Alfie, who was feared by both sides of the criminal divide, the length and breadth of the county. He was a huge, shaggy, black-haired German Shepherd who simply loved biting people. Regrettably, when his blood was up he was singularly unable to differentiate between the good and bad guys, and he had disgraced himself on many occasions by hospitalising cops. Despite his reputation though, the street cops loved seeing him arrive at trouble, and once they were safely out of the way, start to dismember someone.

Alfie wasn't just a biting machine though. He was a fabulous tracker, at his best free-tracking on air scent, though the aim of any of his tracks was always to attack someone, not just to find them and stand around barking. He'd been known to start climbing trees to try and get at his prey.

Young and Alfie were best mates, not just handler and dog. Which was just as well because they had no friends in their respective species group. Alfie hated all other dogs, never missing the opportunity to fight with other police dogs and condemning himself to die a virgin. Young was also friendless, but because he was so dull. His only interest in life was Alfie. There was no doubt in anyone's mind that of the two personalities that formed Delta One, the dominant one was Alfie. It was significant that when Young booked Delta One on duty, no one else on the same radio channel would remark that Bob Young was on duty. To a man the reaction was, 'Alfie's on duty, someone's going to get it.'

The skinny dog cop was married to a dried-up teacher who loathed him, staying with him only for the detached police house that came with the post. He was always looking for female company and always unsuccessfully, but nonetheless tried hard to play on his unlikely resemblance to a porn star, which had given him his nickname of 'Ooh Yah', or in its full form, 'Ooh Yah Pumpen Harder'. He was known around the county, and the wider dog-handling world, simply as 'Ooh Yah' Young, and with his pride and joy handlebar moustache, blond hair worn over the ears in a big side parting and tinted aviator-style glasses, he tried to look the part if nothing else. He was certainly no porn star in the meat and two veg department, as his wife never failed to remind him, referring to him bitterly as 'pencil dick'. He hated the old crone right back, preferring to spend as much time as possible out of the house with Alfie, particularly in the summer when they virtually lived at his local cricket club – their spiritual home.

Young and Alfie were both members there – Young a full playing member, Alfie as a paid-up social member. They could be found at the cricket club almost permanently between April and September, Alfie whiling away the long hot afternoons tethered to a distant tree to keep him out of trouble whilst Young played the game to the best of his distinctly average ability. Once the game had finished, Alfie would join Young in the clubhouse where he had sole rights to the slop trays, and it was not unusual to find the unloved pair asleep in each other's arms in a chair, or more often the changing rooms, as they succumbed to another skinful. What the other members found most unpleasant though was Alfie's almost permanent erection, which would appear like a glowing lipstick when he sat down, and always when he was pissed. They weren't on anyone's Christmas card list, but right at the top of the list of who you'd want around when the wheels came off.

Delta One was assigned to the northern divisions of the county which included Handstead, and whilst Young and Alfie had obligations elsewhere, the reality was that they spent more time in Horse's Arse than anywhere else. Now the shaggy monster howled with delight. He knew where he was headed and that in all probability he'd get to nail someone. Alfie and Young had been at the cricket club all afternoon, and whilst Young had had little to drink, Alfie had got through half a dozen spill trays before they'd left to go on duty. He was fighting drunk and ready for the off.

Carter and Bentham turned around, startled as they heard a vehicle approaching them across the pedestrianised precinct. As the headlights momentarily blinded them, they were relieved to see that it was Piggy in the dirty van, call sign Bravo Nine Nine. The dirty van was, as its name suggested, filthy, but it served a specific purpose on the Division. A battered Ford Transit, it had bench seats along either side at the back, which were separated from the driver by a heavy-duty steel-mesh screen. The van was used to transport the drunks and other unsavoury prisoners into custody, and stank of its many former passengers despite the liberal use of industrial-strength disinfectant.

'You just called in Delta One?' asked Piggy, winding down his window and smiling at them.

'Yeah, got a break-in at the chemist's,' replied Bentham.

'You want to get in? That's Alfie on his way,' said Piggy benevolently.

'Alfie?' said Carter and Bentham in unison. 'Fuck that.'

They dashed to the rear of Nine Nine, opened the doors and scrambled in, gagging immediately at the combined smells of disinfectant, vomit, urine, shit and Piggy's arse.

'Fucking hell,' wheezed Carter, his eyes watering, and dropped his nose inside his tunic, preferring the smell of his armpits, 'you had a corpse in here or something?'

Neither Carter nor Bentham had ever come across Alfie before. He and Young worked exclusively with D Group, but despite the lack of personal contact with the two PCs from another group, Alfie's fearsome reputation had preceded him.

'Never mind the smell, boys – trust me, you're better off in here than out there with that monster,' laughed Piggy, and belched loudly in their faces.

His breath was simply appalling – it had been

rumoured by some of his colleagues that entomologists had approached him with a view to using his breath to kill their specimens and save on expensive ethyl acetate in their killing jars.

Sliding away from his poisonous conversation along the bench, Carter pressed him further about Alfie.

'Is he really that bad?'

'A real beast,' replied Piggy who had, much to their relief, turned back to look out of the windscreen. 'The only person he won't attack, apparently, is his handler – what's his name – the bloke with the big tash and the sex-case specs?'

'Ooh Yah Young?'

'Yeah, that's him. Ooh Yah Young. Skinny bloke, looks like a kiddy fiddler.'

The three of them continued to assassinate Young's character until Delta One rolled to a standstill alongside them. Getting out, Young stretched before he strolled over to Piggy's window with a smile on his face. The three officers in the van barely registered his presence, transfixed as they were on the small grizzly bear going apeshit in the front passenger seat of Delta One. Its huge jaws were clamped over the top of the half-opened window and it appeared to be trying to snap the glass. Its mean, coppery little eyes were fixed on them and there was no doubt that they were its intended target.

'Get your fucking windows up,' shouted Carter desperately at Piggy. 'It's nearly out.'

Piggy did as he was told and smiled limply at Young from behind glass.

'All right boys, what you got for us?' enquired Young.

'Window's gone in at the chemist's,' shouted Carter.

Young cupped his ear to indicate he couldn't hear them through the glass and above Alfie's roaring.

'Chemist, window, over there, broken,' bellowed Carter, waving his arms about like a tic-tac man.

Young grimaced at him like a Scotsman paying a bill before he returned to Delta One, opened the passenger door and grabbed a handful of raging Alfie. With practised ease he clipped the lead he was carrying to the stout steel-link collar Alfie was wearing, and with two hands jerked the choke chain in one violent movement. The watchers in the van were aware of a huge mass of hair, teeth and slobber suddenly flying out of the passenger seat of Delta One and out of sight below them beside the van. The roaring had stopped, and they were just peering closer to their windows to see where it had gone when Alfie leaped on to his back legs and thumped his huge front paws, the size of wicket-keeping gauntlets, on to the side windows. Carter and Bentham screamed so loud Minnie Riperton would have blushed.

'Come on, you big ox,' said Young, snapping hard on the lead, pulling Alfie off the van and in tight to his left knee, and starting to walk towards the shattered shop window. Alfie began to lunge and jump as he sensed he might soon get to do someone, forcing Young to hold on with both hands. They paused and surveyed the gaping hole and inside the obvious signs of entry by intruders. Discarded boxes and bottles lay all over the floor, surrounded by thousands of pieces of glinting glass.

Many dog-handlers would balk at sending their dog into a glass-strewn, darkened shop, but Young had no such anxiety. Alfie's pads were as tough as teak, and in his entire working life to date, in every conceivable situation, had never suffered so much as a scratch. Sensing that his release was imminent, Alfie had dropped his head and shoulders into his attack stance, eyes fixed on the interior of the shop.

'Police officer with a dog! Stand still or I'll send in the dog,' called Young from deep within his stomach, his voice echoing around the deserted concrete precinct. Alfie's ears were pricked and alert for the magic words.

Then: 'Arthur Scargill, Arthur Scargill,' bawled Young to the inky black heavens, and he released the spring catch at the end of the lead.

The magic words, followed by the magic click behind his head, were all that Alfie was waiting for. Straining forward like a thoroughbred racing horse leaving the starting gate, with a deep snarl and with two huge strides he disappeared into the chemist's shop.

Young glanced back at his enthralled audience cowering in the van and grinned. If there was anyone still in there, it wouldn't take long and it was likely to be very messy. He could hear Alfie crashing around inside the shop, knocking over displays and clearing shelves as the beast desperately sought the scent of his prey. After five minutes the noise had subsided and Young's confidence in a result was draining away.

'You checked the back door?' he called to the wide-eyed cops in the van.

'Hasn't got one – all deliveries come in through the front,' called back Carter.

That ruled out one option, mused Young. What the hell was the big bugger up to? He moved over to the shattered window and called into the shop. 'Where is he, big fella? Where is he? Find him, big fella – go on, find him.'

There was only silence from inside. Rapidly losing face, Young returned to Delta One and rooted about behind the seats for his thousand-candle-strength search lamp. Hurrying back to the window, he lit up the interior of the shop but could see no sign of Alfie.

'Bollocks,' he hissed to himself. Then, after checking that there were no guillotine-like shards of glass in the top of the frame waiting to drop on him, he stepped through the window, his boots crunching on the carpet of smashed glass.

'Alfie, where the fuck are you?' he said.

He swept the interior of the relatively small shop with the lamp and just caught the glint of one of Alfie's eyes as the beam ran across the perfume counter at the back.

'Alfie, what have you got, son?' he asked, as he began to

walk towards the silent dog – and then the smell hit him. He stopped dead in his tracks.

'Oh no, you've got to be joking,' he whispered urgently, glancing back at the window in case any of the others had followed him. He needn't have worried – they wouldn't leave Nine Nine until he'd left the area.

'Alfie, you'd better not be,' he continued harshly, as he advanced to the front of the perfume counter, the smell getting stronger.

He was. Alfie was having a huge dump behind the counter, occasionally closing his eyes in concentration and tongue lolling out of the side of his mouth, as the three pints of cider, bitter and lager that had washed down the four packets of pork scratchings and two hot dogs at the cricket club were eased on to the floor of the chemist's.

'You dirty bastard, pack it in,' Young whispered impotently. 'For fuck's sake, Alfie.'

There was nothing he could do but wait for the dog to finish, constantly looking back at the smashed window. As he waited, he gathered together the items he'd need to mask their escape. Once Alfie had padded contentedly back to join him, Young began to empty half a dozen bottles of Hai Karate aftershave. Its advertising slogan 'Be careful how you use it' was ignored as Young began to douse the entire shop interior, using one entire bottle on the offending pile, which bore a striking resemblance to the Devils Tower in *Close Encounters of the Third Kind*. Five minutes later, Young and Alfie stepped back out into the precinct with Alfie trotting obediently at heel.

'No joy then?' called Piggy, winding his window down a couple of inches.

'Nah, long gone,' muttered Young, opening the rear doors of Delta One and putting Alfie into his cage – all a sure sign that he was in disgrace.

'No chance of a track away?' continued Piggy.

'No – he found a rat in the shop, won't get him interested now,' replied Young hurriedly, keen to get on his way out of town before someone found Alfie's present.

Chapter Eleven

The bloody woman was driving him insane. She'd only gone and done it again, all through the item on the *Ten o'Clock News* about the Handstead dispute, but this time it was her fucking newspaper. Jesus, the noise a one-armed woman can make reading a broadsheet newspaper – it was like being next to a building site. And as if that wasn't enough, between prolonged, deafening turns of the pages, she was sipping from a mug of hot tea. Long, noisy slurps like a bath emptying, followed by a loud sigh. *Rustle, rustle, slurp, aaah.* Smelly old George Hayward couldn't take any more. He glared at her, fists clenched into tight balls on the arms of his dusty armchair, and felt the veins in his temples throb.

Twenty minutes later, the Brothers pulled up outside the Haywards' rundown bungalow on the Ashbridge Estate and glanced towards it. The lights were on in the sitting room but they could not hear any of the shouting, screaming and smashing of objects that had prompted the fed-up neighbours to dial 999. The Haywards' tatty, matt-green Reliant Robin was the right way up on the driveway and everything seemed quiet.

'Late Turn were here yesterday,' said H, as he switched the engine off. 'Gave them both a yellow card. Reckon we might end up locking them up this time.'

'Christ, I hope not,' replied Jim, getting out. It was another beautiful evening and promised to be good fighting weather. The last thing he wanted to be doing was locking up a pair of pensioners who should be sitting at home swapping teeth and tablets, not punches.

'Seems quiet enough. Maybe they've kissed and made up,' laughed H.

Jim gave a mock groan and shudder at the thought as they strolled up the concrete slab pathway and H knocked loudly on the peeling front door. It was opened immediately by George Hayward, who looked up at them with wide, scared eyes. He was wearing a pair of dirty dark trousers and an old blue shirt, with a pair of thin braces hanging loose round his waist. He was unshaven and unkempt, and even though they were still a few feet from the interior of the house, the Brothers had already caught their first whiff.

'You've come then,' said George quietly.

'Of course we've come. You've pissed your neighbours off again,' said Jim angrily. 'What's the matter with you two?'

George didn't reply but hung his head. He appeared to be on the verge of breaking down.

'Where's your missus, George? We need to speak to both of you. This has got to stop or else you're both going to get lifted. You're too old to be spending time in the cells, trust me. Come on, where is she?' asked Jim irritably.

'I've done it,' replied George vacantly, still keeping his head down.

'Done what?'

'She was really pissing me off. Her fucking paper was driving me mad.'

'Her paper? What are you on about?' asked H, glancing at Jim with a worried frown on his face.

'And she was slurping her tea. Christ, I couldn't hear the telly for it. She did it on purpose, I reckon. And rubbing her fucking feet together.'

'What the fuck are you on about? Where is she?' asked H, pushing past him into the hall and leaving Jim to talk to George. Wincing at the appalling smell, he walked into the sitting room and immediately saw Brenda Hayward.

'Oh fuck,' he said quietly, also noting the liquid dribbling down the shabby wall above the mantelpiece and the remains of a shattered mug all over the floor.

'Jim,' he called, stepping back into the hall and fixing his mate with a wide-eyed stare. 'Better have a look at this and bring him with you.'

Sighing, Jim took hold of one of George's scrawny arms and guided him over to where H stood, still looking into the sitting room.

'Jesus Christ,' he breathed.

'She was really pissing me off,' said George Hayward, his eyes brimming with tears.

'What the fuck have you done?' asked Jim.

'She wouldn't keep quiet, I couldn't hear a fucking thing on the news. I missed the story about that dispute again.'

'So what did you do?'

'I've stopped her making any more noise, I reckon.'

H returned cautiously into the room and knelt alongside Brenda Hayward. She was lying on her back by the fireplace, her bulging eyes wide open staring sightlessly at the ceiling, her curiously inflated tongue hanging limply out of one side of her mouth. Her lips were a deep blue colour, and the skin under her eyes dotted with vivid red pinpoints. She had an almost purple complexion and her face appeared to be covered in spittle. The area around her neck and throat was a deep red colour and there was obvious bruising. Even to a layman it was obvious she had been strangled.

'Dead as a fucking doornail,' said H, feeling for a pulse around her bruised neck. 'You do this, George?'

'Afraid so. She was pissing me off,' he replied, a single tear rolling down his thin face and through his stubble.

'How did you do it?' asked Jim. 'What with?'

'Just my hands,' replied George, holding the offending items up in confirmation.

It was true. A sixty-three-year-old man had simply lost all self-control and snapped over the most trivial of matters. And then he'd clamped his bare, arthritic hands around the thin throat of the woman he'd been with for over forty years and squeezed with a strength that came from a fiery pit of anger deep inside him until he heard bones cracking and she stopped making that terrible deep choking noise and clawing at his hands with her one good hand. He had literally squeezed the breath out of the woman he had known most of his life, who had borne him a son, and watched as her eyes had glazed over and the sparkle in them that he had fallen in love with all those years ago, went out. In reality, he had killed himself as well. He was not so much consumed with guilt or remorse, as with an overpowering sense of loss. He was now all alone in a world he no longer understood, and destined to see out his final years in a prison cell. Brenda had been many things to him during their years together, not merely the pain in the arse she had become more recently. She was a part of him. She had literally lost her right arm in that industrial accident, but now George had metaphorically lost his – and it was all down to him.

'You want to call this in, Jim?' asked H, looking up at his partner. 'You have him, I had the last one.'

'Nice one, H,' said Jim. 'Hang on to our elderly Boston Strangler, I'll be right back.'

As H sat the now sobbing George Hayward down in his armchair for the last time, Jim strode back to Yankee One and briefly composed himself before transmitting. He had a half-smile on his face as he waited for other radio traffic to clear. He was waiting to deliver a message that would take precedence over pretty much everything else that was going on around the county, certainly on Channel One, and further enhance the reputation he and H enjoyed as street cops. To lock up one murderer as they had done last year with their capture of a junkie who'd butchered a Chinese woman and her daughter, was rare for uniformed officers. Most of the latter could expect to go an entire thirty-year career and never make such a collar; to get another was, he was almost certain, unheard of.

'Delta Hotel, this is Yankee One, active message,' he said urgently as there was a pause in the radio traffic.

In the main Force Control Room at Headquarters eight miles away, the middle-aged female operator frowned as she hit her talk-through button to clear the airwaves and glanced down at her open assignments. Yankee One? They were only at a domestic dispute – what the fuck had they done now?

'Yankee One, go ahead. All units stand by,' she transmitted as her Sergeant appeared over her shoulder and plugged his headset into her console to listen in.

'Delta Hotel, regarding the domestic dispute at Bernhardt Crescent, Ashbridge Estate, Handstead, show one arrest for murder. We have one dead elderly female on the premises and require an FME, SOCO and CID back-up,' came the unmistakable sound of Jim's broad Geordie accent.

As the Sergeant unplugged himself and turned back into the room to go and find his Inspector, who was over in the garage bay washing his car, the operator took a few seconds to also compose herself and mentally went over what she needed to get right as well. First thing was to get hold of her excitement.

'Yankee One's got a murder!' she shrieked at the top of her voice, causing crews across the north of the county to wince at the pitch which could crack glass. The operator was notorious for completely wigging out when things got tasty, with her panicked voice getting higher and louder as she lost control. Her Sergeant was about to leave the room when he heard her shriek again, 'Yankee One's got a murder!' He paused, rolled his eyes to the heavens, then retraced his steps to her control position, where he reached down under her desk and pulled out her headphones jack plug. She looked up at him, bug-eyed.

'Go and put the fucking kettle on,' the Sergeant hissed at her as he plugged himself in, 'and find Mr Jameson. He's washing his car, but try not to burst his eardrums, will you? Tell him we've got another big one at Horse's Arse.'

He glared at her as she shuffled away disconsolately; this was the final straw as far as he was concerned. She'd found street duties too onerous on Division and clearly the Control Room was beyond her as well. She obviously had a glittering career ahead of her as a Senior Officer, he mused.

'Yankee One, this is Oscar Two, technical problems on the Channel One pod. Go ahead to me, please. Confirm one female dead, one arrest for murder at Bernhardt Crescent, Handstead,' he said.

Jim, in common with everyone else on Channel One, knew exactly what had happened. 'The Screamer' had long been a topic of heated discussion around the county, and her demise was welcome.

'Yes, yes, Oscar Two. One dead, one locked up. We need an FME to pronounce life extinct, SOCO to the scene and CID back-up.'

'Leave it with us, Yankee One. You need any further uniform back-up?'

'Negative, Oscar Two. Once we've got CID here we'll get the prisoner back to Hotel Alpha. No further uniforms required.'

'Understood, Yankee One. You got a landline number on scene we can contact you on?'

Jim hadn't noticed a phone in the Haywards' dingy bungalow, but if they had one it would certainly make life easier. They could keep the radio air clear for everyone else and the General Post Office would be helping enormously with police enquiries. And they'd have a bastard of a job getting poor old George Hayward to settle his bill from his cell in Strangeways.

'I'll get back to you, Oscar Two,' promised Jim. 'Yankee One out.'

*

Dan Harrison was sure he'd only just closed his eyes, but the bright red numerals on his bedside alarm clock told him otherwise. Twenty-three thirty-five? That couldn't be right, he'd only just turned off the light. Why was he awake? Where was he? The bloody phone was ringing on the floor beside the bed. Jesus, not again. Now what?

Still struggling to get his brain in gear, Harrison felt around on the bedside table by the dim light of his digital clock until he found the switch on his bedside lamp and groaned as the glare welded his puffy eyes shut. He was exhausted, having worked almost nonstop for the last forty-eight hours. The phone was ringing off the hook and he scrabbled about over the side of his bed until he located it and hauled the handset up to his mouth as he remained face down in his pillow.

'Harrison,' he croaked, keeping his throbbing eyes closed and recoiling from the smell of his own breath off the mouthpiece. He'd been too tired to brush his teeth when he finally got in, and the purely medicinal Bushmills and miniature cigar he'd had to help him get off to sleep revisited him with a vengeance. That had been around ten o'clock – a lifetime ago.

'Sorry to bother you, boss,' said an equally shattered Bob Clarke on the other end of the phone. 'You need to know about this – probably want to come in.'

Not as long as I've got a hole in my arse, thought Harrison to himself, but he knew Clarke wouldn't have phoned him unless it was urgent – and he also knew that

Clarke and his partner John Benson were running on fumes themselves. As the night duty CID at Handstead they'd copped for the Mandy Blackstock rape the night before and had barely been home. It had been the night before, hadn't it? Or was it the day before that? He'd lost all track of time, the days simply merging into one continuous duty. It was how life became for a busy detective when things hotted up. Work, sleep, work. Eat sometimes, wash occasionally, but always work, sleep a little, work a lot more.

'No worries, Bob. What you got?' he asked.

'A domestic murder on the Ashbridge Estate. The uniforms have got it nicely boxed off, with the husband locked up and no loose ends that I can see.'

Harrison was alert and interested now, rolling into a sitting position on the side of the bed and dumping the telephone base set on the bedside table, trying to unravel the tangled telephone cord as he spoke.

'We got the FME and SOCO on scene?'

'Yeah. Doctor Payne has just pronounced life extinct, SOCO are waiting to go and Yankee One's en route to Horse's Arse with the prisoner.'

'You on scene now?'

'Yeah, John's with me.'

'Scene all secured?'

'Yeah. We've borrowed one of the night duty uniforms to stand on the front door to log everyone in and out. We're just waiting for the undertakers now.'

'Sounds tidy, Bob – well done. I'm going to have a quick shit, shave and a shower, and get in. I couldn't sleep anyway,' lied Harrison. 'We can have another chat about your serial rapist if we get a chance.'

'*Our* serial rapist,' corrected Clarke with a short laugh. 'Been busy on that today.'

'Have you had any sleep, Bob? You must be fucked.'

'Couldn't sleep either, boss. Got a real feeling for this guy,' replied Clarke. 'I've got plenty to show you when there's a spare minute.'

'Can't wait, Bob,' said Harrison with a low chuckle and a heavy heart. 'See you in a bit.' He hung up and sat for a moment, peering down at his feet and particularly at the nail on the big toe of his left foot. It was rotten, all black and gnarled and not very nice at all. He'd have to see a doctor about it soon. He bent down to examine it closer before another voice in his head cut in: 'Have a shave and a shower. You've got to go in – get a grip.'

Wearily he got to his feet, stretched and wandered out of his bedroom to the poky bathroom on the other side of the landing. The shirts on wire hangers dangling from the small radiator there reminded him that he hadn't ironed one before he went to bed. 'Bollocks,' he swore as he switched on the shower behind the mildewed shower curtain and leaned against the tiled wall with his eyes closed and a hand under the weak trickle of water, praying that he'd put the immersion heater on.

Chapter Twelve

As Dan Harrison suffered under a cold shower, Pizza and JJ cruised the Park Royal Estate, chatting about the extraordinary events of the previous night and, of course, about what the Brothers had stumbled across. JJ was, to put it mildly, shell-shocked.

'Fucking hell, Pizza,' he said, looking at his mentor with haunted, sleep-starved eyes, 'I'm party to a bloody murder now.'

'Murder?' scoffed Pizza. 'Where do you get murder from? Death by reckless driving, probably.'

JJ threw up his hands in desperation. 'Death by reckless driving; murder – what's the fucking difference? There's a bloke killed and they chucked him over a hedge. Someone's going to find him soon – and then what happens?'

'Relax, JJ. It's going nowhere, is it?'

'Jesus, Pizza – this is all wrong,' JJ fretted, looking out of his open window at the darkened school they were passing.

'It was an accident, JJ,' replied Pizza firmly, adjusting the volume on the main radio set slung under the heater to listen to a message from the Brothers down on the Ashbridge Estate.

'They've come up trumps again, haven't they?' he continued casually. 'Second murder they've locked up in a year.'

'What is it they keep on about – "the harder you work, the luckier you get"?' asked JJ with more than a touch of irony in his voice, happy to discuss something other than the incident that threatened to haunt him for the rest of his career.

'Yeah, something like that. No getting away from it, I reckon. They work their nuts off and sometimes you forget that because they're such punchy bastards.'

JJ didn't respond, continuing to stare out of his window as the cool evening air wafted around his upper body and the awful feeling of impending doom wrapped its fingers around his guts.

Pizza smiled as he glanced at him, asking, 'You get any sleep today?'

'Not a wink.'

'Not got used to sleeping during the day yet?'

'Got fuck all to do with that,' snapped JJ.

'Don't worry about it, mate, things will work out. They always do,' chided Pizza. 'Hey, have a gander at this one – looks like a candidate.' He was pointing at a tatty, dark-coloured Mark One Ford Escort that had pulled out of a side road about 100 yards ahead of them without its lights on. As Pizza closed the gap between the two vehicles, the Escort veered across the central white lines and then violently back to clip the nearside verge. They could see the front seats were occupied and a sole head in the rear.

'Pissed as a parrot,' remarked Pizza happily. 'You had a drink driver yet?'

'No,' replied JJ, cheering up at the prospect. 'You reckon he's pissed?'

'That, or off his face on something else,' Pizza grunted. 'Have a look, will you?'

The Escort had clipped the nearside verge again before regaining its position on the crown of the road as the driver desperately followed the only thing he could see – the central white lines.

'Check the plate,' ordered Pizza.

A vehicle check with the PNC operator on Channel Two confirmed what the two cops had already begun to suspect. There was no current keeper for the vehicle, the previous owner having informed the DVLA that the car had been scrapped eighteen months earlier.

'Pikeys,' they said in unison, as JJ hung up the handset.

'No, no,' said Pizza, correcting themselves with a loud laugh. 'Caravan Utilising Nomadic Travellers.'

'And headed for the Jack Oldings site, probably,' continued JJ.

'Let's put a stop in now before they get any closer,' said Pizza. 'Right – put the blues on, my son.'

As JJ pushed the blue lights toggle to on, Pizza began to flash his headlights and hit the car horn. He was pleasantly surprised to see the Escort almost immediately pull over to the nearside kerb and stop, albeit with both nearside wheels up on the pavement.

'Fucking hell, wonders will never cease,' he muttered. 'Off you go, JJ, get the keys out and get him bagged.' Pizza had been confidently expecting a chase with the Escort, but the simple fact was that the driver had performed a bit of a miracle in just getting the car started and on the road.

Dermot Papper was slaughtered. He was at least still awake, whilst his two older brothers, in the passenger seat and the back, were fast asleep after their all-day drinking binge in rural pubs favoured by the traveller community. Not that the Pappers were travellers in the true sense of the word, living in the permanent gypsy camp on the nearby Jack Oldings roundabout. But travellers in the sense that they didn't pay any tax on the proceeds of their criminal activities, which included burglary and ripping off pensioners for slapping a couple of inches of red tarmac on their drives, or replacing a broken rooftile. And of course, claiming every benefit they and their extended, and sometimes imaginary, families were given without question by the state – which all amounted to a pretty comfortable way of life with very little input from them. The only occasional interruption to this idyll came from the local police, who seemed to have taken great exception to their freeloading and never failed to jump all over them when the opportunity arose.

'This your motor, mate?' asked JJ, as he reached into the Escort to get the keys, recovering instead a small screwdriver that had been jammed into the ignition barrel.

Twenty-three-year-old Dermot Papper looked up at him with eyes that refused to focus, his head rolling like a ship in a heavy sea.

'Fuck off,' he slurred in his thick Irish accent. 'We're going home quiet like – leave us alone.' He began to rummage about around the ignition barrel for the screwdriver, still unsure why he'd bothered to stop for the cops. He didn't normally, but then he wasn't normally that pissed.

'Looking for this, pal?' asked JJ, brandishing the screwdriver. 'You're not going anywhere. Out you get, I need a breath sample from you.'

'Like fuck I will,' said Papper aggressively. 'Give us the screwdriver, you little prick.'

JJ took a step back as Papper swung open the driver's door and unsteadily hauled himself out to stand swaying and blinking in front of the young cop.

'Give us the fucking screwdriver or I'll deck you,' growled Papper. He had had plenty of scraps with cops over the years and fancied himself against this youngster who, even in his drunkenness, he could see was obviously just out of police training school, where they taught them really useful things like wrist and armlocks and about only using their ridiculous truncheons on the arms and legs. It took most cops a few beatings before they switched on to the fact that there was no substitute for a swift kick in the nuts and a baseball bat between the ears. Most cops perhaps, but JJ wasn't most cops and neither was Pizza, who had seen the aggressive move towards his partner and called for some back-up before he got out of the car to join him.

'Any unit Hotel Alpha, back up Bravo Two One in Park Road. Vehicle stopped, three up, may need some assistance,' broadcast the operator in response to Pizza's request.

'We'll have some of that, Psycho,' said Malcy cheerfully in Two Two as they drove out of the deserted underground car park at the Grant Flowers flats where they'd been looking for junkies shooting up. 'Delta Hotel, show Bravo Two Two on our way,' he said quickly into the headset before anyone else got a chance to run to the job. It had been relatively quiet other than the murder at Bernhardt Crescent, and the promise of a bit of action would attract other cops like flies round a cow's arse.

'Delta Hotel, show Delta One running to that as well,' chimed in Ooh Yah Young, who was keen to make amends in Handstead after Alfie's dreadful showing at the chemist's. He'd been hovering on the borders of the Division, backing as many horses as he could on jobs elsewhere in the northern divisions, praying he might get something decent for Alfie to redeem himself with. As things stood, as yet only he knew that Alfie had curled one off in the shop, but it was only a matter of time before the shop owners discovered his calling card. Young and Alfie really needed some credit in the bank before, quite literally, the shit hit the fan. Normally the local cops would have bridled at the prospect of being beaten to a call by anyone, but as Psycho and Malcy heard Young's call sign come up, they smiled broadly at each other.

'Someone's in the shit,' said Psycho happily.

Papper took another step towards JJ to get a better look at him before he planted a right-hander on him. This was his last mistake. Misjudging JJ's physical appearance was the first. JJ's animal instinct seemed to almost detect the chemical reaction in Papper's muscles as he tensed to move, and in a blink the young PC had planted a fearsome straight jab between his eyes. Papper neither saw it coming nor felt it – everything simply went black as he flew backwards against the Escort and slid down the side of it unconscious.

'What the fuck was *that* all about?' enquired Pizza, who had not seen Papper make any move to attack his young partner.

'He was about to plant one on me,' replied his beaming protégé, massaging his fist. '"Get your revenge in first", you always told me.'

'Quite right, quite right,' answered his twenty-two-year-old guru and sage. 'Looks like you might need to get a bit more revenge in, son.' He was indicating the interior of the Escort, where the other Papper boys had been roused by the sound of their brother being put to sleep against the side of the car.

The Pappers both exited the car from the passenger side and staggered round to where Dermot lay with blood trickling from his nose. Then they turned to face Pizza and JJ. Joseph and Brendan Papper were a formidable pair who had a reputation in gypsy circles as very handy bare-knuckle fighters. They feared no one and certainly not this pair of arseholes who were clearly responsible for knocking out young Dermot. And to add insult to injury, the youngest of the cops, who looked like a choirboy, was smiling at them. Fucking *smiling* at them?

'I'm going to wipe that stupid smile off your face, son, and then I'm going to break your legs,' drawled Joseph, the biggest of the brothers at twenty stone. His ruddy red face, capped with a wild mop of black hair, was contorted with rage and he suddenly lunged at JJ. Who had moved a split second before the lunge and was ideally placed to smash him in the side of the face with a huge swinging right-hander. Joseph Papper collapsed face first into the middle of the road and lay still, his nose pumping blood on to the tarmac.

'You cunts!' screamed Brendan, launching himself at Pizza who was nearest to him.

Pizza, who had anticipated the attack, deflected the

punch thrown at him with his left arm and then split Brendan's head open with a clean shot across the top with the wheelbrace he had thoughtfully brought with him.

'Shot, Pizza,' applauded JJ, walking over to examine the prostrate Brendan, who lay on his side with blood pouring down his face from the deep gash in his head. 'Reckon we need an ambulance for these two?'

'Do we fuck,' replied Pizza. 'Ambulances are for taxpayers. Besides, these bastards are like cockroaches; you've got to cut their fucking heads off to kill them.'

JJ was digesting this, his latest lesson in policing Handstead and its awful inmates, when Bravo Two Two came squealing to a stop behind their vehicle. Psycho and Malcy got out, looking disappointed at the mayhem in front of them.

'Great, you've finished,' complained Psycho loudly. 'You might have waited until we got here.'

'We would have, but they kicked off quickly. That big fucker over there went for JJ first,' replied Pizza, 'then Shit for Brains here offered to help me change a wheel.' He smiled and held up the still dripping wheelbrace.

'Fucking hell,' moaned Psycho, 'I was looking forward to this.' He wandered over to Joseph Papper and gave him a prod in the ribs with his boot. The big man began to stir.

'He's coming round!' exclaimed Psycho jubilantly. 'Might be something left for us still.'

As he spoke, Delta One careered to a standstill in the

middle of the road. Young looked furious as he got out and marched over to the group.

'You might have waited,' he whined. 'The big fella needs to get his teeth into something soon. He's had a shocker so far and I was hoping he'd get something here. All pikeys, I take it?'

'Yeah, reckon so,' replied Pizza, as he wiped the wheelbrace clean on the back of Brendan Papper's shirt. 'Unregistered motor, heading towards the Oldings roundabout, Irish accents. Got to be bogtrotters.'

'They all nicked yet?' queried Young, rubbing his chin in deep thought.

'Well, they will be. Why?'

'See, it would be useful to give Alfie a bit of a pick-me-up, if you know what I mean,' continued Young in the same vein.

'What you on about?'

'How about leaving one for Alfie?'

'Leaving him one?'

'Yeah, leave one for the big fella. Lock two of them up and leave me one to do a bit of training with.'

Pizza and the others looked at each other and smiled. Even JJ forgot the huge misgivings he harboured about the Brothers' fatal traffic accident and signed up to the exercise.

'Why don't you take this big bastard?' he said, indicating Joseph Papper. 'He seemed keen to have a pop. I reckon he and Alfie would get on fine.'

It was agreed, and fifteen minutes later the three

Papper brothers had been roused and hauled to their feet, but only Dermot and Brendan had been locked up.

'What about me, you bastards?' shouted Joseph, keen not to have to explain to the camp at Oldings why only he of the three brothers in the car had walked away from the encounter with the police.

'Oh, you're all right, you didn't even get close to me,' said JJ benevolently. 'You get yourself off home, there's nothing for you here.'

'What about my brothers?'

'Both nicked for assault on police and anything else we can think of later,' replied Pizza. 'Go on, fuck off before we change our minds.'

Joseph was in a dilemma. He wasn't looking forward to having to explain to his fellow tarmackers and roofers why he hadn't been nicked, but he was also very aware that there were at least three warrants out for him, not backed for bail, currently in circulation. If he got locked up now, he was going away for a bit.

'You cunts,' he offered. 'Assault on police my arse. There's not a fucking mark on any of you.'

He had a point, but Psycho made a better one. 'Fuck off now, pal, or I'm going to put your details through the computer. Pound a penny to a pinch of shit, you'll be wanted for something, somewhere. What a surprise, I thought as much,' he finished as Joseph Papper turned on his heel and began to stagger away up the road in the general direction of the gypsy site.

Papper had sobered up considerably since he had been the unwilling recipient of JJ's stinging jab, but he was still drunk, and his nose hurt like a bastard. It felt as though it was broken and the punch to the side of his face had loosened a couple of teeth. Still, he'd avoided getting locked up, and those dumb cops hadn't found the two sawn-off shotguns in the boot of the Escort that they'd used to rob three sub-Post Offices in South Manchester earlier in the week. Fucking wankers.

Then: 'Police officer with a dog! Stand still or I'll send the dog!' he heard someone shouting behind him. Papper stopped and turned in the direction of the voice. Squinting, he could see the group of coppers about 100 yards away and his brothers still handcuffed on the ground beside them. Then one of the coppers moved towards him, leading a small black horse. What are they doing with a fucking horse? he thought to himself.

'Police officer with a dog! Stand still or I'll send the dog!' repeated the copper with the horse, before even louder, he leaned his head back and screamed, 'Arthur Scargill, Arthur Scargill!'

'What dog?' Papper asked himself, as the horse began to gallop towards him. And then he sobered up in a flash as his befuddled brain focused on what was approaching him. It certainly wasn't Red Rum, on whom Joseph had won heavily in last year's Grand National, but it was about the same size. Something in his pea-sized, alcohol-sodden brain told him to run, but the message failed miserably to make it to his leaden legs.

He stood transfixed, watching as the horse thundered towards him in the dark, with the cop now yelling, 'Kill him! Kill him!' or words to that effect. When it was about fifty yards away from him, he realised it was, in fact, an alligator with the body of a shaggy bison, and it had its mean coppery little eyes fixed on him.

With a scream, Papper finally managed to get his legs to function, and he turned back the way he had been heading and started to run. He gave a passable impression of a man in a diving suit before the horse overtook him and tried to swallow his head. As Alfie bit deep into his already broken nose, Papper screamed in mortal terror, his scream seeming to echo, so far was his head inside the beast's mouth. As the brute forced him to the ground, Papper gamely landed a few punches to its ribcage but they were as effective as blows to a punchbag. The horse just kept snarling and biting him harder, all over his head and shoulders, and then it suddenly switched tactics and bit him in the nuts.

It was a moment in his life that would stay with Joseph Papper to his dying day. Not just the indescribable, excruciating pain, but the enduring memory of a vision from the very bowels of Hades – a pair of fiery eyes set in a horse's head of unspeakable size, and a set of fangs lined in bared pink lips clamped around his crutch attempting to rip all he held dear and sacred away in a single shake of its head. His mother had always told him it could end like this, the day Beelzebub himself set foot on the earth to take what was rightfully his.

And then Papper passed out, with the mingled sounds of hysterical laughter and snarling ringing in his ears.

George Hayward stood waiting in the cell area at Handstead Police Station, with the Brothers standing either side of him. He was still wearing his tartan slippers and was shaking with fear. Not the fear of what the outcome of his actions held for him – he was resigned to that – but the fear of where he currently found himself. He was clearly in a madhouse.

The big, grey-haired Sergeant behind the single wooden desk had been very kind and sympathetic with him, even offering him one of his cigarettes, and he patiently explained what would happen now. He was about to start taking George's personal details, when the doors to the room had burst open and three recently butchered carcases had been carried in by a group of coppers who were all swearing loudly at the pieces of meat and hitting them with their truncheons. After a few seconds it dawned on George that the three carcases were, in fact, human – and they were still alive. Indeed, the carcases were still very much alive, shouting and screaming back at the frenzied coppers in strange accents and referring to them as 'feckers'.

One of the human carcases was drenched from head to

toe in blood, presumably his own. His entire head and face appeared to be covered in deep gashes, the only break in colour being his frenzied blue eyes. He could have been wearing a Hallowe'en mask, but it was obvious it was all him. His shirt was similarly stained red, but it was his red trousers that were most disturbing. They were torn to shreds around the crutch area, a deep red stain covering the cloth and spreading down the legs as far as the knees. It was the tie-dye fad taken a stage further.

George watched as the three carcases were battered to the floor whilst the nice Sergeant waited for peace and order to be restored. Eventually his voice could be heard, saying, 'What you got, boys? I've got an important one here.'

'Three for assault on police, threatening and abusive behaviour, and that one,' (the officer had difficulty identifying the relevant carcass) 'for refusing to provide a specimen of breath,' replied a panting Pizza, pausing momentarily from clubbing the trio like baby seals. The one with the red trousers roared something again about feckers and shites before he disappeared in a flurry of blows, the Brothers nipping over to get a couple of crafty ones in. Despite their quality arrest, they both felt a little cheated, to have missed out on a bit of fighting.

'Got to get this old boy booked in first,' said Collins above the din. 'Stick them in the detention room and stay with them. I'll be with you as soon as possible.'

He turned his attention back to George Hayward who

was trembling like a leaf, watching in horror as the three bodies were hauled across the floor to the large adjacent detention room, leaving a smear of blood that reminded him exactly of the smears on the ice floes after the Canadian seal hunters had finished.

'What's your name, old-timer?' asked Andy Collins.

'G-George Hayward,' he stammered. 'What was that all about, Sarge? That's not going to happen to me, is it?'

'Good gracious no, George,' laughed Collins, looking up at him. 'That's just pikeys getting some. They don't know any different, just how it is. That's not for decent, law-abiding folk like you, George, don't you worry,' he finished, ignoring the fact that only a few hours earlier, the cantankerous old bugger had manually strangled his wife because her shoes squeaked and reading a paper with one arm was a little noisy.

In truth, the old bastard deserved a visit from the Handstead Canadian Seal Clubbers Appreciation Society as much as the Papper brothers.

Chapter Thirteen

Half an hour later, George Hayward sat in his cell wearing a white paper suit and a pair of black elasticated plimsolls that were two sizes too large that the nice Sergeant had given him. He'd watched forlornly as his worn trousers and shirt had been taken from him by a plain-clothes officer and put into brown bags. Even his slippers had gone the same way. He recognised that it was probably the last time he would ever see a piece of clothing he actually owned. In future, all his sartorial issues would be dealt with by Her Majesty's Government. The nice Sergeant had given him a heavily sugared polystyrene cup of tea and slipped him a couple of his own cigarettes, lighting one for him before he left and slammed the heavy dark green door behind him.

'You ring your bell when you want that other one lit, George,' he called through the open inspection hatch.

'Thank you Sergeant, you've been very good to me,'

called George from the grimy blue plastic-covered mattress he was sitting on.

'Not a problem, George. People like you don't deserve to be locked up in places like this. You've done an awful thing, but this isn't where you should be. We've got to look after old people like you. Bet you've done your bit for Queen and Country, time to repay the debt as best we can.'

Collins's experience was that, given an opportunity like that, most ex-servicemen would happily recount every second of their military careers, however brief, but George didn't respond at all. He just looked down at the floor.

'You did your time, didn't you, George? World War Two or maybe Korea?'

George mumbled a reply Collins didn't catch, so he reopened the door and stood towering over him.

'What did you say?' he asked.

'I wasn't in World War Two or Korea.'

'Why the fuck not? You were old enough,' Collins said angrily.

'I was in prison from 1940 to 1947,' replied Hayward, looking up at him fearfully.

'What the fuck for?'

'Armed robbery at a Post Office in Manchester.'

'What about Korea?'

'Doing another six stretch for counterfeiting.'

'You fucking old scrote!' shouted Collins. 'Give me those fucking fags back, you no-good, sponging, murdering old bastard.'

He grabbed the cigarettes from Hayward's shaking hand and stormed out of the cell, all he believed in of the wartime generation in tatters. Like many of his age, he had been led to believe that the country had pulled together as one during the dark days of World War Two, when the uncomfortable truth was that there had been plenty of people like George Hayward whose criminal lives had been untouched by cataclysmic world events.

'The detectives will be down to interview you later. You make sure you make a full and frank confession, you old crook, or else you'll be smoking your next fag through your arse,' shouted Collins through the inspection hatch before he slammed that shut as well and turned off the cell's lights.

Bitterly disappointed with the evaporation of what he had believed in, Collins made his way to the detention room to deal with the three gypsies. They were now sitting on the low wooden bench glaring defiantly at the cops standing in front of them.

'Want to do the driver first, Alan?' Collins asked Pizza. Before Pizza could reply, Joseph Papper got to his feet.

'You get these cuffs off me, you old grey-haired twat and I'll take the fucking lot of you on. You're fuck all now you haven't got your horse with you.'

'Sit down, you cunt. What you on about?' asked Collins.

'Your nancy boys didn't do all this to me,' said Papper, indicating his extensive injuries. 'Your fucking horse did, but now it's gone and I'll do the lot of you. Just get the cuffs off me and I'll show you bastards.'

'What the hell is he on about a horse for?' Collins asked his troops as he paused at the door.

'Delta One,' answered Pizza, raising his eyebrows in further explanation.

'Got you,' nodded Collins. 'Sit down, you scumbag, you'll get your turn.'

'Will I fuck!' shouted Joseph Papper. 'You get these fucking cuffs off me and I'll take your head off, you old cunt.'

Joseph Papper had made a terrible mistake. One which any number of prisoners in the past had made when dealing with Andy Collins. Andy had gone grey in his late twenties, an event connected with the birth of his twin daughters, and as he'd got older his hair had turned a distinctive battleship grey. Now in his late forties, there was more white than grey, but he was proud of the fact that he still had all his own hair, unlike many of his contemporaries. Its colour had never really been an issue with him, though his daughters had been brought up believing that his original shade was ash blond, and the numerous insults he'd been on the receiving end of were like water off a duck's back. What he couldn't abide was being called *old*.

The cops saw the nerve begin to tic under his right eye and made some room for him. After George Hayward's revelations, this was just what Andy Collins needed.

'Is that right?' said Collins quietly, planting his huge hamlike hands on his hips. 'Tell you what, I'll do a deal with you. I'll take the cuffs off, and you and I'll go for it in here now, OK? If you win, you and your brothers can walk out of here without charge. I win, you behave yourselves, admit everything and don't make any complaints. Agreed?'

'Agreed,' shouted Papper. 'Now get these off,' and he thrust his manacled wrists towards Collins.

It promised to be an interesting encounter. Papper and Collins were roughly the same size, though the gypsy carried a little more weight around the gut, but Collins was twenty years older. Papper was a vicious street-fighter with a well-earned reputation in the bare-knuckle fraternity, but Collins was a real boxer with pedigree. As a youngster he had boxed at middleweight, representing England Schools, and then England in the 1950 Commonwealth Games in Auckland. Narrowly missing out on a medal on a dubious points decision, he had been toying with the idea of turning professional when his family persuaded him to become the third-generation Collins to join the police. There he had dominated police boxing at that weight, representing his Force and then the British Police team which travelled around the world.

The highlight of his police boxing career had been a trip to the United States in 1953 when he'd fought Police Departments across the country, finishing undefeated with a two-round demolition of a huge Irish-American detective from the New York Police Department at a massive boxing event at Carnegie Hall. It was the American cops who had given him the nickname of the Anaesthetist, which had followed him back to the UK and stuck.

Andy hadn't boxed competitively for fifteen years, but kept himself in shape and his hands hard, battering an ancient brown leather punchbag hanging in his garage at home. He had lightning hand speed, with hands the size of shovels which, when encased in boxing gloves, made him look like he was carrying a pair of motorcycle helmets. His punching prowess was legendary around the Force and the local CID often had reason to be grateful that the 'good Dr Collins' had visited a prisoner before they interviewed him and given the guy a local anaesthetic to assist meaningful dialogue. On occasions, however, he'd overdone it and administered a general, rendering the subsequent interview fairly pointless.

The two younger Pappers and the cops moved to the back of the detention room as Collins unlocked Joseph's cuffs and the gypsy vigorously rubbed at his cut and bleeding wrists.

'Right, you old fucker,' he began, clenching his fists and beginning to drop into a fighting position. There was a blur of movement in front of him and he flew backwards against the wall as Collins landed a perfect left-right combination to his jaw. Papper stared up from the floor, blinking wildly as he tried to clear his head and work out what had hit him – half-expecting to see the headlights of a truck that had driven into the detention room. Instead he was greeted by the sight of Collins doing an 'Ali shuffle' and encouraging him to get to his feet.

'Come on, come on. Up you get, you piece of shit, show the *old man* what you've got,' he called.

Papper hauled himself unsteadily to his feet and shook his head to clear his double vision. There was another blur of movement as Collins landed a double combination left-right flurry to his head and jaw. As if fired from a cannon, Papper flew backwards again, cracking his head with a sickening sound against the wall before sliding slowly to the floor. Collins had done both his eyes with the last attack, the eyebrows now split with blood coursing down his face and the eyes already puffy and closing fast.

'Come on, on your feet!' yelled Collins with a manic tone to his voice and glint in his eyes, shuffling across the Detention-Room floor in a fashion that would have done the Thriller in Manila proud. 'The *old man* ain't frightened of you, you big pansy.'

The younger Pappers had never seen anything like it. Joseph was unbeatable, never lost a bare-knuckle fight in his life and now he was getting a hammering from a middle-aged cop. This couldn't be right.

'Come on, Joe, you soft bastard. Finish him off, for the love of God,' called Brendan.

'You think you can do any better than this lump of

shit, you're welcome to take his place,' growled Collins menacingly, moving towards him.

'You're all right,' conceded Brendan, wisely retaking his seat on the bench and relieved to see that his brother was again hauling himself slowly to his feet. Collins had also seen him moving and launched an uppercut from below his hip that crashed into the man's jaw, snapping his head back and putting his lights out. Joseph Papper crashed to the floor for the last time and lay still, dreaming of the demon horse chasing him in the dark.

Half an hour later, he found himself being slapped back to life in the doctor's room by Andy Collins. His huge figure zoomed in and out of focus until Papper could just see the clear image of his tormentor through his eyes that looked like racing dogs' bollocks.

'You all right, you big lump?' asked Collins genially.

Papper smiled mournfully and looked down at the floor but said nothing. His head was thumping, he was covered in blood, and the gaping wounds in his head, face and groin, courtesy of the horse, were agony.

'Don't feel too bad about it. I've done a bit in my time,' continued Collins, patting him on the shoulder.

'Is that right? Where then?' asked Papper weakly.

'Commonwealth Games as a lad.'

'Jesus. You know what, Sergeant, I've fought more of you bastards than I can remember, but I've never had a beating like that before. Hats off to you.' Papper got painfully to his feet and offered Collins a bloodstained handshake. Collins returned it warmly and began to walk Papper out of the room back to the booking-in area.

'Where are the boys?' asked Papper.

'Banged up, mate, like you're going to be. Hope you haven't forgotten our deal, because I've got something for you to sign.'

'What's that then?'

Collins pushed the arrest sheet he had been writing on towards him. 'You read and write OK?' he asked.

'No.'

'No problem. Just put your mark here, here and here.'

'What's this then?'

'First one: "I admit all the offences alleged against me" – just sign there,' said Collins.

'Jesus,' sighed Papper, making his cross by Collins's finger.

'Next one just here: "I do not wish to make any complaint about my treatment whilst in custody" – just there.'

'Fucking hell,' said Papper, doing as he was told.

'Last one: "I promise to behave myself in future" – just here.'

'You're fucking joking,' complained Papper.

'Just sign it. We had an agreement,' Collins reminded him.

'Fuck's sake,' sighed Papper, signing the sheet again alongside Collins's finger. He was already thinking ahead to the beatings he was going to have to give his brothers, to ensure their silence in the future. He had a reputation to preserve, and any mention of his thrashing by Collins could have serious consequences, possibly fatal.

As the Papper boys slept off their hangovers and hammerings in adjacent cells, Pizza and JJ, Psycho and Malcy were joined by Ooh Yah to write up their notebooks for the arrests.

'Have we got enough to charge them with assault on police?' asked Psycho.

'I blocked a punch,' offered Pizza.

'And then did him with a wheelbrace,' added JJ, to loud laughter.

'What I'm getting at is they look like they've been through a meat-grinder. You two are unmarked, get my drift?'

Pizza and JJ looked at each other and agreed with the diagnosis. Other than JJ's slightly bruised knuckles, they were uninjured.

'If we're going to charge them with assault on police we're going to need more than some bruised knuckles. Have you seen the police doctor yet?'

'No. He's on his way.'

'You need some bruising before he gets here,' said Psycho firmly.

'How're we going to do that then?' asked JJ.

'Come on, down to the locker room. I'll take care of it.'

Pizza and JJ got to their feet and with quizzical

expressions on their faces followed Psycho out of the room and down the corridor to the locker rooms. They quickly checked the changing area, toilets and showers to confirm that they were alone, before Psycho began to rummage about in his locker. All manner of material began to pile up on the bench and the floor around him, including a powerful-looking air rifle with a huge telescopic sight.

'What the fuck is that for?' gasped JJ.

'Gypsies,' replied Pizza simply, who had seen it used in the past to shoot up the occupants of an illegal gypsy site.

'What, you shoot them with it?'

'Don't go there, JJ, just leave it,' replied Pizza, looking him straight in the eye.

JJ gulped and shook his head. He was having serious misgivings about his chosen career anyway, what with the dead cyclist he'd seen being dumped over a hedge, and now it appeared that they had a mad sniper on the payroll.

'Here it is,' announced Psycho triumphantly, pulling a filthy towel free from the depths of his locker, old trainers and boots tumbling out onto the floor as he did so.

'What's that shitty old thing for?' asked JJ fearfully.

'You left- or right-handed?' replied Psycho, ignoring the question.

'Right, why?'

'Give us your left arm.'

'Hold on, what the fuck are you on about? What are you doing?'

'You need a bit of bruising for the Doctor to see. Wrap this towel around your arm, it'll reduce the pain.'

'What?' shouted JJ, now seriously alarmed.

'Put the towel around your arm, JJ,' continued Psycho patiently, 'and we'll give your arm a bit of a bashing and bruise it up without leaving too many marks.'

'Are you fucking mad? I'm not letting you smash my arm up!'

'Look at the state of the Pappers, JJ,' Pizza said. 'They're smashed to fuck and we're unmarked. You laid two of them out, so a few bruises are needed.'

'You're joking. What about you? You laid the other one out with a fucking wheelbrace.'

'Yeah, yeah, I know, but in the general context of things that was different.'

Completely failing to see the difference at all and sighing deeply, JJ offered his left arm to Psycho, who immediately wrapped the disgusting towel around his forearm. The towel was covered in the most horrific stains but JJ was not tempted to ask their origins. Rightly, he suspected the answer would be gruesome.

'Right, brace yourself, JJ,' said Psycho, stepping back and pulling his truncheon out of the pocket down the side of his right trouser leg. He raised it high above his head in the style of a Highland warrior with a claymore. The port wine stain on his contorted face could easily have been mistaken for woad, and for a split second he bore a striking resemblance to Sir William Wallace on the field at Stirling Bridge.

'Fucking hell, hold up,' shouted an alarmed JJ. 'Just a few bruises, you said.'

'Lighten up, you big girl,' scoffed Psycho, grabbing JJ's arm, straightening it and positioning it for the blow. 'Close your eyes and grit your teeth.'

With a resigned shake of his head and another deep sigh, JJ did as he was told and without further ado, Psycho smashed his truncheon down on the towel. There was an horrific crack as the radius bone in JJ's forearm broke under the blow and he crashed to the floor, faced screwed up in agony, clutching desperately at the injured limb.

'Oh fuck,' said Psycho, pulling a face and slipping his truncheon away.

'Oh fuck?' exclaimed Pizza. 'Jesus Christ, Psycho, what have you done now, you mad bastard? You were only supposed to bruise his arm, not break the bloody thing.'

'Probably sounded worse than it is,' chided Psycho, crouching down alongside the groaning JJ. 'You OK, son?'

'You've broken my fucking arm, you lunatic,' groaned JJ through gritted teeth, his face pale and sweaty.

'Well, it's something decent for the doc to have a look at, if nothing else,' remarked Psycho, getting to his feet. 'The story is that Papper grabbed your arm and smashed it against the open edge of the car door during a struggle, OK? No one's going to argue with that version of events, and besides, Papper's putting his hands up to everything courtesy of Sergeant Collins.'

'ABH is a big step up from assault on police,' pointed out Pizza, as he helped JJ to his feet, the ashen-faced youngster holding his injured arm close to his chest like a nursing mother.

'You mad fucker,' he groaned, looking at Psycho for the first time. 'A fucking bruise, you said, and you've broken it.'

'You'll be fine, don't worry. Look on it as your first war wound. No one else is going to know how it happened, are they?' said Psycho, patting him paternally on the shoulder.

As he spoke, the Tannoy in the corridor outside burst into life with the Blister announcing that Doc Dougan had arrived and all injured officers should report to him in the doctor's room.

'Perfect timing,' beamed Psycho as he unwrapped his towel from JJ's trembling forearm and they gazed at the deep red and blue dent in his arm. 'Come on, JJ – and don't forget how that animal Papper viciously attacked you.'

JJ didn't reply, allowing himself to be guided back along the corridor and down into the cell area to see Doc Dougan. Once he'd been deposited with the good medic Pizza and Psycho hung around outside waiting for him.

'He going to be OK with this, Pizza?' asked Psycho. He had a slightly worried look on his face.

'You stupid sod,' snapped Pizza. 'You were only supposed to bruise it.'

'It may only be bruised,' pleaded Psycho, but his hopes were immediately dashed as Doc Dougan opened the door and peered out at the whispering cops.

'Looks like the radius bone in his left forearm is cracked. He's going to need an X-ray. Can one of you run him down to A and E?' he asked cheerfully.

'Yeah, I'll take him, Doc,' said Pizza.

'Very nasty attack, very nasty indeed,' said the Doc as he shut the door.

'Just a bruise, yeah?'

'OK, OK,' Psycho sighed. 'He going to be OK with it though?'

'You mean is he likely to put you away?'

'Something like that.'

Pizza paused before replying. 'No, he's as sound as a pound, he won't say anything. But I am worried about the business with the dead cyclist the other night.'

'Worried, how?'

'He's shitting himself about it. We need to have a word.'

'OK. We're off tomorrow, why don't we all meet at the Waggon and Horses lunchtime? We can have a chat then.'

'Speak to the others – we need everyone there.'

'Yeah, will do. He's not going to roll over, is he?'

'Not if we get to him in time he won't. He's a bloody good lad at heart; we just need to put him right.'

The Waggon and Horses pub in nearby Tamworth was a regular haunt for the D Group cops when they finished a night shift. In an attempt to try and get their body clocks back in sync, they would generally try to sleep to about midday and then meet up and get pissed in the hope that they would sleep that night. It worked to a degree, but the day after was often spent nursing a blinding hangover and they were back on to Late Turn the day after that. Nights were a killer in many ways.

The man stood deep in the bushes and waited and watched. He'd been there for half an hour and not moved a muscle, his eyes darting from side to side, the only movement he made. His hands were thrust deep in his coat pockets, his right hand occasionally rolling the open condom he had brought with him. The urges were stronger than ever; even doing that bitch a couple of days ago had only temporarily eased them. She'd been good, he thought to himself, a thin smile on his pale face, very good, but he needed it more now than ever. He'd been able to keep it all under control for longer periods in the past, but he'd got a real taste for it now. A taste for their fear, the whimpering and pleading, their lives in his hands. God, he loved it and he needed it again.

And then he saw her, walking unsteadily along the footpath in Bolton Road. The slut was obviously drunk. He moved forward slightly to see her better and saw her lurch right through the open gate to Bishops Rise School, a regular short-cut for locals heading back to the Park Royal Estate from the town centre.

Perfect! He'd done one of the whores there in the past and knew exactly where he'd jump her. The man was about to break cover and dash over to his ambush point when he saw a car pull up in Bolton Road. Fucking police, they were all over the place tonight. He saw a cop get out of the vehicle and call the girl over, then watched with increasing anger as she staggered back to it. The cop and the girl had a brief conversation and then she got into the back of the car as the cop put his driver's seat forward for her.

Not tonight then, the man thought. There were cops around. He could wait; he'd try again tomorrow.

Chapter Fourteen

Temporary Chief Constable Chislehurst read Detective Chief Superintendent Mills's proposal quickly and pushed it back across his desk to him.

'Can this work?' he asked simply.

'There's no reason why not, Chief. We've got a man on the inside; we can engineer an encounter when we're ready.'

'Chief, you can't be serious,' interrupted Assistant Chief Constable Brian Seagrove. 'This proposal verges on some kind of black op – it's outrageous.'

'Shut up, Brian,' Chislehurst said testily, having recognised that he'd been handed a Get Out of Jail card. 'What timescale for this operation, black or otherwise?'

'Three weeks maximum. If we start the training next week, we can get that done in a week, then all we've got to do is pick a date.'

'No mutual aid requirement?'

'None at all, we keep it completely inhouse.'

Chislehurst nodded. 'And what about the cost implications? This is a big extraction from the divisions. We're going to have to rely on twelve-hour shifts for the period they're away.'

'Roughly three hundred thousand.'

'Jesus Christ!' exploded Seagrove. 'We can't afford that! Chief, where do we expect to find that sort of money?'

'Shut *up*, Brian,' repeated Chislehurst. 'There are all sorts of options. I might run this past the Home Office as a one-off Extraordinary Requirements payment. We can recoup a lot of it from the public affairs budget or put the replacement vehicles plan on hold until the new financial year. We can find it somewhere and it could solve all our problems at Handstead.'

'Chief, this is madness,' said Seagrove loudly. 'Anyone starts asking questions, and we're fucked.'

Chislehurst ignored him and looked again at DCS Mills. 'How clean are things?'

'We'll be OK.'

'Who's our man inside?'

'One of DCI Harrison's U/Cs. Been there a couple of months now, well established with the main players.'

'That was all signed off and approved, was it?' asked Chislehurst, raising his eyebrows.

'Of course,' lied Mills.

'Excellent. I'm sure you'll be able to give us sight of all the necessary appraisals in due course, won't you?'

'Of course,' repeated the DCS, who had already begun the bogus paper trail with Dan Harrison.

'Mr Seagrove, I need a special Force Order to go out within the next few hours. I'll give you the text shortly. And I want the Divisional Commanders here within the hour. We've got a lot of work to get done very quickly,' said Chislehurst, as he leaned back in his chair and contemplated the ceiling.

'Chief,' protested Assistant Chief Constable Seagrove, 'this has got "disaster" written all over it. I urge you to reconsider, please.'

'Just get the Divisional Commanders here, Brian,' said the Chief, without taking his eyes off his ceiling – which he'd noticed could do with a lick of paint. Chief Daniels hadn't given a toss about the décor in the office, but Chislehurst already had plans for a more opulent workplace, much more in keeping with his exalted, though thoroughly undeserved, rank.

'Chief, I'm going to have to insist on my reservations about this operation being formally noted in writing,' continued the desperate Seagrove.

Chislehurst dropped his eyes from his ceiling and regarded him with his cold, reptilian-like eyes.

'Of course, Brian,' he said smoothly. 'I can do that for you if you like, but it'll look a little odd, don't you think, especially with you signing the operation off as ACC Ops.'

Seagrove was momentarily speechless. 'Sign it off? I'm

not signing this pile of crap off,' he eventually blustered. 'Not a chance, it's utter madness.'

'Not the wisest of career choices, Brian,' continued his oily Chief. 'Not when you've got an application in with North Yorkshire for the Chief's position there and I have a conference call with the Chairman of the Police Committee this afternoon. I'm sure North Yorkshire will be looking for evidence of your creative thinking and operational dexterity rather than the news that you chuck your teddy out of the pram at the first sight of trouble.'

'That's outrageous,' blustered Seagrove. 'It's blackmail.'

'No, Brian,' said Chislehurst, getting to his feet, 'it's life at the top of the dung pile. You'll sign it off and everything comes to and from you. That's the chain, Brian, what you're paid for. You tell Mr Mills what to do and he deals direct with the head of this new venture. What are we going to call it?'

'I thought the Special Operations Group, Chief,' offered Mills.

'SOG,' said Chislehurst. 'Yes, I like that – got a nice ring about it. What's the leadership structure going to be?'

'Inspector Phil Gilbert – currently heads up the Patrol Group. I'd give him the whole shooting match, reporting directly to me.'

'And you direct to Mr Seagrove. Yes, yes, keep the chain nice and short, should reduce the chances of misunderstandings and the like. That work for you, Brian?'

Assistant Chief Constable Brian Seagrove slumped

down in his chair, face bright red in a combination of anger and humiliation. He faced the classic senior officer's quandary – do his job or safeguard his career. Any blame when this ludicrous fiasco inevitably went wrong would be heaped on his shoulders, with Chislehurst desperately rowing for shore, and if the impossible happened and it worked, he'd be hogging the cameras. But the last thing Seagrove needed was the scheming old bastard putting the poison in with North Yorkshire.

'I'm not happy about this,' he said meekly, conceding defeat. 'Not happy at all.'

'Your view has been noted,' said Chislehurst sinisterly, leaving his Deputy in some doubt as to whether he'd screw him anyway. 'Get the Divisional Commanders for me, will you?'

'Yes, Chief,' he replied, getting up from his chair to leave the office.

'And don't forget to sign the Operation Order off, will you, Brian? I'd like it on my desk before I meet with the Divisional Commanders.'

Seagrove nodded in mute agreement and left to do his Chief's underhand bidding.

DCS Mills had a smile on his face as he watched him leave. Once upon a time, he himself had harboured hopes to reach the Association of Chief Police Officers stratosphere, but his regular dealings with its members, locally and nationally, had convinced him that he couldn't survive for long in an environment where self-preservation overrode every policing requirement. Sometimes Headquarters reminded him of Caesar's Senate, with all the plotting and scheming going on. The real operational decision-making took place at his level and below, and having witnessed the ambush of Brian Seagrove he was happy to stay where he was.

'There will be no record of the meeting we've just had, Mr Mills,' said Chislehurst as the door closed on Seagrove's career. 'Do I make myself clear?'

'Perfectly, Chief.'

'All your contact will be with Mr Seagrove from here on. I don't need to be involved at all.'

'Understood,' said Mills as he took his leave of Chislehurst. He paused in the carpeted staff officers' annexe and smiled at Inspector Hetherington, who glanced up at him.

'Everything OK, sir?'

'Oh yeah, backs are being very nicely covered and heads put on the block just in case,' he replied.

Mick Hetherington laughed dryly. 'Slippery old bugger, he is. If he'd been Captain of the *Titanic* he'd have been heaving kids out of the lifeboats to get himself a seat.'

'Ain't that the truth,' sighed Mills grimly, as he strode out of the office towards the lifts.

An hour and a half later, the five Divisional Chief Superintendents left Headquarters in a state of panic, with very clear instructions from the Chief ringing in their ears. On their arrival back at their desks, that panic was transmitted to their Chief Inspectors and then again on to the unfortunate Inspectors and Sergeants who ran the Administration Units for each Division.

'It will happen, gentlemen, it will happen today, and I want the names by five p.m. Thank you, that'll be all for now,' Chislehurst had told them calmly.

At six o'clock that evening, in an unprecedented move, a Force Order went out by Telex to all stations, announcing the creation of the Special Operations Group.

With effect from 0700 Monday 3 July 1978, the following officers will be attached to the newly formed Special Operations Group for a period not expected to exceed three weeks. On completion of this unspecified period, officers will return to their previous Divisional postings. All booked leave and rest days for these officers that may fall within this period are cancelled and will only be reinstated under exceptional circumstances and with the authority of the ACC (Ops). On their return to Divisions, all officers will be granted two days' Chief Constable's discretionary leave. The attachment has a requirement of residence and all officers will be provided accommodation within Headquarters. Divisional Commanders will arrange for officers to attend the Headquarters Gymnasium at 0700 Monday 3 July 1978 for a full briefing and accommodation allocation. The attached officers will not be permitted to leave the Headquarters complex, other than in exceptional circumstances, for the duration of the attachment. To accommodate this significant extraction of resources from Divisions, and to allow the extracted officers a rest period prior to commencing this duty, with effect 0700 Thursday 29 June 1978, the Divisional shift pattern will be changed to two twelve-hour shifts – 0700 to 1900 and 1900 to 0700. Divisional Administration Units will publish the new shift rotas by 0700 Thursday 22 June 1978. All officers attached are granted four days' Chief Constable's discretionary leave for the period Thursday 29 June 1978 through to Monday 3 July 1978, to compensate for the likely loss of leave days during the attachment.

There followed a seemingly neverending list of officers' names and collar numbers from the six Divisions. The three units of the Patrol Group were also incorporated into the new SOG as the plan to take on the Albion Army took shape.

A little after 7 p.m., Superintendent Grainger from the Complaints and Discipline Department was led nervously into the Chief's office by his Staff Officer.

'Do come in, Mr Grainger,' said Chislehurst, looking up from the papers he was reading. 'Thanks for coming.'

'Not at all, sir. What can I do for you?'

'I want you to look at some names for me, Mr Grainger,' Chislehurst replied, indicating that his guest should sit in one of the low, faux brown-leather chairs arranged in front of his desk.

'Names?'

'Yes – this lot,' said Chislehurst, walking over to him and handing him a folded copy of the lengthy Telex message that had recently gone out to the Divisions. 'Recognise many of them?' he asked, as he sat in a chair opposite him.

Grainger unfolded the Telex and began to read, the colour draining from his face and his mouth dropping open.

'Well?' pressed Chislehurst.

'There must have been some mistake, Chief. They can't really mean this lot, can they?'

'What's the problem?'

'Well, not to put too fine a point on it, two hundred years ago, most of this lot would have been on prison ships on their way to Australia. Oh my God,' he gasped as he continued to read. 'Not Pearce!'

'Who's Pearce?' asked Chislehurst.

'PC Sean Pearce from Handstead, sir. A complete maniac – very, very dangerous. Sexual deviant as well, I suspect.'

'How come we haven't got rid of him before?'

Grainger shifted uncomfortably in his chair, which emitted disconcerting farting noises as he moved around.

He had made the hunt for Psycho a personal one over the years, but to date Pearce had proved to be a far cannier operator.

'Horrible, devious bastard, sir,' said Grainger, as his left eyelid began to twitch nervously as it always did when Psycho's name came up in conversation. 'He'll come in due course, Chief, but I'm not sure that putting him on this Special Operations Group is a good idea.'

'Desperate times require desperate measures, Mr Grainger,' murmured Chislehurst, again contemplating his ceiling that so desperately needed painting.

'They've got the Holding boys on the list,' replied Grainger in hushed tones, as though he was announcing the Second Coming.

'And they are who?'

After Psycho, the Holding brothers were the biggest cause of Grainger's sleepless nights, hairloss and his peptic ulcer. Richard, Charlie, Ben, Toby and Alfie Holding had all in the past eighteen months passed through the Complaints and Discipline system, causing Grainger and his incompetent team hours of trouble. They were all serving in uniform at different stations around the county, but seemed to manage to get into the shit at pretty much the same time, with Grainger struggling to keep on top of whichever one he was dealing with.

The elder brother Richard was twenty-six and a uniformed Sergeant at Tubbenden Road station, where he had acquired an impressive collection of Regulation 9 discipline notices alleging various abuses of prisoners in the cells. None had ever been proved, but in Grainger's view there was no smoke without fire. Charlie Holding, twenty-five years old, was a uniformed Constable at Liverpool Road station and was currently under investigation for allegedly chinning two hooligans who'd verbally abused him out in the street, breaking the jaw of one of them. He'd been fortunate not to be suspended from duty. Ben and Toby Holding were twenty-two-year-old twins serving at West Darrick station but on different shifts. They were identical twins who, it was rumoured, often worked each other's shifts so that one or the other could have a couple of extra days off. It was impossible to tell them apart, even their brothers having difficulty sometimes. The twins had recently been investigated at length following a pitched off-duty battle in a fish and chip shop, during which the owner had been dipped into his own deep-fat fryer by one of them. And that, of course, had been the problem from Grainger's perspective. *Which one?* Both twins had denied it vehemently, and none of the witnesses could positively identify either.

And then there was young Alfie Holding. At just twenty, he was the most trouble of them all. It was entirely appropriate that he shared the same name as the shaggy-haired monster in the front passenger seat of Delta One. He was the smallest of the brothers but the most violent and vocal, and currently had three complaints on the go, all to do with fighting and one including an allegation that he'd racially abused one of his opponents. Young Alfie was a real handful, but intellectually the brightest of the boys, and despite his tender years had become their leader, especially when they were together.

'I see,' said Chislehurst calmly, as Grainger confirmed what he had suspected his Divisional Commanders would do when presented with his *fait accompli*. The list of 400 officers now attached to the Special Operations Group included every pervert, rapist, mugger, horse stealer, cattle rustler, crop burner, car thief, grave robber and barrack-room lawyer currently serving in uniform across the county. If ACC Seagrove ever got wind of Grainger's assessment of the SOG he'd likely section himself under the Mental Health Act.

'An eclectic cross-section of our uniformed officers then?'

'Eclectic?' replied Grainger in astonishment. 'How about terrifying! What's the plan for the SOG anyway, sir?'

'Something right up their street, Mr Grainger, don't you worry,' replied Chislehurst with a knowing look, but deep inside, his guts were churning like a cement-mixer. It was time, he thought, to distance himself from the chaos about to engulf his unfortunate Assistant Chief Constable (Ops).

Chapter Fifteen

Pizza woke at midday to his alarm clock and lay on his back with his arms behind his head, staring at the curtains which were moving gently in the light breeze. He'd slept like a log despite having the dream again. The house was quiet and empty. Lisa had taken little David over to visit her mother as she usually did when Pizza was on nights, to ensure he got some sleep during the daytime. David had sat on the bed with Pizza gurgling away and chatting with him as Lisa had dried her hair, before she'd whisked him away in a flurry of kisses and protests.

Showered and shattered, Pizza was asleep before the front door had closed. He was back in that crowded room, packed so tight with people that he could barely move. The noise of the multitude of different conversations was deafening, but as usual Pizza was scanning the room. And then he saw him. David 'Bovril' Baines was on the far side of the room, wearing his smart uniform, a smile playing on his handsome features as his lips moved. David 'Bovril'

Baines, his closest friend, gunned down in that shit-hole of a flat by that evil bitch Anna Baldwin. The man who'd died in his arms trying to tell him something. He was once again trying to speak, to share that something with him. Sometimes the image Pizza had was a close-up of his moving lips, other times simply of the heaving mass between him and his friend.

He began to smash his way through the throng, lashing out with his arms, and screaming, 'Move! Move!', carving his way through the chattering masses like a scythe through a field of wheat. He was getting closer and closer, his mate was still there smiling, speaking, and suddenly *for the first time*, Pizza crashed through the last of the crowd and stumbled to his friend's side.

Bovril's face was pale and calm and he looked down at the panting, exhausted Pizza with a serene half-smile. Pizza was dumbstruck; having finally reached his friend he had nothing to say – but then Bovril leaned forward and whispered into his ear.

Pizza rolled out of bed and sat on the edge of it as he relived his dream, which he knew would not return. It had become a millstone and now it was gone. Trotting downstairs, he telephoned the police station section house and eventually a groggy JJ came to the phone.

'Just making sure you're awake, JJ,' said Pizza. 'I'll pick you up in half an hour. We're meeting the others at the Waggon and Horses.'

'Oh bollocks,' groaned JJ. 'I don't fancy that, Pizza, I just want to sleep. I'm knackered, and my fucking arm's killing me.'

'Have a few beers, JJ, and you'll sleep tonight, trust me. If you go back to bed now, you're going to be awake all night and feel like shit tomorrow. See you in half an hour, right?' He slammed the phone down to end any argument and went back upstairs for a shower.

Forty minutes later, Pizza and JJ pulled up in the car park of the Waggon and Horses in Tamworth in Pizza's ancient Hillman Imp. They were both in jeans and sweatshirts, with JJ's left forearm wrapped in a bandage. Dougan had assured him that the arm wasn't broken, after an X-ray at A&E had proved inconclusive.

'I heard the fucker crack,' JJ had pleaded.

'Just a bruise,' smiled the doctor. 'Come and see me in a few days if it doesn't settle down.'

'It's gone black,' JJ confided to Pizza as they settled in the car.

Psycho's wrecked Ford Cortina was already there, as was Jim's Viva, but otherwise the car park was almost deserted. It was why they liked the place. Far enough out of Handstead not to be frequented by any of the shitbags they dealt with on a daily basis, but best of all, there were no fruit machines or juke boxes. Just somewhere quiet to drink, and the landlord Smudger Smith knew who they were and what they craved more than anything else – anonymity and some peace and quiet.

They pushed through the ancient dark oak door into the snug interior, and found the Brothers perched on stools at the bar, silently nursing bottles of Carlsberg. They turned as the door opened and nodded a greeting to Pizza and JJ before resuming their quiet vigil.

'All right, boys, ready for a top-up?' asked Pizza, leaning against the bar alongside them.

'We're OK,' said Jim, glancing up at him and answering as they always did on behalf of each other.

'Anyone else here yet?'

'Psycho's in the bog. Piggy and the Blister are in the restaurant.'

Pizza wandered over to the small restaurant area and glanced in to catch sight of Piggy and Blister ploughing their way through huge plates of cottage pie and chips. The thought of eating anything made him feel ill. In truth, none of them actually felt like drinking either, but the routine was well proven to get their body clocks back on normal human-being time.

Smudger appeared through a set of thick coloured bead curtains that always wrapped themselves around him like a psychedelic octopus and led to a frenzied thrashing-about until he freed himself.

'You all right, lads? What you having?' he asked, as he threw the last tentacle from his shoulder and leaned against the bar wheezing like an iron lung from the exertion of it all.

'Jesus, Smudger, that curtain's going to be the death of

you. Couple of pints of best, please,' laughed Pizza.

As Smudger began to laboriously draw a couple of pints off on a huge hand-drawn pump, Psycho bowled out of the gents. His appearance shocked Pizza, who stood upright as he approached the bar. Psycho was absolutely immaculate. He was freshly shaved, clearly recently barbered, and wearing an expensive pair of dark bell-bottomed trousers and a crisp white shirt with the collar turned over the top of a deep purple, crushed-velvet sports jacket. The black brogues on his feet were shone to a mirror finish and the others looked him up and down in amazement. They were all feeling shabby and tired, but he looked ready for a serious night on the town.

'Fucking hell, Psycho,' said Pizza admiringly, 'you look the dog's bollocks. You got a date or something?'

'Right on both counts, boy,' replied the groomed monster. 'Got a meet at half-three.' He rubbed his hands together eagerly as he spoke, a huge grin on his face.

Pizza leaned close to him and sniffed approvingly. 'Smells good, what you got on?'

'Bay Rum – man's finest grooming tool. You going to get me a drink?'

'Sure. What you having – pint?'

'Nah, just a Coke.'

'*A Coke?*' The group responded as one. Psycho was clearly not well. Giving him a soft drink was akin to filling a car's petrol tank with water.

'A Coke?' repeated Pizza slowly, as Smudger dumped

two foaming pints on the bar towel by his elbow.

'Yeah. Got to be on my best behaviour this afternoon.'

'Large Coke please, Smudger,' said Pizza over his shoulder. 'Ice and a slice?' he lisped to Psycho.

'Don't take the piss, you little shite,' responded the brutish Lothario. 'This is important.'

'Who's your meet?' continued Pizza, as he counted out the right money for Smudger.

'Anne Butler,' Psycho replied triumphantly.

'Hey, Psycho, brilliant. Well done, mate, good luck,' said Pizza, genuinely pleased for Psycho but privately doubting he would ever get anywhere with her. Like many male officers, he simply couldn't see the basic animal attraction that Psycho had for many women.

'She's Early Turn today,' continued Psycho, 'so I'm picking her up from her place about half-three. Can't be pissed or late,' he said, glancing at his watch.

'Plenty of time,' said Pizza. 'Get a table?'

The group moved over to a corner table and were soon joined by Piggy and the Blister. Malcy had told Psycho he wouldn't be joining them, as he'd be spending the day with his wife, so only Ally Stewart was missing. They were chatting quietly, beginning to throw off the inhuman shackles of night duty, albeit temporarily. They'd be back on nights within three weeks.

As they chatted and laughed, Pizza became aware of a middle-aged man who had wandered over to their table from the bar area. He was clearly drunk, clutching a half-empty pint glass and swaying gently. He appeared harmless enough so they ignored him. The man's stubbly old face was permanently set in a grin, his watery eyes sparkling, and the longer he looked at him, the more Pizza thought he knew him. When JJ cracked a joke and he joined in the laughter with a dirty old man cackle, Pizza realised who he'd confused him with – he was the absolute double for Sid James. And then the man planted himself down on the padded bench seat alongside Psycho.

'Can we help you, mate?' asked JJ, as the conversation paused. The man ignored him and turned towards Psycho, who was also blanking him as he drank his pint of Coke.

'I fucked your mum last night,' the old man slurred in a gravelly voice that suggested years of heavy smoking. There was an audible gasp from the others as they looked fearfully at Psycho, who they confidently expected to begin to dismember the horrible old drunk. Instead he continued to drink his Coke quietly and ignore him.

'We did everything,' continued the old man. 'She sat on my face, rubbed her tits up and down my cock. Even let me fuck her doggy-style and told me to give it to her up the arse.'

There was an audible low shriek from the Blister, and the others began to look for safe escape routes from the expected eruption. But Psycho just continued to sip his drink.

'She finished me off by giving me a blow job until I came in her mouth,' went on the elderly drunk loudly.

Then Psycho got to his feet and the group froze as they waited for him to grab the old boy and pull him to pieces. He drained his glass, thumped it down onto the table, wiped his mouth on the back of his huge hairy hand and stared at the Sid James look-alike for the first time.

'Come on, Dad. I'll drop you back at the flat, you've had too much to drink,' he said, patting him gently on the shoulder.

'*Dad?*' shouted H, more in relief than anything else. 'That's your dad?'

'Yeah,' sighed Psycho. 'Mum's kicked him out so he's staying with me for a while. Come on, Dad, I'll get you back and you can sleep it off.' He took the pint glass his dad was about to raise to his mouth out of his hand and put it on the table, then pulled him to his feet.

'Come on,' he said kindly, guiding him unsteadily away from the table and towards the door. 'See you lot Wednesday,' he called, shielding his eyes from the glaring sunshine, out towards the car park.

The others watched him go in stunned silence. It had never occurred to any of them that Psycho might have parents. They had always assumed that perhaps he'd been hatched from a large egg laid by a giant devil chicken, or found orphaned and raised by a pack of wolves – but not parents, not Psycho. They suddenly realised that they actually knew very little about him. They knew he was divorced and lived in his grotty little flat – scene of some extraordinary drinking sessions in the past – on his own, and that when it came to operating on the very fringes of the law, he was without equal. But about Psycho the private individual, they knew absolutely nothing. They weren't even sure how old he was, and none of them would regard him as a personal friend. He was just Psycho, the mad bastard who made their time at work a neverending tapestry of outrageous, hilarious events.

Having deposited his father on the sofa back at his flat, Psycho again checked his appearance in the grimy mirror in his bathroom. He was determined to make the right impression with Anne Butler and had resolved to give her chapter and verse on his past escapades in an attempt to win her trust. He was pretty sure she was attracted to him, but Malcy was right. His disgusting, and well-deserved, reputation was a major obstacle for her to overcome.

The truth had to be the way forward, which was not something that Psycho generally acknowledged, but in Anne's case he was prepared to make an exception.

The last thing he wanted if he got together with her was any skeletons waiting to leap out of cupboards and bite him in the arse. He was developing feelings for her that were totally alien to him and which he found quite unsettling because they made him vulnerable. No woman had ever had that effect on him – not his ex-wife and certainly none of the multitude of women he'd had since.

Sure, he'd had feelings for many of them, but when either they or he terminated the relationship, life had gone on seamlessly. With Anne though, he was desperate to be with her. Not just to shag her, though that had been his initial motivation, but to be with her every moment he could. If his feelings went unrequited, he was genuinely worried how he would cope.

With his mind in turmoil and a leaden feeling of dread in his stomach, Psycho drove to a small private estate in South Handstead and parked up outside Anne's small rented terraced house. As he'd promised himself, he was nice and early, so he sat alone in the car rehearsing his lines. There was no sign of her at half-three, and by four he was becoming desperate. At five o'clock he considered finding a telephone box and ringing the station to find out if she'd left, but decided against it in case whoever answered the phone started asking awkward questions.

At half-five he gave up, driving disconsolately back to his flat where his dad was still out cold on the sofa. Feeling quite empty, he collapsed into the armchair opposite his father and stared at the wall. Eventually he got slowly to his feet with a deep sigh, wandered over to his record player on the sideboard, and soon the flat filled with the sound of Mel Carter's pleading vocals.

Chapter Sixteen

DCI Dan Harrison glanced at the group of officers he'd called into his cramped office and smiled at them. Chief Inspector Pete Stevenson nodded back in acknowledgement as he took his seat in one of the armchairs, whilst DI Barry Bryan responded with a polite, 'Boss,' as he sat down. DCs John Benson and Bob Clarke pulled up the chairs they'd brought with them from the main CID office alongside the A3 size flipchart Clarke had brought with them. Harrison got up to shut the office door and perched himself on the edge of his desk.

'Thanks for coming at short notice,' he began, 'but we may have a serious problem. Has Bob run this past you, John?'

'Yeah, been helping him with the background,' nodded Benson.

'OK, excellent. Pete and Barry, this is going to be news to you then, but what I've asked Bob to do is run through what he thinks he's found, and get your opinions. Ask him questions as he goes along, if you want. This is all tied in with the rape of Mandy Blackstock the other night. Thanks, Bob,' he finished, returning to his chair behind the desk.

Bob Clarke got to his feet and approached the flipchart, keenly aware of the intense air of expectation in the office.

'OK,' he began, lifting the blank sheet over the top of the board to reveal reams of writing in various columns. 'John and I picked up the Mandy Blackstock rape on Thursday night. Fucking horrible one it was as well, but there was something about it that rang bells with me. So, I've been trawling through the crime sheets and I'm pretty sure we've got a serial rapist on the ground.'

'Oh fuck,' said DI Barry Bryan, neatly summarising the feelings of everyone in the office.

'I've gone back eight years to 1970, looking at every undetected rape over that period. There are fourteen still undetected.'

'Fourteen?' replied Bryan. 'Jesus, that's terrible. Not all down to one man, surely?'

'No, but applying what I think are the common traits, I've discounted six of them.'

'Still leaves eight.'

'Yes, eight going back to 1970 which fit the pattern. First one, eighth of July 1970, eleven forty-five p.m., Grosvenor Park. Janet Grayson, seventeen years old. Then September the third 1970, half-past midnight also in

Grosvenor Park, Caroline Chambers, twenty years old. June the eighth 1971, one in the morning in Stream Woods, Vanessa Baker, nineteen years old. August the thirteenth 1972, eleven-thirty p.m. on Tugmutton Common, Ruby Barnes, twenty-three years old. August the ninth 1973, one in the morning in Oakwood Park, Janice Wainwright, twenty years old. June the thirtieth 1974, two in the morning in the grounds of Bishops Rise School, Natalie Pickard, twenty-one years old.' Clarke paused to gauge the reaction of his audience, who were hanging on his every word.

'Nothing in 1975, but then July the thirty-first 1976, eleven-thirty p.m., in Garston Woods, Cilla Cooper, nineteen years old. Nothing last year, but now, on June the fifteenth this year, just after midnight in Stream Woods again, Mandy Blackstock, twenty-two years old.'

'What's the connection between all eight, Bob?' asked Barry Bryan.

'They all have common components. Firstly, every attack took place within a three-hour time slot, anywhere between eleven p.m. and two a.m. They all took place outdoors, in or near woods or heavy undergrowth. All the girls were attacked from behind and incapacitated by ferocious beatings. None of them could provide any sort of description. There were no independent witnesses. All the scenes were identified but absolutely no forensic evidence was obtained from any of them. All the girls were probably raped using a condom. The examinations of all of them provided zero evidence of semen. No condoms were ever recovered, though in five of the investigations, the SIOs have actually recorded their belief that he brought a condom with him and took it away. Every one of the girls was beaten black and blue, way beyond what was required to subdue them.'

'Mandy Blackstock was anally penetrated with a bottle,' interrupted Harrison. 'What about the others?'

'No,' admitted Clarke, 'but it's my belief that our man has stepped up his game. Raping and beating them up isn't doing it for him; he needs more – and Mandy Blackstock is just the first in a brutal escalation.'

'What do you base that theory on, Bob?' asked Pete Stevenson.

'I listened to a lecture on my CID refresher course last year from an FBI guy from Quantico who specialised in serial rapists and murderers. One feature in all of his studies was an increasing use of violence to satisfy the urges these monsters have. But even if you don't subscribe to that theory, there's another more significant trait common to all of these attacks.'

'What's that?'

'I've been through all the SOCO inventories, and in each case, we didn't recover everything the girls were wearing prior to the attack. Like many of the serial guys the FBI bloke had studied, our guy keeps a memento. He's a trophy hunter.'

'We got all Mandy Blackstock's stuff, didn't we?' queried Harrison.

'Nope. We've never found her knickers. They didn't appear on the SOCO inventory so I spoke to the SOCO yesterday. He'd just made an assumption that she hadn't been wearing any, but when I spoke to Mandy in hospital this morning, she was adamant that she was wearing some, and in her statement she says she can recall him literally tearing them off her. All the other girls have items unaccounted for. Bras, knickers, a scarf, tights. They're all missing something and our man's got them.'

'Mandy's knickers could still be in Stream Woods,' argued Harrison.

'Hundred per cent sure they're not. The Patrol Group went through it again this morning. They're not there, they're with our man somewhere.'

'The SOCOs could have made similar assumptions in all the other cases,' said Bryan.

'Possible, yes, but four of the girls still live in Handstead. John and I have re-interviewed all of them. They've confirmed they were wearing the items we never got back. Boss, he's collecting them,' insisted Clarke.

There was silence in the office as the others considered his compelling case. Clarke folded back the page he'd been pointing to, revealing a large 1:500 scale Ordnance Survey map of Handstead. Eight small white, numbered circular stickers were clearly visible dotted around a small area of the map.

'These are the eight attacks since 1970, all within a mile and a half radius of each other. My money's on our man living within or very near this area because he travels on foot.'

'On foot?'

'Oh yeah. Our man knows his business. He knows how we investigate crimes like this. He knows that without any sort of description or witnesses, no forensic evidence, we go back to basics. We start looking through the stop forms and producers just in case they got a lucky pull going to or from the scene. Our guy won't take that risk. He's never too far from home and he keeps off the main roads: he's not going to risk getting a pull. He lives within this radius,' said Clarke, drawing a large blue circle on the map with a marker pen. 'He's in here somewhere,' he finished, tapping the pen on the map. The others gathered round the map looking closely at the numbered stickers and Clarke's circle.

'Takes in the Park Royal and Birchwood Estates, Bob,' said Harrison. 'Still a huge area.'

'True, but it's a start. We can narrow our search to a smaller target area.'

'No attacks in 1975 or 1977 – why's that?'

'No attacks that we know of that we can *attribute* to him,' pointed out Clarke. 'I'm not suggesting this is a comprehensive list. It's possible that we've got indecent assaults on the books that are down to him for 1975 and 1977 that just fell short of rape. Maybe he was disturbed

– it's even possible they weren't reported. I've only looked at our undetected rapes, but I'd put money on him being at it in both those years even though we've found nothing recorded – yet.'

Harrison returned to his chair and rubbed his cheeks as he thought hard. 'Anyone got any questions? Any doubts about what Bob's put up?' he asked wearily.

'Looks good, or rather not good,' said DI Barry Bryan.

'I agree,' concurred Stevenson. 'What do we do with this now?'

'I'll need to take it to Headquarters and make a case to set up a team to re-investigate the whole lot again and look at every undetected sex offence on the books. I dread to think how many more we're going to find.'

'In the interim I think we'll have to up our evening and night presence in this wider radius,' said Stevenson, indicating Clarke's circle on the map.

'How much information are we going to let out of this office?' asked Bryan.

'I don't want to start a panic,' said Harrison, 'especially as we're so far behind this bastard. The press haven't picked up on it yet so I'm not going to spoonfeed it to them. I want to be some way into an enquiry before I give them anything. Last thing we need is headlines like *Night Stalker on the Prowl* or *Beast of Handstead at Large.*'

No one laughed. Harrison wasn't joking.

'Bob and John, I want you to keep digging. Widen the search to include the indecent assaults that we've still got on the books. Barry, I'd like you and one of the DCs to start looking again at these eight jobs. Re-interview the girls John and Bob have already found and find the others. Concentrate on the personal effects and clothing angle. I also want you to get on to the collator, but discreetly. We need to know about any convicted sex offenders living in this specific area. Any sex crimes, flashing, anything, I want to know about them. Pete, I need the uniforms to concentrate their efforts in Bob's target radius between ten p.m. and three a.m. Stop anything that moves and check it out thoroughly. Tell them it's an anti-burglary initiative or something. Any questions?'

There were none, but Harrison hadn't finished.

'Bob, how's the Hayward murder coming along?' he asked.

'All tidy, boss. Full confession, charged and remanded. Dave Cronin's putting the DPP file together. No issues.'

'Thanks. Pete, we need to talk about Pork Sword Man or Zorro or whatever they're calling him now.'

'Yeah, I know, Dan. I've had a few ideas.'

'Go on, what you got? Hope it's not going to involve the CID – we've got plenty on the go as it is,' laughed Harrison.

At this point, the three detectives took their leave of the two men who ran the sub-division. As the door shut behind them, Harrison reached into his bottom drawer and pulled out his ever-present bottle of Bushmills and two glasses.

'You ready for one?' he said. 'Go on, Pete, what you got for me?'

As Harrison poured two large drinks for them, Stevenson outlined a plan to deal with Pork Sword Man.

'I'm looking at using some of our WPCs with a back-up team in the area he seems to favour.'

'Around the church?'

'That's it. Seven offences in and around there in the last month.'

'Which WPCs can we use?'

'That could be the problem. There's only one volunteer so far.'

'Who's that?'

'Amanda Wheeler, know her?'

'Oh come on, Pete, you have got to be kidding me. Unless Pork Sword Man's blind, that's a non-starter,' complained Harrison. 'You'll have to find someone else. You'd be better off putting that lunatic Pearce in a dress.'

'Another problem is going to be manpower. We're going to lose a fair few officers to the SOG in just over a week. We need to run this as soon as we can, or wait until they're all back.'

'Try and get something running before they go, Pete, and we'll go again when they're back. We sending a few?'

'Pretty much all of D Group and every other reprobate we've got on the books.'

Harrison laughed and took a long sip of his drink.

'Who's going from D Group? Shame to lose that lot, got some good guys.'

'The Brothers, Pearce, Ally Stewart, Malcy the Mong Fucker.'

'Malcy the Mong Fucker!' exclaimed Harrison incredulously. 'Who the fuck is Malcy the Mong Fucker?'

'Andy Malcolm, transferred in last year from West Darrick, I think.'

'And he fucks mongs, is that right?'

'Apparently. I don't know the full story, but something along those lines.'

'Jesus, where do these guys get their nicknames from?' said Harrison, shaking his head. 'Still, where he's going he should be in his element. Plenty of mongs in the Albion Army for him to fuck.'

Stevenson grinned and the two men raised their glasses in a toast to future success.

Pizza drove on to the driveway of the house he and Lisa shared shortly after 5 p.m., having first dropped JJ off at the section house. He waited briefly as the clapped-out engine in the rear of the Imp ran on for a few seconds after he'd turned off the ignition, before it gave a loud misfire and was silent. He paused by the side of the car after he'd locked it and looked at the house with a contented smile on his face. It was home in so many ways; his family lived there. His family. He briefly pondered those words and the smile broadened. As he entered the small hallway, the smell of cooking hit him and he could hear Lisa chattering away in the kitchen to David.

'Only me,' he called, dropping his keys on the hall table.

'In the kitchen,' Lisa called.

He was positively beaming as he walked into the brightly decorated but cramped kitchen where David sat in his highchair engrossed with some Lego bricks and Lisa was peeling potatoes at the sink. He strolled behind her, wrapped his arms around her waist and buried his lips into the back of her neck. Her hair and skin smelled delicious. She laughed and threw her head back to accommodate the kisses.

'You're early,' she said, resuming her peeling. 'Wasn't expecting you for a bit. Tea won't be ready for half an hour.'

'No problem, I can wait,' he replied, unravelling from her and planting a kiss on his son's head. David ignored him and Pizza ruffled his mop of blond hair affectionately with his hand.

'Many there?' asked Lisa.

'The usual suspects – only Ally and Malcy didn't show. I gave JJ a lift.'

'How's he settling down?'

'He'll be fine.'

'Did you get to talk to him about the cyclist?'

'No, didn't really get the right opportunity. It'll keep.'

'How'd you sleep today, darling?'

'Out like a light, didn't even hear you two leave. How's your mum?'

'Same old, you know what she's like,' laughed Lisa. 'Sends her love.' She turned round from the sink and looked at Pizza. He was staring at her with a half-smile on his face. God, she was gorgeous and he was filled again with that sense of complete fulfilment he always got when he thought of her and young David.

'You OK?' she asked.

'Everything's fine.'

'Have you been having that dream again?' she continued, her large doe-like blue eyes looking worried.

'The dream? God, no,' lied Pizza easily, 'not had it for a while. I reckon it's gone now – probably some sort of Post Traumatic Stress or some shit like that, but I think I'm over it now.'

'Do you really think so?' she asked, moving to stand in front of him and putting her wet hands on his shoulders. 'Really?' The dream was the only thing that stood between her and the idyllic life she wanted with Pizza and David. 'Oh I hope so, Alan. I hate to see you suffer with it.'

He pulled her close to him and cupped the cheeks of her firm buttocks as she buried her head into his chest. He rested his mouth and nose on the top of her hair and breathed deeply. She smelled of oranges and limes and a good life together.

'Yeah, I'm sure it's gone now,' he said quietly as he

closed his eyes and promised himself that he'd always honour the request Bovril had whispered into his ear in that crowded room – *'Look after Lisa and my son.'*

Six hours later, Psycho stood looking in disgust at his father who was still stretched out on the sofa snoring loudly. Psycho had changed out of his glad rags and was wearing a tatty old tracksuit, and to his own enormous surprise, wasn't pissed. His usual reaction to the sort of setback he'd endured that afternoon would have been to get himself legless, but he'd not touched a drop. Instead, he'd listened to Mel Carter endlessly until it had got dark, checking occasionally that his father was still alive, and he'd drunk a couple of cups of tea. But not a drop of alcohol. He'd phoned his mother shortly after 8 p.m. to let her know that the old man was with him, and whilst she'd sounded pleased to know that he was in safe hands, she hadn't asked him to bring the old bugger home.

'He can't stay with me for ever, Mum,' Psycho had not very subtly pointed out.

'Stick him on a bench in a park with the other winos,' she'd said flatly, 'he'll be in the right company there. Sean, I'm not having him back while he's drinking like that. You have a word with him.'

Psycho had promised he would, especially as he'd be preaching to him from what was almost a moral position of strength, seeing as he'd not had a drink himself for nearly forty-eight hours. He rolled his dad on to his side, switched off the living-room lights and was shutting the door quietly when the telephone rang.

'Hello,' he barked brusquely.

'Sean?'

His mood lightened immediately. 'Oh, it's you,' he said, less aggressively.

'Are you OK?' asked Anne Butler.

'I'm fine. I thought we had a date this afternoon,' replied Psycho, trying to rein in his natural inclination to go for the throat.

'I'm so sorry, I got tucked up with a fatal on the A102. I came across it.'

'Oh shit, you OK?'

'Yeah, I'm fine. Just had a long day. I tried to ring you from a callbox but there was no reply.'

A wave of relief swept over Psycho, not just that she hadn't blown him out but more because he'd controlled his instinct to explode at the perceived slight.

'You still there?' Anne continued.

'Yeah, yeah. Sorry, Anne. I was worried you'd stood me up – sorry.'

'Stood you up? I'd never do that, Sean, that's just plain rude. I'll tell you if I don't want to see you. I just got tucked up at work, that's all.'

'*Do* you want to see me?' asked Psycho, his heart in his mouth.

There was a long pause and he swallowed hard.

'Yes, I do,' she finally replied, 'but I'm wary about you.'

He'd considered trying to bluff and bullshit her but had decided on a different course of action.

'I don't blame you,' he said quietly. 'I've got a terrible reputation which I deserve. You've probably heard all of it, but I want to tell you it all because I want to see you and I don't want you to hear anything about me that I haven't already told you about.' He frowned as he thought over what he had just said. It was definitely he who had said it, but he was no longer sure he recognised himself.

'Am I going to want to hear it all?' Anne asked after she had digested what he'd said.

'I don't know, to be honest. If you walk away after, I'll at least know that I was straight with you, but that wasn't enough. I wouldn't blame you, Anne.'

There was a long silence with just the sound of some static on the line.

'You've been attached to this new SOG thing, haven't you?' she said.

'Yeah, we'll be away for a while.'

'Why don't we meet up when you get back, Sean? I do want to get to know you better, but you frighten me.'

'Please don't be frightened of me, Anne,' said Psycho urgently. 'I'm putting things in order, turning over a new leaf because I've met someone who means a lot to me. I'm trying to become a better person.'

'I don't want you to try and be what you're not, Sean. A lot of your charm and attraction is your wildness and devil may care outlook. But you also do things that are vile, and that worries me.'

'I used to,' corrected Psycho. 'I *used* to do things that were vile, but I've walked away from all that sort of stuff. I want to be different, not change the person I am completely.'

'Listen, why don't we arrange something when you're back from this operation? I do want to see you.'

'Sounds great. I'll ring you the moment I can, OK?'

'Yeah, that'd be fine. Sean, will you promise me something?'

'Of course, anything.'

'Behave yourself whilst you're away.'

'I will, I promise.'

'And please be careful. Take care, won't you?'

'I will,' said Psycho, as she hung up, and he listened to the dialling tone for what seemed an eternity.

Chapter Seventeen

'Listen up, you lot,' shouted Sergeant Andy Collins as the group swapped banter and insults amongst themselves in front of him. 'Got a bit to get through.'

Order was gradually restored and he continued, 'As you'll have seen, most of you are off on your travels with the Special Operations Group, whatever that is, effective tomorrow.'

There were cheers from most of those present.

'All very well for you,' joked Collins. 'Whilst you're off on the piss, we're back here doing twelve-hour shifts until you decide to return.'

Piggy, JJ and the Blister, the only three members of the group not going, sat with their arms folded looking pissed off as the others celebrated.

'You heroes of the SOG have got the rest of the week off until you start at Headquarters on Monday morning. Make the most of it, boys; no way the Chief's going to grant that sort of leave unless there's a shitstorm heading your way.'

The banter died away as the truth of what he had said became apparent to them all. They were heading into the unknown. The secrecy surrounding their attachment was unprecedented, with lots of rumour and speculation flying about as to what their task might be, but the truth was that only a tiny handful of people knew what was planned.

'There's nothing much of interest in the GOB,' (General Occurrence Book) concluded Collins, closing the large, leather-bound book. 'Nasty fatal on the A102 on Monday afternoon, but nothing else really.'

Psycho leaned back in his chair with his eyes closed and smiled as he thought of Anne again, albeit up to her elbows in gore.

'Got a memo from Mr Findlay at Division,' Collins resumed, to audible groans at the idiot's name. 'He's demanding that all officers reacquaint themselves with their definitions and powers under the Sexual Offences Act 1967 – which, as I'm sure you all know, is now the law of the land.'

There were a few blank faces in front of him.

'The Poofs Charter,' he reminded them. 'Apparently, officers from this Division busted up a house with a couple of homos living there and it's all gone tits up. It's all legal down here now, of course, but not in Scotland – where they take a very dim view of all this man love.'

'Legal?' asked Ally, his little red face screwed up in disgust.

'Legal,' confirmed Collins, with a shake of his head. 'Come on, young JJ, you're not long out of Training School, give these cretins the benefit of your knowledge. What's the mnemonic for it?'

JJ desperately racked his brain under the gaze of the group and then spoke.

'P is for in Private, O is for Only two persons present, the next O is for both Over twenty-one, and F is for neither can be Fucking mental,' he said proudly.

Collins led the ripple of polite applause as JJ took a deep, theatrical bow before resuming his seat.

'There you go, the Poofs Charter,' resumed Collins. 'Don't forget it – you've been told.'

'Bloody disgrace,' chuntered Ally, his arms folded like an outraged matron.

'Lighten up, Ally, it's the law now. You don't like it, you can always fuck off back home where they still burn homos at the stake,' said Collins happily.

'It's an abomination, a sin! Anal sex is a crime against humanity,' shouted Ally, as the rest of the group began to catcall and abuse him.

'Nothing wrong with pulling out a bird's inner tube from time to time,' bellowed Psycho above the din.

'I thought you'd changed,' said Malcy archly, turning to look at him with raised eyebrows.

'Oh fuck, yes, of course,' gasped Psycho, like a shocked

debutante who'd just been goosed. 'Fuck yes. It's evil and a sin! Burn the homos, burn the homos!'

'QUIET!' bellowed Collins at the top of his voice as the muster disintegrated into chaos. He was pleased to see them all so buoyant; Psycho particularly seemed to be back to his old self, but they were always just a step away from descending into anarchy. He waited for silence to return.

'I had a chat with Sergeant Rice in Admin before muster and you'll be delighted to hear that the Sexual Orientation Survey that Mrs Bott sent you all last month has been canned,' he went on.

There were loud cheers and he held his hand up for quiet before continuing.

'Apparently, Mr Findlay went absolutely apeshit. As you know, they were all sent out blank for you to fill in your personal details and sexual preferences and orientation. Sergeant Rice tells me that there was nearly a hundred per cent return of the surveys but unfortunately, ninety-eight per cent were in either Findlay's or Mrs Bott's name. Mr Findlay had to ask what a gash guzzler and flange monster were.'

There were roars of laughter from the group, all of whom had completed Bott's ludicrous survey.

'There were apparently a few officers who completed surveys in their own name, one of whom was our very own Ray Malone,' continued Collins, smiling broadly.

'Huh?' gasped Piggy, who had done no such thing.

'Apparently under "sexual preferences" you put "farmyard animals",' said Collins as the group cried with laughter and Psycho looked innocently at his fingernails.

'Did I fuck!' shouted Piggy. 'I never did a survey. I did one for Bott, but not for me.'

'Oh come on, Piggy,' interrupted Psycho. 'It's nothing to be ashamed of. I heard you walked into your bedroom with a sheep under your arm and said, "That's the pig I have to fuck when you're not in the mood", and Mrs Piggy said, "I think you'll find that's a sheep," to which you replied, "I think you'll find I was talking to the sheep." '

Hysteria ensued, and it was several minutes before Collins had wiped away the tears of mirth from his eyes and restored order. Piggy sat and glowered, pleased now not to be joining Psycho and the others on their attachment, which would undoubtedly be a riotous affair at his expense.

Collins assigned them to their beats and vehicles for the Late Turn shift and was about to dismiss them when Psycho politely put his hand up. Collins frowned. The lunatic obviously hadn't finished with Piggy.

'What now, Psycho? Is this relevant?' he sighed.

'Just a quick one, Sarge, if I may. Guys, those of us who are off to save the world next week have got a few days' leave coming up. I was thinking it would be a great idea to have a bit of a blow-out and go racing. There's a meet at Haydock Park tomorrow afternoon. Who fancies it?'

Collins nodded his approval at the excellent suggestion and wished he could have gone along.

'Good idea, Psycho,' he said. 'Sounds like a great day out, boys, and you might not get another chance for a while.'

There was unanimous approval from all those selected for the SOG.

'How do we get there?' asked Malcy.

'Leave that to me,' answered Psycho mysteriously. 'I'll arrange transport. We'll leave from the front of the nick at ten tomorrow morning.'

'Ten?' queried Malcy. 'Why so early?'

'Have to stop for a livener on the way, Malcy,' replied Psycho, like he was talking to an idiot. 'We'll definitely need a livener or two.'

'I wish I was going with you lot,' said JJ, as he and Pizza made their way out of the muster room and up to the front office to collect their radios and the keys for their beat vehicle.

'Still in your probation, JJ, that's the problem,' said Pizza sympathetically. 'There'll be plenty of other chances once you're through.'

'Sounds like an interesting one,' continued his crestfallen partner. 'I really wish I was going.'

'You OK?' asked Pizza.

'Yeah, why?'

'Not just about this trip – everything, I mean.'

'Yeah,' replied JJ flatly.

'I'm not so sure,' said Pizza. 'Come on, let's get a cup of tea before we head out.'

'You sure? Sergeant Collins won't be too happy if he catches us.'

'I've cleared it with him, come on. We need to have a chat and sort a few things out.'

'I'm all right, honestly.'

'Yeah, I know, but let's have a cup of tea just the same,' said Pizza, putting an arm round JJ's shoulders and leading him towards the stairs. They trudged up to the third floor, occasionally exchanging greetings and pleasantries with people they passed until they pushed into the canteen. The bar area was packed with the Early Turn relief getting at it, and the restaurant area still had a few hangers-on from the offices having an extended lunch.

'Grab a table, JJ,' commanded Pizza. 'I'll get these.'

JJ did as he was told, commandeering two seats on a six-seater table, and looked around the busy canteen area. Everyone seemed so well-established in their environment whilst he still felt a bit of an outsider. He'd proved himself well at the pub fight with the Leeds Service Crew last year, but he was still just tolerated by the group; still on the periphery of everything they did. He was at a loss to know what more he could do to be accepted fully by them. Pizza was fine with him, but he was his Tutor Constable, after all. The others were still wary of him.

'There you go, JJ,' said Pizza cheerfully, as he banged down two large stained, white mugs on the table and dropped a pile of sugar sachets and a plastic winder alongside them.

'Cheers, Pizza,' said JJ, emptying a sachet into his mug and stirring the creosote-coloured contents.

'We need to have a chat,' said Pizza.

'What about?'

'You.'

'Oh, is there a problem? I thought I was doing all right. Have I fucked something up?' asked JJ with a worried look on his face.

'On the contrary. I'm really pleased with how you're shaping up. We all are. And Sergeant Collins.'

'Sergeant Collins? What's he said?'

'He suggested I have this chat with you. He reckons you've shown the necessary.'

'Shown the necessary – what's that mean?'

Before Pizza could reply, they were joined at the table by a large man JJ didn't recognise.

'Room for a small one?' asked the man, pulling a chair out without waiting for an answer.

Pizza smiled at JJ, who was taking a sip of his tea.

'What?' asked JJ.

'This is DS Darren Vaughan from Tubbenden Road,' said Pizza, continuing to smile at him.

'Hello, Sarge,' said JJ slowly. 'PC John Jackson.'

'We call him JJ,' said Pizza.

'Nice to see you again, JJ,' said Vaughan with a broad smile before he took a sip of his own drink.

JJ looked from Vaughan and back to Pizza with a puzzled look on his face. They were both staring at him.

'Again? We haven't met before, have we?' he said slowly.

'Don't you recognise me?' asked Vaughan.

JJ looked closely at him, still frowning. Vaughan was easily six feet tall, stocky with collar-length dark hair and thick butcher's-grip sideburns and a huge mono-brow. He was wearing dirty jeans and a lumberjack-style check shirt over a white T-shirt. JJ was sure he hadn't seen him before.

'I don't think so, Sarge,' he said eventually.

'I'm disappointed, JJ. Obviously my demise had absolutely no effect on you at all, you callous bastard.'

'Demise? What are you on about?'

'You toerags ran me over on the Tamworth Road last week and dumped me over a hedge,' said Vaughan with a huge smile.

JJ's eyes widened to the size of saucers and his mouth dropped open as the colour drained from his face at the shock. The dead cyclist he'd seen the Brothers and Psycho chuck over the hedge smiled back at him. The fuckers had set him up.

'You bastards,' he said loudly, getting to his feet. 'You fucking bastards,' was all he could manage.

Pizza and Vaughan were laughing out loud and Pizza reached across to grab JJ's arm.

'Sit down,' he said. 'You're making a scene – people are looking at you.'

JJ slumped back in his chair, still shocked and shaking his head in disbelief.

'It's an old one, JJ,' Vaughan told him, 'but the best I've seen it done. Got you hook, line and sinker, but I've got to say, son, I'm fucking impressed.'

'Impressed, h-how?' stammered JJ.

'You've said absolutely fuck all, JJ,' said Pizza in a serious tone. 'Not a word. You believed you saw the guys doing something awful but you kept quiet. I'm very proud of you, son.'

'Proud? Hardly the right thing to do, was it?' said JJ, his shock diminishing slowly. 'Jesus, I thought they'd killed him and did nothing about it. That's not right, Pizza.'

His mentor nodded. 'True, JJ, but what it was all about was whether the group could trust you – *really* trust you when things got tasty.'

'They trust me? I'm not sure I trust myself any more,' said JJ.

'Don't dwell on it, lad,' said Vaughan sternly. 'No point – it's done. You passed with flying colours – job done.'

'A test, that's what this was all about? It was a fucking test?'

'That's all,' said Pizza. He was worried; he'd not expected this reaction from him at all. What he'd bargained on was the initial shock and then joy and relief that he'd only been had over.

'You're a made man now, JJ. The guys all know you're sound; they can rely on you to watch their backs when the shit hits the fan.'

'It's not right, Pizza,' JJ repeated, looking him firmly in the eye and then at Vaughan in the same steely manner. 'You led me to believe they'd killed someone and then covered it up. And then you expected me to keep my mouth shut about it. What's that a test of – my inability to tell right from wrong, to ignore everything I signed up to do? It's bollocks, Pizza.'

'It was a test of your loyalty to the group, JJ,' said Pizza urgently. 'The group is the cornerstone of everything. You can't do this job on your own.'

'At the expense of right and wrong? What's happened to you? I'm ashamed of what I did, really ashamed. I haven't slept properly since it happened, not because of what I thought *they'd* done, but because *I* did fuck all about it.'

Pizza glanced at Vaughan, who also looked worried. He licked his lips which had gone horribly dry.

'Listen, son, you're looking at this all the wrong way. It happens all the time. Cops pull stunts like this to find out if the new boys can be trusted, that's all. Admittedly, this might have been a bit extreme, but that's all it was – a test.'

'To see how bent and corrupt I am, you mean?'

'Jesus, no. Of course not.'

'Because that's what I am, isn't it? I can be relied on not

to put away coppers who've done something as awful as killing someone and dumping the body over a hedge. Is that what you're looking for?'

'You've got this all wrong, JJ,' Pizza tried again.

'I don't think so. I don't want your trust, any of you, if that's what it's all about. I'm happy to bend a few rules to get the right people off the street, but that's it. You think I'm prepared to keep quiet about this kind of shit again, you've got me all wrong,' said JJ.

'But you *did* keep quiet,' stated Vaughan. 'Why was that then?'

JJ paused for a moment. 'I wish I knew,' he eventually said. 'Peer pressure, loyalty to you, Pizza, loyalty to the others, because I'm a twat. I don't know.'

'Exactly, JJ, exactly,' said Vaughan. 'You know what I'd do this afternoon if I came across one of my team doing something serious like that?'

'Fuck all, I suspect,' snapped JJ. 'Go on, enlighten me.'

'I'd fucking lock him up,' said Vaughan simply.

'Lock him up? What about all this bollocks about looking after each other, then?'

'We all have to draw a line somewhere, there's got to be a limit. I stretch things to get stuff done every day, and my guys know that. But they also know what I won't do. They trust me, and I trust them, but we all know each other's parameters. I've never taken a bribe in my career, but I know many who have. I won't do it for lots of reasons – not least because I don't want to be in some villain's back pocket for a rainy day. I won't take a backhander and my guys know that if I ever saw one of them do it, I'd lock them up. I'm pretty sure some of them take one from time to time, but they know I won't get involved so they keep it away from me. They know they can trust me over pretty much everything else, but I've drawn my line and now you've drawn yours. It doesn't change the fact that your group can trust you.'

JJ remained silent, staring at his cooling mug of tea,

'What would you have done, Pizza, if they'd done this to you?' he asked eventually.

Pizza puffed out his cheeks and sat back as he considered the million-dollar question.

'I really don't know,' he admitted. 'I hope I'd have done the right thing.'

'And what's that?'

'Whatever works for you, the individual.'

'That doesn't really answer the question, does it? Would you have kept quiet?'

'I think I would have done, yes.'

'Knowing it was wrong?'

'I wish it was that easy, JJ, I really do. With this job, if you're in, you're in, but if you're out, you're fucked. If the blokes around you can't trust you and think you'll be off blowing your whistle every time something a bit underhand happens, you're out in the cold. It's a rite of passage we all go through. Mostly, you fit in and get on with it, preserving your integrity as best you can. But please don't lose sight of what's actually happened here.'

'What's happened is that I've compromised what I always thought was clear – right and wrong. What I did was wrong and I knew it.'

'Nobody got killed, JJ, there was no body chucked over a hedge. It was a test, though I have to admit it was way over the top. I wish we'd done something else.'

'I *failed* the test, Pizza. I did the wrong thing and I knew I was doing the wrong thing. What does that say about me?'

'That you're a human being, JJ, flawed like the rest of us, not some fucking saint,' snapped Pizza irritably. 'You're a uniformed cop working in the arsehole of the world, shovelling shit all day, every day. You have to make a choice about where you line up. With the angels and wither and die, or with the devils and demons and ride it out. This isn't a job where you can walk about wearing a fucking halo turning water into wine. It's fucking dangerous and the odds are stacked against us, so we have to rely on each other – and to do that we have to *trust* each other. And sometimes that's going to mean turning a blind eye to what happens around you because the guys doing whatever it is that you disapprove of have gone a step further than you into this fucking furnace of a job to get a result. Get that fucking dog-collar off, JJ, before it chokes you.'

Pizza sat back with a deep sigh and looked at Darren Vaughan. JJ had remained with his head down throughout Pizza's Sermon on the Mount and stayed silent for a long time, chewing on his bottom lip and picking at his fingernails. Eventually, he sighed deeply and looked up at Pizza and Vaughan.

'I love this job already, really love it. I couldn't imagine doing anything else. But I've got a limit, a line in the sand – like you said, Sarge. I crossed over that line that night and I won't do it again. I crossed it because I was weak and fucking stupid, but it'll never happen again. You've got to understand that, or I'm gone. If you can't trust me with the knowledge that I've got a limit, then I'm not your man and I'm glad of it. I want to be a good copper who can tell the difference. There's got to be a difference between them and us. There wasn't the other night and I can't live like that.'

'Neither could I, JJ, neither could I. I sleep easy at night because my conscience is clear, and that isn't going to change. You stick to your principles and just make sure the others know what they are.'

'Is that going to be a problem?'

'No way. They've all got them to varying degrees. Even the Brothers and Psycho have limits, but inherently they're all honest. Well, when I say honest, you've got to remember you're working in Horse's Arse. Things are different here.'

JJ laughed for the first time and nodded. 'Yeah, they certainly are. I'm OK, thanks, Pizza. I think I understand now. What will you tell the others about our chat?'

'Fuck all, JJ. Just that I've told you that you were set up and you took it well. The rest of it stays with us three, OK?'

Vaughan nodded his head in agreement and got to his feet, offering JJ a firm handshake.

'Just do the right thing, JJ,' he said with a smile. 'That's all you can do.'

'I will, Sarge,' replied JJ with meaning. 'I will.'

Chapter Eighteen

Psycho was quickly about his business; he was on a mission to arrange their transport for a day at the Haydock Races and he was determined that it wouldn't cost them a penny. He had a plan and headed straight for the southbound carriageway of the by-pass where he stood a very good chance of pulling it off. Ten minutes later, he stood at the back of his Panda car watching the approaching traffic. He'd considered utilising his infamous homemade *Lights – You Cunt* sign which he always carried with him, but it seemed entirely inappropriate even to him, to use it on a bright sunny June afternoon. That was really only of any use during the winter, and he resolved to give some thought to an all-year sign, *Speed – You Arsehole* maybe? Sounded good.

He didn't have long to wait; in fact, he heard it coming before it had exited the Birchwood roundabout and begun to crawl towards him in a haze of blue smoke.

'Oh yes!' Psycho said triumphantly to himself, stepping

out into the nearside lane and raising his right hand in a textbook, Number One traffic stop sign.

'Fuck it,' muttered thirty-year-old Mark Connell, as he crashed the gearstick into second and tried to coax some more power out of his dilapidated Ford Transit. The vehicle was a death trap and he was sure the cop pulling him over wasn't going to be doing him any favours.

'Afternoon, sir,' said Psycho breezily, as the engine coughed and spluttered to a stop when Connell had pulled up behind the Panda car and switched off. 'Just a routine traffic stop under the Road Traffic Act. Have you got your documents on you?'

Connell had been watching Psycho closely as he'd been speaking, clocking that he was casting an obviously practised eye over the van.

'No, I'm afraid not. They're all at home,' he replied.

'With the tax disc as well?'

'No, no, that's been applied for – should be in the post.'

Psycho smiled and nodded knowingly. 'Of course. You've probably not owned the van long, have you?'

'No, that's right – only a couple of weeks.'

'So you won't have had time to get it registered in your name yet either?'

'That's right, but I've got the logbook at home,' said Connell, wondering where this big, ugly cop was going with this.

'With the MOT and insurance?'

'Absolutely.'

'And your full driving licence?'

'Yes, and that.'

'I don't suppose you've got any identification on you, have you?' asked Psycho pleasantly.

'Would you believe it? I've left my wallet in the office,' replied Connell, patting his trousers and jacket theatrically like a mime act.

'Hmm, we've got a problem here,' said Psycho, pushing his cap on to the back of his head and stroking his stubbly chin. 'How many seats have you got in the back?'

'Ten.'

'Ten, eh?' mused the strange cop. 'Ten's plenty.'

'Plenty for what?'

'Oh, don't mind me, sir,' said Psycho, 'just rambling to myself. No, the problem as I see it is that I'm virtually certain that when I check you and your exquisite vehicle on the Police National Computer, if I could get down to a bookies in time I'd have a little wager on you not having a driving licence and there being no insurance or MOT on the van. And then I'd probably have to get one of those nasty Traffic cops to pop down and give it the onceover, and again, I'd go and have a little bet that that deeply unpleasant man would impound the vehicle as unroadworthy. How am I doing?' he finished with a smile.

Bang on, actually, thought Connell to himself, before he replied aloud: 'Any way out of this spot of bother, Officer?'

'Any way out? *Any way out?*' shouted the apparently outraged Psycho. 'Are you trying to suggest I should turn a blind eye to the numerous traffic offences I've found in exchange for some sort of inducement?'

Connell swallowed hard. 'Oh no, nothing like that, Officer, God forbid. I was thinking, maybe you could give me a chance to get some work done on it. You know, get it roadworthy and things, rather than screw me down.'

'Give you a chance? That's interesting. You know, I'm not a great lover of traffic offences; always felt we just alienate the public by getting so precious about that sort of thing. How could I be sure you've done what needs to be done and don't just disappear?'

'Oh, I'll get it done, Officer, I promise you,' said Connell.

'I trust you, of course I do,' said Psycho, 'but I'd need to be sure you'd done the work – and then, of course, I'd need to see the van roadtested.'

'Of course.'

'Where do you live?'

'Badgers Close, South Handstead.'

'I know it well. Tell you what, I'll follow you home now to make sure you get there safely, and we'll discuss how you're going to get yourself out of this deep shit, OK?' said Psycho, his smile replaced with an expressionless gaze.

'Follow me home?' gulped Connell. 'I was just off somewhere.'

'Not now you're not. It's back to your place or down to

the breaker's yard. What's it to be and what's your name?'

Half an hour later, Connell coaxed the van on to the drive outside his tatty council house on the Park Royal Estate and waited glumly for the beaming Psycho to join him at the front door.

'I could have a look at your documents whilst I'm here,' he said, as Connell forced open the badly fitted door and they stepped into the filthy house that stank of damp.

'I'll have a look round for them,' Connell said sulkily. 'Could be anywhere though. Look, Officer, what's going on here?'

'This is what you're going to do, pal. You're going to get that pile of shit on the drive serviced this afternoon. You'll have a mate somewhere who can do that for you, I'm sure. And then tomorrow morning, you're going to present yourself at Handstead police station at nine-thirty a.m. and we're going to roadtest it.'

'How are we going to roadtest it?'

'You're going to take me and a few mates to Haydock Park races for the afternoon; give it a good run out and then you're going to wait for us and bring us back. That all clear?'

'You're having a fucking l-laugh, aren't you?' stammered Connell.

'Do I look like I'm having a laugh?' asked Psycho sternly. 'Now what I need is a little insurance to make sure you turn up, don't I?'

Speechless, Connell watched as Psycho strode into the adjacent living room and gazed in undisguised disgust at the squalor. But, as he'd expected, there was a large, expensive television set on a glass table in the corner. There always was.

'You'll get this back tomorrow evening after we've given your van a proper run out,' he said, as he unplugged it and lifted it off the table.

'You can't take that,' protested Connell. 'I've only just bought it on the never-never.'

'You'll get it back tomorrow evening,' repeated Psycho, as he pushed past him. 'Don't be late, will you? Nine-thirty prompt. Some refreshments for the trip would be nice as well.'

He carefully put the television set on to the back seat of his beat vehicle and waved cheerfully at Connell who was scowling at him from the doorway.

'Nine-thirty, Mark. Have a good one,' he called before driving off.

He returned directly to Horse's Arse, where he recorded the television set in the Miscellaneous Property Register before locking it away in the Property Store, and went off to the Report Writing Room to make a telephone call. The Brothers were in there writing up their pocket books for a prisoner they'd just brought in and who was currently being patched up by the police surgeon in the doctor's room.

'Transport's all sorted for tomorrow, boys – no cost.

Don't be late, and let the others know if you see them before I do, will you?'

He made his phone call, wrote a few notes in his pocket book and then popped upstairs for a well-deserved cup of tea and a gossip with big Sweaty Sylvie McGraw, the Late-Turn short order cook.

His phone was ringing as DCI Dan Harrison got back into his office. He ignored it as he took off his jacket and hung it on the wire hanger on the back of the door. Whoever it was, they weren't going to take 'no' for an answer, however, so he picked it up as he sat down.

'DCI Harrison,' he said sharply.

'Hello, boss, it's Sergeant Jones in the cells,' said the voice on the other end. 'Sorry to bother you.'

'What's up, Sarge?' he said wearily.

'We've got a guy locked up down here – been here for the last three days waiting to be interviewed. Is there any chance of it happening today?'

'Three days?' shouted Harrison. 'How the fuck has that happened?'

'Long story, boss, but it appears DCs Benson and Clarke had a quick chat with him but never came back to interview him properly.'

'What's he in for?'

'Burglary. Got potted coming out of the back of a house with some cash, I think.'

'Clarke and Benson have been well tucked up recently,'

explained Harrison. 'Probably dropped off their radar. Is this bloke kicking off about it?'

'Not really, but he's told me he just wants to admit everything and get out of here.'

'They're in the office now,' said Harrison. 'I'll get them to pop down and sort it out. Does anyone else know about how long he's been locked up?'

'No, no – just us,' assured Jones. He understood now how things worked at Horse's Arse. Not that it would have been much consolation for the prisoner, but he was at least fortunate that he'd been left in a cell where he was occasionally fed and watered. If he'd been forgotten about in the prisoner's cupboard in the CID office, his ordeal would have been ten times worse.

Harrison strode into the main CID office where he found Clarke and Benson sifting busily through a mountain of manila-coloured files. They looked up as he came in.

'I've just had the station Sergeant on the phone, boys. Have you got a burglar in the cells to talk to?'

'Oh fuck,' said Benson, looking at Clarke. 'The Romanian. Bollocks – we forgot all about him. Sorry, boss, we'd teed him up nicely and then copped for the Mandy Blackstock rape. We've not been back to see him since.'

'The Sergeant says he's ready to spill his guts to you. Just nip down there and deal with him, will you? Just get the cough and I'll ask DI Bryan to arrange for someone else to put the paperwork together, all right?'

'Sorry, boss. On it now,' said Benson, grabbing a pen and a couple of green-backed contemporaneous interview notebooks. As Harrison left the room, Benson pulled a face at Clarke.

'Fuck, forgot all about this bloke.'

'He hasn't forgotten about your knob though, has he?' laughed Clarke, as they left the office and trotted downstairs to the cell area.

Ten minutes later, the dishevelled Florint Dimitrescu leaped to his feet in the interview room he'd been put in, as Clarke and Benson entered. He looked terrified, and backed against the far wall as Benson fiddled with his belt buckle.

'You keep trousers on, OK? I tell everything,' he pleaded.

'I hope you will, old son,' said Benson, 'otherwise you know what's coming.'

'I tell everything,' Dimitrescu repeated nervously, retaking his seat but never removing his eyes from Benson. 'We steal many houses, take TVs and audios.'

'Who's we?'

Dimitrescu babbled some names that neither detective could make out.

'Write their names and addresses on this,' said Clarke, sliding a sheet of paper and a pen across the desk to him, 'and make sure we can read your writing.'

'Yes, yes, we make many steals from houses, they very bad men.'

'Of course they are,' said Benson pleasantly, 'so you can tell us where you've all been so busy.'

'All over, all over, many houses. Stealing cash money, TVs, audios. They do very bad things sometimes.'

'Where's the gear now?'

'All in his house,' replied Dimitrescu, pointing to the name on the top of his sheet of paper.

'OK, we'll pay him a visit shortly, but you're still not telling us everything, are you, pal?' said Benson threateningly.

'No, no – you keep trousers up, please. No need, no need. We do bad things and they take photo snaps.'

'Photos? What are you on about?'

'We leave cameras with pictures.'

'You're not making any sense, mate,' said Benson, reaching for his belt buckle.

'No, no!' shrieked Dimitrescu. 'Trousers stay up, please. We stick toothbrushes up arses and take pictures to leave for owner.'

Benson and Clarke looked at each other and smiled. Sometimes, even they could be surprised.

Pizza was feeling as horny as a billy goat when he got home shortly after eleven. The house was still and quiet as he tiptoed up the stairs and into the bathroom. He'd glanced into David's nursery but it was pitch black and impossible to see anything. Bundling his sweaty uniform into the wash basket, he showered quickly, washing the grime of Horse's Arse away until he felt fresh and clean and with a raging diamond-cutter. Drying himself quickly, he crept across the landing and opened the bedroom door. Stepping into the room, he could just about make out the shape of Lisa on the far side of the bed, the single white sheet pulled up to her shoulders. The room smelled of her and he inhaled deeply.

'I'm in the mood for love,' he began to sing softly as he slid under the sheet and moved himself close to her, pressing his erection into the small of her back and nuzzling her neck. She moaned, and stirred as he did so, and he slid his hand over her small waist and across her smooth stomach, up towards her breasts. Suddenly, he felt his index finger grabbed by a small hand and sharp teeth sink in. Shocked, he lifted himself upright.

'Daddy go night-night now,' said little David from under the sheet alongside his mother, as Lisa's shoulders shook with laughter.

Chapter Nineteen

'You have got to be fucking joking!' exclaimed H, as he and the others stood outside the station, looking at the high-revving, smoking Transit van the following morning. Mark Connell was keeping the manual choke open to keep it running, whatever the cost. 'It's a death trap.'

'It's got a tax disc for a Vauxhall Viva in the window,' said Pizza.

'That's an improvement on yesterday,' said Psycho, completely unmoved by the barrage of complaints that had come his way after Connell had arrived. 'The fact is, it's costing us bugger all. Mark here volunteered to run us to Haydock out of the goodness of his heart, didn't you, Mark?'

Connell glared at Psycho but kept quiet, praying the pile of junk would get him through the day and he'd get his telly back.

'Come on – all aboard the Sunshine coach,' called Psycho. 'Haydock Park, here we come.' He jumped into the front passenger seat whilst the others reluctantly filed into the back, complaining about everything.

'You ungrateful bastards,' shouted Psycho, as they tried to get as comfortable as possible. 'It's not costing you a penny and all you can do is moan. Mark's even laid on refreshments for us, haven't you, mate?'

'On the floor behind my seat,' he replied sullenly, as he manoeuvred the heap out of the slip road and on to Bolton Road East. H began to rummage about in the rubbish behind the driver's seat and hauled out a Boots plastic carrier bag. Peering in, he saw a collection of sandwiches which, on closer examination, all had sell-by dates of yesterday.

'You've been scratching about in the bloody bins,' shouted H.

'I didn't get them out of the bins,' protested Connell above the roar of the engine. 'They always give what's left over to the tramps, so I got down there first last night.'

'Fucking great – tramps' leftovers,' complained Jim Docherty. 'What's to drink then?' H pulled out a large cardboard box and looked closely at it. 'What the fuck is Valhalla lager?'

'Valhalla, that's where Vikings go to die, isn't it?' asked Malcy.

'It's where we'll be going if we drink any of this shit,' replied H. 'Where the fuck can you buy this stuff, anyway?'

'The pound shop in the town centre,' said Connell glumly.

'So how much did you shell out for twenty-four cans, Big Spender?'

'A quid.'

'Jesus Christ. Psycho, your mate's trying to poison us with his on-board refreshments – if he doesn't get us with his van first. Where on earth did you find him?'

'It's a long story, boys. Another time maybe. Look on the bright side, we're going to the races for fuck all,' replied Psycho, before he turned back to keep an eye on his surly driver.

'Do a left here, Mark,' he suddenly said.

'I need the motorway,' protested Connell.

'Do a left; we're picking someone up on the way.'

'You never mentioned picking anyone up. Where are we going?'

'Do a left and head for Kray Hill. Just follow the signs.'

There were loud protests from the back of the van as it lurched off the main road and began to crawl along narrow country lanes.

'What is this – a bloody Magical Mystery Tour?' shouted Pizza. 'We need to get on to the motorway, not out in the sticks.'

'What are you up to, Psycho?' asked Malcy, leaning forward to whisper into his hairy ear. 'Why are we going this way?'

'We're picking her up. She needs cheering up – you

both do,' he replied without turning round.

'We can't just pick her up and take her out for the day. There are rules and regulations.'

'She's not all wired up to a life-support system or anything, is she? No wires and tubes hanging out of her?'

'No, she's paralysed from the waist down, not a cabbage.'

'There you go, then. She's coming out with us.'

'What if she was on a life-support system?' asked Malcy.

'We'd bring it with us. She needs a day out, mate,' said Psycho, turning to smile at his friend.

'*Falconer Hospital – Paraplegic Centre*,' read Jim aloud as the Transit headed up a long gravel drive towards a magnificent Edwardian country house. 'What the fuck are we doing here?' There was a clamour of complaint but no explanation was immediately forthcoming.

'Turn the van round for a quick exit, Mark, and keep the engine running. We'll be as quick as we can,' said Psycho. 'Come on, Malcy,' he went on, as the van came to a screeching halt on the wide gravel apron in front of the house, 'you'll have to lead.'

'What the fuck are we doing here?' shouted Jim again at the top of his voice.

Psycho leaned back into the van and eyeballed them all. 'We're picking someone up, you'll see in a minute,' he said, and then he followed Malcy at a jog to the front doors of the building.

'This is all bollocks,' wailed Mark Connell as he slowly moved the Transit through a painful twenty-point turn. The vehicle had the turning circle of the *QE2* and seemed to weigh as much. His arms were burning from the exertion as he finally got it lined up back down the drive, and he gunned the engine hard.

'What the fuck are we doing here?' he asked desperately, sweat dripping off his frightened face. 'What are they doing – kidnapping a cripple or something?'

Karen Malcolm looked up from her bed as the door to her private room opened, and she smiled as she saw Malcy walk in. He was with a huge bear of a man who looked like a pirate.

'Andy, what are *you* doing here? I wasn't expecting you,' she said, as he wrapped his arms around her and kissed her.

'Hello, beautiful. All a bit last-minute, I'm afraid, but we're here to take you out for the day. This is my mate, Sean Pearce.'

'Psycho, I've heard lots about you,' she said, shaking his huge, oven-warm hand. 'Sister Murray will go mental if she comes in,' she whispered.

'Better get going then,' said Malcy, reaching underneath her and lifting her like a small child.

'You can't just take me out, Malcy; they've got rules and things here. I need my medication.'

'Got it,' said Psycho, grabbing the numerous bottles

and pots on the table by the bed. 'You know what you've got to take and when, don't you?'

'Yes,' she laughed, 'the instructions are all on them anyway. Where are you taking me?'

'Haydock Park races, sweetheart,' said Malcy. They began to move towards the door when it crashed open and Sister Murray, alerted by the screaming engine of the get-away Transit outside on the drive, stormed into the room.

'Mr Malcolm, what do you think you're doing?' she bellowed in her broad Belfast accent. 'You know your visits are to be closely supervised after your unfortunate incident, and why is your wife out of bed?'

'She's coming out for the day,' he replied quietly.

'She most certainly is not,' thundered the dried-up old hag. 'Return her to her bed right now.'

Sister Murray epitomised everything that could possibly be unsuitable for a career in nursing. Her long, pale, pinched face was set in a permanent scowl that suggested lively haemorrhoids, and her bedside manner would have appealed to Judge Jeffries. She was cold, heartless, rude and abrupt with her staff, and even worse with her unfortunate charges. She was the last person in the world that a young woman like Karen Malcolm, in the depths of despair, needed. It was an accepted fact around the hospital that the appalling, middle-aged spinster had handed out towels at Belsen during a working holiday. Psycho moved in front of Malcy and Karen and smiled down at the scowling Angel of Death.

'Fuck off, Horse Face,' he said politely, and gently eased her to one side. 'We'll be back with her later; don't wait up.'

Sister Murray was apoplectic with rage but unable to form a meaningful sentence. Instead, she followed them down the corridor, spluttering and spitting and waving her arms about impotently and watched, crimson-faced, as Psycho wrenched open the sliding side door of the screaming Transit van.

'Get the number of that van, you idiot,' she managed to screech at the young girl on the reception desk, who'd rather liked the large brute who'd winked at her as he walked out. 'And call the police, you stupid girl.'

'Who the fuck is this?' asked Pizza as they caught sight of the grinning Psycho, Malcy and Karen.

'This, gentlemen, is my wife, Karen. Karen, meet some of D Group, Horse's Arse.'

Karen flashed them a smile that won their hearts as it had won Malcy's some years ago, and shyly said, 'Hello,' as Malcy manhandled her on to the bench seat opposite the door. As he dived on to the jump seat and Psycho slammed the door behind them, Malcy noticed that the others were all staring at him. They all looked unbelievably guilty and shamefaced.

'Yes, she's paralysed from the waist down. A car accident on a holiday in Egypt,' he explained, saving any of them from asking any further questions and causing any embarrassment.

'She's a babe,' blurted H involuntarily, forgetting himself for a moment. Karen looked at him before laughing out loud. For the first time in many months, she was beginning to see herself as her husband still saw her. She was a beautiful, intelligent, desirable woman who couldn't use her legs. Nothing more or less. And they thought she was a babe.

'Go, go, go!' yelled Psycho, leaping into the front passenger seat. 'Get this fucking thing out of here before the cops turn up.'

'Fucking great – more cops. What have you done, kidnapped her or something? Just what I need, isn't it?'

'Stop your fucking moaning and put your foot down. We need a drink after that,' growled Psycho.

The Transit trundled back down the long driveway, obscuring itself in a large noxious cloud of exhaust fumes, flat out at 30 m.p.h. before lurching through the gates on to the main road. In the reception at the hospital, Sister Murray was screaming abuse at the 999 operator who was patiently trying to explain that by the sounds of things, Mrs Malcolm had been a more than willing victim of the 'kidnap'.

'And the big ugly beast of a man told me to fuck off, called me Horse Face,' the Sister reported, enraged, as the young receptionist stifled a laugh. The operator made a sound like a horse blowing through its muzzle and put down the phone.

*

An hour and a half later, following a stop for a drink in a pub on the East Lancashire Road, the Transit pulled into the car park at Haydock Park racecourse, scattering other racegoers keen to avoid the poisonous gas cloud that accompanied it. The noisy occupants then bailed out, stretching, complaining, laughing loudly and ready for a great day out in the sunshine.

'You make sure you're here when we finish, Mark,' said Psycho menacingly before he left the vehicle. 'If we can't find you, I'm going to come looking for you.'

'I'll be here,' said Connell resignedly. 'How long are you going to be?'

'Last race is about six p.m.,' he replied, peering at the copy of the *Racing Post* on his lap. 'Say about half-past six, and then we want to find somewhere to get something to eat.'

Connell sighed and dropped his forehead on to the worn steering wheel. Psycho looked at him and then patted him on the shoulder.

'Appreciate it, Mark. See you later,' he said cheerfully and got out to join the others.

Malcy had Karen in his arms again and they made their way over to the main stand, producing their warrant cards to the startled gate attendant who eventually let them in for free.

'If you need any help this afternoon, you know where to find us,' called Jim, as they climbed towards the upper tier, acknowledging the unwritten agreement that went with the production of a warrant card. It was a fairly standard practice with cops around the country; 'briefing' their way into sports stadiums, music concerts, night clubs and travelling on trains and buses for free, but with the expectation that if the need arose, they'd turn out to assist on-site staff with a problem. 'Two on the Blue' or 'the Blue Rover' was how the practice was known locally, and as they glanced at the crowds in the stand as they took their seats, it looked as though most of the Merseyside and Lancashire Forces were there for the day as well. If any fee-paying racegoers kicked off today they could expect to be confronted by an army of freeloading cops.

As they began to study their race cards and form guides, they all saw a problem immediately. Furtive glances were being cast, but no one could see a way round it. Karen Malcolm had spotted it as well and lanced the boil quickly.

'I fancy the fifty to one shot in the two-fifteen,' she said loudly. 'Andy, can I put a tenner on it to win?'

The group looked at her with wide smiles and then began to laugh with her as Malcy pulled her close to him. Raspberry Ripple with Joey Malone on board was a good outside bet and she'd taken another huge step forward in coming to terms with her life of immobility.

'Back him for a place, honey,' said Malcy softly.

'He's going to win, Andy,' she said, looking up at him and touching his face tenderly. 'Like I am.'

They all backed the horse, and heavily too, more in

hope than expectation, but win he did, and absolutely ecstatic and croaky from screaming him home, they carried their lucky talisman high on their shoulders and adjourned to the champagne bar, where they spent the rest of the afternoon celebrating and placing table bets with the Tote girls.

It was an amazing afternoon. Karen felt alive again. For the first time since that hot afternoon in Mersa Alam when the drunken vegetable farmer in his Toyota had taken out her moped head on, she wanted to live. Her life since waking up in hospital in Birmingham and subsequently in the Falconer Hospital had been grim; spent in the company of medical professionals and tearful family members in clinical, antiseptic surroundings that reinforced her belief that her life was over. She had been sure that was as good as it was going to get. But now she was interacting again with real, vibrant people. Men who were flirting with her, talking to her as Karen the person, not the paraplegic with a colostomy bag. For the first time since the accident, she saw that Malcy was really genuine in what he'd been telling her ever since she'd woken up and realised she was without feeling from the waist down. He still loved her, and fancied her, too.

And she really liked the mates he had brought along with him. True, they were a bit uncouth and loud, but they were real people. And that Sean 'Psycho' Pearce? He was big, brutish, and at first glance, pig ugly. But she could detect something under that armour-plated exterior as he fussed about her like a mother hen. She could see what so many women picked up on. He was vulnerable, yet exuded the persona of a man confident with himself and his place in society. His outrageous sense of humour and penchant for doing the unthinkable was, she suspected, his defence mechanism against getting hurt. And he was very lonely.

'You need a good woman, you know, Sean,' she said to him as Malcy left the table for another bottle of champagne.

'Working on it, darling,' he said, smiling at her. 'Shame you're all loved up with Malcy,' he continued, 'as I'd cheerfully slip you a crippler.'

After a brief pause as they both digested his appalling faux pas, they dissolved in howls of laughter that continued until Malcy returned.

'You need to keep her close, Malcy,' said Psycho, wiping the tears from his face. 'You let her go and I'm in there like a rat up a drainpipe.'

Malcy grinned broadly at them both, noticing that for the first time in as long as he could remember, Karen was glowing with the spirit and vigour that had so attracted him in the first place. She was alive again, all thoughts of ending things banished to the pit of despair she had spent so long looking into.

'You keep your filthy hands to yourself,' he growled with a smile. 'That's my wife you're talking about.' He dropped the new bottle of champagne into the ice-bucket and sat down next to Karen as the raucous conversation and banter got back to full tilt.

The drive back to the Falconer Hospital was quiet. Mark Connell had driven in sullen silence after receiving a crack round the head after complaining about the bottle of pale ale and bag of crisps that Psycho had brought back to the van.

'Is that it? A bottle of pale ale and a bag of crisps? I've been hanging about all fucking afternoon for you bastards. Look at the state of you – pissed as parrots and I get a bottle of pale ale? You shites.'

Outraged, Psych had lamped him. 'You ungrateful prick,' he shouted. 'You should be locked up and you know it.' He checked to make sure that Karen and Malcy were comfortable before issuing his next instructions.

'Right, we're starving. Find us a nice restaurant on the way back – off we go.'

Just after midnight, the van drove through the main gates to the hospital and stopped. The lights to the vehicle were switched off and the group gazed up at the darkened building. Only twin, ornate carriage lamps and the desk lamp on the front reception were visible. The manicured lawns on either side of the driveway stretched away into the dark, the only sound being the complaints of the still misfiring engine and an owl outside.

'We'll carry you in from here, Karen, if you don't mind,' said Psycho, looking back at her, her head nestled on Malcy's chest. She looked radiant and peaceful. 'We don't want to bump into Sister Murray, do we?'

He laughed as a chorus of, 'Hi Ho Silver, away!' rang out around the van, and then got out and dragged the side door open. Malcy staggered out with Karen in his arms and the group followed them out, each kissing and hugging Karen before they got back in.

Malcy and Psycho walked silently on the grass towards the building, checking constantly for signs of life. It wouldn't have surprised them if Sister Murray had come at them out of the dark in full assassin's kit, but as Psycho pointed out, she was probably stretched out on Dr Frankenstein's work-bench having a personality fitted.

'Looks like it's old Jeff on the desk,' said Malcy as they approached the doors. 'He's OK.'

Psycho knocked gently on the window and the night porter, who'd been snoozing, leaped to his feet in panic as he caught sight of the monster outside. Then he saw Karen waving at him in Malcy's arms. Jeff Bainbridge hurried over to open the doors and stood back to let them in.

'Where on earth have you been, Miss Karen?' he beamed. 'Sister Murray's been going mental all day, apparently.'

'Had a win on the gee-gees, Jeff,' she murmured sleepily, the six glasses of champagne and her medication getting the better of her.

'That's for you, old fella,' said Psycho, handing him a bottle of champagne. 'Let's get her back to her room.'

Soon Karen was back in bed, sheet pulled up to her chin and looking heavy-eyed at Malcy and Psycho.

'I had a great day, boys. Thanks for everything.'

'Love you, honey,' whispered Malcy, sitting beside her and leaning to kiss her.

'Love you too, Andy. You promise me, you and Sean will take care on this Special Ops thing you're going on?'

'We will, I promise,' he said softly.

'I'll keep an eye on him,' Psycho told her, looming over the bed and kissing her on the forehead.

'Come and see me when you get back?'

'Promise,' replied Malcy. 'You get off to sleep now.'

As he got off the bed, she opened her eyes fully and looked at him. 'Andy, I want to come home soon. Can I do that?'

'We'll sort it out when I get back, darling. I want you home as well.'

'Then the boys can come and visit us,' she said sleepily, her eyelids beginning to close.

Malcy and Psycho looked at her as she drifted off and they turned to leave.

'And another thing, Sean,' she called softly, her eyes flickering open, 'you be good to her.'

The Transit van was back on the main road headed towards Handstead when the light in Karen Malcolm's room was switched on and Sister Murray stormed in.

'Mrs Malcolm,' she hissed, 'this is outrageous. Where have you been? I've reported your unauthorised absence to the hospital authorities and there will be serious repercussions, I can assure you.'

Karen opened a bleary eye and focused on the old witch. 'Empty my bag and clean me up, then leave me in peace,' she said, and then whispered to herself, 'Horse Face.'

Shortly after 1 a.m., Mark Connell pulled his Transit van up to the verge in the slip road outside Handstead police station. The group fell out, singing and shouting their goodbyes before going in unsteady searches for their own vehicles. Psycho and Malcy watched them go.

'Are we all square now then?' asked Connell sourly. 'Can I have my telly back?'

Malcy looked quizzically at Psycho. 'His telly?' he asked. 'You never nicked his telly?'

'No,' scoffed Psycho. 'Just a bit of insurance, that's all. Hang on and I'll go and get it. Two minutes, Malcy, and I'll run you home.'

He jogged up the steps to the nick, was buzzed in by the bored night shift front desk PC and soon appeared in the office.

'What are you doing here so late, Psycho?' asked the PC.

'Just got to restore some property to the guy in that Transit outside actually,' he replied. 'Give us the Property Store keys, will you?'

Five minutes later he was back, carrying the large

television. Putting it down for a minute, he tossed the keys on to the desk.

'Thinking about it,' he said, 'you might also want to restore *this* property.' He rummaged in his pockets, eventually retrieving a piece of paper which he unfolded and handed to the PC.

'That's the guy outside in the van,' he went on. 'You do a PNC check on him and I think you'll find he's wanted on a no-bail warrant for non-payment of fines,' he said happily.

Chapter Twenty

The large gymnasium at Headquarters was heaving; absolutely packed to the seams with every chair taken and officers hanging from the wooden wall-bars over by the large windows. The noise of 400 coppers talking loudly was making the whispered conversation between Detective Chief Superintendent Mills and Inspector Phil Gilbert a difficult affair.

'Is everything sorted out?' asked Mills.

'Yeah, got back late Saturday. Our man's staying at the Haven Hotel.'

'Fucking hell, Phil, how much is that costing us?'

'Eighty quid a night, boss. Best we get this training done on the hurry up before we blow the budget on his bar bill.'

'His bar bill?'

'He likes a drink. I was out with him around Soho and the West End on Friday. He drinks like a fucking fish.'

'Great. Where is he now?'

'Out the back. Don't worry, he's fine. He seems to have the constitution of an ox.'

'He better had. Keep him off the piss, for Christ's sake, Phil. This is too important. I'll make a start, I think.'

Tucking the folder he'd been examining under his arm, he strode to the front of the hall and stood patiently waiting for the room to fall quiet. Gradually, his presence was noted and the loud chattering of excited men fell away until there was silence. Mills cast his eyes over the assembled throng and was reminded of Wellington's alleged comment on the eve of Waterloo – 'I don't know what effect these men will have on the enemy, but by God, they frighten me.'

Temporary Chief Constable Chislehurst had telephoned Mills over the weekend to update him on Superintendent Grainger's assessment of the personnel now attached to the SOG and on whom so much depended – not least Chislehurst's appointment as the permanent Chief Constable.

'I think it's only fair to warn you, Mr Mills, that the Divisional Commanders have, without exception, opened their sewers and sent you the contents. I fear you may have your hands full.'

'What we've got planned won't tax them intellectually, sir. In fact, it might just be right up their street,' he'd replied with a heavy heart.

'I do hope so, Mr Mills, for your sake,' said Chislehurst

ominously. 'There's a great deal riding on a successful outcome to the operation.'

'I'm well aware of what's at stake, sir.'

'We're not just talking about the reputation of the Force, you know.'

'No, sir,' replied Mills flatly, fully aware that top of Chislehurst's list of priorities was his own palsied career. There wasn't a back he wouldn't stab or an important backside he wouldn't try and get his head up in order to get what he wanted.

'Keep me informed of progress – on an informal basis. There's no need for Mr Seagrove to know that you're doing so. I'd like you to be in a position to move as soon as possible,' said Chislehurst, before hanging up and telephoning the Chairman of the Police Committee.

'Air Vice-Marshall, so sorry to bother you on a Sunday, but I thought you'd like an update on the operation I discussed with you on Friday to deal with the Albion Army picket,' he smarmed.

'It's that unctuous toad Chislehurst,' hissed Air Vice-Marshall Quintin Quartz-Halogen to his wife as he covered the mouthpiece of the telephone with his hand.

'Oh goodness, tell him you're just off out hunting or something. He loves all that guff. I'm just about to serve lunch, Quintin, do be quick.'

'Make it quick, Chislehurst,' barked the retired Air Vice-Marshall. 'Got a couple of thousand grouse to blow out of the air before lunch.'

'Grouse? I thought that all kicked off in August,' queried Chislehurst.

'August?' bellowed Quartz-Halogen, desperately seeking salvation as he realised the oily senior cop was right. He'd never picked up a gun in his life, and certainly not killed anything.

'*August?* Damn your eyes, man,' he shouted. 'I had a few left over from last year that got away. They're a bit older and slower now – excellent practice for August. Now what the blazes are you ringing me for on a Sunday?'

'The operation we discussed on Friday. I just wanted to let you know that I have a few concerns over Assistant Chief Constable Brian Seagrove's planning and tactics for the operation.'

'Then address them, Mr Chislehurst,' said Quartz-Halogen, his moustache bristling.

'Too late, I fear, Air Vice-Marshall,' oozed Chislehurst with the charm of a pickpocket. 'I'm afraid we're way past any changes or re-planning.'

Twenty miles away, as ACC Brian Seagrove sat down at the dinner table with his family, he shifted uncomfortably as he felt a muscle between his shoulderblades go into spasm.

'You all right, darling?' asked his wife, as she saw him wince and clutch at his shoulder.

'It's probably just the stress,' he groaned. 'If I didn't know better, that felt like Chislehurst slipping a dagger into my back.'

He and his family laughed, but Seagrove's laughter was desperate and strained. His arse was in a sling courtesy of his Temporary Chief and the stakes were high.

'Thank you, gentlemen,' said DCS Mills in a firm voice as silence filled the gymnasium. 'Welcome to Headquarters. I am Detective Chief Superintendent Mills in charge of crime operations across the Force. Over there in the corner is Inspector Phil Gilbert from the Patrol Group. And you, gentlemen, are, until further notice, the Special Operations Group.'

He paused for dramatic effect before continuing, 'Your attachment to this Group was deliberately quick and the details kept deliberately vague. It doesn't take much imagination to have worked out that whatever is planned for the Group is significant. Actually, it's vital to this Force. But the details of the assignment will be kept secret from you until a couple of hours before you are deployed. I know there's been a great deal of speculation about what the assignment is. Forget it – don't ask either me or Mr Gilbert what it may be. We won't tell you until the last moment. You will be wondering why you're required to be resident at Headquarters. In a word – secrecy.'

He scanned the sea of faces; they were engrossed.

'You will be the sole residents in the Headquarters complex for the duration of the training for this operation. The training will be done at night to avoid any contact with staff who work here during the day. All other training courses have been cancelled, so the only other staff on this site at night will be the Control Room staff, and they have strict instructions to remain there. You will not be permitted to leave site at all. The public telephone kiosks in the restaurant area have been disabled, but you will be allowed to use the telephones in the Training Centre to contact your families. As you'll no doubt be aware, those telephones are recorded. You will not discuss your training or anything you see or hear whilst you are here during those phone calls. Any breaches of that requirement will be dealt with by way of severe disciplinary procedure – up to, and including, dismissal from the Force.'

Again he paused, noticing that many of the officers in front of him were casting nervous glances at each other.

'Gentlemen, you are likely to be present at an event that will be remembered and discussed within this Force for years to come. Bear that in mind if you find yourselves asking "what the fuck am I doing here?"'

Loud laughter across the hall punctured the growing tension in the air and Mills smiled.

'Some of you will probably also be wondering how you got to be picked to join the Special Operations Group. I'll be honest with you, boys. You have the worst disciplinary records in your home Divisions. You are regarded there as arrogant, aggressive, unruly, belligerent, punchy risk-takers. These are all qualities that are needed in aces for this operation.'

There was another loud laugh.

'Your Divisions don't have a high regard for you, whereas I and Inspector Gilbert hold you in the highest esteem. You are just what your Force needs now, at a time when its reputation is at stake. All the attributes you have that make you stand out like sore thumbs on Division, will be utilised by the Special Operations Group, and when you return to your everyday duties, your colleagues will look at you and know that you were there. Right, get yourselves over to the Administration block. You'll be allocated your rooms; settle yourselves in, get something to eat, use the swimming pool, get some sleep and relax. We start tonight, back here at six p.m. We're going to show you a training film for starters.'

The room exploded with the noise of loud talking and the scraping of chairs as the Special Operations Group began to file slowly out. Phil Gilbert strolled over to Mills who had remained where he was standing, watching them leave.

'Very inspiring, boss,' he said admiringly. 'Very *Henry the Fifth*.'

Mills laughed. 'I was thinking of giving them the full eve of Agincourt speech, but I wasn't sure most of them would have understood it. I think I'll give them a blast of something along those lines on the day, though.'

'"And gentlemen in England now a-bed shall think themselves accursed they were not here",' murmured Gilbert, '"and hold their manhood cheap".'

'Just as long as there's not too much holding of manhoods in the meantime,' laughed Mills. 'Listen, after they've watched the film this evening, I want to see you and the four Sergeants in my office, OK?'

'Sure. Are you going to let them in on the operation?'

'Not bloody likely. No, I just want to start putting the four units together. I'll keep your thirty guys from the Patrol Group together. Have you got any preferences as to who joins them?'

'I'd keep the Handstead boys together on that unit. They'll be awesome.'

'OK – see you at six,' said Mills. 'I've got to update Mr Seagrove.'

He followed the slow exodus out of the gymnasium, sizing up individual officers as he went.

'They may very well be the dregs of a prison ship, but they're the best hope this Force has got to get itself out of the shit,' he mused to himself.

The Park Royal pub was packed as usual. It was full of the ever-present visiting Albion Army members from around the north of the country, and the cretinous, resurgent Park Royal Mafia who had seized on their presence in the town as an opportunity to get back into business. One day, they reasoned, the Albion Army would move on, leaving them to inherit the poisoned earth they would leave behind.

The Mafia had been largely without a clear leader or

figurehead since the mysterious demise of Bobby Driscoll a couple of years ago, ironically just a few yards away from where the picket of the Red Star Electrics factory was taking place. His successors, Andy Travers and Hugh Briggs, had only briefly filled his shoes, flirting dangerously with a well-connected Turkish gangster before disappearing from the face of the earth last summer. There had been plenty of speculation about what had become of them, but their vanishing act had convinced any others tempted to fill the vacancy that it clearly wasn't conducive to a long and healthy life.

The Mafia had subsequently morphed into a loose collective of independent groups of thugs, not controlled by any one individual, doing their own disorganised thing but still keeping the name of the Park Royal Mafia in the back of the town's subconscious. And then Wallace Moffatt and the Albion Army had breathed life into their pointless, violent existence.

Moffatt had absolutely no interest in becoming their leader. He saw very clearly that they were just a bunch of aimless young losers, but as they appeared to hang on his every racist outburst and diatribe, he was content to keep them on side until he had achieved his goal of bankrupting his former employers. The Albion Army, however, saw them a little differently. They were ideal cannon-fodder. Violent, stupid and gullible, they clearly had scope for use at any future trouble spots where the Army chose to rear its ugly head. The Park Royal Mafia were being groomed as the Albion Army's first mercenary army, and by the sound of things, were very close to achieving a spectacular maiden success in Handstead.

Wallace Moffatt stepped through the frosted-glass double doors and surveyed the scene in front of him. The noisy drinkers were predominantly young men in their early twenties, heads shaved to at least a number one, the majority of them in jeans worn high over twelve-lace Doctor Marten boots and braces over T-shirts or Ben Sherman pique polo-shirts. Acres of bare flesh bore tattooed evidence of allegiance to the Albion Army, and the Cross of St George flag and the Confederate flag were a common adornment to all.

The air was heavy with smoke and crude conversations, and Moffatt frowned as he sought the man he had come to join. The last thing he wanted was a shouted, political debate with one of the knuckle draggers; he had far more important things to discuss. His search was ended when Andy Miller barged his way through the mêlée from the bar, clutching a couple of pints of lager which were spilling copiously from the barging.

'You're late,' Miller shouted. 'Grab that table over there, shall we?'

'Yeah – sorry, mate. I got tucked up on the phone to London,' replied Moffatt as he squeezed his huge stomach behind the circular table. It was fixed, like all the furniture in the pub, to prevent it being dispatched through windows.

'What did they want?' asked Miller, taking a sip of his pint. 'Anything important?'

'Routine mostly. They wanted to know how we're getting on up here, whether we needed any more troops – that sort of thing.'

'What did you tell them?'

'That we're OK, we'll get there in the end.'

'Yeah, no doubt about that,' agreed Miller.

The two drank in silence, watching the stormtroopers getting pissed. Moffatt seemed distant and preoccupied.

'Are you all right, Wallace?'

'Yeah, fine. Maybe a little pissed off about the call.'

'Why? No problems, are there?'

'No, I don't think so. It was just the way the conversation went. You know, like they were saying, "What the fuck are you boys doing up there? How long is it going to take to sort out those fucking rag heads?" Just a feeling I got, that's all.'

'You're imagining it,' said Miller, leaning forward to keep his voice low. 'They're getting blinding publicity from this carve-up. They've got to be happy with that.'

'I'm not so sure. I just got a feeling in my water that they'd be happier if it was all done and dusted soon.'

'I don't reckon it will be long, but not soon,' said Miller, taking another swig.

'It'd be nice to know how things are going inside the factory,' Moffatt said gloomily. 'Have you talked to your copper mate lately? He heard anything?'

'I saw him a couple of nights ago but he'd heard nothing new. He's shitting himself he'll get found out but I reckon he'd tell me if anything juicy came across his desk.'

'What does he do again?'

'Fuck knows, works in an office somewhere.'

'What rank is he?'

'I haven't got a clue – never asked him. Why?'

'I just wondered, that's all,' said Moffatt, looking unblinking at Miller who had put his pint down and was staring back at him.

'Are you getting at something, Wallace, because if you've got something on your mind, spit it out, why don't you!'

'Well, he hasn't given us much and you don't know a lot about him, do you?'

'I told you, I met him in the snooker club and we got chatting. His name's Alan, I gave him my home number and he's phoned a couple of times and we've had a few beers.'

'He's given us fuck all of any use though, has he?'

'Well, he's hardly likely to give chapter and verse to a complete fucking stranger, is he? I mean, he's seriously on offer. He doesn't know me from Adam. He's given us a few useful bits – credit where credit's due.'

'Like what?' scoffed Moffatt.

'He gave me the name of the transport company that took on the contract to bus all the Pakis in.'

'That was hardly top secret, was it? Fuck me, the name was all over the back of the buses.'

'That's true, but he gave us that information the day before they started.'

'Yeah,' admitted Moffatt grudgingly, 'but there was fuck all we could do with it.'

'Maybe not immediately, but it's come in handy since.'

'We'd have got that anyway,' said Moffatt, getting irritated. 'Are you sure about this bloke? He's not lining you up for something, is he?'

'Of course I'm not sure about him – I hardly know him, do I? Let's face it, Wallace, if he was in the game of lining me or anyone else up, he'd have had plenty of opportunity to do it before now. If you're not happy with him, I'll cut him off.'

'No, no, don't do that,' replied Moffatt hurriedly. 'I suppose anything is better than nothing.'

'I can't even ring him to gee him up,' said Miller with a deep sigh.

'It makes sense, I suppose,' huffed Moffatt as he drained his pint. 'Keeps himself safe in case you're a wrong 'un.'

They both laughed and Moffatt pointed at Miller's half-finished pint.

'Come on, you big girl's blouse, get that down you. We've got a long night ahead of us.'

Once he'd drained the glass and handed it over, Phil Eldrett sat back against the faded and torn padded upholstery bench and watched Moffatt wade through the heaving bar like Moses parting the Red Sea. The fat bastard was getting a bit twitchy. How long would it be before he insisted on meeting his contact at the nick? Stalling him for a bit longer wouldn't be a problem; after all, he himself supposedly knew very little about him and had no way of contacting him. Right now though, his major problem was trying to drink as little as possible. Every pint he ordered for himself was a shandy, and he took every opportunity to pour some away or spill it, but the alcohol consumption of Moffatt and the shaven-headed bigots was prodigious. The last thing he could do was show out by not drinking the same. His liver couldn't take a lot more; he needed to have another meet with Harrison, and soon.

Chapter Twenty-One

'How's the training going?' asked ACC Brian Seagrove as he took his place at the head of the table in the Conference Room on the seventh floor at Headquarters for what was scheduled to be a regular Friday morning meeting.

DCS John Mills closed the file he'd been leafing through and discreetly adjusted his jacket to feel the small tape recorder in his inside pocket. Only he and Seagrove were present. There was no one there to take the minutes of their meeting; the meetings could always be denied and Mills was determined that he wasn't going to get nailed up if it all went wrong. He'd spent some time testing the effectiveness of the small recorder secreted in his pocket and was happy it would pick up enough in a quiet room.

'The back wheels are smoking, sir; we need to let the handbrake off soon,' he replied.

'Good. No issues then?'

Mills wondered if he was getting information from

somewhere. Maybe the Control Room staff who were present on the Headquarters complex at night were feeding titbits back to him. There seemed little point in mentioning the now fairly frequent fighting between members of the four units of the Special Operations Group as inter-unit rivalry was fostered and nurtured during their night training.

'Everything's going to plan. I'd say we were ahead of schedule. They're getting pretty pissed off with all the classroom work but they've taken to the actual tactics very quickly. We've kept it as simple as possible.'

'That's all very well, but we should start thinking about some likely dates for the off,' replied Seagrove, who'd been busy doing exactly that. His interview for the Chief's post with North Yorkshire had been confirmed for Friday 21 July and he was determined that either the catastrophe or success should be out of the way before he travelled north. He could take steps to reduce the shit that would inevitably hit him in the aftermath of it all going wrong and grab as much credit if it, by some kind of miracle, went right.

'Have you had any thoughts on that score?' Seagrove asked Mills.

'No, not really. We need to coordinate that with Dan Harrison. He's going to have his man tee up the Albion Army to make it work. He really needs to be at these meetings.'

'I'm not sure that's a good idea,' said Seagrove

dismissively, eager to keep witnesses to his machinations to a bare minimum.

'His man is going to need time to make it work,' said an increasingly exasperated Mills. 'He's going to have to give the Albion Army enough notice to make sure they turn up.'

As a career detective, Mills was keenly aware that success in any kind of operation like this was dependent on timing, timing and more timing. Whilst he was keen to let his SOG off the leash, it would all be pointless if the targets of their plan hadn't been given the time to put their heads into the noose. Seagrove seemed to think it was something that could be arranged with a couple of hours' notice, which was the case in his experience of handling budgets.

'How much time?'

'At least forty-eight hours, probably more,' replied Mills, opening his folder again. 'Dan Harrison's man had a meeting with the main player, Wallace Moffatt, on Monday evening. He's apparently been talking to some senior Albion Army figures in London and come away with the feeling that they think there should be a solution up here soon.'

'Well, that sounds positive. They seem to want to bring things to a head, so let's accommodate them.'

'We've got to consider Harrison's man in all this. He's in very deep and he's on offer. Anyone gets wind of who he really is and he's going to disappear. Whatever we agree on as the cover story to instigate this, has got to be believable.'

Seagrove sat back and considered what Mills had said. He was a man of little imagination, unable to comprehend what the undercover officer was going through, now totally immersed in the shit he was there to flush away. He was living on his nerves, having to think in a split second before he said anything unless he compromised himself, always fearful that one day, someone would glance at him twice in dim recognition, always lying awake at night listening for soft footfalls on the landing outside his flat before the front door was kicked off its hinges.

'Could we go next week?' he eventually asked.

'Late next week might be possible.'

'How about a week today?'

'Friday the fourteenth of July? I can't see why not, but we've got to run this past Dan Harrison. He's going to have to get his man comfortable with that date. He's the one who's going to call the shots, deliver the hand grenade for us.'

'That gives us plenty of time,' insisted Seagrove impatiently.

'Sir, we don't have any feel for the nature of the relationship between Harrison's man and Moffatt. Moffatt might have serious reservations about him and just be setting him up. Maybe the call to London was a load of bollocks and the desire to move things on was just a ruse to flush him out. If he suddenly comes up with gold standard information straight after that conversation, then he's out in the open as far as they're concerned. It's too obvious and they won't stand on ceremony, trust me. They'll top him and there's fuck all we can do about it.'

'OK,' agreed Seagrove reluctantly. 'What's the cover story that we're going to slip into them?'

'Dan Harrison and I had a chat about that. We like an idea around the coaches used to transport staff in.'

'Go on, how's that going to work?'

'Well, it appears that the whole aim of the picket is now to stop staff getting into work. There's been widespread intimidation and staff being followed home, cars and houses vandalised, that sort of thing. If the Albion Army were led to believe that there was going to be a concerted effort to break the picket by bussing in contract workers who were going to live on the premises until the strike was resolved, we reckoned the Albion Army would pull out all the stops to prevent them getting in. It should encourage them to turn out their A team, don't you think?'

Seagrove looked worried. 'Jesus, yes. Are we going to be able to cope with a huge turnout by the Albion Army? How many could they put on the street?'

'Three months ago, at their peak attendance, Special Branch estimated they had four to five hundred outside the factory gates, not including the local boneheads from the Park Royal Mafia.'

'And you think we can deal with them with four hundred from the SOG?'

'Those are blinding odds, sir. We're estimating the SOG could deal with eight hundred on a two to one ratio – a thousand at a stretch.'

'A thousand!' exclaimed Seagrove loudly. 'Are you sure?'

'We're not looking to lock too many up, remember,' replied Mills quietly, 'just give them a hammering. We'll go after the ringleaders if we can, but the object of the exercise, as you know, is to send out a clear message. We don't have the resources or cell space to start arresting too many of them, and frankly, nicking them means taking our guys off the street. It'd defeat the whole object of the exercise.'

Seagrove didn't like the sound of things at all. He'd envisaged a bit of a scrap with a few prisoners locked up, job done, but clearly Mills had plans for some sort of pogrom.

'I see,' he said after a long pause. 'And you consider this approach appropriate under the circumstances, do you?'

'It's what the Chief made clear that he wanted,' replied Mills with a smile as he felt the small tape recorder whirring quietly in his jacket pocket. 'Extreme problems require extreme solutions,' he finished, unaware that he was paraphrasing Temporary Chief Constable Chislehurst's own remark to Superintendent Grainger.

'Indeed, indeed,' responded Seagrove, regretting for the first time his decision that these meetings should never be minuted. 'I'm sure he'd have sanctioned it at a higher level. I understand he's had some contact with the Home Office over the issue, as well as the Police Committee. I have some reservations about your tactics, but under these unique circumstances, they're probably what's required.'

You spineless, oily old bastard, thought Mills to himself, but he replied, 'I'll get on then, sir. I need to speak to DCI Harrison and get the ball rolling. I just hope his man can make Friday the fourteenth fit. I'll let you know.'

'Yes, please keep me informed, Mr Mills,' said Seagrove as he watched him leave the room.

DCS Mills returned to his office on the third floor and dialled Dan Harrison's number. He answered immediately.

'Hi Dan, how's things over there?'

'The same old shit, boss, different day,' answered Harrison wearily. 'What can I do for you?'

'How's the rape enquiry going?'

'We've got some leads to follow through, but it's slow work without any forensics,' said Harrison, who had no intention of letting Mills in on Bob Clarke's serial rapist theory – not yet anyway.

'Don't bust a gut on it, Dan; it looks like another non-starter if that's the case,' said Mills. 'Run it for another week or so and then put it away, OK?'

'OK, boss, is that what you were ringing for?'

'Not entirely,' Mills told him. 'I've just come from a meeting with the human jellyfish upstairs.'

Harrison chuckled. 'What did he want? Is everything OK?'

'Oh yes, rowing for shore as you'd expect, but we've got to get this operation up and running.'

'Have you got a date in mind?'

'How about a week today? Friday the fourteenth.'

Harrison whistled softly. 'A week? It's not a lot of time but we could probably slip that in. Is your SOG ready to go? They've not had long.'

'They're raring to go. Let's face it, Dan, out and out violence isn't exactly rocket science. How soon do you think your man can get this date into Moffatt and the Albion Army?'

'I'll see him tonight. I think he'll be quite relieved actually. He's been there a long time and it's starting to tell. He's on the piss with them most nights.'

Mills laughed. 'It's a tough job, isn't it, but someone's got to do it.'

Harrison wasn't laughing. 'I'd rather stick pins in my eyes than do what he does. I couldn't do it, could you?'

'No, sorry, I didn't mean to sound flippant. He's doing a fantastic job for us. Look after him, Dan, and let me know how he does, will you?'

'I will do, boss. How's Mr Seagrove bearing up generally?'

'Like I said, rowing for shore because his name's on the paperwork.'

'I take it you were all wired up?'

'What do you think?' Mills responded. 'One last thing, Dan, have we got a jump-off point sorted out yet?'

'Yeah, we've got the keys to the old bakery on the industrial estate. It's only a quarter of a mile from Red Star Electrics. What I'd suggest is we start moving the SOG on to the site in dribs and drabs the night before we do it. Their vehicles can all be parked up in the old loading bays or go back to Headquarters until it's all finished and they're needed again. Then your troops can make their way on foot to deal with the bad guys.'

'Four hundred hairy-arsed coppers strolling down the road?'

'You're not going to need to deploy them until we're sure the picket is all in place. The Special Branch spotters will be able to give us the info we need, and don't forget, we don't have to make a move until we're good and ready. There's no rush getting to the factory gates. We just don't want to get blown out getting the SOG into the bakery.'

'Agreed. Seagrove went for the story about the factory bussing in contractors to live on the site until the dispute was over, so the Albion Army will be expecting to see a convoy of hired coaches. Tell your man to put that story into Moffatt, will you?'

'I'll speak to him tonight,' repeated Dan Harrison, 'and I'll speak to you again soon, boss.' He hung up and reached into his bottom drawer to fetch out his bottle, glancing at his wristwatch as he did so. It was only 10.30 a.m. and he didn't normally start this early, but circumstances at the moment certainly weren't normal. Pouring himself a large one, he sat back in his creaking chair, pondering his huge workload.

The impending confrontation with the Albion Army was probably near the bottom of his list of things to worry about, alongside Pork Sword Man. Harrison was as satisfied as he could be that, when the wheels dropped off over the creation of the Special Operations Group, he'd be fairly safe. He expected some criticism of his arbitrary decision to infiltrate Phil Eldrett into the swamp that was the Park Royal Estate, but the fact remained that his decision was operationally sound. The lack of any official sanction would be the only issue he'd have to deal with, and he was confident that if push came to shove, the Force would never admit that Eldrett had been planted without formal approval. That would be an admission of a staggering lack of leadership and Headquarters would never allow that. Certainly not with two of the top three bosses seeking to slither a little further up the promotion ladder. No, there would be plenty of retrospective authorities winging about if it came to that.

Pork Sword Man could safely be left to Pete Stevenson and the uniforms when they got back from their attachment to the SOG – but Bob Clarke's serial rapist theory really worried him. Not that he would have to deal with one, but what his investigation would, in all likelihood, uncover about the ineptitude of some of the previous investigations. At best, some of them would have been cursory. Nonexistent in the majority of cases, was what he expected. Too often, detectives in charge of rape investigations where there was little or no forensic evidence, simply did the bare minimum before consigning the enquiry file to a dusty cupboard. A common mindset was that rape wasn't really that high on the crime scale and not worth expending too much energy or resources on. It wouldn't take long for the fact that they had a serial rapist on the loose to leak out of the station and end up first with the local press, and then the national media. Then the pressure would really be on. They were at least eight years behind this bastard and he was cunning and bloody dangerous. If he existed at all.

Harrison knew what the reaction would be if he bothered to run Clarke's theory past any of his fellow DCIs around the Force. Forget it. Why make any more work for yourself with an absolute no-hoper? Wait until you've got a rapist locked up sometime in the future and bleed him dry; maybe fit him up with a couple extra to clear the books a bit.

But whilst Harrison flew by the seat of his trousers and bent rules like they were going out of fashion, doing nothing wasn't his style. Deep down in his guts, he knew Clarke was right. They had a real problem on their hands and absolutely nothing to start looking for him with. And

God help them all when the press got hold of it, particularly some of those aggressive, investigative types.

Even worse would be having to go back to DCS Mills and start pleading for additional manpower to set up a dedicated team to go after their man. There would be little appetite to acknowledge the problem in the first place and even less to start haemorrhaging the Force overtime budget as the team got stuck into sixteen-hour days, seven days a week as they started to play catch-up. Harrison was determined not to let the matter wither and die. Bob Clarke was right – they had a serial rapist on their ground and he was becoming more violent. His escalation could only result in a murder soon and time was running out.

With a deep sigh, Dan Harrison picked up his phone and called Bob Clarke. To his surprise, Clarke answered quickly.

'Thought you might be out and about, Bob,' Harrison said. 'Have you got any good news for me?'

'You probably won't regard it as good news, boss,' replied Clarke, 'but we've traced the other girls who'd moved away. They've all confirmed that items of clothing were never recovered by us. He's definitely collecting trophies.'

'I never doubted your theory, Bob,' said Harrison in a tired voice. 'I just hoped that perhaps you were wrong, or something didn't fit the pattern. But you're right, I'm afraid. Have we got anything back on any of the other actions?'

'The square root of fuck all, sorry.'

'It's to be expected, I suppose, if he's as cunning as you reckon he is. Keep digging, Bob, and let me know if anything crops up, will you? Soon as you've put your spreadsheet together, let me have a look, OK?'

'I should be done in a couple of hours. Are you going to be about?'

'Give me a ring, Bob, I should be here,' said Harrison, pouring himself another large one.

Chapter Twenty-Two

'Those cunning little gupta bastards,' said Wallace Moffatt with a grim smile across his sweaty, podgy face. 'There's nothing they wouldn't stoop to, is there?'

'That's what he said, Wallace, sounded kosher,' said Andy Miller, his loyal lieutenant of the last six months, draining his pint. 'You want another?' he asked nonchalantly.

'In a moment, Andy. Friday, he said – he's sure it's due Friday?'

'That's what he told me, but I only spoke to him for a few seconds.'

'He said they're going to bus a load of contractors in who'll live in the factory until it's all over? Where the fuck are they going to get them from?'

'Fuck knows – you want another? I'm as dry as a witch's tit.'

'How did you meet him again?'

'Completely by accident. Like I told you, I can't get

hold of him and he hadn't rung me, but I bumped into him coming out of the cinema in Ashwell with his missus.'

'And he offered that up?'

'He was asking how things were going for us. I told him we were getting close to shutting the place down and he just came out with it. He said the owners and the cops had come up with the idea of breaking our picket by bussing a load in and leaving them on-site until we gave up.'

'Living in permanently?'

'Yeah, I suppose so. They'd have to bring in their food and water and camp beds and stuff probably. Who knows?'

'Sneaky little brown cunts,' said Moffatt softly, his piggy eyes furrowed in deep thought. 'Then we'll have to make sure their buses don't get in, won't we?'

'That's not going to be easy, is it?'

'They won't stand a fucking chance once we've got the proper help up here.'

'Proper help – what's that mean?'

'I need to put a call in tonight. We'll have plenty of help available on Friday morning. Those devious little bastards,' he said, almost admiringly.

'Fancy another?' asked Phil Eldrett, happy that the baited hook appeared to have been swallowed in its entirety by the obnoxious fat whale sitting opposite him.

'Yeah, get us another pint, Andy, and a little chaser. We've got something to celebrate. After Friday, that fucking factory is *history*.' And Wallace Moffatt slapped his hands together joyfully, his face set in a malicious sneer that managed to make him even uglier than normal.

Shortly after 1 a.m., the telephone on the table by his bed woke Dan Harrison from a sweaty, Bushmills-induced half-sleep. He scrabbled about in the dark looking for the switch to his bedside lamp, but only succeeded in sending the lamp crashing to the floor before he grabbed the phone and rolled back onto his damp pillow.

'Harrison,' he said rustily, his mouth feeling like a desert.

'He bought it,' said the voice at the other end.

'Phil, is that you?' said Harrison, instantly alert and wide awake.

'He bought it without question,' Eldrett slurred.

Harrison chuckled. 'Are you pissed again?'

'I'm slaughtered. I can't keep this up, boss.'

'If he's bought it, you won't have to keep it up much longer. Are you OK?'

'I'm just pissed. And tired,' said Eldrett in a subdued tone.

'Not much longer now, Phil. Stay with it – where are you?'

'Back at the flat.'

'You get some sleep, son. Well done.'

'I've had enough, boss,' continued Eldrett slowly. 'I can't do this any more.'

'You'll have time to let your liver recover soon enough. Christ, you've drunk enough to sink a battleship over the past few months.'

'I mean all of it. It's too much, I've lost everything,' Eldrett went on.

Dan Harrison frowned as he listened to him. He knew Eldrett's marriage had failed and was aware how much he was missing his two young sons, but Harrison hadn't really appreciated how much his star undercover officer had unravelled as a consequence. Of course, a lot of what he'd just said was the alcohol talking, but he'd never heard him so depressed.

'Sleep on it, Phil,' he said urgently. 'We'll talk soon. You've got a shedload of leave due to you. Why don't you have a nice long holiday somewhere hot and think things over? Maybe you and your missus can sort things out.'

'I've had enough, I want to stop,' said Eldrett, his voice sounding small and remote in the dark.

Harrison had long forgotten how the disintegration of his own marriage had affected him. His own daughters were now strangers to him. He dreaded Christmas, his birthday and particularly Father's Day, but religiously sent cards to his girls in the vain hope that one day they would respond. But his personal life remained an empty space and he had thrown himself further still into his job, working all the hours he could to forget what he had sacrificed. Clearly, Eldrett had recognised what he had lost as well and decided it was too high a price.

'I understand, Phil, really I do,' said Harrison softly. 'We'll talk when this is all over. I don't want to lose you, old son, but I know where you're coming from and it's rough. You get some sleep, OK?'

'OK, boss. I'm sorry, but I can't do this any more.'

'I know. We'll call it a day after Friday. Are you going to be there?'

'Yeah, I'll have to be; it'd look strange if I wasn't.'

'Keep your head down, Phil, it's not going to be pleasant. Can you get yourself somewhere where you can slip away when it kicks off?'

'I doubt it. What's the plan, boss?'

'I'd tell you if I thought it would help, Phil, but the less you know, the better. You understand that, don't you?'

Eldrett knew he was right. If between now and Friday his cover was blown, there was very little he could reveal to the Albion Army regardless of what they did to him before they topped him and he disappeared from the face of the planet. He knew DCI Harrison would move heaven and earth to protect him, but that he would also have planned for him getting uncovered by the Army. There had to be a limit to what he knew to ensure the operation succeeded.

'I know,' he replied wearily. 'See you sometime on Friday, OK?'

'Ring me, Phil, as soon as you can. You can come home on Friday.'

Eldrett didn't reply. He didn't have a home to return to

currently, but maybe it wasn't too late to remedy that. Perhaps he and Sarah could bridge the gulf that had opened up between them and raise their boys together. He hung up and stretched out on the grubby sofa in his dingy flat on the Park Royal Estate, closed his eyes and began to sob as the enormous weight of his loss crushed him.

In his bedroom, Dan Harrison retrieved the lamp from the floor and lay back on his bed, deep in thought. If Eldrett gave up his undercover work was going to be an enormous loss to crime investigation in Handstead, but the poor bloke had clearly reached his limit and enough was enough. God, the jobs he'd pulled off in Horse's Arse and elsewhere in the county – how would they ever find someone with his skills again? Still, he'd be going out on a real high. Breaking the Albion Army picket at the Red Star Electrics factory would be a fitting finale to his time with Harrison.

The DCI rolled over and tried to get back to sleep, but his mind was racing again. Soon he was in his sparse kitchen, pouring himself a medicinal glass of Bushmills and pondering an uncertain future. He stood at his kitchen window and stared out at the silent, sleeping town. Every house he could see was in darkness, its occupants probably sleeping soundly, blissfully unaware of what went on to try and keep them safe, to bring law and order to their lawless town. He was reminded of George Orwell's comment that people only slept soundly in their beds at night because rough men stood ready to do violence on their behalf. Was the serial rapist asleep in one of those darkened houses, or out and about on its quiet streets and darkened pathways?

Sometimes Harrison wondered if it was all worth it, all the scheming and sacrifices that people like himself and Eldrett and many others made for an entirely ungrateful public – and for senior officers whose only priority was to ensure that nothing nasty ever stuck to them, yet who would shamelessly grab as much credit as they could for jobs they knew little about.

Phil Eldrett's despondency had got to him and he was starting to question his own priorities. What would he do when he retired? He had no one to share his spare time with, few friends outside the Job and no hobbies to pursue. All he knew was the Job, and without it he had nothing.

Shortly before midnight on Thursday 13 July, Inspector Phil Gilbert and Detective Chief Superintendent John Mills sat in a hired Ford Capri parked up on the Ridgemount Industrial Estate. They were both in civilian clothes and the use of a hired vehicle was a deliberate choice. The local toerags would all know the unmarked vehicles used by the CID, and even if they didn't know the registration numbers the cops showed little imagination with their exclusive use of Mark Two Ford Escorts, usually in Air Force blue or beige and always minus the hubcaps.

Mills was not taking any chances. They had driven slowly around the estate for over an hour and not encountered a living soul. There appeared to be no overnight security officers anywhere other than at the Red Star Electrics factory, and they had only been brought in three months ago as fears of a night-time attack on the premises had grown. The estate was still and quiet, the only sign of life having been a mangy old dog fox sniffing round a dead magpie. Now they sat outside the deserted premises of the Crusty Bread Company, long since departed, and now the intended jump-off point for Operation Chaka.

'Seems all quiet, boss,' said Gilbert, leaning forward to check in the Capri's nearside wing mirror.

'Yeah, we should be OK. Have you got the keys?'

Phil Gilbert held aloft a large bunch of keys from the footwell in front of him.

Mills nodded. 'Call them in, Phil. Two at a time, fifteen minutes apart.'

Gilbert picked up the hand-held main set radio that he'd placed between his thighs, checked that it was correctly locked into the dedicated Channel Two, and transmitted quietly.

'Delta Hotel, Operation Chaka is a go. Contact the Control Inspector, please, and get them on the move. Two coaches at a time; fifteen minutes apart. Issue destination details to the four Unit Sergeants now.'

'Understood,' said the controller, who didn't have a

clue what Operation Chaka was all about and frankly didn't give a damn. 'Operation Chaka is a go.' He cleared the air and glanced down at the envelope Sellotaped above his radio position on which was written in bold red capitals – FOR THE CONTROL INSPECTORS' EYES ONLY IN THE EVENT OPERATION CHAKA GOES LIVE – and signed by Assistant Chief Constable Brian Seagrove.

'Sir,' called the operator over his shoulder to the raised pod in the centre of the room where his Inspector sat. 'One for you – Operation Chaka just went live,' and he held up the envelope.

Five minutes later, the Control Room Inspector walked into a small classroom in the Training Centre where the four Special Operations Group Sergeants were huddled over a large map spread out on two tables they'd pushed together. They looked up as he came in and stopped talking.

'Operation Chaka is a go,' he said nervously. 'I've got your destination details here. Your vehicles are to depart immediately, two at a time at fifteen-minute intervals, and you will rendezvous with Inspector Gilbert in Swallowfields on the Ridgemount Industrial Estate in Handstead.'

'OK, thanks,' said one of the Sergeants as they went back to their map. The Inspector hadn't made to leave so the four of them looked up at him.

'Do you need anything else?' asked the Inspector, hopeful that they might let him in on the big secret.

'No,' answered the same Sergeant, folding up their large map. They continued to stare at the Inspector, who had started to colour up. Then he gave up, turned on his heel and hurried back across the car park, where eleven forty-seater coaches, with curtains drawn, were waiting for the Special Operations Group, drivers snoozing on the back seats. Whatever Operation Chaka was, mused the Inspector, it promised to be a fucking bloodbath and he prayed he and his shift were safely in bed before it kicked off.

The four SOG Sergeants went immediately to the vast accommodation blocks on the far side of the parade square, where they and their units had spent so much time in the past week, and began to call them out. The atmosphere in the blocks was tense. The men had all been in full kit since 8 p.m., checking and re-checking what they would be using, rehearsing their lines, waiting for the off. The shouting and joking and messing around was gone, replaced with the grim determination that came with the knowledge that very soon, something very big was going to take place, of which they would be an integral part. But they still didn't know what or where. Numerous sweepstakes were underway on all the units, but the strict secrecy that Mills had sought had been achieved. Very few people were in the know.

'Grab your kit, boys, we're off,' called Sergeant Richard Holding. 'Get on to your designated coaches as quickly and quietly as you can. Keep the curtains drawn at all times. Come on, this is it.'

In the other blocks, the other Sergeants were similarly engaged, and within fifteen minutes ten out of the eleven designated coaches were full, engines running, waiting to go. The officers on board remained quiet, and while some closed their eyes in a bid to relax ahead of what promised to be a long day, all were coiled like springs, eager to be released for whatever their extraordinary training had been in aid of. The eleventh coach, which had only been required in the event that one of the others broke down, left early and began its return to the depot, leaving the four SOG Sergeants in the car park checking their clipboards.

'Have we got everyone? No one's deserted, have they?' asked one of the original Patrol Group Sergeants. The others confirmed that all 400 SOG officers were on board.

'OK, numbers one and two can get on their way. The others will follow at fifteen-minute intervals. I'll be on coach ten. See you there, boys,' he said with a grim smile, shaking the others' hands.

Twelve minutes later, the first two coaches rolled into Swallowfields on the Ridgemount Industrial Estate with their lights off and continued slowly until the driver of the lead coach was flagged down by Inspector Gilbert, who stepped into the road. He boarded it, looked down the aisle at the tense faces, and smiled at them.

'Ready to go, boys? It won't be long now.'

There were a few muttered acknowledgements and

returned smiles, but none were in the mood for clamour. Not yet anyway.

'Get it in there,' Gilbert told the driver, indicating the now open gates to the old bakery, 'round the back to the loading bays. Once you've dropped off, you can go back to Headquarters, OK?'

He then turned back to the passengers.

'This is the drop-off location, boys. Once you're off the coach, go through the loading bays and into the main body of the factory. There are snack-packs and water, tea and coffee waiting for you there with Mr Mills. Get yourselves as comfortable as you can. Once you're all in, Mr Mills will give you the full story. Try and relax, this is going to be fucking great.'

There were a few tense laughs, but any step into the unknown was always going to generate some nerves.

By 3 a.m. the huge empty bakery, whose walls were impregnated with the smell of its former, more peaceful occupation, was packed with the 400 Special Operations Group officers. At the far end of the old bread production area, twenty hot-water urns steamed away alongside a mountain of bottled water. Arc lights powered by small petrol generators outside the rear of the building provided the only dim light in four corners of the area. There were no tables or chairs, so most of the officers were sprawled on the filthy floor in groups chatting quietly.

There had been a few rows as usual about the

disappearance of the only half-decent hot drinks, the long tubes of hot chocolate acquired by the early arrivals for their own units, leaving only the almost undrinkable tea and coffee. The coffee in particular could have been used to creosote garden fences. And the contents of the snack-packs had generated a lot of trading. Those officers unfortunate enough to get lumbered with the disgusting portions of fruit cake went in search of those with Penguin biscuits, and any with processed cheese and chutney sandwiches either swapped them for anything or went hungry.

Despite the numbers crammed into the room, the noise was little more than a businesslike hum. There was no shouting or raucous laughter, just the drone of low, tense voices and the almost palpable spark of testosterone-fuelled nervous energy in the stuffy air. From the street outside, the factory appeared as it had done for the last six years – deserted and forlorn. In fact, it seethed with aggressive life, eager to burst into the fresh air and get on with things.

DCS John Mills stepped to the front of the crowd of officers and stood patiently waiting for silence. It came a lot quicker than the first day the SOG had met him. Within seconds, every face in the vast hall had turned to him, waiting for an explanation of what they were about to embark on. All 400 were soon on their feet.

'Good morning, gentlemen,' began Mills, casting his

eyes around the hall. 'Welcome to Operation Chaka.'

There were a few knowing murmurs and whispers before he continued, 'An explanation, in case one is needed: this Operation is named after Chaka Zulu, possibly the greatest Zulu chief and the creator of the Zulu nation that took on, and nearly beat, one of the most powerful empires ever known – the British Empire. Under the circumstances, the use of his name is entirely appropriate. As you know, you are now formed into four units of one hundred men. Whilst smaller than the units they used, your formations are based on the Zulu Impi. They were formidable warriors and we expect the same from you.'

Mills could still see many furrowed brows and frowns. It was time to enlighten them all.

'Later this morning, you will be deployed in the style of Zulu Impis against the Albion Army picket that will be in place outside the Red Star Electrics factory.'

There was a loud intake of breath and a few shouts of, '*Yes!*' and Mills was amused to note a number of officers begin to take money off their colleagues as they clearly won the sweepstakes that they had all been running. He held his hands up to silence the excited murmuring.

'You've trained hard, you're ready to go. It won't be long now. I was going to give you a few lines from William Shakespeare but I don't think that's needed,' he said to loud laughter.

He paused again and looked long and hard at the men

in front of him, on whom so much depended. How ironic, he mused, that these unloved dregs of the Force now held the future reputations and career of certain senior officers in their grubby hands. Not least his own, but in truth he had moved beyond that very self-centred stance over the last weeks as he had got to know them. They were generally regarded in their Divisions as the scum of the earth, but collectively they were an extraordinary salvation, bringing their innate love of violence and all things devious and underhand to an operation designed to combat an evil entity.

Mills had warmed to the reprobates of the Special Operations Group in a fashion he could barely believe. They were his babies and now he felt as close to them as he had ever felt to any squad he had been a part of during his career. He would fight their corner whatever happened, and he expected repercussions in the corridors of power at the conclusion of the events destined to happen in a few hours' time. If it failed, the snakes at Headquarters would be looking for scapegoats. He knew he'd be lined up for that role, but he was determined his SOG would not be.

'You've got a few hours to try and relax, boys, so use it if you can. The Special Branch observation points are going in about now to monitor the arrival of the pickets so we'll have a good idea of numbers before you move. You'll go in as you've practised and you'll go in hard and loud. We haven't made any provisions for you to take any prisoners,' he finished, to a huge roar which exploded from the group. It occurred to him that the noise might well be audible outside and he urgently signalled for quiet.

'My fault,' he laughed. 'We've got to keep the noise down. Surprise is the key to this operation. Relax, boys, we'll let you know when it's time.'

As the 400 buoyant SOG officers began to mill about and talk excitedly, Mills and Gilbert conferred again.

'Are the Special Branch observation posts in, Phil?'

'Just checked, boss. All in and in radio contact. Nothing's come through yet, but they're expecting the first arrivals about five a.m.'

'OK, good. Have we got the Traffic boys ready to put the roadblocks in around the estate once they're all in?'

'Yes. They're ready to go.'

'Just so long as they understand that means *no one* gets on to the estate – but especially the media.'

'It was made perfectly clear. If there's one thing we can rely on them for, it's being a fucking pain in the arse. Nothing will get in once they've shut the roads.'

'It had fucking better not,' said Mills grimly. 'We want as few independent witnesses to this as possible.'

'Do you fancy a drink, boss?'

'Yeah, thanks. Get me a hot chocolate, will you, Phil?'

'That could be difficult,' chuckled Gilbert, 'but I'll see what I can do.'

As Gilbert disappeared into the crowd to see if he could beg, borrow or steal a cardboard cup of hot chocolate for him, Mills flicked through his operation folder and came across his hastily scrawled notes, which included Henry V's stirring speech on the eve of Agincourt. He laughed to himself as he read the line again about gentlemen in England now a-bed. Very true, he thought to himself. There were certain gentlemen currently in bed who considered themselves cursed and they hadn't slept a wink. Their lack of sleep, however, had nothing to do with any regrets at missing out on the fun. Temporary Chief Constable Chislehurst and Assistant Chief Constable Brian Seagrove were dreading today and had been up most of the night fretting about it. Chislehurst had phoned Seagrove just after 1 a.m., ostensibly to wish him good luck, but in reality to let him know that if it all went wrong, it was down to him. And if it went wrong, that was the end of his hopes to become the next Chief Constable of North Yorkshire. Neither had given a moment's thought to the 400 SOG officers who now milled around in the dusty old bakery, waiting for the word to take on a likely larger adversary and save their miserable careers.

Chapter Twenty-Three

Just after 5.30 a.m., the Special Branch observation posts on the outskirts of the industrial estate began to report the first arrivals. A convoy of eight hire vans turned up, followed by numerous vehicles, registered to addresses from all round the country, and then came crowds of walkers. These were the local foot soldiers of the Park Royal Mafia, arriving for their date with destiny. Soon the road leading down to the cul-de-sac where Red Star Electrics stood was filling with noisy, aggressive pickets. They were in a great mood. As they arrived in front of the factory gates they were delighted to see that the dozen uniformed coppers that they normally encountered had taken refuge inside the factory compound and looked less than enthusiastic about confronting them. The abuse and insults soon began flying. Keen eyes were watching the pickets arrive from points all around them through binoculars.

'We've counted four hundred and seventy past the

junction with Swallowfields,' radioed the team watching the only road down to the cul-de-sac.

In the old bakery, SOG officers were clustered around hand-held main sets listening to the build-up.

'We've got a head count of four five eight in front of the gates,' reported the Special Branch team situated high in the attic of Red Star Electrics itself.

DCI Dan Harrison was with that team, eagerly sweeping his binoculars over the heaving pickets, trying to find Phil Eldrett. He'd far rather he was a no-show today but knew that his bona-fides dictated that he'd have to be there. And then he saw him, deep in the crowd and talking earnestly into the ear of the repulsive Wallace Moffatt. He watched as the fat man's piggy eyes screwed up in amusement and then he threw his head back and laughed like a drain at something Eldrett had said.

'Over here, mate,' called Harrison to the photographer standing behind him. 'Right in the middle and just to the right of two skinheads in combat jackets – you got them?'

The photographer moved quickly, throwing his camera with the long telephoto lens to his eye and moving the lens over the crowd.

'Fat bloke, shaved head, wearing a pale blue sleeveless shirt?' he asked. 'That's him – Wallace Moffatt. Talking to a tall fair-headed skinhead in a white T-shirt.'

'Yeah, got them,' said the photographer, hitting the button and the motor beginning to whir as he took a dozen shots.

'Can you try and get as many of those two as you can, mate,' said Harrison, 'but especially the tall skinhead. We need to know who he speaks to.'

'OK, boss, no problems. We've got a photographer on the other side of the road as well. Do you want me to get him to do the same as well?'

'Yeah, good idea. Thanks.'

The Special Branch photographer picked up the landline phone that had been specially installed and was soon talking to the observation point located on the upper floor of a cable manufacturing company.

By 6.30 a.m. the crowd of aggressive pickets had swelled again.

'We're counting six-fifty plus at the factory gates,' transmitted Harrison. 'Anyone getting any more dribs and drabs coming on to the estate?'

'Ones and twos,' reported the observers plotted up near Swallowfields. 'Nothing significant – reckon you've got most of them with you now.'

'Zulu One, Zulu One, are you monitoring this?' called Harrison, using DCS Mills's designated call sign.

'All received,' responded Mills, glancing at his wristwatch. 'Give them a few more minutes. Roadblocks can go in at six forty-five a.m.'

'Understood,' responded Harrison, before picking up the landline to send that instruction to the main Force Control room and get the Traffic boys on the move.

'Get kitted up, boys,' called Mills, back in the vast hall

of the bakery. 'You move in ten minutes. You're up first, Phil,' he said to Gilbert, who was standing alongside him, checking his kit. 'You all set?'

'All ready, boss,' he replied, his stomach churning with apprehension and not a little fear. 'All right if I say something to the boys?'

Mills nodded his agreement and then called loudly for silence which he got immediately.

'We're on the move soon, guys,' said Phil Gilbert. The only sound in the building was his voice as the generators had been switched off once it had got light, and quiet though it was, his voice seemed to be carried to the back of the hall on the shafts of sunshine streaming into the vast room. The beams of light were filled with the flour dust that they were all now covered in, and gave the impression that the place was on fire. Gilbert looked at his dirty warriors, faces pale, and strained with apprehension.

'There's maybe seven hundred of them out there and four hundred of us.' He paused to let them digest what appeared to be dreadful odds.

'Four hundred of us – all of whom will fight tooth and nail. How many of that lot do you think will go head to head with us? One hundred, two hundred? If we're lucky, more than that, but you know as well as I do that the majority will shit themselves and look to get away as soon as we move in. The trouble is, they've got nowhere to go, but they won't want to hang around for a scrap with us. If the majority do have a go, it'll be as a means to get away.

We have total surprise on our side; they'll never have seen anything like us before. These odds are meaningless, boys; we're going to be fighting amongst ourselves to get at them.'

There was an audible release of tension as the officers began to laugh at the thought of what awaited the Albion Army members and the Park Royal Mafia gathered on the picket at the factory gates. None of the SOG officers had really given much thought to the shock and awe their appearance and tactics might engender in the pickets. To a man they'd been hugely impressed by what they'd seen in the course of their training, and now it began to dawn on them that soon they'd get to see it for themselves in real live Technicolor.

'Check your kit, check the kit of the man next to you,' called Gilbert above the increased chatter. 'We go in ten minutes.'

'Cry havoc and let loose the dogs of war, eh, Phil?' asked DCS Mills with a wide smile on his face.

'Something like that, boss,' replied Gilbert, 'but not as eloquent.'

'Had the same effect, I reckon,' said Mills, as he patted him affectionately on his NATO helmet. 'You take care out there, Phil, OK?' he continued, looking at his face encased in the tight confines of the dark blue, visored helmet.

Gilbert was already sweating heavily, a combination of the tension building up inside him and the warmth in the old bakery. The clear blue sky visible through the skylights in the roof, and the warm beams of sunlight hitting the dusty floor like searchlights, promised another hot day outside. Not ideal conditions in which to operate vigorously in full riot kit, but they were all young and fit and their bellies were full of fire. The weather was the least of their worries.

The chanting outside the gates of the factory had reached fever pitch. It was deafening. The National Anthem had been bellowed ad nauseam but 'Jerusalem' had been a bit of a disaster as it became obvious that very few of the shaven-headed bigots knew many of the words. Now the usual chants of, 'There ain't no black in the Union Jack,' and, 'Paki, Paki, Paki, out, out, out,' echoed around the cul-de-sac, bouncing back and forth off the surrounding buildings until the words were lost in each other. The contorted faces of the pickets were bathed in sweat as the hot July sun began to rise behind them, and some had already discarded their tops to display their tattooed torsos which were already beginning to pink up. It was a great day to smash Red Star Electrics. The coaches carrying the scab contractors would be here any time – and then they could really get to work.

'Did you hear that?' shouted Wallace Moffatt to Phil Eldrett, who was still standing next to him shouting himself hoarse. Moffatt had turned and was looking back up the long incline behind them that led up the cul-de-sac.

'No, what?' shouted Eldrett, turning to follow his gaze.

'Sounded like thunder. Or a train.'

Some of the others had also heard it though, and gradually the entire picket stopped chanting and turned to look in the same direction. The road behind them was deserted. The only sound was the twittering of birds in the trees that lined the road and the far-off roar of traffic from the motorway. Then they heard it again. A low rumbling sound that could have been distant thunder, but which faded away into silence. Then it came again, slightly closer. Not thunder, there was no chance of that in the perfect blue sky marked only with the distant vapour trails of airliners far above them. More like a steam engine or some other large machine pumping away. The pickets remained silent, looking back up the road, totally engrossed by the approaching noise.

'Here we go,' muttered Dan Harrison as he kept his binoculars trained on the crest of the road. 'It's going to happen.' He quickly swung the binoculars down to the crowd to pick out Phil Eldrett and saw him glance back towards the Red Star Electrics factory and up towards the window in the attic where he knew the observation team was located. He looked confused and worried.

'Get the fuck out of there, Phil,' whispered Harrison to himself. 'Get the fuck out.' He swung the binoculars back up to the crest of the road in time to see the sole figure of a cop in full riot kit and carrying a small round shield and a long baton walk to the crest and then stand still facing the massed pickets. For what seemed like an eternity, the cop stood still, his arms by his sides.

'Zulu One, Zulu One,' transmitted Harrison into his radio. 'They're in place and ready to go.'

DCS Mills didn't respond to the message. He no longer had any control over the Special Operations Group. Everything that happened now would be dictated by developments and decisions on the ground. He dropped to his haunches and sipped from a cup of hot chocolate that he'd finally found, listening to the excited voices on the radio.

Inspector Phil Gilbert stood and watched the Albion Army pickets gathered about 200 yards ahead of him. They were moving anxiously around like a pan of simmering water, clearly asking one another what the fuck this was all about. He could feel the sweat trickling down his spine into the top of his trousers, and his entire body was cooking inside the heavy blue, fire resistant overalls he was wearing. His head felt like it was about to burst inside his pressure cooker of a helmet, yet he felt no real discomfort. All his senses seemed to have been fine-tuned. He could hear the creaking of his leather boots as he flexed his feet and his heavy leather gauntlets as he squeezed the handle of his shield and the ribbed handle of his baton. He could hear his heart thumping inside his head as he waited, and waited; turning up the tension little by little, as he'd been taught.

'What the fuck is all this about?' asked Moffatt nervously, turning to Eldrett.

'Fuck knows,' he replied, being totally honest with Moffatt for the first time since they had become allies.

'Your man never mentioned anything about this then?'

'No, not a word. I told you, he just said they were going to bus a load of contractors in.'

'Well, where the fuck are they then?' shouted Moffatt angrily.

'How the bloody hell would I know?' responded Eldrett in a similar tone. 'I told you everything he told me, which wasn't a lot.'

'So what the fuck is going on here now?' continued Moffatt, turning back to face the lone copper who was still standing motionless, just watching them.

'I don't know,' replied Eldrett truthfully. 'I really haven't a clue.'

Suddenly, the sole copper raised his shield and baton high above his head and seconds later, lines of coppers similarly dressed and equipped moved to either side of him from where they had been out of sight below the crest of the road. They formed up in ranks 50 wide on either side and 400 deep, and stood mutely watching the wide-eyed pickets. The road was completely blocked by the silent, menacing coppers and it was beginning to dawn on some of the pickets, Wallace Moffatt included, that they were trapped like rats with nowhere to go except through this seemingly solid wall of tooled-up policemen.

'Oh fuck,' said Eldrett, as he realised what was about to happen.

'What the fuck is this?' shouted Moffat, grabbing him by his sweaty T-shirt with both hands.

Eldrett angrily pulled his hands away and glared at him. 'We're in the shit, is what's happening,' he said sharply.

'Well, who are this lot then?'

'I don't know, but I doubt they're local. There's too many of them.'

'So what do we do now?' said Moffatt nervously, as his confidence and bravado seeped away under the relentless gaze of hundreds of silent police officers.

'We fight them, Wallace,' replied Eldrett simply and looking at him with contempt. 'We fight them because they're sure as hell not here to talk to us.'

Moffatt gazed at the bullet-headed cretins who surrounded him, all looking for some advice and guidance from him, their untouchable and all-conquering leader, but he had nothing to offer them. A classic bully, he was now completely exposed as full of nothing but shit, finally fronted up by an even bigger bully. And the bigger bully now staring at him was clearly intent on making a mess of him.

'What do we do, Wallace?' asked a frightened, spotty glue-sniffer from the Park Royal Mafia, one of the many feral youths from the estate who had signed up for what had been sold as a day booting some Pakis about but now seemed to have 'total fucking disaster' written all over it.

Before he could say anything, the first copper who had wandered into view began to sing and chant at the top of his voice, stamping his feet as he did so, moving along the lines of silent, motionless coppers. The time Phil Gilbert and the other members of the Special Operations Group had spent in the classroom with Dr Samuel Buthelezi, cultural attaché at the South African Embassy in London, was about to pay off. The huge sums spent on the good doctor's considerable bar bills and his expensive hotel accommodation were about to prove a good investment, as Gilbert and the SOG put into practice everything he had taught them. In passable Zulu, Gilbert began to sing in a decent baritone, the chant lifting up and down as he had seen in *Zulu* and *Zulu Dawn*.

'Izika pai, izika pai, zoh me, Sali-lah,
Izika pai, izika pai, zoh me, Sali-lah.'

'Zi-tour, zi-tour, zoh me, Sali-lah,' continued Gilbert alone, stamping his feet and raising his shield and baton towards the frozen Albion Army pickets. Then the other 400 responded, *'Zi-tour, zi-tour, zoh me Sali-lah,'* this time rhythmically stamping their feet, raising clouds of dust.

'Zinga be hynd zoh me, Sali-lah,
Zinga be hynd zoh me, Sali-lah.'

'What the fucking hell is going on?' asked a desperate Wallace Moffatt. He and many of his companions were looking for an escape route. There appeared to be only one way out – through the singing, chanting, lunatic coppers.

Gilbert continued the singing, raising the tension in the air as he did so, leading the SOG in the chants Dr Buthelezi had painstakingly taught them.

'We shall slay, we shall slay. Is it not so, my brothers?
Our spears shall blush blood-red. Is it not so, my brothers?
For we are the sucklings of Chaka. Blood is our milk, my brothers.
Awake, children of the Umletwa, awake!
The vulture wheels, the jackal sniffs the air.
Awake, children of the Umletwa – cry aloud ye ringèd men.
There is the foe, we shall slay them. Is it not so, my brothers?
S'gee! S'gee! S'gee!
Yonder is the kraal of the white man – a little kraal, my brothers.
We shall eat it up, we shall trample it flat, my brothers.
But where is the white man's cattle, where are his oxen, my brothers?'

The entire Special Operations Group were now singing and stamping their feet in unison, a permanent cloud of dust enveloping them. It was a terrifying sight – and then they began to advance slowly towards the pickets in crouched attack-style, their shields held close to their bodies, batons thrust aloft. Then they rushed forward twenty paces, shouting a loud, low *'Ooh'* sound before they stopped and began to beat their shields. It was the noise of the distant thunder or approaching train that Wallace Moffatt had heard earlier.

Still the Albion Army picket had not responded. They appeared to be rooted to the spot, the majority saucer-eyed at the spectacle. Inspector Gilbert upped the tempo of the singing and shield hammering, beginning to dance around in front of the SOG like a demented dervish. The sound crashed about the transfixed pickets as effectively as any fusillade of gunfire. Most were incapable of any sort of response.

Gilbert increased the tempo until all 400 SOG officers were chanting, stamping and surging forward like a sea threatening to burst through a dam, hammering wildly at their shields. He waited until the SOG resembled a drag car with its back wheels about to burst until he released them.

'Jii!' he screamed at the top of his voice. 'Death!' And with the rest of the group following his cry, the SOG raced headlong at the pickets. *'Jii, jii!'* they howled, as they covered the ground between them like an incoming, unstoppable tide.

Chapter Twenty-Four

'It's started,' transmitted Harrison tersely, as he watched the SOG sprinting towards the factory gates, and in the disused bakery DCS John Mills stretched out on the dirty floor amongst the rubbish with his hands behind his head and smiled.

Inspector Phil Gilbert's assessment of the likely opposition they would face had been spectacularly wrong. Fewer than fifty of the Albion Army pickets had the stomach to face such an onslaught. Whilst the others fled like the cowards they were towards the factory fence line, they turned to face the wall of screaming coppers sprinting towards them. But that was all they did. The shock the SOG had generated was almost total and the defiance they showed towards them was little more than token.

The first wave of a hundred SOG hit them full on, sweeping them away as they disappeared under a hail of baton blows and boots. And then the entire SOG fell on the disintegrating body of the pickets, smashing them with blows to the head and body and vicious swipes with the edges of their shields. Those pickets with their backs to the factory fence began to try and climb it to reach safety, but were greeted with truncheon blows from the coppers stationed safely inside. The air rang to the sound of the still shouting SOG and the crack of batons on heads, breaking bones and the screams of the panicked pickets. The dusty road was littered with their groaning or more usually unconscious bodies, and their blood soon had the road surface slick and sticky. And still the SOG went for them. Any attempt at surrender was ignored, with pickets being felled like nine-pins as the attack continued. It was a massacre.

In the middle of the mêlée, Phil Eldrett had grabbed the traumatised Moffatt and begun to haul him towards the edge of the battle. He had spotted the doorway of the cable manufacturing company and it appeared to him that the bulk of the fighting was now confined to the centre where the pickets had been forced. There was less activity to the sides where escape might be possible as the SOG surged through them like a knife through butter. He began to barge his way through the screaming throng, raising his forearm to ward off a baton blow to his head. He felt the bone crack and cried out with pain, continuing to push on, dragging Moffatt with him. And then they burst through the crowd and he realised they were out of the worst of it.

'Run – for fuck's sake, run!' he shouted. Moffatt looked at him with sightless eyes. He was completely out of it.

'Fuck you,' hissed Eldrett, dropping his arm and beginning to sprint away up the road. Dozens of other bleeding pickets had also managed to break away from the cull and were also headed in the same direction. The great Albion Army picket of the Red Star Electrics factory had been completely smashed by the Special Operations Group Impis and now all that was left for the survivors was the desire to escape unscathed.

Eldrett was running as fast as he could, but as he glanced over his shoulder, his blood ran cold. Three of the coppers had split away from the core of the fighting and were chasing him. Clearly, these three had him in their sights, and when they caught up with him, they would show him no mercy.

Dan Harrison was desperately searching through his binoculars for a glimpse of Phil Eldrett. Then he saw him pulling Moffatt through the crowd. What the fuck was he doing? He should leave that fat lump of shit and get the fuck out of there. He watched as the pair broke free from the edge of the fighting and then breathed a sigh of relief as Eldrett abandoned Moffatt and began to sprint away. He continued to watch and saw Moffatt felled by a huge blow to the back of his cannonball-shaped head and then he saw three of the SOG start to go after Eldrett.

'Oh fuck,' he murmured, throwing the binoculars on

to the desk and racing out of the observation post and down the stairs four at a time.

Eldrett was keeping a good distance between himself and his pursuers, but the effort was starting to tell on him. His copious alcohol intake over the past few months had impacted badly on his previous decent levels of fitness and now he was suffering. His lungs felt like they were about to burst and his legs were burning from the unfamiliar exercise. He was fucked, but he daren't stop.

Racing around a corner, he headed for the factories at the bottom of the road where he could see it curved left, glancing over his shoulder again. The other coppers were still coming after him, their faces set in grim determination beneath their blue helmets, off which the fierce sun reflected like sparks. Jesus, would these bastards ever give up?

He rounded the bend, running in the middle of the road, and came to an abrupt halt. His heart racing, he realised he was in a dead end. Turning quickly, he saw the three coppers run round the bend behind him and also come to a stumbling halt. Like him, they bent forward, hands on their knees, panting heavily from the brief but wild chase. Sweat ran down Phil Eldrett's nose and he watched the steady drops begin to fall into the dust at his feet. None of them was going anywhere and he was in the shit.

'Listen, guys,' he said breathlessly, standing upright

and holding his hands out to the three coppers who were staring at him. 'We're on the same side.'

'Well, well, Mr Whitey sure wants to be our friend now, don't he?' snarled Alfie Holding, unfastening the strap under his chin and ripping his NATO helmet off. He dropped it to the road and wiped the sweat from his face with a gloved hand. 'Seems to me we ain't never been on the same side. Suddenly today you want to be my brother, is that it? I don't think so, *white boy*,' Alfie said in an exaggerated Jamaican patois.

Eldrett realised how he would appear to the black officer who now stood in front of him. He'd been part of the Albion Army picket and dressed accordingly; his head shaved, always in the Albion Army uniform of T-shirt, braces and high-lace boots.

'Look, mate, I'm an undercover police officer,' he pleaded. 'I work for DCI Harrison at Handstead. You can check with him. Nick me now or something if you're not sure, but we're definitely on the same side.'

Alfie Holding laughed loudly. 'You an undercover cop? Man, that's something. You got your warrant card with you?'

'Of course not. I can't carry shit like that with me on a job like this, can I? Come on, be reasonable.'

'Us be reasonable?' demanded Ben Holding, also taking off his helmet and moving alongside his younger brother. 'You're the arsehole been shouting your mouth off about the niggers and coons and wogs and Pakis taking over your fucking country. Us be reasonable? Nah, I don't think so, Mr White Boy. You're going to get your nasty white arse kicked, brother.'

'Listen, I'm an undercover cop, for fuck's sake. I was never anything to do with those cunts. I've been working undercover amongst them for months,' said Eldrett nervously as the three cops began to walk slowly towards him. His mouth had gone dry and he licked his lips.

'You're making a big mistake,' he continued, backing away from them.

'You made the mistake, you white arsehole,' said Toby Holding, also throwing his helmet to the ground. 'You ran down a dead end, boy.'

The three Holding boys, third-generation West Indian but Manchester born and bred, laughed loudly. All their lives they had endured taunts and barbs from racists such as they now faced. Even after their father had recognised the inherent dangers of staying in Manchester, where it was only a matter of time before they all got nicked for fighting with the racists they encountered, and had moved his family out to Handstead, it had continued. Every day of their lives, something would happen to them that related to the colour of their skin. Maybe just a look, or simply being ignored, but it happened all the same. The colour of their skin was what seemed to matter – not the colour of their souls or their capabilities – and now they had one of their lifelong tormentors at their mercy.

Things hadn't got a lot better for them when they

joined the police, one after the other. True, Richard had bucked the trend and got himself promoted to Sergeant, but invisible walls and ceilings had been put up to keep the outsiders in their place, despite their obvious qualities. There were still coppers around who made no secret of their dislike for blacks – particularly blacks who had the temerity to put on a uniform. Some of the senior officers they had encountered were true dinosaurs. Alfie had met one Superintendent who had referred to him as a 'fuzzy wuzzy'.

Worse, as they had become isolated in their chosen, largely white profession, they'd become increasingly ignored by the black community, who had their own problems with the police and regarded them as traitors. 'Uncle Tom' and 'Coconut' were the terms regularly used to describe the brothers by the black people they met whilst they were in uniform. Hardly surprisingly, the Holding boys were prickly, unruly and very bitter. But now they had the chance for a bit of payback.

'Another problem, white boy, is we ain't taking no fucking prisoners today,' hissed Alfie, taking a step towards Eldrett and raising his baton high above his head. 'Especially no Albion Army arseholes.'

'I'm not with them, for Christ's sake, I'm a copper like you,' shouted Eldrett desperately.

At that moment, Alfie Holding lunged forward and landed a crashing blow with his baton to the top right of Eldrett's head. Phil had tried to flinch away as he saw the blow coming, but missed with his raised arm and took the blow at its fullest force. He crashed on to the road surface on his back, deeply unconscious and with a trickle of blood already oozing from his right ear.

'Nice shot, Alfie,' said Ben Holding, walking over to stare at Eldrett's prostrate body. 'White shit,' he sneered contemptuously. 'Come on, boys, time we weren't here, and I bet there's plenty of racist white arse to kick back at the factory.'

Strapping their helmets back on, the Holding brothers turned and trotted away up the cul-de-sac. At the main junction, a fat middle-aged white man who had clearly been running hard, paused to stare at them, his puce red face streaming with sweat, but they ignored him and hurried back towards the action at the factory.

Phil Eldrett lay in the dust in the dead end, his life ebbing away, the pool of blood under his right ear growing steadily larger and the colour slowly draining from his face. The blow from Alfie Holdings's baton had fractured the front right bone in his skull, torn the membrane around his brain and set in motion a subdural haemorrhage. The trauma had rendered him instantly unconscious; he had barely felt the blow it had been so quick, but now he was bleeding to death and needed help urgently.

DCI Dan Harrison rounded the corner at a canter and stopped dead in his tracks.

'Oh no,' he whispered to himself, before running to

Eldrett's side and kneeling alongside him. He felt for and eventually found a faint pulse in his neck. Getting to his feet, Harrison rummaged in his suit pocket for his hand-held radio and switched it on with trembling fingers. Quickly selecting the main Force Channel One he cut across the radio traffic with a shouted message.

'Delta Hotel, this is Bravo Hotel Alpha Three,' he said, using his divisional radio call sign. 'Active message.'

As was the norm with an active message, all radio traffic was cleared and he was instructed to proceed with his message.

'I need an ambulance urgently to Heritage Close on the Ridgemount Industrial Estate, Hotel Alpha. I have a man down with serious head injuries. I repeat, man down with serious head injuries.'

As the operator acknowledged the immediate request to the ambulance service for dispatch, Harrison sat down alongside Eldrett and stroked his head.

'Hang in there, Phil,' he whispered. 'Stay with me. We'll get you sorted out, I promise.' His eyes had filled with tears and he was consumed with guilt about what had befallen his man, probably at the hands of his own colleagues. But there was little he could do about it now; he'd have to come up with a solution when the dust had settled. Right now, all that mattered was that Phil Eldrett survived.

'Stay with me, Phil,' he whispered again, but this time into his ear. 'Stay with me, son.'

*

'Eldrett was Harrison's man, I take it?' asked Temporary Chief Constable Chislehurst as he selected a lamb chop from the platter on the table in the Senior Officers' dining room at Headquarters.

'Apparently, yes,' answered Assistant Chief Constable Brian Seagrove, his mouth full.

'Do we know how he came by his injuries?'

'Not yet. He's deeply unconscious so he's not said anything to anyone.'

'How serious *are* his injuries?' asked Chislehurst, deciding to have an extra chop.

'He's got a fractured skull and internal bleeding.'

Chislehurst glanced down at the rare cooked chop he'd just selected and thought better of it. 'Life-threatening?'

'Touch and go. It could go either way, apparently.'

'Well, let's hope for your sake, Mr Seagrove, that he pulls through,' said Chislehurst, fixing his ACC with a cold, reptilian smile.

'For *my* sake?' queried Seagrove, his cheeks bulging like a greedy hamster.

'A dead police officer on the books for an operation you were overseeing isn't going to do your promotion prospects a lot of good, is it?' replied Chislehurst, taking his seat and unfolding his crisp, white linen napkin which he placed on his lap.

'It won't look good for any of us,' reminded Seagrove. 'And other than that, it was an unqualified success.'

'How many arrested?'

'Just the twelve.'

'Twelve, out of a mob of over six hundred? Doesn't sound like a good return to me!'

'The strike is finished, the Albion Army won't be back and besides, locking them up was never part of the plan, was it?'

'I understand that A and E departments around the county have reported quite an increase in the number of skinheads presenting themselves with broken limbs and cracked heads,' continued Chislehurst.

'Yes, so it seems.'

Chislehurst raised his eyebrows. 'It was an operation sanctioned by you, Mr Seagrove,' he went on, 'in your role as ACC Operations – in case you'd forgotten. Has this Eldrett chap got any family?'

'I believe he's separated from his wife, two young sons as well.'

'It's a terrible tragedy for them,' mused Chislehurst, looking at his meal. 'Pass the salt, would you?'

Early that evening, Sarah Eldrett was washing up dishes in the sink from their early supper, watching her boys kicking a football about in the garden with her new man. She was a slim, attractive brunette, who'd retained her figure after the birth of her sons, but her green eyes were dull and tired, and her once-glowing skin had lost its lustre. The breakdown of her marriage had taken a heavy toll on her.

The boys were taking part in the game reluctantly as usual. Tom was trying hard to build a relationship with them, she thought wistfully to herself, but as her sons constantly reminded both of them – he wasn't their dad. The boys were failing to come to terms with their parents' separation and were deeply unhappy with the presence of the new man in their mother's life. And he was shit at football, they said, whereas their dad used to be able to do loads of ball-juggling tricks. The older boy had even expressed the view that Tom was a prick. It was going to be a difficult process.

She heard the phone ringing in the hallway and glanced up at the clock on the kitchen wall above the door. It was 6.15 p.m., so it would probably be Phil. He always tried to ring to speak to the boys at about this time. The routine was something the boys clung to, and in truth, she liked the opportunity to chat, albeit briefly, with the man who had been such a significant part of her life. Drying her hands on a tea towel, she trotted out to the hall and picked up the phone.

'Hello you,' she answered breezily, expecting to hear her estranged husband respond in the same vein.

'Mrs Eldrett?' asked a voice she didn't recognise on the other end.

'Yes, who's this?'

'I'm DCI Dan Harrison from Handstead police station. I need to talk to you.'

Sarah Eldrett listened in silence as Dan Harrison

explained what had happened to her husband.

'You're the one he does all these jobs for, aren't you?' she said bitterly when he'd finished.

'Yes, I am.'

'This was bound to happen one day, the jobs you give him to do,' she said, her voice full of recrimination.

'He was unlucky today, Mrs Eldrett. I'm sorry.'

'He was unlucky the day he met you, Mr Harrison. In fact, we were all unlucky the day your paths crossed.'

'I understand how you feel about me, and I am truly sorry – believe me. The doctors tell me that he's fit and strong and he's got every chance of pulling through. His operation went very well.'

'You'll forgive me if I don't get too cheery, won't you?' she snapped.

'I'm sorry,' sighed Dan Harrison from the callbox in the reception area of the Intensive Care Unit at Handstead General Hospital. 'I can get a car to pick you up in twenty minutes and bring you here. Can you arrange for someone to look after the kids, or if you like I'll get a WPC to sit with them until you get home?'

'I'll sort something out, but I could do with a lift to the hospital.'

'Someone will be with you in twenty minutes,' said the subdued Dan Harrison as he replaced the phone. He wasn't surprised by Sarah Eldrett's reaction to the news or to him, but it still cut him to the quick – reinforcing his own feeling that much of the blame for Phil Eldrett's injury lay with him, personally.

Sarah Eldrett walked back into her kitchen and gazed out at the boys and Tom playing football. She tapped on the window and motioned for Tom to come in. The boys looked relieved to see him go and continued to play with increased vigour once he had gone.

'What's up, Princess?' asked the manager of the supermarket where she worked and her new lover.

'Can you look after the boys for me?' she asked. 'I need to go down to the hospital.'

'The hospital? Why, what's happened?'

'Phil's been attacked. He's unconscious. They've had to operate on his skull,' she replied, her eyes filling with tears.

'Phil?' queried Tom, his face hardening. 'He's nothing to you any more, is he?'

'What the hell does that mean?' she demanded. 'Can you look after them or not?'

'I had plans for us tonight,' said her stony-faced boyfriend, who had made no move to comfort her. 'Listen, Sarah, he's not your concern any more. I'm sure he's got plenty of friends on the Force who can go down to be with him. Or his parents maybe?'

Sarah Eldrett stared at him, wondering what in the world she had seen in the balding little twat who combed what hair he had left forward to try and hide his bald patch. The little twat she had chosen in preference to

Phil, who had gone through so much with her.

'I'll get my mother over to sit with them, don't you worry,' she said flatly, walking out to the hallway and picking up the phone again.

'Don't be like that, Princess,' whined Tom, as he followed her out like a puppy. 'I just don't want to see you hurt by him any more. He's really not your problem now.'

Sarah Eldrett held the phone against her chest and turned to look at him.

'*Not my problem?*' she spat contemptuously. 'He's my husband and the father of our sons. He'll always be my problem, as you put it – but *you* won't. I don't want you here any more. You can leave now and don't come back.'

'Princess,' pleaded Tom. 'Come on, you don't mean that. We're good together, we've got a great future together.'

'Go away, Tom, and don't come near me again,' she replied. 'Now leave me alone. I've got to visit my husband.'

Chapter Twenty-Five

Chief Inspector Pete Stevenson's honey-pot operation to take out the Pork Sword Man was not going well. Since the return of the Horse's Arse officers who'd been attached to the Special Operations Group, he'd run it on a couple of days, but volunteers to take part had been few and far between. Indeed, the only female volunteer to be the honey pot had been the Blister, and her involvement had led to a number of complaints from members of the public, outraged about a fat woman displaying her dubious wares on the grass outside the church. One elderly woman had even put in a 999 call to inform the police, whom she supported through thick and thin, that there was a dreadful, fat prostitute touting for business in the area.

Stevenson had begun approaching surrounding Divisions for a more presentable WPC to be the Horse's Arse bait, but to date there had been no takers.

*

Psycho was in seventh heaven as he strolled along the canal tow-path holding Anne Butler's hand. It was a beautiful afternoon with a light breeze keeping the temperature pleasant. It may as well have been fifty degrees plus, for all he cared. He was out with Anne and she was holding his hand as though she wanted to.

They walked quietly, passing other couples in similar embraces, and he simply glowed. He had telephoned Anne as soon as the Special Operations Group had been released from Headquarters the day after the massacre at the Red Star Electrics factory, and made arrangements for their date today. She was on a day off, and whilst he was due to work a Late Turn, he had taken one of the Chief Constable's Discretionary Rest Days that the SOG had been promised.

'We've got a lot to talk about, haven't we, Sean?' she said as they passed a line of brightly painted barges.

'Yes, we have,' admitted Psycho glumly, fearful that what he needed to tell her would finish their relationship before it even got off the ground.

'It's probably best if I ask you the questions and you can fill in the gaps if I miss anything – if that's OK?' she went on, looking up at him.

Psycho was again cleanly shaved and his hair neatly groomed, but he looked miserable.

'OK,' he said softly.

'You were married once, weren't you?'

'Yes, a long time ago.'

'What happened?'

'She left me because I shagged her best friend,' replied the morose Psycho, keeping his eyes down. Telling the truth was killing him, but he had promised himself that he had to go for broke and tell her everything. He couldn't afford for her to find out things subsequently – assuming, of course, that she was willing to overlook his appalling track-record to date and give him a chance.

'How many women have you slept with?'

Oh no, the million-dollar question. *'You promised to tell the truth, get on with it,'* insisted his conscience.

'Dozens,' he admitted.

'Who were they?'

'I really can't remember all their names. Lots of them were drunken one-night stands.'

'And prostitutes?'

Psycho swallowed hard, glanced at her as his face coloured up, and then back down at the tow-path as they continued their slow pace.

'Yes,' he said.

'How many prostitutes?'

'Oh God,' said Psycho, stopping to look desperately at her. 'I really don't know.'

'More than ten?' asked Anne, taking him by the arm and leading him along the path again.

'Probably,' he replied mournfully, convinced now that his hopes were dashed beyond redemption.

'Tell me about you and Amanda Wheeler.'

Psycho shook his head, his despair complete. Anne had obviously been well-briefed about him and done her research.

'Yes, we used to shag each other occasionally.'

'God, what's the matter with you, Sean?' asked Anne crossly. 'Have you got no respect for yourself?'

'I know,' he said miserably. 'I've lost the plot completely. I'm sorry.'

'When did you last use a prostitute, Sean?'

'Christ, ages ago. Last year sometime, I think.'

'And what about the Blister?'

'The same, I think. Last year, sometime – why?'

'I'm interested, that's all,' replied Anne thoughtfully. 'Tell me, why has it been so long since you went with any of them?'

Psycho paused for a moment and then stopped again to look at her and drink in everything he loved about her but was sure he was going to lose.

'Because I met you,' he said simply, his throat tightening as he spoke. 'Because I wanted to be someone you could care about – not the wild animal I was becoming.'

'I *do* care about you, Sean, but you really worry me,' said Anne, as they continued to walk. 'I've seen a side of you that I find very attractive, but you also have a dark side that seems to dominate you most of the time.'

'It did – that's true,' he admitted, 'because I let it. I know it's there and I let it take over because it was easier than resisting it. You know, life's a doddle when you don't give a fuck.'

'That's a hell of a way to live.'

'It worked for me,' shrugged Psycho. 'I didn't get hurt, but it's not how I want to carry on.'

'Why?'

There was another lull in their conversation and they walked in silence, ducking under the heavy, low branches of a weeping willow as Psycho considered what to say next.

'Because I met you,' he finally repeated.

Anne stopped and turned to face him. 'Do you think leopards can change their spots?' she asked him.

'What do you mean?'

'Do you think that people can change extreme behaviour patterns?'

'If something's important enough to them, yes. And this *is* important to me.'

They carried on walking in silence. Significantly, certainly in Psycho's troubled mind, Anne had not let go of his hand as they had talked; her tiny, perfectly formed hand remained encased completely in his.

'I don't know, Sean,' she said after a while. 'I just don't know. I do have feelings for you, but I don't want to make another mistake.'

'Another mistake?'

'Andy was a huge mistake,' she said, referring to her former live-in boyfriend. 'He was a jealous control freak.

I recognised that when we first got together but I hoped he'd change. If anything, he got worse.'

'Anne, all I can say in my defence is that you know pretty much everything about me. I don't have any skeletons in my closet waiting to ambush you, and I've already turned over a new leaf because I know I need to. If I'm honest with myself, I had to change – not just because of how I feel about you, but how I feel about myself.'

'How *do* you feel about yourself?'

'Right now, much better,' he replied. 'I am a different, better person and whatever does or doesn't happen between us, I'm going to stay the person I am now.'

'I'm not sure I fancy a shadow of the old Psycho,' she laughed. 'Half of the attraction to you was your wildness.'

'It all went too far,' said Psycho, encouraged by her smile. 'I was doing things that went beyond the pale sometimes. I reckon I'll still sail close to the wind, but there's got to be a limit. Especially if I want to be with you.'

'You don't know much about *me*, do you, Sean?' she said, swinging their hands as they walked.

'I reckon I know all I need to.'

'I might have a very dark, murky past,' she went on with a broad smile, her blue eyes sparkling with the promise of a hidden, rampant sexual appetite.

'God, I hope so,' said Psycho, smiling for the first time since they had begun walking and talking. Anne squeezed his hand.

'Let me think about things, Sean, OK? I don't want to rush in and get burned again. Do you understand?'

'Of course. At least you haven't said you'd like us to be friends because you love me like a brother,' he replied with a chuckle.

'I've got lots of friends,' she said. 'I'm not after another one.' She looked up knowingly at him and smiled softly.

The tow-path had brought them to the foot of the gardens and graveyard at the rear of the church in the town centre. As usual, the manicured lawns were covered in office workers enjoying their lunch-hours in the glorious sun; the air full of the sound of numerous conversations and laughter. Glancing up towards the church, Psycho noticed that one of the fleet of unlicensed ice-cream vans that plagued the town had taken advantage of the captive audience and was plying a roaring trade from outside the main doors to the church itself.

'Look at that saucy bastard,' he laughed. 'Fancy an ice cream?'

'Hmm, yes please,' she said. 'Can I have a ninety-nine?'

'Coming up. Grab that seat and I'll be right back,' said Psycho, indicating a weathered wooden bench at the edge of the canal before he hurried through a nearby rusty gate in the fence and across the lawns towards the van.

Ten minutes later, he'd relieved the grumpy ice-cream seller of two free double 99-flake cornets and then moved him on. He was negotiating his way through the irate crowd of red-faced sunbathers complaining to the seller about pulling down his shutters, when he heard the scream. It was Anne.

'Sean!' she yelled at the top of her voice. 'Sean – help me!'

He pushed through the scrum, emerging on to a gravel path and immediately saw Anne, still on the canal tow-path. She was wrestling with a large man who was desperately trying to throw her away from him. Psycho could see her hanging on to his dark top, and then the man begin to hit her across the face with fierce, powerful slaps.

The change in Psycho's demeanour was not dissimilar to that undergone by the Incredible Hulk; the only difference being that Psycho's face went red with rage. With a bellow of her name, he threw his two cornets to the ground and began to sprint across the grass towards the gate he had come through. He raced through two carefully laid out picnics and flattened a spindly accountant who had got to his feet to see what all the shouting was about, covering the distance in a time Alan Wells would have struggled to match. The only sound he could hear was Anne screaming his name. His arms and legs were pumping like pistons and he slowed briefly to pass through the gate and as he did so, he saw the big man finally smash Anne to the ground and begin to run away in the other direction along the tow-path. In a flash, Psycho was by her side, lifting her to her feet and relieved to see that she wasn't cut but had a slight reddening around her right eye.

'It's Pork Sword Man,' she stammered, tears streaming down her face.

'Call three nines,' shouted Psycho, before he kissed her on the forehead and set off again. His feet barely touched the tow-path as he flew after the man who had attacked his woman. His focus was totally fixed on him: it was as though the cross-hairs of a telescopic sight formed in his eyes and transferred on to the fleeing man's back.

Pork Sword Man had got about a 100 yard start on Psycho, but the canal tow-path was not the best place he could have chosen to outrun the irate partner of a woman he'd just punched to the ground. There was nowhere to hide. The metal rail fence to the left was just climbable but it would take time and he had little of that; and to the right was only the deep, green canal.

Pork Sword Man glanced fearfully over his shoulder, panting with the exertion of the unfamiliar exercise; he then caught sight of his pursuer. The latter was huge and clearly in the mood to smash him to a pulp. Turning back to face the way he was running, Pork Sword Man could feel his legs turning to jelly and he was sure his lungs were beginning to bleed. He was badly overweight and cursing himself for not thinking through this, his latest flashing, a little better. Previously, he'd always been able to disappear into the tight, crowded lanes around the church before anyone had even begun to think about chasing him. But that blonde bird had been too good an opportunity to miss, sitting there all alone on that bench with her head up her arse. She had to be done, but he'd not given himself an escape route other than the long, straight tow-path. And now he had some raging nutter on his tail.

'You're fucking dead!' yelled his chaser, reminding him, not that he needed it, that he was in the shit. He was quite sure now that his lungs had haemorrhaged; he could taste the telltale metallic signs in his mouth. He couldn't go on, he'd have to go toe to toe with him. He came to a stumbling halt and turned to face the man chasing him.

Psycho saw the fat bloke turn and realised that Anne had been spot on. Through the signature Zorro face mask, he could see the man's frightened piggy eyes staring intently at him. His fat, round head was glistening with sweat and he was panting like a greyhound. Psycho came to a halt a few feet away from him and looked at him as he gulped for air. He was surprised at how fresh he felt after his sprint of nearly 400 yards. Adrenalin-fuelled, he guessed. And now he stood just a few feet away from the man who'd slapped Anne about and had been spoiling other women's *al fresco* dining for the last month or so.

Other than Pork Sword Man's panting and Psycho's heavy breathing, the only sounds on the tow-path were of birds twittering in the nearby woods. A wood pigeon cooed in the branches of an adjacent yew, as the sun beat down on the pair, reflecting brightly off the millpond-still surface of the canal like a mirror into Pork Sword Man's eyes. He stood upright and shaded his masked eyes.

'You fuck off now and I won't give you a slap,' he growled at Psycho.

'That's very generous of you,' said Psycho with a smile.

'Yeah, I'm like that. Go on, fuck off. Why are you getting involved anyway? The bitches love it really.'

'Bitches?' queried Psycho, the smile disappearing from his face to be replaced by a steely mask.

'Blondie was well up for it back there, she was – could hardly take her eyes off my cock. Fuck them, they deserve it. Go on, fuck off.'

'Bitches?' repeated Psycho, louder this time.

Pork Sword Man swallowed hard. This big bastard wasn't backing off an inch. Generally in his experience, people wilted when he fronted them up with a bit of aggression and some threats, but not this one. He was going to have to take him out. It wouldn't be the first time he had chosen that solution, but it would, however, be the last.

Taking a step towards Psycho, his face set in a sneer, he raised an aggressive finger at him to reinforce the point. As many before him had found to their considerable cost, coming within grabbing distance of Psycho was a fatal error. In one lightning movement, Psycho grabbed the wrist as it came forward, pulling the fat man violently towards him and with perfect timing, smashed his forehead into the bridge of his nose. The collision reverberated around the surrounding trees, sending flocks of birds spiralling out of their hiding places in alarm.

Psycho felt the nose shatter under his forehead and the instant flow of warm blood before Pork Sword Man flew backwards and lay unconscious on the tow-path, the blood gushing in torrents down his jowls and over his neck on to the tarmac path.

Psycho was himself temporarily dazed from the force of the blow he had delivered, staggering slightly as he shook his head to clear it. He leaned forward and placed his hands on his knees, controlling his breathing, watching Pork Sword Man should he show any signs of recovery. But he was well away and likely to be for some time.

Just then, Psycho heard his name being shouted and turned to look back the way they had run. Coming round a slight curve in the tow-path was Anne, running towards him, slightly ahead of two uniformed coppers he recognised from the Early Turn relief. Standing upright, he raised his arms in triumph, his red sweaty face creased with a huge smile.

'Sean, you got him. Are you OK?' gasped Anne, as she reached him and threw herself against his heaving chest and wrapped her long, slim arms around his waist. Psycho folded her up in his arms and closed his eyes as he breathed deeply into her scalp, sucking in her wonderful fragrance.

'I'm fine, gorgeous,' he sighed. 'He's sleeping it off. Are *you* all right?' He pushed her gently away from him to look closely at her face. The reddening around her eyes and cheeks was clear, but he couldn't see any cuts or bruises forming.

'I'm fine,' she laughed. 'Just a few bruises, perhaps. Hey – he's a bit of a mess.' She was peering round Psycho and watching as the two uniformed cops rolled the now stirring and groaning Pork Sword Man on to his front and handcuffed him.

'Have you nicked him, Psycho?' asked one of them.

'Of course – no reply after caution,' he replied with a chuckle.

'Do you know who he is?'

'Not a clue,' said Psycho, turning and walking over to him. Reaching forward, he pulled up the Zorro mask and smiled at the watery, hate-filled little eyes that blazed at him.

'Don't recognise the ugly fucker,' he remarked casually. 'Fuck me, look at the mess you're making.' He winked at Pork Sword Man. 'There's always someone bigger and more horrible than you around, old son, and you met him today. Lock him up for me, boys. Anne and I'll follow you back in my motor and get our statements done. And don't forget, I'm the arresting officer, collar number 1408 and he's potted for assault and indecent exposure.'

'Got you, Psycho,' grinned the other uniform cop. 'Come on, fat boy, back to the station.'

Pork Sword Man cast a murderous look at Psycho as he was dragged past him back down the tow-path. Psycho took Anne's hand again and they followed them back at a stroll, occasionally giving each other's hands a squeeze and smiling at each other.

'Have you made any plans for today, Sean?' asked Anne, as they got into his car five minutes later.

'No, nothing arranged – why?' he answered.

'Why don't you pop over to my place after we're done and I'll cook us some dinner?'

'That would be great,' Psycho almost shouted, his face split in a huge smile. 'That would be fantastic.'

'And bring a toothbrush,' said Anne, turning to look at him and fluttering her eyelashes.

Chapter Twenty-Six

DCI Dan Harrison was busy completing an actions list to present to DCS Mills in an effort to get a squad put together to go after their serial rapist, when there was a knock at the door and DC John Benson put his head into the room.

'Have you got a moment, boss?' He was smiling broadly.

'Yeah, sure. What are you so pleased about?'

'The uniforms have just locked up Pork Sword Man,' he replied happily.

'Fucking great!' exclaimed Harrison. 'Pete Stevenson's going to be over the moon. His honey-pot operation was going nowhere. We've got a few jobs we can clear up with him. What a great result. What happened – who got him?'

'He flashed an off-duty WPC – Anne Butler off A Group, and slapped her about a bit when she tried to get hold of him. He ended up getting himself lifted by Sean Pearce.'

'Pearce? Psycho Pearce? How did *he* get involved?'

'He and Butler were having a stroll along the canal tow-path apparently,' replied Benson with a leer.

'Were they indeed?' said Harrison, smiling. 'Good for them. Pork Sword Man is locked up downstairs, I take it?'

'Yeah, he's with Doc Dougan now. Pearce flattened his nose all over his face when he lifted him. He looks like his face's been ironed. He came on a bit strong apparently, so he had to be restrained. He's complaining like a bitch now.'

'I should hope he did have to be restrained; comes with the territory, especially when you lay hands on one of our WPCs. Have we identified him yet?'

'That's the best news of the lot, boss,' said Benson, walking over to his desk and handing him an arrest record sheet. He was smiling so broadly, it had to hurt.

Harrison took the sheet of paper from him and read it, his mouth dropping open in shock before he put his head back and whooped with joy.

'You fucking beauty!' he yelled, before he regained his composure though he continued to grin like the Cheshire Cat. 'John, you deal with this – and do it by the numbers, OK?'

'Will do, boss.'

'I mean no funny business, John. Get it all down on paper and chop his fucking legs off.'

'Understood,' said Benson smartly, retrieving the

arrest sheet from Harrison and leaving the office.

As the door shut, Harrison opened his bottom drawer and got out his bottle of Bushmills and a glass. He was drinking far too much of the stuff, but to hell with it; he hadn't had much to celebrate recently. Poor Phil Eldrett was still unconscious in hospital and questions were being asked about his role in Operation Chaka, but this was something to cheer about.

'Fuck me,' he mused to himself as he swilled his first mouthful around his palate before he swallowed it. 'Wallace Moffatt. Who'd have thought it?'

There was a God, after all.

Two hours later, Dan Harrison was putting the finishing touches to his report when there was another knock at the door. Hurriedly, he shut his bottle and glass away and looked up as John Benson put his head round the door again.

'Can you spare me a moment, boss?'

'Sure, John. Make it quick though, will you? I've got to run this lot past John Mills at Headquarters,' he replied, indicating the pile of papers on his desk.

'Bob's stuff?' asked Benson.

'Yeah. The very same, I'm afraid. What's on your mind?' He motioned Benson to take one of the chairs alongside the low coffee-table in front of him.

'It's Moffatt.'

'Go on. Any problems?'

'Something's not right but I can't put my finger on it.'

'Like what? He's not putting his hands up yet – you want me to have a chat with him?'

'No, no, nothing like that. He's coughed flashing Anne Butler and giving her a slap today, no problem with that. He's not having any of the other jobs though. He's pretty sure of himself; he knows we're going to struggle to prove any of them unless he admits them.'

'Is he suggesting we've got more than one pervert running about in a Zorro mask?'

'Something like that,' chuckled Benson, 'but I've charged him with today's offences.'

'Good, and remand him in our custody until we can get him to court tomorrow.'

'Yeah, all arranged. He's all printed and photographed, but something's bugging me about this bloke.'

'We'll have to write all his other jobs off, John, or slip them in as TICs at a later date. Has he got a solicitor?'

'Yeah, some fat, slippery bastard from Mayes and Caldwell. Alex Thaw – do you know him?'

'No, never heard of him. Never mind, these things happen, John. At least we've got him bang to rights on substantive offences today that we can prove. Now – what's the problem?'

'I've got a feeling in my water, that's all.'

Harrison groaned out loud. 'Oh no, John, not you as well. First Bob with his serial rapist and now you with Moffatt. Don't do this to me, please,' he begged.

Benson gave a short laugh, but insisted: 'Sorry, boss, but he's just not right.'

'Not right? How's he not right?'

'He's too clean.'

'Jesus, John, too clean. What's that mean?'

'Moffatt's an obnoxious, racist, perverted bigot – right?'

'Agreed, but so what? We deal with creatures like him all the time. Where are you going with this?'

'He's got absolutely no previous at all,' replied Benson, handing him a piece of paper with the result of a PNC search on it.

As Harrison scanned it, Benson went on, 'Absolutely nothing. Not as a juvenile, not as an adult, absolutely zero. How many people like Moffatt have you ever dealt with who're so clean? He's lily-white, boss, not even any outstanding parking or motoring offences. It doesn't add up. Unless we've got unbelievably lucky and bagged him first time out, none of this adds up.'

Harrison looked at his detective with a frown on his face. Benson was right. It was virtually unheard of for an individual with the mindset such as Moffatt had, not to have come to the attention of the police before. It just didn't happen.

'You've got his prints?' Harrison asked.

'Yes, here,' replied Benson, holding aloft the two sets of inky finger and thumb sets and the single full palms form.

'What do the Fingerprints Section say about them?'

'No trace.'

'OK, what do you want to do next?'

'Get them checked nationally.'

'Christ, John, that'll take weeks. He'll be convicted and out and about before we get that check back.'

'Unless we can get it done on the hurry-up.'

'On the hurry-up? How?'

'With your mate down at the Yard. Flying Squad, isn't he?'

'Paul Johnson, yeah. Ask him to get the Yard's Fingerprint Bureau to do a national search? It's a tall order, John.'

'We could narrow the search down a bit for them – confine it to convicted sex offenders,' Benson suggested.

'Just sex offenders? Why?'

'If he's got previous, chances are it's for something similar to what he did today.'

'It's a lot of fucking work for a flasher, John,' said Harrison grimly. 'A hell of a lot of work.'

'It'd tie up all the loose ends, boss, and we'd know for sure. Who knows, he might be wanted somewhere else in the country.'

Harrison paused to consider what Benson was saying. He hated loose ends and Benson was right. Something didn't quite add up.

'OK,' he said eventually, 'I'll contact Paul. Leave the prints with me. We'll have to get them down to London this afternoon if he can arrange it. You go down to the cells and get Moffatt banged up until tomorrow. Tell the Station Sergeant we're hanging on to him on the grounds that we believe he's a recidivist and likely to commit further offences if he's bailed. Assuming Paul can get the prints checked, I'll ask him to liaise direct with you. I'm going to be at Headquarters for quite a while.'

'Thanks, boss,' said Benson, getting to his feet. 'Something's just not kosher.'

'I know, I know,' Harrison sighed, picking up his address book to find DI Paul Johnson's number at the Yard. 'Go on, John, get him banged up.'

Twenty minutes later, having endured the usual barrage of insults and jibes about northern monkeys from his old pal at the Yard's famous Flying Squad, Dan Harrison telephoned the Traffic Section operator in the main Force Control Room.

'This is DCI Harrison at Handstead. I need a motorcyclist on the hurry-up to take documents from Handstead to the Yard,' he said when the phone was eventually answered.

'The Yard?'

'New Scotland Yard,' said Harrison irritably.

'In London?'

'That's right, London.'

'I'll need to get authority to assign a traffic motorcyclist outside the county, sir,' said the operator. 'I'll speak to my Inspector.'

'It's already authorised,' lied Harrison. 'I got the authority from Assistant Chief Constable Seagrove five minutes ago.'

'OK, hold on, sir, let me see who we've got available,' said the operator.

Harrison drummed his fingers impatiently on his desk blotter, listening to the clamour in the Control Room for a few minutes before the operator came back on the line.

'Tango Four's on his way to you, sir,' she said. 'Should be about five minutes.'

'Excellent. Tell Tango Four that the documents will be waiting for him in the front office at Handstead, and they're to be delivered into the hands of DI Paul Johnson of CO8, fourth floor at the Yard. In London,' he added sarcastically.

'CO8?' queried the operator,

'The Flying Squad,' replied Harrison wearily.

'Ooh, the Sweeney – how exciting,' trilled the operator, who never missed an episode of the series that was cult viewing.

'Thank you, goodbye,' said Harrison abruptly, putting down the phone and then placing Moffatt's prints into a plain brown A4 envelope. Scrawling a quick note of thanks to his mate and asking that he get back with any result to DC John Benson as soon as possible, he sealed the envelope, grabbed his other paperwork and jacket and strode out of his office.

Dropping the envelope for DI Johnson in the front

office with clear instructions for the front office PC, he went out to collect his car from the rear yard and was soon in the light afternoon traffic in Bolton Road East, making for Headquarters. He had quickly forgotten Moffatt and his lack of a criminal past. There was too much else going on: the possibility of a serial rapist and, of course, Phil Eldrett.

Eldrett been unconscious now for five days. The craniotomy surgery he'd had within two hours of the attack on him had successfully relieved the pressure and swelling on his brain, but he was not responding otherwise. With various tubes and wires hanging from him he looked a sorry mess, but the surgeons had been confident that he was young enough and strong enough to pull through. When that would be, however, they had no idea – and worse, until he came round they would have no idea what permanent damage had been inflicted on him. That was what bothered Dan Harrison most. What if Eldrett had been left a dribbling, brain-damaged wreck?

He'd spent time at Eldrett's bedside every night, carefully arranging his visits with the Intensive Care Unit staff to coincide with Sarah Eldrett's brief absences. He was the last person she would want to see with her husband – since, according to her, he was responsible for everything that had happened to him and to them as a couple. Harrison didn't agree with her but could see where she was coming from. Hopefully Phil hadn't made too much of a sacrifice; only time would tell.

*

Just after 6 p.m., John Benson and Bob Clarke were busy at their desks working their way relentlessly through the piles of paper that threatened to engulf them. Dan Harrison was back from his meeting at Headquarters with DCS Mills and had got the green light to get a squad together and start work on getting behind the serial rapist that they all now agreed they had on the ground. Harrison had popped into the main CID office on his return.

'We got anything back from the Yard yet?' he asked.

'No, nothing yet,' answered Benson, looking up at him.

'Do we know if the prints were definitely delivered?'

'I haven't heard anything.'

'I bet that wanker's stopped to have a look at someone's bald tyres or something,' said Harrison bitterly. 'Give the Control Room a ring, John, see if Tango Four's booked back on in the county, will you?'

Benson was just finishing the crime report he was writing up before making that call when his desk phone rang.

'CID, John Benson,' he said, tucking the phone under his chin and speaking as he continued to write.

'Have they invented pens up there yet, son?' said DI Paul Johnson from his office at the Yard. 'If not, grab a bit of chalk or something and listen to this little lot.'

Half an hour later, Benson knocked again on Dan Harrison's closed door. Opening it, he detected the telltale aroma of Bushmills and smiled at his boss. The old boy was really going for it these days, but he put the hours in and it seemed to keep him going. The bloke never seemed to go home.

'You OK, John?' asked Harrison, wiping his mouth with the back of his hand. 'You look very pleased with yourself.'

'Just heard back from your mate at the Yard. Cast your eyes over this, boss,' said Benson, dropping a wad of paper in front of Harrison. Sighing, the big man began to read and then his cheeks flushed.

'Holy fucking shit, John,' he whispered slowly without looking up. 'Holy *shit*.' He leafed carefully through the dozen or so pieces of paper he had been handed and then got quickly to his feet.

'This changes everything,' he said, his face creased in concentration. 'Get your coat, we've got a visit to make.'

The door to the shabby semi-detached house on the Park Royal Estate was opened by a thin, pale woman with lank shoulder-length hair. The black rings under her eyes highlighted the fear and worry in them.

'I'm DCI Dan Harrison, this is DC John Benson,' said Harrison by way of an introduction, holding his warrant card up for her to see. 'Are you Mrs Moffatt?'

She ignored his warrant card and the question.

'What the fuck do you bastards want?' she spat. 'You've got him locked up – isn't that enough for you?'

'We need to talk to you. Can we come in?'

'Come in? You're fucking joking, aren't you? What the fuck else do you want? Looking to fit him up with something else, are you?'

'I don't need to fit him up, Mrs Moffatt. He's put his hands up to everything, but we do need to talk.'

'I've got fuck all to talk to you about, you bastard. Go on, fuck off.' She began to close the peeling door, but Dan Harrison put his foot against it and stepped over the sill.

'Get out of here,' screamed the enraged woman. 'You haven't got a warrant, you've got no right to force your way in here.'

'If you won't talk to me for your sake, Mrs Moffatt, then do it for theirs,' said Harrison softly, motioning to the two young girls in pyjamas who had come to the top of the stairs, disturbed by the commotion at the front door.

'Go back to your room, you two!' shouted Mrs Moffatt. Then she said angrily, 'Now look what you've done. Coming round here bothering people on some fucking witch-hunt. Fuck off, I said.'

'Right, so you won't talk to me, Mrs Moffat, but you can bloody well listen,' said Dan Harrison, who'd had enough, pushing her back into the hallway followed by Benson and then closing the front door firmly behind them.

Chapter Twenty-Seven

At 11.15 p.m., Dan Harrison and John Benson walked purposefully into an interview room in the cell block where Wallace Moffatt and his Legal Aid solicitor, Alex Thaw, had been waiting for the last twenty minutes. The delay had been intentional, as Harrison turned up the pressure.

The interview room was typical of its type. Pale yellow gloss walls, absolutely bare so the prisoner had only his interviewers to concentrate on, and lit by a single fluorescent striplight and what natural light seeped in through the opaque bullseye glass windows high in the wall. A battered wooden table was riveted to the floor in the centre of the room, and four similarly ancient chairs, also riveted, stood two each side of the table. For detectives like John Benson and Bob Clarke, the riveted furniture had been a definite step backwards in terms of interview technique. A chair wrapped around the head of a bolshy, silent prisoner had proved very persuasive in the past.

A middle-aged woman carrying a notepad walked in behind Harrison and Benson, pulling a blue plastic chair with her which she positioned at the back of the small room. Wallace Moffatt sat with his arms folded defiantly, his face set in an arrogant sneer. A large plaster covered his broken nose and his small piggy eyes were blackened and puffed from his encounter with Psycho that afternoon.

'I'm DCI Dan Harrison, this is DC John Benson and that's Mrs Audrey Giles. She takes shorthand notes. I thought it prudent that we get this interview recorded verbatim,' said Harrison, offering Alex Thaw a handshake.

'This is most irregular and inconvenient, Chief Inspector,' began Thaw. 'My client has made admissions and been charged with alleged offences today. Why are we here again?'

'I'll come to that in a moment,' replied Harrison. 'Are you OK with the interview being taken down in shorthand so there's no confusion later? Of course, you'll be given a copy of the transcript as soon as it's available.'

'No objections at all, Chief Inspector, but why are we here? Have you seen the time?'

'Yes, getting late, isn't it – but I always say, don't put off until later what you can get done now. The reason we're here now is because there appears to be a little confusion – some anomalies in your client's account of things.'

'There's no confusion,' interrupted Moffatt bitterly. 'I'm going to have that bastard's job.' With a stubby finger he indicated his shattered nose and blackened eyes. In addition to his injuries courtesy of Psycho, Moffatt also sported quite an impressive crease across the top of his bald head. It was a legacy of his encounter with a SOG officer outside the Red Star Electrics factory after Phil Eldrett had left him to it. Moffatt had eventually made his escape from the scene, but the top of his head still hurt like a bastard.

'Have you made a formal complaint yet?' asked Harrison.

'We will be doing so in due course, Chief Inspector,' chimed in the solicitor, resting a hand on Moffatt's upper arm to silence him. 'In the meantime, perhaps you would explain what you mean by "confusion and anomalies". My client has been quite frank with you in interview.'

'Hmm, we'll see,' said Harrison, looking long and hard at Moffatt, who glared back at him. 'First, I must remind your client that he is still under caution and doesn't need to say anything unless he wishes to do so, and—'

'Yes, yes, yes,' interrupted Thaw irritably, 'we understand he's still under caution. Can we get on?'

'Of course,' said Dan Harrison pleasantly, opening the folder in front of him. 'Would you confirm that your name is Wallace John Moffatt, born second of February 1938 and living at 23 Harvey Road on the Park Royal Estate in Handstead?'

'What the fuck is this?' asked Moffatt angrily. 'You woke me up for this bollocks?'

'Just answer the question, please,' said Harrison quietly.

'*Yes*, for fuck's sake!'

'This is your arrest sheet and property record?' continued Harrison, sliding the two sheets of paper across the desk so Moffatt and Thaw could see them.

'So fucking what?'

'And that is your signature under the list of personal property? Seven pounds, thirty-eight pence made up of one five-pound note, two one-pound notes and small change, a black leather belt, a cigarette lighter and a packet of Benson and Hedges, a blue plastic key ring with three keys on: a Chubb, a Yale and an unmarked key, and sundry papers. That's your property and your signature?'

'Yes,' said Moffatt, his anger increasing. 'Look – this is all bollocks, Mr Thaw.'

'I have to agree, Chief Inspector,' said the solicitor. 'Where is the confusion and anomaly here?'

'Bear with me, Mr Thaw, I'm getting there,' replied Harrison politely, retrieving the arrest sheets and producing the fingerprint forms saying, 'And would you confirm that these are your fingerprints and that is your signature appearing on each form?'

Moffatt glanced at the forms on the desk. 'Christ all-bloody-mighty. Yes – satisfied?'

Harrison pulled the forms back and replaced them in his folder, smiling at Thaw and Moffatt.

'Well, there's the first anomaly,' he said softly.

'Anomaly – how?' said Thaw, glancing at Moffatt who was licking his lips nervously.

'We had those prints checked at New Scotland Yard this afternoon,' went on Harrison in the same low, serious tone. 'We had them checked at a national level, not just locally. And guess what?'

'What? Get to the point, Chief Inspector,' said Thaw crossly.

'Those fingerprints don't belong to someone called Wallace John Moffatt,' said Harrison, leaving the statement hanging in the air. Thaw again looked at Moffatt, whose eyes were darting anxiously around the room, the colour draining from his fat face. There was a long, pregnant pause.

'No, Wallace John Moffatt doesn't really exist – or rather he didn't until November 1969. These fingerprints belong to one Alan David Evans, born on the same day as the subsequent Mr Moffatt, in Tiger Bay, Cardiff, to Barbara Jane Evans, father unknown.'

There was no response from Moffatt, so Harrison continued, 'So, what do we know about Alan David Evans? A great deal, I'm afraid. This is a copy of a case file antecedent form completed by a Detective Inspector Ivor Owen of the Cardiff Borough Police on 11 November 1960. It gives some pretty unpleasant details about offences committed by our Mr Evans on 9 November 1960. It appears, Mr Thaw, that the delightful Mr Evans befriended a divorcée who lived on an estate in Cardiff and eventually moved in with her. This unfortunate woman had two teenage daughters. On 9 November

1960, the appalling Mr Evans concealed himself in a wardrobe in the girls' bedroom and waited for them to return from school. The girls' mother was at work. When the girls came up into their bedroom, Mr Evans attacked them. He raped them both, forcing each to watch as he raped the other. And then he threatened to kill them if they breathed a word of what he had done to anyone. Fortunately, the girls were made of sterner stuff. They told their mother, and Mr Evans had his collar felt by our colleagues from Cardiff. He appeared at Cardiff Assizes on the fourth of January 1961 and pleaded Not Guilty to the two counts of rape. He forced the two young girls to endure a hostile cross-examination. Fortunately, justice prevailed, and Mr Evans got two Guilty verdicts. He was sentenced to fifteen years, but thanks to our piss-poor justice system, was paroled after just eight years – eight fucking years, can you believe it? – on the ninth of February 1969. How am I doing, Mr Evans?' snarled Harrison, leaning forward, his face grey with controlled anger.

The former Alan David Evans stared back at him, his face a mask of shock and fury.

'I did my time,' he eventually managed.

'Not nearly enough, many would think,' said Harrison. 'Anyway, let's move on, shall we?'

'Hold on,' interrupted the solicitor. 'My client's real name is Alan David Evans, is that what you're saying?'

'No, his real name – legally – is Wallace John Moffatt.

You changed your name by deed poll in September 1969, didn't you, Mr Moffatt – or Mr Evans?'

'It was all legal and above board; I was entitled.'

'Of course it was. You took advantage of a loophole that was probably explained to you in prison by the other perverts and nonces, didn't you? You changed your name by deed poll and effectively reinvented yourself,' Harrison said disgustedly.

The solicitor relaxed a little. 'I can understand you needed to clarify this matter, Chief Inspector, but unless my client is wanted for offences elsewhere then I can't see where this is going. So he changed his name by deed poll; that's not against the law, is it?'

'Certainly not, Mr Thaw, but let me finish. So once the nasty, vicious rapist Mr Evans becomes Mr Moffatt, he decides life in Cardiff is a little hot. It's a small town, people know him and remember him. Those young girls had a large family who would cheerfully string him up. So, probably calling on old prison contacts, the new Mr Moffatt turned up in Handstead in early 1970, soon took up with Janet Price whom he'd met in a club, and married her in June 1971 – the eighteenth, to be precise. And guess what? Janet Price was a divorcée with two young daughters aged three and two back then. They're fine-looking young girls of ten and nine now.'

There was an electric silence in the small stuffy room. Moffatt was swallowing hard but keeping quiet.

'You were up to your old tricks, weren't you, you

fucking animal?' Harrison said bitterly. 'History repeating itself. You're just waiting to start on those two girls unfortunate enough to have a pig like you as a stepfather.'

'Hold on, Chief Inspector, that's outrageous,' protested Alex Thaw. 'So my client did time for rape and changed his name by deed poll. Unless you have anything else, I don't see that he's done anything wrong and this interview is at an end.'

'Shut up, Mr Thaw,' hissed Harrison menacingly. 'I've got loads more, so pin your ears back.'

'How dare you talk to me like that!' exploded the irate, pompous little solicitor.

'This is the last time, Mr Thaw,' warned Harrison. 'Next time I'm going to chin you.'

'So I changed my fucking name, so what? You've got fuck all else,' growled Moffatt.

'Fortunately, that's not the case,' said Harrison, pulling a large brown paper sack from between the chairs he and Benson were sitting on. 'I feel a bit like Father Christmas.'

Moffatt scowled but said nothing. Harrison could see a single bead of sweat rolling down the side of his face. He was definitely rattled.

'Once we'd identified you as a convicted rapist, your status in another enquiry became apparent,' Harrison went on.

'What other enquiry?' protested Thaw. 'This is the first time I've heard anything about another enquiry.'

'We're currently investigating eight unsolved rape

offences in Handstead going back to July 1970. You were living here then, Mr Moffatt, in a bail hostel in Grange Road – do you remember it?'

There was no reply, but Moffatt was licking his dry lips desperately.

'As you'll appreciate, in an investigation like that with apparently very little to go on, one line of enquiry is always to look at what our known sex offenders were up to on the days in question. But of course, we didn't know you were here, did we? But now we do and we've been very busy.'

'Chief Inspector, if you've got evidence pertinent to my client, then please get on,' insisted Thaw. 'Otherwise we're done.'

'I paid your unfortunate wife a visit this evening' said Harrison softly.

'You cunt!' screamed Moffatt, getting to his feet. 'He can't fucking do that, can he?'

'Sit down, Mr Moffatt,' said Harrison, who had not flinched. 'During a criminal investigation I can talk to who I want and they can give me as much information, or as little, as they want. Your wife was quite enlightening – eventually.'

'He can't do this, can he?' Moffatt shouted again to Thaw. 'She can't be forced to give evidence, can she?'

'Just be quiet, Mr Moffatt,' counselled Thaw. 'That is highly irregular, Chief Inspector.'

'Not at all, Mr Thaw. Mrs Moffatt was, as I'm sure you

won't be surprised to hear, completely unaware of your client's former name and conviction.'

'You've told his wife? That's scandalous!' shouted Thaw. 'You have absolutely no power to disclose such information, and certainly no right to do so.'

'I had every right, Mr Thaw. Now just shut the fuck up and listen, because I haven't finished.'

Glowering at him, the solicitor settled back in his chair and glanced at Moffatt. Sweat was pouring off his face and he was wiping it away with both hands.

'Anyway, Mrs Moffatt was extremely helpful once I'd let her in on your nasty little secret, and she gave me this.' Harrison delved again into his bag of tricks and produced a small green notebook. Flicking through the pages which appeared to contain close, spidery handwriting, he looked up at Moffatt.

'Did you know your wife kept a diary?' he asked him. Then: 'I'll take that as a no,' he went on as Moffatt stayed quiet. 'Yes, she's kept a diary since 1971 because she suspected you were having affairs.'

'Affairs? How on earth is that relevant!' scoffed Thaw.

'It's relevant because she was recording times and dates every time he went missing and she suspected he was with other women.'

The solicitor looked again at Moffatt, who was now drenched with sweat.

'As an example, let's have a look at her entry for

twentieth June, just last month, shall we? That's the date, incidentally, that Mandy Blackstock, our last victim, was attacked. Let me find it . . . yes, here we are. "W out again at ten, no explanation – again! Heard him in late around one. Bastard, one day I'll find them." And let's have a look at ninth August 1973. "W sleeping in spare room. Heard him creep out to see her at eleven-thirty." Janice Wainwright was attacked in Oakwood Park about half-past one that morning. Compelling stuff, isn't it?'

'Hardly, Chief Inspector,' said Thaw. 'It's purely circumstantial. I'm sure we could all produce dozens of men whose wives couldn't account for their husbands' whereabouts at the times of these attacks. It doesn't prove anything.'

'You're quite right, sir, it's purely circumstantial, but interesting all the same. And all recorded by her for the day she envisaged she'd be taking him to court to divorce him on the grounds of his adultery. But what really caught my eye was the fact that not only has she made entries that coincide with the dates of the eight attacks I'm investigating, but there are several other dates when he went walkabout in the small hours. Interesting, isn't it?'

'Not at all, purely circumstantial in my view.'

'Do you think your client could account for his whereabouts on any of the dates in question? I can certainly say where he wasn't.'

'He doesn't have to, Chief Inspector,' snapped Thaw. 'You're embarking on a fishing expedition here and I've no intention of assisting you with it. Have you got any more than wild speculation?'

'I wouldn't describe it as speculation, but I'll move on. Tell me, Mr Moffatt, do you own a lock-up garage?'

Moffatt looked at Thaw, who nodded.

'No, I don't drive,' he answered sullenly.

'No, that's right. You're a disqualified driver, aren't you? Or at least David Alan Evans is. Do you have access to a garage then?'

'No.'

Harrison rummaged about in the brown paper bag again and pulled out a clear plastic property bag sealed with a white plastic tag and with a green *Prisoner's Property* tag on it.

'Your property?' asked Harrison.

'Yes, you know it is.'

Harrison tore open the bag and held up the blue plastic key ring with the Chubb, Yale and a flat, dull grey metal key on it.

'Can you tell me what these fit?' asked Harrison.

'My front door, obviously.'

'What about this flat one?'

'Fuck knows.'

'It's on your key ring, one of only three. You must know what it's for, surely?'

'I told you, I don't know. I must have found it or something and stuck it on there.'

'A key that you found? You stuck it on your key ring

with two door keys that you use every day? It doesn't sound very plausible, does it?'

'He's answered your question, Chief Inspector,' interrupted Thaw. 'He doesn't know what it's for. Can we get on?'

'Of course,' said Harrison, reaching into the paper sack yet again and pulling out a key with a yellow *Property Subject of Enquiry* tag on it. He placed it flat on the table in front of Moffatt and Thaw. Then he moved it slowly towards the flat metal key on Moffatt's key ring until they were side by side.

'Do you recognise this other key?' asked Harrison, tapping the key with the yellow tag.

Moffatt was swallowing so hard it was audible to everyone in the room. 'No,' he answered hoarsely.

'Look,' said Harrison, like an excited science teacher talking through a successful classroom experiment to an enthralled class. He moved the key on to the one on Moffatt's key ring and held them together in the air for them all to see.

'They're a perfect match. Actually they were made at the same time,' said Harrison with a smile, 'and you've got one of the pair on your key ring.'

Neither Moffatt nor Thaw spoke, but Moffatt was breathing heavily and wiping his soaking face constantly.

'Guess where I got this key from, Mr Moffatt?' asked Harrison. He didn't bother to wait for a reply. 'Your wife gave it to me.'

Moffatt gasped audibly and gulped for air as Thaw cast him anxious glances.

'These keys were cut for a lock-up garage owned by your wife's father in Drakes Drive, a couple of streets away from your home. The old boy doesn't use it any more though he still pays the rent for it. He gave these keys to your wife years ago. And you've got one of them on your key ring. Can you explain that?'

Moffatt had begun to shake.

'It's difficult, I know, but there you go. Anyway, once I'd left your wife, I went to see a local Magistrate and obtained a search warrant to search your father-in-law's garage. Here's a copy of the warrant, Mr Thaw,' said Harrison, slipping a sheet of paper across the desk. 'DC Benson and I went to the garage about nine p.m. Do you recognise this?'

Reaching into the brown paper bag, Harrison placed a large Huntley & Palmers biscuit tin, decorated with jolly Santas and prancing reindeer, on the desk. The tin was covered in aluminium fingerprint dust.

'Yes, it's been fingerprinted,' he said, as he noticed the solicitor peering closely at it. 'Do you recognise it, Mr Moffatt?' he repeated.

Moffatt was panting and staring at the ceiling, the sweat staining the cell issue tracksuit top he was wearing.

'That'll be another no then, which is odd when you take into consideration that the only fingerprints found on that tin belong to Wallace John Moffatt, previously known as the dreadful Alan David Evans. Can you explain that?' asked Harrison.

The only sound in the room was the rasping from Moffatt as he desperately sought to breathe. Harrison looked at him with a glare full of loathing.

'The contents of this tin were . . . interesting,' he said after a lengthy pause listening to Moffatt wheezing. 'Recognise any of these?' He went back into the brown paper bag and very slowly and deliberately laid out twelve smaller brown paper bags with small cellophane windows. Each was sealed and tagged with blue *Property Subject of Crime* tags.

'A lady's white bra,' announced Harrison, picking up the first of the bags and reading from the white exhibit label. 'A pair of women's tights, another woman's bra, a lady's gold-coloured metal wristwatch, a lady's blue check scarf, and this one was of particular interest,' he said, looking at another bag. 'It contains a pair of torn lady's knickers with bloodstains.'

Moffatt appeared by now to have gone into shock. He was staring at the ceiling with his mouth wide open.

'And this,' said Harrison, pushing a sheet of paper across the desk to Thaw, 'is a statement made earlier this evening by Mandy Blackstock from her hospital bed, positively identifying those knickers as the ones she was wearing when she was assaulted on June the twentieth this year. I'm pretty sure that forensics will confirm the blood on them belongs to her. You couldn't help it, could you,

Wallace? You were very smart and planned things very cleverly, but you just had to keep a little something, didn't you? We found your trophies, Wallace.'

The solicitor stared open-mouthed at Harrison and then at his client. 'I, I . . .' he began before giving up.

'Wallace John Moffatt, I am arresting you on suspicion of the rape of Mandy Blackstock in Stream Woods, Handstead, on June the twentieth 1978,' said Dan Harrison, getting to his feet. 'You do not have to say anything unless you wish to do so, but whatever you say may be given in evidence. Got you, you horrible, fat, obnoxious, racist piece of shit!' he shouted. 'I've fucking got you!' He turned to the shorthand note-taker at the back of the room.

'You can leave that last bit out, darling,' he said, smiling at her. She drew a line through her notes and smiled back, hugely impressed by what she had heard and recorded. Harrison had simply destroyed Moffatt and rendered him an immobile lump. It had been magnificent.

'Shit, I nearly forgot,' said Harrison, sitting down again. 'Wallace John Moffatt, I am also arresting you on suspicion of indecent assault on Teresa Price and Dawn Price – you fucking beast. You don't have to say anything, but you already know that, don't you? You'll be delighted to hear that the girls and their mother are upstairs with some of my officers now, making detailed statements. Wallace, old son,' said Harrison, leaning forward and whispering, 'next time you see the outside of a prison cell you'll be a very, very old man. That's if you ever get out alive, because I'm going to make sure that the other cons know exactly who you are and what you've done.'

'I n-need some time with my client, Chief Inspector,' stammered the shattered solicitor.

'He's got plenty of that, Mr Thaw,' said Harrison, getting to his feet and stretching the tension of the interview out of his shoulders. He glanced at his wristwatch. 'Interview terminated at 00.15,' he called over his shoulder to the still smiling shorthand note-taker.

'You take all the time you want with him, Mr Thaw, but don't keep him up too late. We'll be back to interview him again tomorrow morning. He's got a long day ahead of him. You can have your chat back in his cell; I'm not going to waste anyone's time standing outside this interview room door.'

The solicitor didn't protest and whispered urgently into his traumatised client's ear. Moffatt didn't respond for nearly a minute, but eventually got painfully to his feet. Swaying slightly, he grabbed the edge of the table to steady himself before he looked at Harrison. His eyes were watery and scared, and all his arrogance and aggression were gone. His bottom lip began to tremble.

'Don't go all soft on us now, Wallace,' said Harrison harshly. 'Where you're going, the soft ones don't fare very well. Best you harden up or you're going to end up with an arse like the Japanese flag. Won't be long now, mate, before you're lying in the dark on your prison bunk bed and the monster in the bunk above you whispers, "Come here, Wallace, and suck Mummy's cock".'

Moffatt dropped his head. He was completely broken.

'Bang him up, John,' said Harrison contemptously, 'and put Mr Thaw in with him for a chat.'

John Benson, who had remained silent throughout the extraordinary interview, took hold of Moffatt and manhandled him out of the interview room and back to his cell with his silent, shell-shocked solicitor trailing after them.

Harrison turned again to look at the shorthand note-taker.

'Are you OK, Audrey?' he asked her, concerned.

'Yes, I'm fine, Mr Harrison, thanks. Just a little stunned, I think.'

Harrison chuckled. 'Yeah, sometimes you come across things that are a little out of the ordinary, don't you? Don't suppose you'll have heard anything like that before.'

'God, no. I can't believe people like that exist, or do things like that. And they live amongst us and we just don't know they're there. You know, I'm pretty sure my kids go to the same school as his daughters.'

'You keep that to yourself, Audrey,' counselled Harrison. 'We've saved those poor little buggers from a lifetime of misery, but life's still going to be difficult for them, once all this becomes common knowledge.'

'Of course I will, poor little mites,' she said, getting to

her feet and beaming at Harrison again. 'I'll get these notes typed up tonight and leave them on your desk.'

'Thanks, love, appreciate you putting yourself out like this at short notice,' said Harrison, as he opened the interview-room door for her.

After banging both Moffatt and Wade up, Benson returned to the booking-in area where Dan Harrison was waiting for him with their brown paper bag of tricks. The custody charge board now showed Moffatt locked up for rape and indecent assault in addition to the earlier ABH and indecent exposure on Anne Butler. Benson smiled at him and extended a firm handshake.

'Fucking quality, boss,' he said simply.

'All fell into place, didn't it, John?' replied Harrison. 'Grab the bag for me, will you – reckon we've earned a drink after that.'

They trudged back up the stairs to the CID floor and into Harrison's office.

'Is Bob still about?' he asked, as he placed his bottle and glasses on the desk.

'No, he went home about half-six, I think. He was Early Turn today,' replied Benson, taking his glass from Harrison.

'Give him a ring, John. Tell him he was right and we got a brilliant result.'

Benson left to ring his mate from the main CID office and Harrison slumped back in his chair. Taking a swig of his Bushmills, he closed his eyes and put his head back.

Suddenly he felt exhausted, close to collapse. The tiredness swept over him like a huge breaker crashing on to a beach and he wanted to close his eyes for ever. It was hardly surprising. He had done almost nothing but work for the last three weeks, keeping numerous balls in the air, trying to maintain control of everything. He barely slept, he was drinking too much, and what little he ate was junk. At least he'd cut down on his miniature cigars, but his health was suffering and he knew it.

Right now, what he needed most was sleep. Days and nights of the stuff. Then he could begin to tackle the rest.

Chapter Twenty-Eight

Dan Harrison sat bolt upright in bed wondering what the hell was going on. He was bathed in sweat and his head was thumping, but he didn't know what was happening or where he was. He was in his own bedroom, he eventually realised, and it was the bloody phone ringing – *again.* He'd been in the deepest of sleeps he'd enjoyed in months – and now, once more, he'd been rudely awakened. He glanced at the piercing red digits on his clock. Fucking hell – 3.20 a.m.

'Harrison,' he groaned in a thick, flat voice he barely recognised.

'It's Sarah Eldrett,' said the faint voice at the other end. His heart stopped and his blood ran cold. *Oh no, please God, no*. Not this, he pleaded to himself.

'Hello Sarah. Where are you? What's happened?'

'At the hospital,' she said, so quietly he could barely hear her. In the background were the metallic echoes and distant sounds of the Intensive Care Unit. She had stopped talking and then he could hear the sound of her weeping. The lump in his throat threatened to choke him.

'Sarah, please, what's happened?' he said urgently.

'It's Ph-Phil,' she stammered. 'You said you wanted me to ring you if anything changed.'

'Yes, yes, of course. What is it?' he urged with a leaden feeling in his stomach.

'Oh God,' she cried, her sobs louder.

'Sarah, talk to me!' shouted Harrison. 'What's happened? Please tell me.'

'It's Phil,' she repeated. 'He came round at three o'clock.' Then she began to weep loudly.

A sob wracked Harrison's body and he dropped the phone into his lap. He closed his eyes and gave silent thanks to an Almighty he didn't believe in before picking up the phone again and trying to compose himself.

'I'm so pleased, Sarah,' he eventually croaked. 'How is he?'

'Talking, but a bit sore,' she replied, sniffing, and he could hear her blowing her nose. 'The doctors say they don't think there's any permanent damage, but they've still got a lot of tests to do.'

'Of course. God, I'm so pleased for you both, Sarah. I'm so happy,' said Harrison, as the tears coursed down his stubbly face on to the crumpled bedsheets. 'I'm so very happy.'

'He asked me to give you a message,' she said softly.

'Me?' asked Harrison in a strangled voice.

'He told me to tell you that he recognised two of the men who attacked him.'

Harrison's tears stopped and he was immediately alert to the impending danger. He was now sitting bolt upright in the dark, his mind racing as he considered what he might have to do now. There was no investigation currently underway into how Eldrett had come by his injuries, because on the face of it, the cause was unknown. The only person who knew for definite what had happened was Eldrett himself, and until now he had been saying nothing. Harrison had a very good idea of what had occurred in the cul-de-sac but he could not have identified the Holding brothers. Now, potentially, he had a disaster on his hands.

'Did he? That can wait for now, Sarah. Let's get him better and I'll deal with that in due course,' he said.

'He said it was important that you dealt with it quickly,' she insisted. 'He recognised two of them as members of something called the Park Royal Mafia. Does that mean anything to you? He said you'd understand what that meant and what you need to do.'

Harrison breathed deeply and lay back on his pillows with a wide smile. Eldrett was giving him the solution to his problem.

'I'll deal with it, lass,' he said. 'Send him my best and tell him I'll be in to see him later today. You try and get some sleep as well, OK? You must be shattered. I'm so pleased for you, I really am.'

'You've been in to see him every day, haven't you, Mr Harrison?' she asked.

'Yeah, I worry about him. He's one of my boys,' laughed Harrison.

'That's what he said. Thank you, Mr Harrison, good night,' and Sarah Eldrett hung up.

Dan Harrison lay for a while staring up at the light-fitting on the ceiling, listening to the dialling tone on the phone which remained on his chest. Sometimes, he thought to himself, it just doesn't get any better than this. What a job, what a fucking amazing job.

Bravo Jubilee

Charlie Owen

THE FILTH AND THE FURY . . .

Summer 1977: it's no holiday in the sun in Handstead New Town, a north Manchester overspill. Known to the local cops as Horse's Arse, it's preparing to celebrate the Queen's Silver Jubilee, but lob in football violence, rampant police hooliganism and an expanding LSD market – and there'll be a riot going on . . .

Local gangster Sercan Ozdemir has underestimated DCI Harrison, head of the CID. Blood on the floor in an interview room is all in a day's work for Harrison. And Ozdemir knows that if his crime family discover he's been doing his own thing, they'll pull his face off.

Meanwhile the uniformed cops, Psycho, Pizza, The Brothers, Ally and the others, hurl the rule book out of the window and continue to hold the tide of criminal scum at bay for as long as they can in a town they despise . . .

Praise for Charlie Owen:

'A kaleidoscope of unbridled moral mayhem. [Charlie Owen] narrates with a genuinely deft, distinctly non-regulation-issue wit' *Telegraph*

'After just three books, the policemen in this wonderful series seem like old friends. Raw, crude, ugly and brazenly real . . . shocking and funny, a great read' *Guardian*

'Gene Hunt would be proud . . . entertaining, chaotic and hilarious' *Manchester Evening News*

'Will have you gripped from page one . . . rude, crude and grittier than the M8 on an icy day' *Daily Record*

978 0 7553 4568 7

headline